D0207527

A Blunt Instrument

Georgette Heyer

sourcebooks
landmark

Copyright © 1938 by Georgette Rougier
Cover and internal design © 2010 by Sourcebooks, Inc.
Cover photo credit © The Advertising Archives

Sourcebooks and the colophon are registered trademarks of
Sourcebooks, Inc.

All rights reserved. No part of this book may be reproduced in any form
or by any electronic or mechanical means including information storage
and retrieval systems—except in the case of brief quotations embodied
in critical articles or reviews—without permission in writing from its
publisher, Sourcebooks, Inc.

The characters and events portrayed in this book are fictitious or are
used fictitiously. Any similarity to real persons, living or dead, is purely
coincidental and not intended by the author.

Published by Sourcebooks Landmark, an imprint of Sourcebooks, Inc.
P.O. Box 4410, Naperville, Illinois 60567-4410
(630) 961-3900
Fax: (630) 961-2168
www.sourcebooks.com

Library of Congress Cataloging-in-Publication Data
Heyer, Georgette.
  A blunt instrument / Georgette Heyer.
      p. cm.
  1. Hannasyde, Inspector (Fictitious character)--Fiction. 2. Police-
-England--Fiction. 3. Murder--Investigation--Fiction. 4. Country
homes--England--Fiction. I. Title.
  PR6015.E795B58 2010
  823'.912--dc22
                          2009046824

Printed and bound in the United States of America.
VP 10 9 8 7 6 5 4 3 2 1

Also by Georgette Heyer

Romance

The Black Moth
These Old Shades
The Masqueraders
Beauvallet
Powder and Patch
Devil's Cub
The Convenient Marriage
Regency Buck
The Talisman Ring
The Corinthian
Faro's Daughter
Friday's Child
The Reluctant Widow
The Foundling
Arabella
The Grand Sophy
The Quiet Gentleman

Cotillion
The Toll Gate
Bath Tangle
Sprig Muslin
April Lady
Sylvester
Venetia
The Unknown Ajax
Pistols for Two
A Civil Contract
The Nonesuch
False Colours
Frederica
Black Sheep
Cousin Kate
Charity Girl
Lady of Quality

Historical Fiction

Simon the Coldheart
The Conqueror
An Infamous Army

Royal Escape
The Spanish Bride
My Lord John

Mystery

Footsteps in the Dark
Why Shoot a Butler?
The Unfinished Clue
Death in the Stocks
Behold, Here's Poison
They Found Him Dead

A Blunt Instrument
No Wind of Blame
Envious Casca
Penhallow
Duplicate Death
Detection Unlimited

One

A BREEZE, HARDLY MORE THAN A WHISPER OF WIND, STIRRED the curtains that hung on either side of the long window, and wafted into the room the scent of the wisteria covering the wall of the house. The policeman turned his head as the curtains faintly rustled, his rather glassy blue eyes frowning and suspicious. Straightening himself, for he had been bending over the figure of a man seated behind the carved knee-hole desk in the middle of the room, he trod over to the window and looked out into the dusky garden. His torch explored the shadows cast by two flowering shrubs without, however, revealing anything but a nondescript cat, whose eyes caught and flung back the light for an instant before the animal glided into the recesses of the shrub. There was no other sign of life in the garden, and after a moment of keen scrutiny, the policeman turned back into the room, and went to the desk. The man behind it paid no heed, for he was dead, as the policeman had already ascertained. His head lay on the open blotter, with blood congealing in his sleek, pomaded hair.

The policeman drew a long breath. He was rather pale, and the hand which he stretched out towards the telephone shook a little. Mr Ernest Fletcher's head was not quite the right shape; there was a dent in it, under the coagulated blood.

The policeman's hand was arrested before it had grasped the telephone receiver. He drew it back, felt for a handkerchief, and with it wiped a smear of blood from his hand, and then picked up the receiver.

As he did so, he caught the sound of footsteps approaching the room. Still holding the instrument, he turned his head towards the door.

It opened, and a middle-aged butler came in, carrying a tray with a syphon and a whisky decanter and glasses upon it. At sight of the police constable he gave a perceptible start. His gaze next alighted on the figure of his master. The tumbler on the tray shuddered against the decanter, but Simmons did not drop the tray. He stood holding it mechanically, staring at Ernest Fletcher's back.

PC Glass spoke the number of the police station. His flat, unemotional voice brought Simmons's eyes back to his face. 'My God, is he dead?' he asked in a hushed voice.

A stern glance was directed towards him. 'Thou shalt not take the name of the Lord, thy God, in vain,' said Glass deeply.

This admonishment was more comprehensible to Simmons, who was a member of the same sect as PC Glass, than to the official at the Telephone Exchange, who took it in bad part. By the time the misunderstanding had been cleared up, and the number of the police station repeated, Simmons had set the tray down, and stepped fearfully up to his master's body. One look at the damaged skull was enough to drive him back a pace. He raised a sickly face, and demanded in an unsteady voice: 'Who did it?'

'That'll be for others to find out,' replied Glass. 'I shall be obliged to you, Mr Simmons, if you will shut that door.'

'If it's all the same to you, Mr Glass, I'll shut myself on the other side of it,' said the butler. 'This – this is a very upsetting sight, and I don't mind telling you it turns my stomach.'

'You'll stay till I've asked you a few questions, as is my duty,' replied Glass.

'But I can't tell you anything! I didn't have anything to do with it!'

Glass paid no heed, for he was connected at that moment with the police station. Simmons gulped, and went to shut the door, remaining beside it, so that only Ernest Fletcher's shoulders were visible to him.

PC Glass, having announced his name and whereabouts, was telling the Sergeant that he had a murder to report.

Policemen! thought Simmons, resentful of Glass's calm. You'd think corpses with their heads bashed in were as common as daisies. He wasn't human, Glass; he was downright callous, standing there so close to the body he could have touched it just by stretching out his hand, talking into the telephone as though he was saying his piece in the witness-box, and all the time staring at the dead man without a bit of feeling in his face, when anyone else would have turned sick at the sight.

Glass laid down the receiver, and restored his handkerchief to his pocket. 'Lo, this is the man that made not God his strength, but trusted in his riches,' he said.

The sombre pronouncement recalled Simmons's thoughts. He gave a sympathetic groan. 'That's true, Mr Glass. Woe to the crown of pride! But how did it happen? How do you come to be here? Oh dear, oh dear, I never thought to be mixed up with a thing like this!'

'I came up that path,' said Glass, nodding towards the French windows. He drew a notebook from his pocket, and the stub of a pencil, and bent an official stare upon the butler. 'Now, Mr Simmons, if you please!'

'It's no use asking me: I don't know anything about it, I tell you!'

'You know when you last saw Mr Fletcher alive,' said Glass, unmoved by the butler's evident agitation.

'It would have been when I showed Mr Budd in,' replied Simmons, after a moment's hesitation.

'Time?'

'I don't know – not for certain, that is. It was about an hour ago.' He made an effort to collect his wits, and added: 'About nine o'clock. I was clearing the table in the dining-room, so it couldn't have been much later.'

Glass said, without raising his eyes from his notebook: 'This Mr Budd: known to you?'

'No. I never saw him before in my life – not to my knowledge.'

'Oh! When did he leave?'

'I don't know. I didn't know he had left till I came in just now. He must have gone by the garden-way, same as you came in, Mr Glass.'

'Was that usual?'

'It was – and it wasn't,' replied Simmons, 'if you know what I mean, Mr Glass.'

'No,' said Glass uncompromisingly.

'The master had friends who used to visit him that way.' Simmons heaved a sigh. 'Women, Mr Glass.'

'Thine habitation,' said Glass, with a condemnatory glance round the comfortable room, 'is in the midst of deceit.'

'That's true, Mr Glass. The times I've wrestled in prayer –'

The opening of the door interrupted him. Neither he nor Glass had heard footsteps approaching the study, and neither had time to prevent the entrance into the room of a willowy young man in an ill-fitting dinner-jacket suit, who paused on the threshold, blinked long-lashed eyelids at the sight of a policeman, and smiled deprecatingly.

'Oh, sorry!' said the newcomer. 'Fancy finding you here!'

His voice was low-pitched, and he spoke softly and rather quickly, so that it was difficult to catch what he said. A lock of lank dark hair fell over his brow; he wore a pleated shirt, and a deplorable tie, and looked, to PC Glass, like a poet.

His murmured exclamation puzzled Glass. He said suspiciously: 'Fancy meeting me, eh? So you know me, do you, sir?'

'Oh no!' said the young man. His fluttering glance went round the room and discovered the body of Ernest Fletcher. His hand left the door-knob; he walked forward to the desk, and turned rather pale. 'I should shame my manhood if I were sick, shouldn't I? I wonder what one does now?' His gaze asked inspiration of Glass, of Simmons, and encountered only blank stares. It found the tray Simmons had brought into the room. 'Yes, that's what one does,' he said, and went to the tray, and poured himself out a stiff, short drink of whisky-and-soda.

'The master's nephew – Mr Neville Fletcher,' said Simmons, answering the question in Glass's eye.

'You're staying in this house, sir?'

'Yes, but I don't like murders. So inartistic, don't you think? Besides, they don't happen.'

'This has happened, sir,' said Glass, a little puzzled.

'Yes, that's what upsets me. Murders only occur in other people's families. Not even in one's own circle. Ever noticed that? No, I suppose not. Nothing in one's experience – one had thought it so wide! – has taught one how to cope with such a bizarre situation.'

He ended on an uncertain laugh; it was plain that under his flippancy he was shaken. The butler looked at him curiously, and then at Glass, who, after staring at Neville Fletcher for a moment, licked his pencil-point, and asked: 'When did you see Mr Fletcher last, if you please, sir?'

'At dinner. In the dining-room, I mean. No, let us be exact; not the dining-room; the hall.'

'Make up your mind, sir,' recommended Glass stolidly.

'Yes, that's all right. After dinner he came here, and I wandered off to the billiard-room. We parted in the hall.'

'At what hour would that have been, sir?'

Neville shook his head. 'I don't know. After dinner. Do you know, Simmons?'

'I couldn't say, sir, not precisely. The master was usually out of the dining-room by ten to nine.'

'And after that you didn't see Mr Fletcher again?'

'No. Not till now. Anything you'd like to know, or can I withdraw?'

'It'll save time, sir, if you'll give an account of your movements between the time you and the deceased left the dining-room, and 10.05 p.m.'

'Well, I went to the billiard-room, and knocked the balls about a bit.'

'Alone, sir?'

'Yes, but my aunt came to find me, so I left.'

'Your aunt?'

'Miss Fletcher,' interpolated the butler. 'The master's sister, Mr Glass.'

'You left the billiard-room with your aunt, sir? Did you remain with her?'

'No. Which all goes to show that politeness always pays. I silently faded away, and now I'm sorry, because if I'd accompanied her to the drawing-room I should have had an alibi, which I haven't got. I went upstairs to my own room, and read a book. I wonder if I can have fallen asleep over it?' He looked doubtfully towards his uncle's chair, and gave a faint shudder. 'No, my God, I couldn't dream anything like this! It's fantastic.'

'If you'll excuse me, Mr Glass, I fancy that was the front-door bell,' interrupted Simmons, moving towards the door.

A few moments later a police-sergeant, with several satellites, was ushered into the study, and in the hall outside the voice of Miss Fletcher, urgently desiring to be told the meaning of this invasion, was upraised in some agitation.

Neville slid out of the study, and took his aunt by the arm. 'I'll tell you. Come into the drawing-room.'

'But who are all those men?' demanded Miss Fletcher. 'They looked to me exactly like policemen!'

'Well they are,' said Neville. 'Most of them, anyway. Look here, Aunt Lucy –'

'We've been burgled!'

'No –' He stopped. 'I don't know. Yes, perhaps that was it. Sorry, aunt, but it's worse than that. Ernie has met with an accident.'

He stumbled a little over the words, looking anxiously at his aunt.

'Try not to *mumble* so, Neville dear. *What* did you say?'

'I said an accident, but I didn't mean it. Ernie's dead.'

'Dead? Ernie?' faltered Miss Fletcher. 'Oh no! You can't mean that! How could he be dead? Neville, you know I don't like that sort of joke. It isn't *kind*, dear, to say nothing of its being in very questionable taste.'

'It isn't a joke.'

She gave a gasp. '*Not?* Oh, Neville! Oh, let me go to him at once!'

'No use. Besides, you mustn't. Terribly sorry, but there it is. I'm a trifle knocked-up myself.'

'Neville, you're keeping something back!'

'Yes. He's been murdered.'

Her pale, rather prominent blue eyes stared at him. She opened her mouth, but no words passed her lips. Neville, acutely uncomfortable, made a vague gesture with his hands. 'Can I do anything? I should like to, only

I don't know what. Do you feel faint? Yes, I know I'm being incompetent, but this isn't civilised, any of it. One has lost one's balance.'

She said: 'Ernie *murdered*? I don't believe it!'

'Oh, don't be silly,' he said, betraying ragged nerves. 'A man doesn't bash his own skull in.'

She gave a whimper, and groped her way to the nearest chair, and sank into it. Neville lit a cigarette with a hand that trembled, and said: 'Sorry, but you had to know sooner or later.'

She seemed to be trying to collect her wits. After a pause she exclaimed: 'But who would *want* to murder dear Ernie?'

'Search me.'

'There has been some dreadful mistake! Oh, Ernie, Ernie!'

She burst into tears. Neville, attempting no consolation, sat down in a large armchair opposite to her, and smoked.

Meanwhile, in the study, PC Glass was making his painstaking report to his superior. The doctor had gone; the cameramen had taken their photographs; and the body of Ernest Fletcher had been removed.

'I was on my beat, Sergeant, walking along Vale Avenue, the time being 10.02 p.m. When I came to the corner of Maple Grove, which, as you know, sir, is the lane running between Vale Avenue and the Arden Road, at the back of the house, my attention was attracted by a man coming out of the side gate of this house in what seemed to me a suspicious manner. He set off, walking very fast, towards the Arden Road.'

'Would you know him again?'

'No, Sergeant. It was nearly dark, and I never saw his face. He had turned the corner into Arden Road before I had time to do more than wonder what he was up to.' He hesitated, frowning a little. 'As near as I could make out, he was a man of average height, wearing a light-coloured soft hat. I don't know what gave me the idea there was something wrong about his coming out of Mr Fletcher's garden-gate, unless it was the hurry he seemed to be in. The Lord led my footsteps.'

'Yes, never mind about that!' said the Sergeant hastily. 'What did you do then?'

'I called out to him to stop, but he paid no heed, and the next instant had rounded the corner into the Arden Road. That circumstance led me to inspect these premises. I found the garden-gate standing open, and, seeing the light from this window, I came up the path with the intention of discovering whether anything was wrong. I saw the deceased, like you found him, Sergeant. The time, as verified by my watch and the clock there, was 10.05 p.m. My first action was to ascertain that Mr Fletcher was dead. Having assured myself that he was past mortal help, I effected a search of the room, and made sure no one was hiding in the bushes in the garden. I then called up the station on the telephone, the time being 10.10 p.m. While I was waiting to be connected, the butler, Joseph Simmons, entered the room, bearing the tray you see upon that table. I detained him, for interrogation. He states that at about 9 p.m. a person of the name of Abraham Budd came to see the deceased. He ushered same into this room. He states that he does not know when Abraham Budd left the house.'

'Description?'

'I hadn't got to that, sir. Mr Neville Fletcher came in at that moment. He states that he saw the deceased last at about 8.50 p.m., when they left the dining-room together.'

'All right; we'll see him in a minute. Anything else?'

'Nothing that I saw,' replied Glass, after a moment's scrupulous thought.

'We'll look around. Looks like an open-and-shut case against this man you saw making off. Friend Abraham Budd, eh?'

'Not to my way of thinking, Sergeant,' said Glass.

The Sergeant stared. 'Oh, it isn't, isn't it? Why not? The Lord been guiding you again?'

A flash of anger brought Glass's cold eyes to life. 'The scorner is an abomination to men!' he said.

'That's enough!' said the Sergeant. 'You remember you're speaking to your superior officer, if you please, my lad!'

'A scorner,' pursued Glass inexorably, 'loveth not one that reproveth him: neither will he go unto the wise. The man Budd came openly to the front door, making no secret of his name.'

The Sergeant grunted. 'It's a point, I grant you. May not have been a premeditated murder, though. Fetch the butler in.'

'Joseph Simmons is well known to me for a godly member,' said Glass, on his way to the door.

'All right, all right! Fetch him!'

The butler was discovered in the hall, still looking rather pale. When he entered the study he cast a nervous look towards the desk, and drew an audible sigh of relief when he saw the chair behind it unoccupied.

'Your name?' asked the Sergeant briskly.

'Joseph Simmons, Sergeant.'

'Occupation?'

'I am – I was employed as Mr Fletcher's butler.'

'How long have you been with him?'

'Six-and-a-half years, Sergeant.'

'And you state,' pursued the Sergeant, consulting Glass's notes, 'That you last saw your master alive at about 9 p.m., when you showed a Mr Abraham Budd into this room. Is that correct?'

'Yes, Sergeant. I have the person's card here,' said Simmons, holding out a piece of pasteboard.

The Sergeant took it, and read aloud: 'Mr Abraham Budd, 333c Bishopsgate, EC. Well, we know where he's to be found, that's one thing. You state that he wasn't known to you, I see.'

'I never laid eyes on the individual before in my life, Sergeant. He was not the type of person I have been in the habit of admitting to the house,' said Simmons haughtily.

Glass dispelled this pharisaical attitude with one devastating pronouncement. 'Though the Lord be high, yet hath he respect unto the lowly,' he said in minatory accents, 'but the proud he knoweth afar off.'

'My soul is humbled in me,' apologised Simmons.

'Never mind about your soul!' said the Sergeant impatiently. 'And don't take any notice of Glass! You listen to me! Can you describe this Budd's appearance?'

'Oh yes, Sergeant! A short, stout person in a suit which I should designate as on the loud side, and a bowler hat. I fancy he is of the Jewish persuasion.'

'Short and stout!' said the Sergeant, disappointed. 'Sounds to me like a tout. Did the deceased expect a visit from him?'

'I hardly think so. Mr Budd stated that his business was urgent, and I was constrained to take his card to Mr Fletcher. My impression was that Mr Fletcher was considerably annoyed.'

'Do you mean scared?'

'Oh no, Sergeant! Mr Fletcher spoke of "damned impertinence", but after a moment he told me to show Mr Budd in, which I did.'

'And that was at 9 p.m., or thereabouts? Did you hear any sounds of altercation?'

The butler hesitated. 'I wouldn't say altercation, Sergeant. The *master's* voice was upraised once or twice, but I didn't hear what he said, me being in the dining-room, across the hall, until I withdrew to my pantry.'

'You wouldn't say that a quarrel took place between them?'

'No, Sergeant. Mr Budd did not strike me as a quarrelsome person. In fact, the reverse. I got the impression he was afraid of the master.'

'Afraid of him, eh? Was Mr Fletcher a bad-tempered man?'

'Dear me, no, Sergeant! A very pleasant-spoken gentleman, usually. It was very seldom I saw him put-out.'

'But was he put-out tonight? By Mr Budd's call?'

The butler hesitated. 'Before that, I fancy, Sergeant. I believe Mr Fletcher had a – a slight difference with Mr Neville, just before dinner.'

'Mr Neville? That's the nephew? Does he live here?'

'No. Mr Neville arrived this afternoon to stay with his uncle for a few days, I understand.'

'Was he expected?'

'If he was, I was not apprised of it. I should mention, in fairness to Mr Neville, that he is – if I may say so – a somewhat eccentric young gentleman. It is by no means an unusual occurrence for him to arrive here without warning.'

'And this difference with his uncle: was that usual?'

'I should not like to give a false impression, Sergeant: there wasn't any quarrel, if you understand me. All I know is that when I took sherry and cocktails to the drawing-room before dinner it seemed to me that I had interrupted an altercation. The master looked to be distinctly annoyed, which was a rare thing, in my experience, and I did hear him say, just as I came in, that he wanted to hear no more about it, and Mr Neville could go to hell.'

'Oh! And what about Mr Neville? Was he annoyed?'

'I shouldn't like to say, Sergeant. Mr Neville is a peculiar young gentleman, not given to showing what he feels, if he feels anything, which I sometimes doubt.'

'Well I do, frequently,' said Neville, who had come into the room in time to hear this remark.

The Sergeant, unaccustomed to young Mr Fletcher's noiseless way of entering rooms, was momentarily startled. Neville smiled in his deprecating fashion, and said softly:

'Good-evening. Isn't it shocking? I do hope you've arrived at something? My aunt would like to see you before you go. Do you know who killed my uncle?'

'It's early days to ask me that, sir,' replied the Sergeant guardedly.

'Your words hint at a prolonged period of suspense, which I find peculiarly depressing.'

'Very unpleasant for all concerned, sir,' agreed the Sergeant. He turned to Simmons. 'That'll be all for the present,' he said.

Simmons withdrew, and the Sergeant, who had been eyeing Neville with a good deal of curiosity, invited him to sit down. Neville obligingly complied with this request, choosing a deep armchair by the fireplace. The Sergeant said politely: 'I'm hoping you may be able to help me, sir. I take it you were pretty intimate with the deceased?'

'Oh no!' said Neville, shocked. 'I shouldn't have liked that at all.'

'No, sir? Am I to understand you were not on good terms with Mr Fletcher?'

'But I was. I'm on good terms with everyone. Only I'm not intimate.'

'Well, but, what I mean, sir, is –'

'Yes, yes, I know what you mean. Did I know the secrets of my uncle's life? No, Sergeant: I hate secrets, and other people's troubles.'

He said this with an air of sweet affability. The Sergeant was a little taken aback, but rallied, and said: 'At all events, you knew him fairly well, sir?'

'We won't argue the point,' murmured Neville.

'Do you know if he had any enemies?'

'Well, obviously he had, hadn't he?'

'Yes, sir, but what I'm trying to establish –'

'I know, but you see I'm just as much at a loss as you are. You weren't acquainted with my uncle?'

'I can't say as I was, sir.'

Neville blew one smoke ring through another, and watched it dreamily. 'Everybody called him Ernie,' he sighed. 'Or Ernie dear, according to sex. You see?'

The Sergeant stared for a moment, and then said slowly: 'I think I get you, sir. I've always heard him well spoken of, I'm bound to say. I take it you don't know of any person with a grudge against him?'

Neville shook his head. The Sergeant looked at him rather discontentedly, and consulted Glass's notebook. 'I see you state that after you left the dining-room you went into the billiard-room, where you remained until Miss Fletcher came to find you. At what hour would that have been?'

Neville smiled apologetically.

'You don't know, sir? No idea at all? Try and think!'

'Alas, time has hitherto meant practically nothing to me. Does it help if I say that my aunt mentioned that a most peculiar visitor was with my uncle? A fat little man, who carried his hat in his hand. She had seen him in the hall.'

'Did you see this man?' asked the Sergeant quickly.

'No.'

'You don't know whether he was still with your uncle when you went up to your room?'

'Sergeant, Sergeant, do you think I listen at keyholes?'

'Of course not, sir, but –'

'At least, not when I'm wholly incurious,' explained Neville, temporising.

'Well, sir, we'll say that some time between 9.00 and 10.00 you went up to your room.'

'At half-past nine,' said Neville.

'At – A moment ago, sir, you said you had no idea what time it was!'

'Oh, I hadn't, but I remember now one solitary cuckoo.'

The Sergeant shot a startled look towards Glass, standing motionless and disapproving by the door. A suspicion that the eccentric Neville Fletcher was of unsound mind had darted into his brain. 'What might you mean by that, sir?'

'Only the clock on the landing,' said Neville.

'A cuckoo-clock! Well, really, sir, for a moment I thought – And it struck the half-hour?'

'Yes, but it's quite often wrong.'

'We'll go into that presently. Which way does your room face, sir?'

'North.'

'It's at the back of the house, then? Would it be possible for you to hear anyone coming up the side path?'

'I don't know. I *didn't* hear anyone, but I wasn't trying to.'

'Quite,' said the Sergeant. 'Well, I think that'll be all for the present, thank you, sir. Of course, you understand that you will not be able to leave this house for a day or two? Just a matter of routine, you know. We'll hope it won't be long before we get the whole thing cleared up.'

'Yes, let's,' agreed Neville. His gaze dwelt speculatively on a picture on the wall opposite the fireplace. 'It wouldn't be robbery, would it?'

'Hardly, sir, but of course we can't say definitely yet. It isn't likely a burglar would come when Mr Fletcher was still up, not to mention the rest of the household.'

'No. Only the safe is behind that picture – just in case you didn't know.'

'Yes, sir, so the butler informed me. We've been over it for finger-prints, and as soon as we can get Mr Fletcher's lawyer down we'll have it opened. Yes, Hepworth? Found anything?'

The last words were addressed to a constable who had stepped into the room through the window.

'Not much, Sergeant, but I'd like you to have a look at one thing.'

The Sergeant went at once; Neville uncoiled himself, got up, and wandered out of the room in his wake. 'Don't mind me coming, do you?' he murmured, as the Sergeant turned his head.

'I don't see as there's any objection, sir. The fact is, a man was seen sneaking out by the side gate just after 10 p.m., and unless I'm mistaken he's the chap we're after.'

'A – a fat man?' suggested Neville, blinking.

'Ah, that would be too easy, wouldn't it, sir?' said the Sergeant indulgently. 'No, just an ordinary looking chap in a soft hat. Well, Hepworth, what is it?'

The constable had led the way to the back of a flowering currant bush, which was planted in a bed close to the house. He directed the beam of his torch on to the ground. In the soft earth were the deep imprints of a pair of high-heeled shoes.

'They're freshly made, Sergeant,' said Hepworth. 'Someone's been hiding behind this bush.'

'The Women in the Case!' said Neville. 'Aren't we having fun?'

Two

B Y HALF-PAST ELEVEN THE POLICE, WITH THE EXCEPTION of one constable, left behind to keep a watch over the house, had departed from Greystones. Miss Fletcher, gently interrogated by the Sergeant, had been unable to assist the course of justice. The news of the finding of the imprints of a woman's shoes did not seem either to shock or to surprise her. 'He was such an *attractive* man,' she confided to the Sergeant. 'Of course, I don't mean – but one has to remember that Men are not like Us, doesn't one?'

The Sergeant had found himself listening to a panegyric on the late Ernest Fletcher: how charming he was; how popular; what perfect manners he had; how kind he had always been to his sister; how gay; how dashing; how generous! Out of this turmoil of words certain facts had emerged. Neville was the son of Ernie's brother Ted, many years deceased, and certainly his heir. Neville was a dear boy, but you never knew what he would be up to next, and – yes, it *did* annoy poor Ernie when he got himself imprisoned in some horrid Balkan state – oh, nothing serious, but Neville was so hopelessly vague, and simply lost his passport. As for the Russian woman who had appeared at Neville's hotel with *all* her luggage before breakfast one morning in Budapest, saying he had invited her at some party the night before – well, one couldn't exactly approve, of course, but young men did get drunk sometimes, and anyway the woman was obviously no better than she should be, and really Neville was not like that at all. At the same time, one did rather feel for Ernie, having to buy the creature off. But it was quite, quite untrue to say that Ernie didn't like Neville: they hadn't much in common, but blood was thicker than water, and Ernie was always so understanding.

Questioned more closely, no, she knew of no one who nourished the least grudge against her brother. She thought the murderer must have been one of these dreadful maniacs one read about in the papers.

The Sergeant got away from her, not without difficulty, and very soon left the house. Aunt and nephew confronted one another in the drawing-room.

'I feel as though this were all a horrible nightmare!' said Miss Fletcher, putting a hand to her head. 'There's a policeman in the hall, and they've locked dear Ernie's study!'

'Does it worry you?' asked Neville. 'Was there anything there you wished to destroy?'

'That,' said Miss Fletcher, 'would be most dishonest. Not but what I feel sure Ernie would have preferred it to having strangers poking their noses into his affairs. Of course I wouldn't destroy anything important, but I'm sure there isn't anything. Only you know what men are, dear, even the best of them.'

'No, do tell me!'

'Well,' said Miss Fletcher, 'one shuts one's eyes to That Side of a Man's life, but I'm afraid, Neville, that there have been Women. And some of them, I think – though of course I don't *know* – not what I call Nice Women.'

'Men are funny like that,' said Neville dulcetly.

'Yes, dear, and naturally I was very thankful, because at one time I made sure Ernie would get caught.'

'Caught?'

'Marriage,' explained Miss Fletcher. 'That would have been a great blow to me. Only, luckily, he wasn't a very *constant* man.'

Neville looked at her in surprise. She smiled unhappily at him, apparently unaware of having said anything remarkable. She looked the acme of respectability; a plump, faded lady, with wispy grey hair and mild eyes, red-rimmed from crying, and a prim little mouth, innocent of lip-stick.

'I'm now definitely upset,' said Neville. 'I think I'll go to bed.'

She said distressfully: 'Oh dear, is it what I've told you? But it's bound to come out, so you had to know sooner or later.'

'Not my uncle; my aunt!' said Neville.

'You do say such odd things, dear,' she said. 'You're overwrought, and no wonder. Ought I to offer that policeman some refreshment?'

He left her engaged in conversation with the officer on duty in the hall, and went up to his own room. After a short interval his aunt tapped on his door, desiring to know whether he felt all right. He called out to her that he was quite all right, but sleepy, and so after exchanging good-nights with him, and promising not to disturb him again, Miss Fletcher went away to her own bedroom in the front of the house.

Neville Fletcher, having locked his door, climbed out of his window, and reached the ground by means of a stout drain-pipe, and the roof of the verandah outside the drawing-room.

The garden lay bathed in moonlight. In case a watch had been set over the side entrance, Neville made his way instead to the wall at the end of the garden, which separated it from the Arden Road. Espaliers trained up it made the scaling of it a simple matter. Neville reached the top, lowered himself on the other side, and let himself drop. He landed with the ease of the trained athlete, paused to light a cigarette, and began to walk westwards along the road. A hundred yards brought him to a crossroad running parallel to Maple Grove. He turned up it, and entered the first gateway he came to. A big, square house was sharply outlined by the moonshine, lights shining through the curtains of several of the windows. One of these, on the ground-floor to the left of the front door, stood open. Neville went to it, parted the curtains, and looked into the room.

A woman sat at an escritoire, writing, the light of a reading-lamp touching her gold hair with fire. She wore evening dress, and a brocade cloak hung over the back of her chair. Neville regarded her thoughtfully for a moment, and then stepped into the room.

She looked up quickly, and gave a sobbing gasp of shock. The fright of her eyes gave place almost immediately to an expression of relief. Colour rushed into her lovely face; she caught her hand to her breast, saying faintly: 'Neville! Oh, how you startled me!'

'That's nothing to what I've been through tonight,' replied Neville. '*Such* fun and games at Greystones, my dear: you wouldn't believe!'

She shut her blotter upon her half-finished letter. 'You haven't got them?' she asked, between eagerness and incredulity.

'All I've got is the jitters,' said Neville. He strolled over to her, and to her surprise went down on his knee.

'Neville, what on *earth* – ?'

His hand clasped her ankle. 'Let's have a look at your foot, my sweet.' He pulled it up and studied her silver kid shoe. 'O my prophetic soul! Now we are in a mess, aren't we? Just like your pretty little slippers.' He let her go, and stood up.

Swift alarm dilated her eyes. She glanced down at her shoes, and twitched the folds of her frock over them. 'What do you mean?'

'Can it, precious. You called on Ernie tonight, and hid behind a bush outside the study window.'

'How did you know?' she asked quickly.

'Intuition. You might have left it to me. What was the use of dragging me into it if you were going to muscle in? God knows I was unwilling enough.'

'That's just it. I didn't think you'd be any good. You're so unreliable, and I knew you hated doing it.'

'Oh, I did, and I am, and I wasn't any good, but all the same it was damned silly of you not to give me a run for my money. Did *you* get them, by the way?'

'No. He only – laughed, and – oh, you know!'

'Well isn't that nice!' said Neville. 'Did you happen to knock him on the head?'

'Oh, don't be silly!' she said impatiently.

'If that's acting, it's good,' said Neville, looking at her critically. 'Did you see who did?'

She was frowning. 'Did I see who did what?'

'Knocked Ernie on the head. My pretty ninny, Ernie's been murdered.'

A sound between a scream and a whimper broke from her. 'Neville! Oh no! *Neville*, you don't mean that!'

He looked at her with a smile lilting on his mouth. 'Didn't you know?'

Her eyes searched his, while the colour receded slowly from her face. 'I didn't do it!' she gasped.

'I shouldn't think you'd have the strength,' he agreed.

They were interrupted by the opening of the door.

A slim young woman with a cluster of brown curls, a monocle screwed into her left eye, entered the room, saying calmly: 'Did you call, Helen?' Her gaze alighted on Neville; she said with every appearance of disgust: 'Oh, you're here, are you?'

'Yes, but I wouldn't have been if I'd known you were, hell-cat,' responded Neville sweetly.

Miss Drew gave a contemptuous snort, and looked critically at her sister. 'You look absolutely gangrenous,' she remarked. 'Anything the matter?'

Helen North's hands twisted nervously together. 'Ernie Fletcher's been murdered.'

'Good!' said Miss Drew, unperturbed. 'Neville come to tell you?'

Helen shuddered. 'Oh don't! It's awful, awful!'

'Personally,' said Miss Drew, taking a cigarette from the box on the table, and fitting it into a long holder, 'I regard it as definitely memorable. I hate men with super-polished manners, and charming smiles. Who killed him?'

'I don't know! You can't think I know!' Helen cried. 'Sally! – Neville! – oh, my God!' She looked wildly from one to the other, and sank down on to a sofa, burying her face in her hands.

'If it's an act, it's a good one,' said Neville. 'If not, it's mere waste of time. Do stop it, Helen! you're making me feel embarrassed.'

Sally regarded him with disfavour. 'You don't seem to be much upset,' she said.

'You didn't see me an hour ago,' replied Neville. 'I even lost my poise.'

She sniffed, but merely said: 'You'd better tell me all about it. It might be good copy.'

'What a lovely thought!' said Neville. 'Ernie has not died in vain.'

'I've always wanted to be in on a real murder,' remarked Sally thoughtfully. 'How was he killed?'

'He had his head smashed,' replied Neville.

Helen gave a moan, but her sister nodded with all the air of a connoisseur. 'A blow from a blunt instrument,' she said. 'Any idea who did it?'

'No, but Helen may have.'

Helen lifted her head. 'I tell you I wasn't there!'

'Your shoes belie you, sweet.'

'Yes, yes, but not when he was killed! I wasn't, I tell you, I wasn't!'

The monocle dropped out of Miss Drew's eye. She screwed it in again, bending a searching gaze upon her sister. 'What do you mean – "yes, but not when he was killed"? Have you been round to Greystones tonight?'

Helen seemed uncertain how to answer, but after a moment she said: 'Yes. Yes, I did go round to see Ernie. I – I got sick of the noise of your typewriter, for one thing, and, for another, I – I wanted particularly to see him.'

'Look here!' said Sally, 'you may as well spill it now as later! – what is there between you and Ernie Fletcher?'

'As a purist,' said Neville, 'I must take exception to your use of the present tense.'

She rounded on him. 'I suppose you're in on it, whatever it is? Then you'll dam' well tell me.'

'It isn't what you think!' Helen said quickly. 'Truly, it isn't, Sally! Oh, I admit I liked him, but not – not enough for that!'

'If you can tell Neville the truth you can tell it to me,' said Sally. 'And don't pull any stuff about going to see him because of my typewriter, because it won't wash.'

'Tell her,' advised Neville. 'She likes sordid stories.'

Helen flushed. 'Need you call it that?'

He sighed. 'Dear pet, I told you at the outset that I considered it too utterly trite and sordid to appeal to me. Why bring that up now?'

'You don't know what it is to be desperate,' she said bitterly.
'No, that's my divine detachment.'

'Well, I hope you get pinched for the murder,' struck in Sally. 'Then what price divine detachment?'

He looked pensive. 'It would be awfully interesting,' he agreed. 'Of course, I should preserve an outward calm, but should I quail beneath it? I hope not: if I did I shouldn't know myself any more, and that would be most uncomfortable.'

Helen struck the arm of the sofa with her clenched hand. 'Talk, talk, talk! What's the use of it?'

'There is nothing more sordid than the cult of utility,' replied Neville. 'You have a pedestrian mind, my dear.'

'Oh, do shut up!' begged Sally. She went to the sofa, and sat down beside Helen. 'Come on, old thing, you'd much better tell me the whole story! If you're in a jam, I'll try and get you out of it.'

'You can't,' Helen said wretchedly. 'Ernie's got IOUs of mine, and the police are bound to discover them, and there'll be a ghastly scandal.'

Sally frowned. 'IOUs? Why? I mean, how did he get them? What are they for, anyway?'

'Gambling debts. Neville thinks he probably bought them.'

'What on earth for?' demanded Sally, the monocle slipping out again.

Neville looked at her admiringly. 'The girl has a mind like a pure white lily!' he remarked. 'I am now taken-aback.'

Sally retorted hotly: 'I haven't got any such thing! But all this price-of-dishonour business is too utterly *vieux jeu*! Good Lord, I wouldn't put it in any book of mine!'

'Are you an escapist?' inquired Neville solicitously. 'Is that why you write improbable novels? Have you felt the banality of real life to be intolerable?'

'My novels aren't improbable! It may interest you to know that the critics consider me as one of the six most important crime novelists.'

'If you think that you're a bad judge of character,' said Neville.

Helen gave a strangled shriek of exasperation. 'Oh, don't, don't! What does any of that matter at a time like this? What am I to *do*?'

Sally turned away from Neville. 'All right, let's get this thing straight,' she said. 'I don't feel I've got all the data. When did you start falling for Ernie Fletcher?'

'I didn't. Only he was so attractive, and – and he had a sort of sympathetic understanding. Almost a touch of the feminine, but not quite that, either. I can't explain. Ernie made you feel as though you were made of very brittle, precious porcelain.'

'That must have added excitement to your life,' said Neville reflectively.

'Shut up! Go on, Helen! When did it all begin?'

'Oh, I don't know! I suppose from the moment I first got to know him – to know him properly, I mean. You mustn't think that he – that he made love to me, because he didn't. It wasn't till just lately that I realised what he wanted. I thought – oh, I don't know what I thought!'

'You didn't think anything,' explained Neville kindly. 'You floated away on a sea of golden syrup.'

'That's probably true,' said Sally. 'You were obviously right under the ether. What did John think, if anything?'

Her sister coloured, and averted her face. 'I don't know. John and I – had drifted apart – before Ernie came into my life.'

Neville, apparently overcome, sank into a chair, and covered his face with his hands. 'Oh God, Oh God!' he moaned. 'I'm being dragged into this repulsive syrup! Dearest, let *us* drift apart – me out of your life, before I start mouthing clichés too. I know it's insidious.'

'I must say,' remarked Sally, fair-mindedly, 'That I rather bar "drifted apart" and "came into my life" myself. Helen, do try not to sentimentalise yourself; it all looks too darned serious to me. I thought you and John weren't hitting it off any too well. Some women don't know when they've struck ore. What went wrong between you? I should have thought John was the answer to any maiden's prayer.'

'Oh, it's so hard to explain!' Helen said, her eyes brimming with tears. 'I was so young when I married him, and I thought everything was going to be like my dreams. I'm not excusing myself: I know John's a fine man, but he didn't understand me, and he didn't want what I wanted – life, gaiety and excitement!'

'Didn't you love him?' asked Sally bluntly.

'I thought I did. Only everything went wrong. If only John had been different – but you know what he's like! If he'd shaken me, or even beaten me, I'd have pulled myself up. But he didn't. He simply retired into his shell. He was busy, too, and I was bored. I started going about without him. Sally, I tell you I don't know how it began, or how we got to this pitch, but we're utterly, utterly estranged!' The tears were running down her cheeks. She said with a catch in her voice: 'I'd give anything to have it all back again, but I can't, and there's a gulf between us which I can't bridge! Now *this* has happened, and I suppose that'll end it. I shall have dragged John's name in the mud, and the least I can do is to let him divorce me.'

'Don't be such an ass!' said Sally bracingly. 'John's much too decent to let you down when you're in trouble. You don't divorce people for getting into debt, and if your IOUs are found in Ernie Fletcher's possession it'll be obvious that you weren't a faithless wife.'

'If they're found, and it all comes out, I'll kill myself!' Helen said. 'I couldn't face it. I could *not* face it! John doesn't know a thing about my gambling. It's the one thing that he detests above all others. Neville's a beast, but he's perfectly right when he says it's a sordid story. It wasn't Bridge, or the sort of gambling you have at parties, but a – a real hell!'

'Lummy!' said Miss Drew elegantly. 'Gilded vice, and haggard harpies, and suicides adjacent? All that sort of thing?'

'It wasn't gilded, and I don't know about any suicides, but it was a *bad* place, and yet – in a way – rather thrilling. If John knew of it – the people who belonged to it – Sally, no one would *believe* I wasn't a bad woman if it was known I went to that place!'

'Well, why did you go there?'

'Oh, for the thrill! Like one goes to Limehouse. And at first it sort of *got* me. I adored the excitement of the play.

Then I lost rather a lot of money, and like a fool I thought I could win it back. I expect you know how one gets led on, and on.'

'Why not have sold your pearls?'

A wan smile touched Helen's lips. 'Because they aren't worth anything.'

'*What?*' Sally gasped.

'Copies,' said Helen bitterly. 'I sold the real ones ages ago. Other things, too. I've always been an extravagant little beast, and John warned me he wouldn't put up with it. So I sold things.'

'Helen!'

Neville, who had been reposing in a luxurious chair with his eyes shut, said sleepily: 'You said you wanted copy, didn't you?'

'Even if it didn't concern Helen I couldn't use this,' said Sally. 'Not my line of country at all. I shall have to concentrate on the murder. By the way, Helen, who introduced you to this hell? Dear Ernie?'

'Oh no, no!' Helen cried. 'He absolutely rescued me from it! I can't tell you how divine he was. He said everything would be all right, and I wasn't to worry any more, but just be a good child for the future.'

'Snake!' said Sally hotly.

'Yes, only – it didn't seem like that. He had such a way with him! He got hold of those ghastly IOUs, and at first I was so thankful!'

'Then he blackmailed you!'

'N – no, he didn't. Not quite. I can't tell you about that, but it wasn't exactly as you imagine. Of course, he did use the IOUs as a weapon, but perhaps he didn't really mean it! It was all done so – so *laughingly*, and he was very much in love with me. I expect I lost my head a bit, didn't handle him properly. But I got frightened, and I couldn't sleep for thinking of my IOUs in Ernie's possession. That's why I told Neville. I thought he might be able to do something.'

'Neville?' said Miss Drew, in accents of withering contempt. 'You might as well have applied to a village idiot!'

'I know, but there wasn't anyone else. And he is clever, in spite of being so hopeless.'

'As judged by village standards?' inquired Neville, mildly interested.

'He may have a kind of brain, but I've yet to hear of him putting himself out for anyone, or behaving like an ordinarily nice person. I can't think how you ever succeeded in persuading him to take it on.'

'The dripping of water on a stone,' murmured Neville.

'Well having taken it on, I do think you might have put your back into it. Did you even try?'

'Yes, it was a most painful scene.'

'Why? Was Ernie furious?'

'Not so much furious as astonished. So was I. You ought to have seen me giving my impersonation of a Nordic public-school man with a reverence for good form and the done-thing. I wouldn't like to swear I didn't beg him to play the game. Ernie ended up by being nauseated, and I'm sure I'm not surprised.'

'You know, you're not hard-hearted, you're just soulless,' Sally informed him. She glanced at her sister. 'Was I invited to stay to be a chaperon?'

'Yes, in a way. Besides, I wanted you.'

'Thanks a lot. What happened tonight?'

'Oh, nothing, Sally, nothing! It was silly of me, but I thought if only I could talk quietly to Ernie, and – and throw myself on his generosity, everything would be all right. You were busy with your book, so I got my cloak, and just slipped round by the back way to Greystones, on the off-chance of finding Ernie in his study.'

'It looks to me as though it wasn't the first time you've called on Ernie like that,' interpolated Sally shrewdly.

Helen coloured. 'Well, no, I – I have been once or twice before, but not after I realised he had fallen in love with me. Honestly, I used to look on him as an exciting sort of uncle.'

'More fool you. Carry on! When did you set out on this silly expedition?'

'At half-past nine, when I knew you'd had time to get absorbed in your silly book,' retorted Helen, with a flash of spirit. 'And I knew that Ernie was in his study, because when I turned up into Maple Grove from the Arden Road, I saw a man come out of the Greystones side gate, and walk off towards Vale Avenue.'

'Abraham,' said Neville. 'Well, that settles him, at all events. Pity: the name had possibilities.'

'I don't know what you're talking about. I let myself into the garden, and walked up the path to Ernie's study. Ernie was there, but I soon saw I'd made a mistake to come. He was – almost horrid – as horrid as a person with charm like his could be.'

'That's what comes of getting me to become a pukka sahib,' said Neville. 'You can't blame Ernie.'

'How long did you stay with him?' demanded Sally. 'Think! it's probably important.'

'I don't have to think: I know,' said Helen. 'Ernie said something about my being found with him at a compromising hour, and I looked at the clock, and said if he thought a quarter to ten a compromising hour he must be actually a Victorian, though I'd thought him merely Edwardian.'

'Good!' approved Sally.

'Yes, I was in a rage,' admitted Helen. 'And I walked straight out, the way I'd come.'

'Straight home?'

Helen hesitated, her eyes on Neville, who was regarding her with an expression of sleepy enjoyment. 'No,' she said, after a pause. 'Not quite. I heard the gate open, and naturally I didn't want to be seen, so I dived behind a bush beside the house.'

'Who was it?' asked Sally quickly.

'I don't know. I couldn't see. A man, that's all I can tell you.'

Sally looked at her rather searchingly, and then said: 'All right, go on!'

'He went into the study. I think he closed the window behind him; I didn't hear anything except a sort of murmur of voices.'

'Oh! Did you beat it while you had the chance?'

Helen nodded. 'Yes, of course.'

'And no one but Ernie saw you?'

'No.'

'And you didn't go dropping handkerchiefs about, or anything like that?'

'Of course I didn't.'

'Then there's nothing except the IOUs to connect you with the murder!' Sally declared. 'We've got to get hold of them before the police do.'

Helen said: 'Oh, Sally, if only I could! But *how*? They aren't in his desk –'

'How do you know?' asked Sally swiftly.

'Why, I – something Ernie said,' faltered Helen.

'I shouldn't set much store by anything he said. Of course, they may be in a safe, but we'll hope he didn't go in for safes. Neville, this is your job.'

Neville opened his eyes. Having surveyed both sisters in his peculiarly dreamy way, he dragged himself out of his chair, and wandered over to the table where the cigarette-box stood. He selected and lit one, produced his own empty case, and proceeded to fill it. 'All this excitement,' he said softly, 'has gone to your head.'

'Oh no, it hasn't! You're staying in the house; you said you'd help Helen. You can jolly well find those IOUs before Scotland Yard gets on to the case.'

'Scotland Yard!' gasped Helen.

'Yes, I should think almost certainly,' replied Sally. 'This is the Metropolitan area, you know. They'll probably send a man down to investigate. Neville, are you willing to take a chance?'

'No, darling,' he replied, fitting the last cigarette into his case.

'You would fast enough if they were your IOUs!'

He looked up. 'I daresay I should. But they aren't mine. I won't have anything to do with them.'

'If you had a grain of decency, or – or *chivalry* –'

'Do stop trying to cast me for this beastly Gunga Din rôle!' he implored. 'Find someone else for the job! You must know lots of whiter men than I am.'

'Very well!' said Sally. 'If you haven't the guts to do it, I have, and I will!'

'I don't want to blight your youthful ardour, sweet one, but I think I ought to tell you that there's a large, resolute policeman parked in the front hall.'

Her face fell. 'I never thought of that,' she said slowly. An idea occurred to her. 'Do you mean he's keeping a watch over the household?'

'Well, he's certainly not a paying-guest.'

She started up. 'You utter, abysmal idiot, what did you come here for if the house was being watched?'

'To get some cigarettes. We've run out.'

'Oh, don't be a fool! Don't you realise you'll have led them straight to Helen?'

'Oh no! No, really I haven't,' Neville replied, with his apologetic smile. 'I climbed out of my window, and over the wall.'

'You – Did you really?' exclaimed Sally, her thunderous frown vanishing. 'I must say I should never have thought it of you.'

'Atavism,' he explained.

'Oh, Neville, how on earth did you manage it?' Helen asked, a note of admiration in her voice.

He looked alarmed. 'Please don't get misled! It wasn't a bit heroic, or daring, or even difficult.'

'It must have been. I can't think *how* you did it! I should never have had the nerve.'

'No nerve. Merely one of the advantages of a University education.'

'Well, I think it was fairly sporting of you,' said Sally. 'Only it doesn't help us to solve the problem of how to get those IOUs.'

'Don't strain yourself,' Neville recommended. 'You can't get them. They're probably in Ernie's safe, just like you suggested.'

'There are ways of opening safes,' said Sally darkly, cupping her chin in her hands. 'I suppose you don't happen to know the combination?'

'You're right for the first time tonight. God, how I hate women!'

'Sally, you don't really know how to open safes, do you?' asked Helen, forgetting her troubles in surprise.

'No, not offhand. I should have to look it up. Of course, I know about soup.'

'What sort of soup?' inquired Neville. 'If we're going to talk gastronomy I can be quite intelligent, though seldom inspired.'

'Ass. Not that kind of soup. The stuff you blow open safes with. I forget exactly what it's made of, but it's an explosive of sorts.'

'Is it really?' said Neville. 'What lovely fun! Won't it go big with the policeman in the hall?'

'I wasn't thinking of using it, even if I knew how to make it, which I don't.'

'That must be your weak woman's nature breaking through the crust, darling. Get the better of it, and don't stop at the safe. Blow the whole house up, thus eliminating the policeman.'

'Have a good laugh,' said Sally. 'After all, you aren't in this jam, are you?' She got up, and began to stride about the room. 'Well, let's face it! We can't open the safe, and we don't know how to get by the policeman. In fact, we're futile. But if I created this situation in a book I could think of something for the book-me to do. Why the devil can't I think of something now?'

Neville betrayed a faint interest. 'If we were in one of your books, we should all of us have much more nerve than we really have, to start with.'

'Not necessarily.'

'Oh yes! You always draw your characters rather more than life-size. We should have more brains, too. You, for instance, would know how to make your soup –'

'Any where to buy the – the ingredients, which actually one just *doesn't* know,' she interpolated.

'Exactly. Helen would go and scream blue murder outside the house, to draw the policeman off while you blew up the safe, and I should put up a great act to regale him with on his return, telling him I thought I heard someone in the study, and leading him there when you'd beaten it with the incriminating documents. And can you see any one of us doing any of it?'

'No, I can't. It's lousy, anyway. It would be brought home to us because of Helen's being an obvious decoy.'

'Helen would never be seen. She'd have merged into the night by the time the policeman got there.'

'Let's discuss possibilities!' begged Helen.

'I'll go further, and discuss inevitabilities. We shall all of us sit tight, and let the police do the worrying. Ernie's dead, and there isn't a thing we can do, except preserve our poise. In fact, we are quite definitely in the hands of Fate. Fascinating situation!'

'A dangerous situation!' Sally said.

'Of course. Have you never felt the fascination of fear? Helen has, in that gambling-hell of hers.'

'Not now!' Helen said. 'This is too awful. I only feel sick, and – and desperate!'

'Take some bicarbonate,' he advised. 'Meanwhile, I'm going home to bed. Oh, did I say thank you for the cigarettes? By the way, where is John supposed to be?'

'In Berlin,' replied Helen listlessly.

'Well, he isn't,' said Neville. 'I saw him in London today.'

She came to her feet in one swift movement, paper-white, staring at him. 'You couldn't have! I know he's in Berlin!'

'Yes, I saw him,' murmured Neville.

He was by the window, a hand on the curtain. Helen moved quickly to detain him. 'You thought you saw him! Do you imagine I don't know where my own husband is?'

'Oh, no!' Neville said gently. 'I didn't say that, precious.'

Three

'WELL, IT DOESN'T LOOK SUCH A WHALE OF A CASE TO me,' said Sergeant Hemingway, handing the sheaf of typescript back to his superior. 'No one in it but the one man, on the face of it.'

'True,' agreed Hannasyde. 'Still, there are points.'

'That's right, Superintendent,' nodded Inspector True. 'That's what I said myself. What about them footprints? They weren't made by the old lady: she doesn't wear that kind of shoe.'

'Housemaid, saying good-night to her young man,' said the experienced Hemingway.

'Hardly,' said Hannasyde. 'She wouldn't choose a bush just outside her master's study.'

'No, nor there wasn't anything like that going on,' said the Inspector. 'The cook is a very respectable woman, married to Simmons, the butler, and the housemaid is her own niece, and this Mrs Simmons swears to it both she and the kitchen-maid never stirred outside the house the whole evening.'

'It's my belief those footprints'll be found to be highly irrelevant,' said Hemingway obstinately. 'All we want is this chap your man – what's-his-name? – Glass saw making off. Nothing to it.'

Hannasyde cocked an eyebrow at him. 'Liverish, Skipper?'

'I don't like the set-up. Ordinary, that's what it is. And I don't like the smashed skull. Just doesn't appeal to me. Give me something a bit recherché, and I'm right on to it.'

Hannasyde smiled a little. 'I repeat, there are points. The murdered man seems to have been universally liked. No motive for killing him even hinted at.'

'You wait till we've done half-an-hour's work on the case,' said Hemingway. 'I wouldn't mind betting we'll find scores of people all stiff with motives.'

'I thought you said all we had to do was to find the man PC Glass saw?'

'I daresay I did, Chief, and what's more I was probably right, but you mark my words, we shall find a whole lot of stuff just confusing the main issue. I've been on this kind of case before.'

'The way I look at it,' said the Inspector slowly, 'we want to find the instrument it was done with.'

'Yes, that's another of the points,' replied Hannasyde. 'Your man Glass seems quite certain that the fellow he saw wasn't carrying anything. What sort of a chap is he? Reliable?'

'Yes, sir, he is, very reliable. That's his conscience. He's a very religious man, Glass. I never can remember what sect he belongs to, but it's one of those where they all wrestle with the devil, and get moved by the Lord to stand up and testify. Well, I'm Church of England myself, but what I say is, it takes all sorts to make a world. As a matter of fact, I was thinking of detailing Glass to you, to give you any assistance you may need, Superintendent. I reckon he's one of my best men – not quick, you know, but not one to lose his head, or go flying off at a tangent. Seems only right to put him on to this case, seeing as it was him discovered the body.'

'All right,' said Hannasyde absently, his eyes running down the typescript in his hand.

The Inspector coughed. 'Only perhaps I'd better just warn you, sir, that he's got a tiresome habit of coming out with bits of the Bible. One of these blood-and-thunder merchants, if you know what I mean. You can't break him of it. He gets moved by the spirit.'

'I daresay Hemingway will be able to deal with him,' said Hannasyde, rather amused.

'I knew I wasn't going to like this case,' said Hemingway gloomily.

Half-an-hour later, having made a tour of the grounds of Greystones, inspected the footprints behind the flowering currant bush, and cast a jaundiced eye over the stalwart, rigid form of PC Glass, he reiterated this statement.

'If thou faint in the day of adversity, thy strength is small,' said Glass reprovingly.

The Sergeant surveyed him with acute dislike. 'If you get fresh with me, my lad, we're going to fall out,' he said.

'The words are none of mine, but set down in Holy Writ, Sergeant,' explained Glass.

'There's a time and a place for everything,' replied the Sergeant, 'and this isn't the place nor the time for the Holy

Writ. You attend to me, now! When you saw that chap sneaking out of this gate last night, it was just after ten o'clock, wasn't it?'

'It was, Sergeant.'

'And getting dark?'

'As you say, Sergeant.'

'Too dark for you to see him very clearly?'

'Too dark for me to distinguish his features, but not too dark for me to take note of his build and raiment.'

'It's my belief it was too dark for you to see whether he was carrying anything or not,' said the Sergeant.

'His hands were empty,' replied Glass positively. 'I will not bear false witness against my neighbour.'

'All right, skip it!' said the Sergeant. 'Now, you've been in this district some time, haven't you?'

'For three years, Sergeant.'

'Well, what do you know about these Fletchers?'

'Their eyes stand out with fatness; they have more than heart could wish.'

'Yes, that's a lot of use, isn't it? What about the nephew?'

'I know nothing of him, either good or ill.'

'And the late Ernest?'

A sombre look came into Glass's face. 'He that pursueth evil pursueth it to his own death.'

The Sergeant pricked up his ears. 'What evil?'

Glass looked sternly down at him. 'I believe him to have been wholly given up to vain show, double of heart, a fornicator, a –'

'Here, that'll do!' said the Sergeant, startled. 'We're none of us saints. I understand the late Ernest was pretty well liked?'

'It is true. It is said that he was a man of pleasing manners, filled with loving kindness. But the heart is deceitful above all things, and desperately wicked: who can know it?'

'Yes, that's all very well, but where do you get that fornication idea? From those footprints, eh?'

'No. Joseph Simmons, who is in the way of light, though a foolish man, knew some of the secrets of his master's life.'

'He did, did he? We'll see!' said the Sergeant briskly, and turned towards the house.

He entered it through the study window, and found his superior there, with Ernest Fletcher's solicitor, and Neville Fletcher, who was lounging bonelessly in an armchair, the inevitable cigarette drooping from the corner of his mouth.

'Then, if that is all, Superintendent,' the solicitor was saying, 'I will take my leave. Should you require my further services, there is my card.'

'Thank you,' said Hannasyde.

The solicitor picked up Ernest Fletcher's Will, and replaced it in his brief-case. He glanced rather severely over the top of his pince-nez at Neville, and said: 'You are a very fortunate young man, Neville. I hope you will prove yourself worthy of the benefits your poor uncle has conferred on you.'

Neville looked up with his fleeting smile. 'Oh, so do I! I shall try hard not to let all this vulgar wealth corrupt my soul.'

'It's a great responsibility,' said the lawyer gravely.

'I know, that's what depresses me. People will expect me to wear a hat, and look at tape-machines.'

'I hope you will do more than that,' replied the lawyer. 'Now, if you please, I should like to have a word with your aunt. Perhaps you could take me to her.'

Neville obligingly rose, and opened the door for him. They passed out of the room together, and Sergeant Hemingway, who had been standing silent in the window, said: 'Who's the bit of chewed string, Chief?'

'The heir,' answered Hannasyde. 'Neville Fletcher.'

'Oh! well, I don't grudge it him. He looks as though he hasn't got tuppence to rub together, let alone hardly having the strength to stand up without holding on to something.'

'You shouldn't go by appearances, Sergeant,' said Hannasyde, a twinkle in his eye. 'That weary young man holds the record for the high jump. Got a half-blue at Oxford, so the solicitor informed me.'

'You don't say! Well, I wouldn't have thought it, that's all. And he's the heir? What did I tell you? Motive Number One.'

'I'll remember it if I draw a blank on that unknown visitor,' promised Hannasyde. 'Meanwhile, we've found this little lot.'

The Sergeant came to the desk, and looked over Hannasyde's shoulder at three slips of paper, all signed by Helen North. 'IOUs,' he said. 'Well, well, well, she *did* splash money about, didn't she? Know what I think, Super? There's a nasty smell of blackmail hanging round these bits of paper. I believe friend Ichabod wasn't so far off the mark after all, with his pursuit-of-evil stuff.'

'My name is not Ichabod, Sergeant, but Malachi,' said Glass stiffly, from the window.

'It had to be,' said the Sergeant. 'What price those footprints, Chief?'

'The medical evidence goes to show that it is in the highest degree improbable that a woman could have struck the blow which killed Ernest Fletcher. Still, I agree that these notes will bear looking into.'

'Young Neville know anything about this Helen North?'

'I haven't asked him. In the event of those IOUs having no bearing on the case, I'm not anxious to stir up any mud.' He glanced up to see Glass staring at him with knit brows. 'Well? Does the name convey anything to you?'

'There's a man of that name living with his wife not five minutes' walk from this house,' replied Glass slowly.

The Sergeant pursed his lips in a soundless whistle. Hannasyde said: 'Know anything about them?'

'No, sir.'

'Address?'

'You will find the house in the road which runs parallel to Maple Grove. It is called the Chestnuts.'

Hannasyde jotted it down. The Sergeant, meanwhile, was turning over a collection of photographs and snapshots laid on the desk. 'Looks like you weren't so far out, Glass,' he remarked. 'I have to hand it to the late Ernest. He certainly knew how to pick 'em. Regular harem!' He picked up a large portrait of a dazzling blonde, dressed, apparently, in an ostrich-feather fan, and regarded it admiringly. 'That's Lily Logan, the dancer. What a figure!'

Glass averted his eyes with a shudder. 'Can a man take fire in his bosom, and his clothes not be burned? As a jewel of gold in a swine's snout, so is a fair woman which is without discretion!'

'That's what you think,' said Hemingway, laying Lily Logan down, and looking critically at another smiling beauty. 'Went the pace a bit, didn't he? Hullo!' His eyes had alighted on the portrait of a curly-headed brunette. He picked it up. 'Seems to me I've seen this dame before.'

'As his female acquaintance seems to have consisted largely of chorus girls, that's not surprising,' said Hannasyde dryly.

'Yours lovingly, Angela,' read out the Sergeant. 'Angela…' He scratched his chin meditatively. 'Got something at the back of my mind. Do you seem to know that face, Chief?'

Hannasyde studied the photograph for a moment. 'It does look a little familiar,' he admitted. 'Some actress, I daresay. We'll check up on them presently.'

Hemingway held the photograph at arm's length. 'No, I'm pretty sure I don't connect her with the stage. No use asking you, Glass, I suppose?'

'I do not wish to look upon the face of a lewd woman,' Glass said harshly. 'Her end is bitter as wormwood, sharp as a two-edged sword.'

'Look here, what's the matter with you?' demanded the Sergeant. 'Some actress given you the air, or what?'

'I have no dealings with actresses.'

'Well, then, stop panning them. How do you know anything about this poor girl's end, anyway?' He laid the portrait down.

'Anything else, Chief?'

'Nothing so far.'

At this moment the door opened and Miss Fletcher came in. She was dressed in deep mourning, and her plump cheeks were rather pale, but she smiled sweetly at Hannasyde. 'Oh, Superintendent – you are a Superintendent, aren't you?'

He had risen to his feet, and unobtrusively slid the big blotter over the heap of photographs. 'Yes, that's right, madam.'

She looked at the mass of papers on the desk. 'Oh dear, what a lot you must have to do! Now, tell me, *would* you like a little refreshment?'

He declined it, which seemed to disappoint her, and asked her civilly if she wished to speak to him.

'Well, yes,' she admitted. 'Only *any* time will do. You're busy now, and I mustn't disturb you.'

'I'm quite at your disposal, Miss Fletcher. Won't you sit down? All right, Glass: you can wait outside.'

'You have such a kind face,' Miss Fletcher told him. 'Quite unlike what one expected. I feel I can *talk* to you. Are you *sure* you won't have something? A little coffee and a sandwich?'

'No, really, thank you. What was it you wanted to say to me, Miss Fletcher?'

'I'm afraid you'll say I'm wasting your time. So silly of me not to have asked dear Mr Lawrence while he was here!

We have known him for so many years that I always say he is more like a friend than a solicitor, though of course there is no reason why he shouldn't be *both*, as indeed I hope he feels he is. It was particularly foolish of me, because it is just the sort of thing he would know.'

'What is it, Miss Fletcher?' asked Hannasyde, breaking into the gentle flow of words.

'Well, it's the reporters,' she confided. 'Poor things, one knows they have their living to earn, and it must be very disagreeable work, when one comes to think of it, and one doesn't want to be unkind –'

'Are they worrying you?' interrupted Hannasyde. 'All you have to do is to tell your butler to say that you have no statement to make.'

'It seems so very disobliging,' she said doubtfully. 'And one of them looks dreadfully under-nourished. At the same time, I should very much dislike to see my photograph in the papers.'

'Of course. The less you say to them the better, Miss Fletcher.'

'Well, that's what I thought,' she said. 'Only my nephew is so naughty about it. It's only his fun, but you never know how much people will believe, do you? I suppose you wouldn't just *hint* to him that he oughtn't to do it? I feel that what *you* said would carry more *weight* than what I say.'

'What's he been up to?' asked Hannasyde.

'Well, he's told one of the reporters that he's employed here as the Boots, and when the man asked him his name he said it was Crippen, only he didn't want it to be known.'

Hannasyde chuckled. 'I don't think I should worry very much about that, Miss Fletcher.'

'Yes, but he told another of them that he came from Yugoslavia, and was here on very secret business. In fact, he's in the front garden now, telling three of them a ridiculous story about international intrigue, and my brother at the back of it. And they're taking it down in their notebooks. Neville's such a *marvellous* actor, and of course he speaks Serbian, from having travelled in the Balkans. But I don't think he ought to deceive those poor men, do you?'

'No, I don't,' said Hannasyde. 'It's most unwise to play jokes on the gentlemen of the Press. Hemingway, go and ask Mr Fletcher if I can have a word with him, will you?'

'Thank you *so* much!' said Miss Fletcher gratefully. 'Poor Neville, one always has to remember that he hasn't known a mother's love. I feel that accounts for so much, don't you? Not that he isn't a dear boy, of course, and I'm very fond of him, but he is like so many of the young people nowadays, so strangely *heartless*! Nothing seems to matter to him, not even a thing like this.' Her lips trembled; she groped for her handkerchief, and dabbed her eyes with it. 'You must forgive me: I was very much attached to my dear brother. It doesn't seem to me as though any of this can really have happened.'

'It must have been a terrible shock to you,' said Hannasyde sympathetically.

'Yes. You see, my brother was such a charming man. Everyone liked him!'

'So I understand, Miss Fletcher. Yet it seems that he had one enemy at least. Have you no idea who that might be?'

'Oh, no, no! I can't think of anyone. But – I didn't know all his – friends, Superintendent.' She looked up anxiously, but Hannasyde said nothing. 'That was one of the things I came to talk to you about,' she ventured. 'I'm afraid you will think it rather odd of me to mention such things, but I have made up my mind that I ought to.'

'You may be perfectly frank with me, Miss Fletcher,' he said encouragingly.

She fixed her eyes upon a point beyond his shoulder. 'My brother,' she said in a faint voice, 'had affairs with – with women.'

Hannasyde nodded.

'I never inquired into them, and of course he never spoke of them to me, but naturally I knew. In my young days, Superintendent, ladies did not discuss such matters. Nowadays things are different, and young people seem to talk of everything, which I can't help feeling is a pity. It is much better to shut one's eyes to some things, don't you agree? But it has occurred to me – I thought it all over during the night – that whoever killed my brother may – may have done so from jealousy.'

'Yes, that is a possibility,' Hannasyde said.

'Yes. Of course, if it *was* so, it will have to come out. I quite realise that. But if you find it wasn't, or – or fail to discover the man who did it – do you think my brother's – private affairs – need be known?'

'Certainly not,' Hannasyde replied. 'I quite understand your feelings in the matter, Miss Fletcher, and I can assure you that I shall respect them as much as I possibly can.'

'*So* kind!' she sighed. 'I have such a dread of the papers printing horrid things about my poor brother – perhaps getting hold of letters. You know the sort of thing I mean, I expect.'

'You need not be afraid of that,' he assured her. 'There are no such letters as you refer to.'

'Oh, how *thankful* I am!' she breathed. 'You have taken a load off my mind!'

She got up, as Sergeant Hemingway ushered her nephew into the room, and bestowed a tremulous smile upon the Superintendent. Neville came in talking in his soft, rapid way, and it was plain from Hemingway's strained, appreciative expression that his discourse was of an entertaining nature. When he saw his aunt he broke off in mid-sentence, and recommended her to make no statement to the police except in the presence of her lawyer. Miss Fletcher explained to Hannasyde that this was only his fun, and made her way to the door.

Neville closed it behind her, saying plaintively: 'Of course, I know one has to obey the summons of the Law, but you interrupted me at a most delicate moment, Superintendent.'

'I'm sorry,' replied Hannasyde, adding with a gleam of humour in his eye: 'International complications?'

'Yes, I had just worked in a Montenegrin patriot with a knife. The whole story was unfolding itself beautifully, but I've lost the thread now.'

'Take my advice, and don't try to fool the Press. Suppose – though it's improbable – that your International story did get published?'

'Oh, but I do hope it will!' Neville said. 'Really, it's a lovely story, and I've taken pains with it. I don't usually, but old Lawrence seems to think I ought to try to become more earnest. Did you want me for anything in particular? Because if not I'm in the middle of telling your Sergeant about an experience which befell me in Skopje. It isn't exactly a polite story, but I find he has a lovely dirty mind. In fact, we're practically affinities.'

The reminiscent grin which still lingered on the Sergeant's face vanished. A dusky blush mounted into his cheeks, and he gave an imploring cough.

'I daresay,' replied Hannasyde. 'But this is hardly the time to indulge in smutty anecdotes, do you think?'

'Oh, I don't agree with you!' said Neville engagingly. 'Given the right company, there's no real close season for dirty stories.'

'Tell me, Mr Fletcher, did you know your uncle well?'

'I expect it'll save time if I say no,' answered Neville. 'I can see we are on the verge of talking at cross-purposes.'

'Why?' Hannasyde asked bluntly.

'Oh, one doesn't know people. Mothers say they know their children through and through. Fallacy. Rather disgusting, too. Indecency inherent in over-probing, and results misleading, and probably disquieting.'

'Oh!' said Hannasyde, who had followed this rapid and telegraphic speech with some difficulty. 'I see what you mean, but it doesn't answer my question. As well as one person may know another, did you know your uncle?'

'No. Interest being the natural forerunner to understanding.'

'You'd none in him?'

'Nor anyone, 'cept objectively. An' I'm not sure of that either. Do you like people?'

'Don't you?'

Neville spread his hands out, slightly hunching his thin shoulders. 'Oh, some – a little – at a distance.'

'You seem to be an ascetic,' said Hannasyde dryly.

'Hedonist. Personal contacts pleasant at first, but leading to discomfort.'

Hannasyde regarded him frowningly. 'You have peculiar ideas, Mr Fletcher. They're not getting us anywhere.'

A smile flickered in Neville's eyes. 'Eschew my company. You see, I don't want to get anywhere. Prolonged intercourse with me bad for your temper.'

'You are probably right,' returned Hannasyde with a touch of asperity: 'I won't detain you any longer.'

'Oh, can I go back to my entrancing reporters?'

'If you think it wise – or desirable.'

'Like feeding goldfish,' said Neville, drifting out by way of the window.

The Sergeant watched him go, and drew a long breath. 'What I call a turn in himself,' he said. 'He's certainly a new one on me.'

Hannasyde grunted. The Sergeant cocked an intelligent eye at him. 'You didn't take to him, did you, Chief?'

'No. Or believe him.'

'I'm bound to say I don't entirely follow his talk – what I can hear of it, which isn't much.'

'I think he knows more than he pretends, and doesn't want to be questioned. However, he'll keep. I've nothing on him – so far.' He looked at his wrist-watch, and got up. 'Take charge of those papers, and the photographs, will you? I'm going now to call on Mrs North. I'll leave Abraham Budd to you. Find out from Headquarters, while you're in town, if they've got anything out of the finger-prints.'

He had no difficulty in finding his way to the Chestnuts, and, upon sending in his card, was ushered presently into a pleasant morning-room at the back of the house. There he found not only Helen North, but Miss Drew also, who was seated at a table in the window with a portable typewriter in front of her.

Helen came forward a few steps, saying nervously: 'Good-morning. I'm Mrs North. I understand you want to see me?'

'Yes,' Hannasyde replied. He glanced towards the window, and added: 'Perhaps if I might have a word with you alone it would be best.'

'Oh no! I mean, I would like my sister to remain. Won't you sit down? I – I've never entertained a detective before!'

'I should explain, Mrs North, that I am investigating the murder of Ernest Fletcher, who I believe was an acquaintance of yours.'

'Yes. Yes, I quite understand. Please go on!'

'You knew that Mr Fletcher had been murdered?' he asked.

Before she could answer, Sally cut in. 'In common with the butcher, the baker, the milkman, all the servants, the postman, and the paper-boy.'

He looked at her appraisingly, but did not answer, merely inclining his head slightly.

'News gets round so frightfully quickly in the suburbs,' Helen said, again with her uneasy, artificial laugh.

'Yes,' he agreed. 'I expect it does. When did you last see Mr Fletcher, Mrs North?'

'What's your reason for asking that question?' demanded Sally.

'I am investigating a murder, Miss –'

'I'm Sally Drew. You can hardly think that my sister knows anything about a murder.'

'I'm quite ready to believe that she doesn't,' he replied, with a good-humoured inflexion in his voice which surprised her. 'But I have a reason for asking Mrs North certain questions, and a right to do so.'

'Oh, of course!' Helen said quickly. 'Only it's rather difficult to say when I saw Ernie Fletcher last. Let me see now…it was probably in town. Oh yes, we were both at a party last week!'

'Are you quite sure that you haven't seen him since then?'

He kept his eyes on her face, taking note of the fluctuating colour in her cheeks, the frightened, wary look in her eyes that told plainly of indecision.

'Why, no, I – I don't think so!'

'You did not, by any chance, see him last night?'

'Last night?' Helen repeated. 'Of course not! Whatever made you think I might have?'

'I have reason to think that some woman visited him yesterday evening.'

'Good gracious, why should it be me, I wonder!'

He said in his quiet way: 'Please don't misunderstand

me, Mrs North. I am quite prepared to find that the woman was not you. Indeed, I'm sorry to be obliged to worry you with these questions. But I'm sure you'll realise that the presence of a woman at Greystones last night must be investigated, for it is just possible that she, whoever she is, may be able to throw a little light on the murder.'

'How?' she said quickly.

'She may, quite unwittingly, have seen the murderer.'

'Oh!' she exclaimed, shuddering. 'But it's preposterous to suppose that *I* –'

He interrupted, saying in a matter-of-fact way: 'Well, Mrs North, the question can be settled quite easily. What size in shoes do you wear?'

A quiver ran over her face; she threw a glance towards her sister, who stepped promptly into the breach. 'Five-and-a-half, don't you, like me?'

'Yes,' she admitted. 'Yes, I do. I think most women of our height do.'

'Thank you,' said Hannasyde. 'I wonder if you would lend me the shoes you were wearing last night?'

'Lend you my shoes! Really, Superintendent, that's quite impossible!'

'Why, Mrs North?'

'Well, you must *see* – Oh, this is idiotic! *I* had nothing to do with Ernie Fletcher's death!'

'Then you can have no possible objection to lending me your shoes for half-an-hour,' said Hannasyde.

'Of course she hasn't,' said Sally. 'What's more, you shall have mine as well. I knew Ernest Fletcher too, so presumably there is just as much reason to suspect me of having been at Greystones last night as my sister.'

'Not quite,' he replied.

Helen sat down suddenly on the sofa. 'I can't stand this!' she said in a choking voice. 'There's no reason why you should come and badger me! Simply because I happened to know Ernie Fletcher –'

'Not entirely,' he said. 'Are not these yours, Mrs North?'

She looked at the slips of paper which he had taken from his pocket-book. The colour rushed into her face, but some of her strained rigidity left her. 'Yes. They're mine,' she answered. 'What of it?'

'They call for some kind of explanation, as I think you'll agree,' he said. 'Did you owe these various sums of money to Mr Fletcher?'

'No. That is, not in the way you seem to think. He bought up those debts, to get me out of a – a hole, and I was – I was repaying him bit by bit.' She glanced up fleetingly, and added, twisting her handkerchief between her fingers: 'I did not wish my – my husband to know. He – I – oh, this is impossible!'

'I quite appreciate your reluctance to discuss your affairs, Mrs North. It may make it easier for you to be frank with me if you can bring yourself to believe that except in so far as they may relate to the case I am at work on I have no interest in them, and certainly no desire to create any unnecessary – er – scandal.'

'There's nothing to make a scandal about!' she said. 'Mr Fletcher was just a friend. The whole arrangement was perfectly amicable. I don't know what you are imagining, but –'

'You can put an end to any imaginings of mine by being open with me, Mrs North. I have told you that I appreciate your point of view, but you must see that the discovery of these notes of yours in Ernest Fletcher's safe is a circumstance which must be fully inquired into. If you can satisfy me that you did not visit Greystones last night I shall have no further need to worry you with interrogations which you must naturally find unpleasant. But if you can bring no proof forward in support of your denial, and persist in refusing to let me compare your shoes with the footprints we have found in the garden at Greystones, I can have no alternative to pursuing my inquiries further. In which event, I fear there will be little hope of your evading the sort of publicity you must wish to avoid.'

Sally got up from her seat by the table, and walked forward. 'That,' she said, 'sounds remarkably like a threat, Superintendent.'

'I expect it does,' he agreed equably. 'It isn't, though. I am only trying to point out to your sister that her wisest course is to be entirely frank with me. If I have to question her servants as to her whereabouts last night –'

'I get it,' said Sally, grimacing. She took a cigarette from the box on the table, and fitted it into her holder. She glanced speculatively at Hannasyde, and took a lighter from her pocket. The little flame spurted up; she lit her cigarette, once more looked at Hannasyde, and then said tersely: 'He's right, Helen. And what he says about having no interest in your affairs is true. He's got nothing on you, but obviously you've got to be eliminated.'

Helen looked frightened, but after a pause said: 'I did call on Ernie Fletcher last night. I've explained that he was a – a great friend, though *years* older than me. I looked on him as a sort of uncle.'

'Quite,' said Hannasyde. 'Had you any particular purpose in paying this call?'

'No, not exactly. My sister was busy, and I was bored. It was quite early, and I thought I'd just look in on Ernie.'

In spite of herself she coloured, but Hannasyde merely asked: 'At what hour did you arrive at Greystones?'

'It must have been at about five-and-twenty to ten. I know I left this house at half-past nine.'

'Just tell me everything that happened, Mrs North.'

'Really, there's so little to tell. I went by way of the Arden Road, because for one thing it's quicker than going all the way up this road, and along Vale Avenue, and for another – I expect this seems odd to you, but it isn't really – I didn't much want to see Miss Fletcher, so I thought I'd go in by the garden-entrance, on the chance of finding Ern – Mr Fletcher in his study.' She broke off, and exclaimed wretchedly: 'Oh, this is too impossible! It sounds as though I had some horrid assignation! But I hadn't, I hadn't!'

'Don't go over at the knees,' recommended her sister. 'It's obvious you hadn't, or you'd have thought up some convincing reason for calling on Ernie.'

'Oh, don't! Do you suppose I can't see what a false impression anyone must get, not – not knowing the terms I was on with Ernie?'

'The only impression the Superintendent's got is that you're a paralytic ass,' responded Sally cheerfully. 'Why you chose to enter by the garden-gate has got nothing to do with him, so get on with your story!'

'I don't know where I was. Oh yes! Well, Mr Fletcher was in his study – oh, I forgot to tell you that I saw a man coming out of the gate, just as I turned up into Maple Grove. I – I don't know whether that's any use to you?'

'Can you describe him, Mrs North?'

'No, except that he was rather stout and short. You see, it was dusk, and I didn't see his face. He walked off towards Vale Avenue. Well, I found Mr Fletcher in his study, as I said.'

'Was he alone?'

'Oh yes!'

'And then?'

'Well – well, nothing, really. We had a – a talk, and then I said I mustn't be late, and – and just left.'

'Do you know what the time was then?'

'Yes, it was a quarter to ten.'

'A quarter to ten?' he repeated, raising his head from his notebook.

'Yes. There was a clock on the mantelpiece, and I happened to notice the time.'

'Then you were only with Mr Fletcher for ten minutes?'

'I suppose so. Yes, it must have been about that.'

'A very short call, Mrs North, was it not?'

'I don't see why – What do you mean?'

'Merely that it strikes me as odd that having, as you yourself state, gone to see Mr Fletcher because you were bored, you stayed so short a time with him. Did anything happen to make you anxious to leave at once?'

'No. No, of course not. Only I could see he was busy, and I didn't want to be a nuisance.'

He made a note in his book. 'I see. So you left the study at 9.45. Did you return home by the way you had come?'

'Yes. But not immediately. I heard the garden-gate open, and – and it occurred to me that it would look rather odd – my being there at that hour. I didn't want anyone to see me, so I hid behind a bush.'

'Mr Fletcher, then, did not accompany you to the gate?'

'No,' she faltered. 'There was no reason why he should.'

'Oh!' said Hannasyde. 'Very well, Mrs North: you hid behind a bush. Did you see who it was that entered the garden?'

'No, I didn't. I mean, in the dusk, and – and only being able to peer through the bush, I couldn't get a clear view. I only know it was a man. He looked quite ordinary, but he had a hat on, and I didn't see his face.'

'What sort of hat, Mrs North?'

'A Homburg, I think.'

'Light or dark?'

She hesitated. 'I think it was a light one.'

'Did you happen to notice whether he carried a walking-stick?'

'No. No, I'm sure he didn't.'

'Did he go up to the house?'

'Yes, he went into Mr Fletcher's study.'

'Did you hear what happened then?'

'No. As soon as it was safe to do so I went away, of course. I don't know anything more.'

Hannasyde shut his notebook, and, looking straight across

at Helen, said bluntly: 'Mrs North, are you prepared to state that your visit to Mr Fletcher was not in connection with these notes of yours?'

'I don't understand. I've told you –'

'I don't think you've told me the whole truth.'

'I don't know why you should say that, or what you may choose to suspect, but –'

'I suspect that Mr Fletcher was threatening to use these notes against you, Mrs North.'

'That's absurd! I tell you he was a friend of mine!'

'Yes, you have told me that, but I find it difficult to reconcile that statement with the presence of the IOUs in his safe. If his motives in obtaining possession of them were as chivalrous as you say they were, it would surely have been more natural for him either to have destroyed them, or to have given them back to you?'

'Are you suggesting that he was trying to blackmail me? It isn't true! Good heavens, what could he possibly want to blackmail me for?'

'Perhaps he wanted something from you which you were unwilling to give, Mrs North.'

She flushed. 'Oh – ! You've no right to say that! Besides, how could he blackmail me? It isn't a sin to get into debt!'

'He might have threatened to lay your IOUs before your husband, might he not?'

'He wouldn't – he wasn't like that!' she said faintly.

'Where is your husband, Mrs North?'

'He's in Berlin. He went last week, and won't be back till next Wednesday.'

Even as the words left her lips he saw her face change. The click of an opening door had sounded. Hannasyde turned quickly. A man had entered the room, and was standing on the threshold, his hand resting on the doorknob, his cool, rather stern grey eyes surveying the group in the middle of the room.

Four

H ANNASYDE HEARD THE FRIGHTENED GASP THAT CAME
from Helen, and glanced once towards her. She was
very white, gazing as though benumbed at the newcomer. It
was Sally who spoke.

'Hullo, John!' she said nonchalantly. 'Where did you
spring from?'

John North closed the door, and walked forward. 'How do
you do, Sally?' he responded. His voice was a deep one, and
he spoke with a certain deliberation. He was a well-built man
of average height, good-looking, and with a manner quietly
assured. Having shaken hands with his sister-in-law, he nodded
at his wife, saying: 'Well, Helen? Sally keeping you company?'

'Yes, she's staying here,' Helen answered breathlessly. 'John,
what are you doing here? I thought you were in Berlin!'

'I got through my business there more quickly than I
expected.' He looked at Hannasyde in a measuring way, and
said: 'Will you introduce me, Helen?'

She threw an imploring look at Hannasyde, but said: 'Yes,
of course. It is Superintendent – oh dear, I'm afraid I have
forgotten your name, Superintendent!'

'Hannasyde,' he supplied.

'Yes, from Scotland Yard, John. Rather a dreadful thing has happened – well, a *ghastly* thing! Ernest Fletcher has been murdered.'

'That doesn't seem to me to explain the presence of the Superintendent in my house,' he said calmly. 'May I know what you are doing here, Superintendent?'

Before Hannasyde could reply Helen had hurried into speech. 'Oh, but don't you see, John? The Superintendent is trying to discover someone who might be able to throw any light on the mystery, and hearing that I knew Ernie, he came to see if I could help. Only of course I can't. The whole thing seems absolutely incredible to me.'

His brows rose a little. 'Are you making a house-to-house visitation of all Fletcher's acquaintances, Superintendent? Or do you suspect my wife of having knocked him on the head? I hardly think she possesses the necessary strength.'

'You are well informed, Mr North. Where did you learn that he had been knocked on the head?'

John North looked at him with a faint smile in his eyes. He drew a folded newspaper from under his arm, and handed it to Hannasyde. 'You may study the source of my information if you wish,' he said politely.

Hannasyde glanced down the columns of the evening paper. 'Quick work,' he remarked, folding the paper again, and giving it back. 'Were you acquainted with the deceased, Mr North?'

'I knew him, certainly. I should not describe my acquaintance with him as very close. But if you are interrogating everyone who knew him, perhaps you would like to come into the library, and interrogate me?' He moved to the door as he spoke, and opened it. 'Or have you not yet finished questioning my wife?'

'Yes, I think so.' Hannasyde turned to Helen, meeting her anguished look with the flicker of a reassuring smile. 'Thank you, Mrs North: I won't take up any more of your time. Good-morning, Miss Drew.'

'You haven't seen the last of me by a long chalk,' Sally told him. 'I don't think my name conveys anything to you, which is rather levelling, but I'm a writer of crime novels, and I have never before had the opportunity of studying a crime at close quarters. What is of particular interest to me is your handling of the case. One is always apt to go wrong on police procedure.'

'I suppose so,' answered Hannasyde, looking rather appalled.

She gave him a sudden, swift smile. 'You've taught me one thing at least: I've always made my detectives a bit on the noisome side up till now.'

He laughed. 'Thank you!' He bowed slightly to Helen, and went out of the room before John North, who was still holding the door for him.

'This way, Superintendent,' North said, leading the way across the hall. 'Now what is it you would like to ask me? You have established the fact that I was acquainted with Fletcher.'

'But not, I think you said, very well acquainted with him?'

'Not so well acquainted with him as my wife was,' replied North. 'You will probably find that his closest friends were all of them women.'

'You did not like him, in fact, Mr North?'

'I can't say I was drawn to him,' admitted North. 'I should describe him as a ladies' man. The type has never appealed to me.'

'Did you consider him a dangerous man – with ladies?'

'Dangerous? Oh no, I shouldn't imagine so!' North said, a suggestion of boredom in his voice. 'My wife, for instance, regarded him, I believe, somewhat in the light of a tame cat.'

'I see. So, speaking as a husband, you would not consider it worth while to be – let us say – jealous of him?'

'I cannot pretend to speak for anyone but myself. But I take it that you do not want me to. I was not jealous of him. Is there anything else you wish to ask me?'

'Yes, I should like to know when you returned from the Continent, Mr North?'

'I arrived in London yesterday afternoon.'

'But you did not come down to Marley until this morning?'

'No, Superintendent, I did not.'

'Where did you go, Mr North?'

'To my flat, Superintendent.'

'Where is that, if you please?'

'In Portland Place.'

'Was that usual?'

'Quite.'

'You will have to forgive my bluntness, Mr North, but I must ask you to explain yourself a little more fully. Do you and Mrs North inhabit separate establishments?'

'Not in the sense which you appear to mean,' replied North. 'I may be wrong, but you seem to attach a sinister importance to my having chosen to remain in London for the night. My wife and I have been married for five years, Superintendent: we are long past the stage of living in one another's pockets.'

There an edge to the deliberate voice, which Hannasyde was quick to hear. As though aware of it himself, North added lightly: 'I am often kept late in town. I find the flat convenient.'

'I see. Did you dine there?'

'No, I dined at my club.'

'And after dinner?'

'After dinner I returned to the flat, and went to bed.'

'You were alone there? Or are there any servants?'

'Oh, I was quite alone! It is a service flat, and I had given my valet leave to go out for the evening. I'm afraid I cannot – at the moment – bring forward any corroborative evidence, Superintendent. Perhaps you would like to take my finger-prints?'

'No, not at present, thank you,' returned Hannasyde. 'In fact, I hardly think I need detain you any longer.'

North walked over to the door. 'Well, you know where you can find me if you should want to ask me any further questions. My business and flat addresses are both in the London Telephone Directory.'

He led the way into the hall, and across it to the front door. A pale grey Homburg lay on the gate-leg table, beside a pair of wash-leather gloves. Hannasyde's eyes rested on it for a moment, but he made no comment, merely picking up his own hat from the chair whereon he had laid it.

Having seen him off the premises, North returned unhurriedly to the morning-room, entering it in time to hear his sister-in-law say trenchantly: 'You must be suffering from mental paralysis! You can't possibly hope to keep it from –'

She saw who was coming into the room, and snapped the sentence off in mid-air. North closed the door, tossed the newspaper he was still carrying on to the table, and said suavely: 'What can't she possibly hope to keep from me?'

'Did I say from you?' demanded Sally.

'It was sufficiently obvious.' He began methodically to fill a pipe. An uncomfortable silence fell. Helen was sitting with her gaze fixed on North's face, and her hands tightly clasped in her lap. As he restored his pouch to his pocket he raised his eyes, and for a moment looked steadily into hers. 'Well? Isn't it so?'

She evaded the question. 'What brought you home so unexpectedly, John?'

'Does that really interest you?' he inquired.

She said in a low, unsteady voice: 'You came back to spy on me!'

A hard look came into his face. He said nothing, however, but felt in his pocket for matches, and began to light his pipe.

A less intense note was introduced by Miss Drew, who said brightly: 'Would you by any chance like me to withdraw tactfully? I should hate to think I was cramping either of your styles.'

'No, don't go!' Helen said. 'John and I have nothing private to discuss.' She glanced up at North, and added with an attempt at nonchalance: 'It would be interesting to know why you elected to come home in the middle of the morning. You can't have felt an overwhelming desire for my company, or you'd have come last night.'

'No,' he replied imperturbably. 'We are rather beyond that, aren't we? I came when I read about Fletcher's murder.'

'There! What did I tell you?' said Sally. 'The answer to the maiden's prayer! Not that I'm fond of the protective type myself, but I should be if I were a pretty ninny like you, Helen.'

'Oh, don't be absurd!' Helen said, a catch in her voice. 'So you thought I might be mixed up in the murder, did you, John?'

He did not answer for a moment, but after a pause he said in his cool way: 'No, I don't think I suspected that seriously until I found a Superintendent from Scotland Yard in the house.'

She stiffened. 'Surely you understand the reason for that! He came simply –'

'Yes, I understood.' For the first time a harsh note sounded in his voice. 'The Superintendent came to discover whether the woman's footprint in the garden was yours. Was it?'

'Count ten before you answer,' recommended Sally, her eyes on North's grim face. Golly, she thought, this isn't going to be such plain sailing as I'd imagined.

'Oh, why can't you be quiet?' Helen cried sharply. 'What are you trying to do?'

'Stop you telling useless lies. You may be all washed-up, you two, but I don't see John letting you get pinched for murder if he can help it.'

'I didn't murder him! I didn't! You can't think that!'

'Were the footprints yours?' North asked.

She got up jerkily. 'Yes! They were mine!' she flung at him.

Sally gave a groan. 'How not to break the news!' she said. 'For God's sake, try to stop looking like something carved out of the solid rock, John! Holy mackerel, to think I've written books about people like you, and never believed a word of it!'

North disregarded her, addressing his wife. 'No doubt I shall seem to you unwarrantably intrusive, but I should like to know why you visited Fletcher in this apparently clandestine fashion?'

'I went to see him because he's – he was – a friend of mine. There was nothing clandestine about our relations. I don't expect you to believe that, but it's true!'

Sally polished her eyeglass. 'Questioned, Miss Sally Drew, an eminent writer of detective fiction, corroborated that statement.' ·

'You are a somewhat partial witness, Sally,' North said dryly. 'Oh, don't look so belligerent, Helen! I merely asked out of curiosity. It's really quite beside the point. What seems to me to be more important is what, if anything, you know about the murder?'

'Nothing, nothing!'

'When were you with Fletcher?' he asked.

'Oh, early, quite early! I left his study at a quarter to ten. John, I know it sounds strange, but I went to see him on a perfectly trivial matter. I – I wanted to know if he'd go with me to the Dimberleys' affair next week, that's all.'

He paid no heed to this, but picked up the newspaper and studied the front page. 'I see that Fletcher's body was discovered at 10.05 p.m.,' he remarked. He looked steadily across at his wife. 'And you know nothing?'

'I saw a man come up the path,' she said in a low voice. 'That's why I hid behind the bush.'

He folded the newspaper very exactly. 'You saw a man come up the path? Well? Who was it?'

'I don't know.'

'Do you mean you didn't recognise him?'

'Yes – that is, I couldn't see him distinctly. I – I only know that he went into the study, through the window.'

'Have you told the police this?'

'Yes, I – I told them.'

'Did the Superintendent ask you if you would be able to recognise this mysterious man if you saw him again?'

'No. I told him that I couldn't see at all clearly, and only had a vague impression of an ordinary sort of man in a light hat.'

There was a slight pause. 'In a light hat? Oh! And would you recognise him again?'

'No, I tell you! I haven't the least idea who it was!'

'I hope the Superintendent believed you,' he remarked.

'Why?' demanded Sally, who had been watching him closely.

He glanced indifferently down at her. 'Why? Because I have no desire to see my wife in the witness-box, of course.'

'Oh, my God, I shan't have to give evidence, shall I?' gasped Helen. 'I couldn't. I'd rather die! Oh, what a ghastly *mess* it all is!'

'It is indeed,' he said.

Sally, who had been rhythmically swinging her monocle on the end of its cord, suddenly screwed it into her eye, and asked: 'Does the Superintendent suspect you of having had anything to do with it, John?'

'I've no idea what he suspects. Helen's connection with the crime has evidently given him food for thought. He probably suffers from old-fashioned ideas about jealous husbands.'

She cocked her head on one side. 'I should have thought you were capable of being a trifle primitive. What's more, your somewhat unexpected appearance on the scene must look a bit fishy to him.'

'Why should it? If I'd murdered Fletcher I should hardly have come down here today.'

She considered this dispassionately. 'Dunno. It's a point, of course, but it would have looked bad if you'd lain low, and he'd found out that you weren't in Berlin at all.'

'Give me credit for a little common sense, Sally. When I commit a murder I can assure you I shall take good care to cover my tracks.' He glanced at his wrist-watch. 'Ask them to put lunch forward, will you, Helen? I've got to go back to town.'

'I'll go and tell Evans,' offered Sally, and went out, firmly shutting the door behind her.

Helen mechanically straightened an ornament on the mantelpiece. 'Are you – are you coming back?' she asked.

'Certainly I'm coming back,' he replied.

She hesitated, then said in a low voice: 'You're very angry about this…'

'We won't discuss that. The mischief is done, and I imagine my possible anger is unlikely to make you regret it more than you are already doing.'

She lifted her hand to her cheek. 'You don't believe me, but I wasn't having an affair with Ernie.'

'Oh yes, I believe you!' he returned.

Her hand fell. 'You do believe me? You didn't think I was in love with him – ever? I thought –'

'You thought because I personally disliked the man, and your intimacy with him, that I was jealous,' he said sardonically. 'You were wrong. I always knew he was not the type you fall for, my dear.'

She winced. 'It is not fair to say I fall for anyone. It sounds – rather Victorian, but I've been perfectly faithful to you.'

'I am aware of that.'

'You have made it your business to be sure of that!'

'It was my business,' he replied hardly.

'Why did you behave as you did over my friendship with Ernie, then? You knew you could at least trust me not to indulge in a vulgar intrigue!'

'It wasn't you, but Fletcher whom I mistrusted,' he said. 'I warned you that I wouldn't stand for that particular friendship, didn't I?'

'What right had you to expect me to drop him or any other of my friends? You allowed me to go my own road, and you went yours –'

'This is a singularly unprofitable discussion,' he interrupted. 'You chose to go your own road, but if I remember rightly I made it clear to you two years ago that I would not tolerate either your debts or your indiscretions. Six months ago I requested you to keep Ernest Fletcher at arm's length. You have been almost continuously in his company ever since.'

'I liked him. I didn't love him!'

'You can hardly have expected the world to know that.'

'But you knew it!'

He looked at her with narrowed eyes. 'I knew that Fletcher had a peculiar fascination for women.'

'Yes! That's true, and I did feel that fascination. But love – ! Oh, no, no, no!' She turned away in some agitation, and walked rather blindly towards the window. With her back to the room, she said after a moment: 'Why did you come down here today? You suspected I was – mixed up in this, didn't you?'

'Yes,' he said. 'I did.'

'I wonder you came, then,' she said bitterly.

He did not answer at once, but presently he said in a gentler voice: 'That's silly, Helen. Whatever our differences we are man and wife, and if there's trouble brewing we're both in it. I hope, however, that it'll blow over. Try not to worry about it – and don't say more than you need if Superintendent Hannasyde questions you any further.'

'No. I'll be very careful,' she replied.

Miss Drew reappeared at that moment, with the tidings that luncheon would be ready in five minutes.

'Thanks. I'll go and wash,' North said, and went out.

Sally eyed her sister's back speculatively. 'Tell him the truth?'

'No.'

'Fool.'

'I couldn't. It's no use arguing: you just don't understand.'

'He'd prefer the true story to the obvious alternative.'

'You're wrong. He knows there was nothing between Ernie and me.'

'*Does* he?' said Sally.

Helen wheeled round. 'What do you mean?'

'I'm not sure. But somehow he didn't give me that impression. If he knew there was nothing between you and Ernie, I don't quite see the reason for the very definite animus against Ernie.'

'He never cared much for him. But as for animus, that's absurd!'

'Oh no, it isn't, and you know it isn't, my girl! John's wasting no tears over Ernie's death. Moreover, it wouldn't altogether surprise me to learn that he knows more than you think he does.'

'Once a novelist always a novelist!' said Helen, with a little laugh.

'Too true! And that being so, I think I'll wander round to take a look at the scene of the crime after lunch.'

'You can't possibly do that!'

'What's to stop me?'

'It isn't decent!'

'Decent be blowed! I shall go and rout that poor worm Neville out. He's another person who conceivably knows more than he chooses to admit. I hope the police aren't underrating him; immense potentialities in Neville.'

'Potentialities for what?'

'You have me there, sister,' replied Sally. 'I'm damned if I know, but I'm going to have a shot at finding out.'

Luncheon was announced a moment later, and the subject of Ernest Fletcher's death was abandoned. Throughout the meal, Helen said little, and ate less. Miss Drew maintained a cheerful flow of small talk, and North, having eaten a hurried meal, left the table early, informing his wife that he would be back to dinner.

After the ladies had finished their coffee, Sally gave it as her considered opinion that Helen would be the better for a rest. Somewhat to her surprise Helen fell in with this suggestion, and allowed herself to be escorted upstairs. When Sally lowered the window-blinds she said: 'You aren't really going round to Greystones, are you?'

'Yes, I am. Taking a message of condolence from you to poor old Miss Fletcher. I shall say you are writing to her, of course.'

A faint voice from amongst the banked-up pillows said: 'Oh! I ought to have done that!'

'Time enough when you've had a nap,' said Sally, and withdrew.

Half-an-hour later, when she presented herself at the front door at Greystones, it was to be met by the intelligence that Miss Fletcher, like Helen, was resting. She was spared the necessity of inquiring for Neville by that willowy young gentleman's strolling out of the drawing-room into the hall, and inviting her to enter and solace his boredom.

Simmons made it plain by his cough and general air of pious gloom that he considered the invitation unseasonable, but as neither Sally nor Neville paid the slightest heed to him, there was nothing for him to do but to retire to his own domain, on the far side of a baize door leading out of the hall, and draw, for his wife's edification, an unpleasing picture of the fate awaiting the hard-hearted and the irreligious.

Meanwhile, Neville had escorted his visitor into the drawing-room. 'Come to see the sights, darling?' he inquired. 'You're too late to see the dragging of the lily-pool.'

'Ah!' she said. 'So they're after the weapon, are they?'

'Yes, but there's no pleasing them. I offered them Aunt Lucy's Indian clubs, a mallet, and the bronze paper-weight on Ernie's desk, but they didn't seem to like any of them.'

'So there was a bronze paper-weight on his desk, was there? H'm!'

'Well, no,' said Neville softly, 'There wasn't. I put it there.'

'What on earth for?'

'Oh, just to occupy their minds!' said Neville, seraphically smiling.

'It'll serve you right if you get pinched for the murder,' Sally told him.

'Yes, but I shan't. I was right about Honest John, wasn't I?'

'Yes. How did you know he was back?'

'News does get about so, doesn't it?'

'Rot!'

'All right, precious. I saw him drive past the house on the way to the station. Flying the country?'

'Not he. John's not that sort. Besides, why should he?'

Neville regarded her with sleepy shrewdness. 'Do not bother to put on the frills with me, sweet maid. It is worrying for you, isn't it?'

'Not in the least. My interest in the murder is purely academic. Why do they think the instrument is still on the premises? Because of what Helen said?'

'They don't confide in me as much as you'd think they would,' replied Neville. 'What did Helen say?'

'Oh, that she was sure the man she saw wasn't carrying anything!'

'Bless her little heart, did she? Isn't she fertile? First, she didn't see the man at all; now she knows he wasn't carrying anything. Give her time and she'll remember that he had bandy legs and a squint.'

'You poisonous reptile, just because it wasn't light enough for her to recognise the man –'

'Oh, do you think it wasn't?' asked Neville. 'You've a kind heart, and no Norman blood.'

'Oh! So you think she did recognise the man, and that it was John, do you?'

'Yes, but I have a low mind,' he explained.

'You've taken the words out of my mouth.'

'I know.'

'Well, I've got the same kind of low mind, and the thought that crosses it is that you're probably the heir to Ernie's money. Correct?'

'Yes, rather,' said Neville cordially. 'I'm practically a plutocrat.'

'Yes?' said Sally. 'Then it'll be a nice change for you, Mr Neville Fletcher, after having been up to your eyes in debt!'

Five

～

THIS SUGGESTION, HURLED AT HIS HEAD LIKE A CHALLENGE, was received by Neville with unruffled placidity. He appeared to consider the matter dispassionately, remarking at length: 'Well, I don't know that I altogether agree with you.'

'What?' said Sally scornfully. 'You don't agree that a fortune is better than debt?'

'Depends what you're accustomed to,' said Neville.

'Don't be a fool! You don't imagine I'm going to swallow that, do you?'

'No.'

'Then what on earth's the use of saying it?'

'I mean I haven't speculated on the processes of your mind,' explained Neville. 'Unprofitable occupation, quite without point.'

'Look here, Neville, are you sticking to it that you've no objection to being snowed under by debts?' demanded Sally.

'Yes, why not?'

'It doesn't add up, that's why not. There's nothing more uncomfortable than not having any money, and being dunned by tradesmen. Receiving To Account Rendered by every post, with a veiled threat attached, and totting up the ghastly totals –'

'Oh, but I don't do anything like that!' Neville assured her. 'I never open bills.'

'Then you get County Courted.'

'You soon get used to that. Besides, Ernie hated it, so he got into the way of paying my outstanding debts. Really, the whole thing worked out very well. Now I've got his money I shall never have a moment's peace. People will badger me.'

'Well, you can employ a secretary.'

'I shouldn't like that at all. I should have to have a house to put him in, and servants to run it, and before I knew what had happened I should find myself shackled by respectability.'

This point of view struck Sally quite forcibly. 'I must say, I hadn't looked at it like that,' she admitted. 'It does sound rather lousy. What do you want to do?'

'Nothing, at the moment. But I may easily want to wander off to Bulgaria next week. It's a place I hardly know.'

'You'll still be able to, won't you?'

'First class ticket to Sofia, and a suite at the best hotel? Not if I know it!'

Sally was so much interested that she was beguiled into pursuing the subject of foreign travel. Neville's disjointed yet picturesque account of incredible adventures encountered during the course of aimless and impecunious wanderings held her entranced, and drew from her at length a rather wistful exclamation of: 'Golly, what fun you must have had! I wish I were a man. Why haven't you written a book about all this?'

'That,' said Neville incorrigibly, 'would have invested my travels with a purpose, and spoilt them for me.'

'You're definitely sub-human,' said Sally. She eyed him curiously. 'Does anything ever worry you?'

'Yes. Problem of how to escape worry.'

She grinned, but said: 'I hate paradox. Does this little situation worry you?'

'What, Ernie's murder? No, why should it?'

'Does it strike you that you've got a pretty good motive for having killed Ernie?'

'Naturally not.'

'The police will think so.'

'Too busy chasing after the unknown man seen by Helen and Malachi.'

'Who?'

'Haven't you met Malachi?' said Neville, roused to sudden interest. 'Oh, I must introduce you at once! Come on!'

'Yes, but who is he?' demanded Sally.

He took her wrist and led her out into the garden through the long window. 'He's the bobby who discovered the crime.'

'Good Lord, did he see Helen's man too? That wasn't in the paper John brought home!'

'Oh, here we live at the hub of the crime!' said Neville.

'Just a moment,' interposed Sally, pulling her hand away. 'I want to take a look at the general lay-out. Anyone mounting guard over the study?'

'Not now. Nothing to be seen.'

'I might get an idea,' Sally said darkly.

'Morbid mind, professional interest, or family feeling?'

She ignored the implication of this last alternative. 'Professional interest.'

They had rounded the corner of the house, and come in sight of the path leading to a gate set in the fence separating the garden from Maple Grove. A thick bed of shrubs concealed the fence from view, and was being subjected to a rigorous search by two hot and rather dishevelled policemen. Sally cast them a cursory glance, and transferred her attention to the house. 'Which is Helen's bush?'

He pointed it out to her, and she went to it, inspected the footprints, and would have concealed herself behind it had it not been for the prompt action of PC Glass, who, having observed her arrival with some disapproval, now abandoned his search in the shrubbery to admonish her.

'It's all right,' said Sally. 'I'm not going to obliterate the prints, or anything like that. I only want to get an idea of what anyone hidden here, in the dark, could actually see. I'm interested in crime.'

'Remove thy foot from evil,' recommended Glass severely. 'These things are in the hands of the police.'

'Don't you bother your head about me: I've made a study of murder. I may be able to help,' said Sally.

'Like me,' murmured Neville. 'I tried to help, but no one was grateful.'

A cold eye was bent upon him. 'Bread of deceit is sweet to a man,' said Glass. 'But afterwards,' he added forebodingly, 'his mouth shall be filled with gravel.'

Sally, having by this time satisfied herself that very little could be seen from behind the currant bush, emerged. 'Is that out of the Bible?' she inquired. 'Nearly all the best things are, except those that come out of Shakespeare. Can I go into the study, Neville?'

'Do!' he said cordially.

'What is your business here?' demanded Glass. 'Why do you desire to enter that room?'

'I'm a novelist,' explained Sally. 'Crime stories.'

'You were better at home,' he said sombrely, but made no further attempt to stop her.

Followed by Neville, who had produced a Bible from his pocket, and was swiftly flicking the pages over, Sally entered the study, and stood just inside the window, looking round. Neville sat down on the edge of the desk, absorbed in his search through the Proverbs.

'Where was he found?' Sally said abruptly.

Neville jerked his head in the direction of the chair behind the desk.

'Facing the window?'

'Yes. Don't bother me!'

'Actually seated in his chair?'

'Mm. I've got a goodish bit here about the lips of the strange woman, but that's not the one I want.'

'And the murderer is supposed to have entered by way of the window, which Ernie was directly facing?'

'Flattery is the tongue of the strange woman…no, that's not it.'

'Oh, do take your head out of that! Don't you see that if the murderer entered by way of the window Ernie must have been entirely unsuspicious? He apparently didn't even get up from his chair!'

'Got it!' said Neville triumphantly. '*She is loud and stubborn; her feet abide not in her house.* That's you. I'm going to tell Glass.' He slid off the edge of the table, and departed in search of the policeman.

Left alone, Sally sat down in an armchair, dropped her chin in her cupped hands, and frowned upon her surroundings. Neville soon reappeared, saying: 'He reproved me. Seemed to know the context.'

'What was that?' asked Sally absently.

'Not polite. Only two kinds of women in the OT. This was the other kind. Solved the whole mystery?'

'No, but as I see it one fact stands out a mile. It wasn't John.'

'All right; have it your own way.'

'Yes, but don't you see?' she insisted. 'Ernie wasn't expecting to be murdered. If John had walked in, wouldn't he – No, I suppose it doesn't absolutely follow. One doesn't expect even jealous husbands to murder one.'

'Oh, is John jealous?' said Neville. 'I thought he was quite complaisant.'

'That's what a great many people think, but –' She stopped. 'Forget it!'

'Crediting me with an earnest desire to incriminate Honest John?' inquired Neville. 'Non-existent, believe me.'

'Nevertheless I should probably be wise not to say too much to you,' said Sally bluntly.

'That's all right with me too,' he assured her. 'As a subject for conversation, I find that Ernie's murder palls on one.'

She looked at him. 'You're a cold-blooded fish, Neville. I didn't like Ernie, but gosh, I'm sorry for him!'

'What a waste of emotion!' he remarked. 'What's the use of being sorry for a dead man?'

'There's something in that,' she admitted. 'But it's hardly decent to say so. Oh, damn it all, this is a rotten mess! Why the dickens couldn't you have got hold of those IOUs before it all happened?'

'Oh, have they been found?' said Neville.

'Of course they have!'

'John pleased?'

'He doesn't know anything about them. Helen won't tell him.'

He blinked. 'Let me get this straight, just in case of accidents. What is Helen's story?'

'That she went round to see Ernie on some trivial matter. Yes, I know it's insane, but she probably knows her own business best. John wasn't particularly encouraging, and as he's apparently rabid on the subject of gambling and debts, I daresay she's right not to tell him. If you run into John, you'd better know nothing about it.'

'You go home and tell Helen about the bread of deceit,' said Neville. 'I don't think she's being very clever.'

'No, poor darling, but she's all in. I've left her on her bed, and I hope she'll be feeling a bit better by the time I get back – more able to cope. I don't think she slept much last night.'

'Well, let's hope she doesn't do anything silly,' said Neville. 'She probably will, but with any luck she'll merely confuse the issue.'

'She happens to be my sister,' said Sally frigidly.

'Yes, it's the best thing I know of her,' agreed Neville.

Sally, taken by surprise, showed signs of being overcome.

'And the worst thing I know of you,' added Neville dulcetly.

Sally cast him a withering look, and left the study to exercise her charm on the younger of the two policemen still searching the shrubbery.

Helen, meanwhile, was not, as her sister had supposed, upon her bed, but closeted with Superintendent Hannasyde at the police station.

Upon Sally's leaving the house, she had lain for some few minutes, thinking. After glancing once or twice at the telephone she had at last sat up in bed, with the sudden energy of one who has come to a difficult decision, and lifted the receiver off its rest. 'I want to be put through to the police station,' she told the operator calmly.

She was connected almost immediately, and asked for Superintendent Hannasyde. The voice at the other end of the wire desired her, somewhat suspiciously, to divulge her identity. She hesitated, and then said: 'I am Mrs John North. If Superintendent Hannasyde –'

''*Old* on a minute!' said the voice.

She waited. Presently a fresh voice addressed her, and she recognised the Superintendent's even tones.

She hurried into speech. 'Superintendent, this is Mrs North speaking. I wonder if I could see you? There's something I wish to tell you.'

'Certainly,' he replied. 'I'll come up to your house.'

She glanced at her watch. 'No, don't do that. I have to go into town and I can quite easily call in at the police station, if that would be convenient to you?'

'Quite convenient,' he said.

'Thank you. I'll be there in about twenty minutes, then. Goodbye!'

She laid the receiver down and, flinging back the eiderdown, slid off the bed on to the floor. She pulled up the blinds which Sally had so thoughtfully lowered, and in the relentless glare of sunlight sat down at her dressing-table, and studied her face in the mirror. It was pale, with shadowed eyes. 'Heavens! What a guilty-looking sight!' she said under her breath, and with quick, nervous hands, pulled open a drawer and exposed an array of face-creams, lotions, and cosmetics.

Ten minutes later she was pulling on her gloves, her eyes resting critically on her own reflection. Her make-up had been delicately achieved; the face that confronted her from under the brim of a shady hat was faintly tinged with colour, the corn-coloured curls neatly arranged in a cluster in her neck, the eyebrows lightly pencilled, the lovely mouth a glow of red.

On her way down the stairs she encountered her maid, who exclaimed at her, bemoaning the fact that Madam was not resting after all.

'No, I've got to go out,' Helen answered. 'If Miss Drew should get back before me, tell her I've gone into the town, will you, but shall be back for tea.'

She drove herself to the police station, and was taken at once to the somewhat comfortless office where Hannasyde was going through a pile of documents.

He got up as she came in, and favoured her with a rather keen look. 'Good-afternoon, Mrs North. Will you sit down?'

She took a chair on the side of the desk opposite to him. 'Thank you. Do you know, the only time I've ever been to a police station before was about a dog I once lost?'

'Indeed?' he said. 'What is it you wish to say to me, Mrs North?'

She raised her eyes to his face. 'I want to tell you something which I ought to have told you this morning,' she said frankly.

'Yes?'

His voice betrayed nothing but a kind of polite interest. She found it a little disconcerting, and stumbled over her next words. 'It was silly of me, but you know how it is when one is suddenly confronted – or no, perhaps you don't. It's always you who – who asks the questions, isn't it?'

'I have had plenty of experience of people who either concealed the truth, or told me only a part of it, if that is what you mean, Mrs North.'

'I suppose it is,' she admitted. 'Perhaps you can understand, though, how awkward it was for me, when you – well, exposed my – my indiscretions this morning. I won't attempt to deny that I was badly rattled, not because of the murder, because I had nothing to do with that, but because I'm not the sort of woman my dealings with Mr Fletcher might have led you to suppose, and – and there could be nothing worse from my point of view than to have an indiscretion – like that – made public. The only idea in my head this morning was to admit as little as I need. You – you *do* understand that, don't you?'

He nodded. 'Perfectly, Mrs North. Please go on!'

'Yes. Well, since I saw you I've had time to think it over, and of course I realise that when it's a question of murder it would be terribly wrong of me to keep anything back. Moreover –' she smiled shyly across at him – 'you were so very nice about it, not – not giving me away to my husband, that I feel sure I can trust you.'

'I had better make it clear, Mrs North, that while I have not the smallest desire to create any unnecessary unpleasantness in connection with this case, my consideration for your feelings cannot interfere with the execution of what I may decide to be my duty.'

'Of course not; I quite appreciate that.'

He looked at her. A few hours earlier she had been nervous to the point of distraction, but she had herself well in hand now. She met his eyes deprecatingly, but quite squarely, and was sure enough of herself to employ little feminine tricks to beguile him. She was a lovely woman; he wondered what the brain behind her soft blue eyes was evolving. She was probably playing a part, but so well that he could not be sure of it. It was easy to believe that she had concealed some of the truth earlier in the day; the reasons she put forward for having done so were quite credible; but it would not be so easy to know how much of whatever revelations were to come was to be believed.

He said impersonally: 'Well, Mrs North? What is it that you are going to tell me?'

'It is about what happened after I hid behind that bush, outside Mr Fletcher's study. I said that as soon as the man who came up the path had entered the house I went away. Actually, I didn't go away.'

His keen eyes narrowed slightly. 'Indeed! Why not?'

She began to fidget a little with the clasp of her handbag. 'You see, what I originally said about my interview with Mr Fletcher wasn't true. It – it wasn't amicable. At least, not on my part. Mr Fletcher, as you suggested this morning, Superintendent, did want something from me which I – which I was more than unwilling to give. I don't want to give you a false impression. Looking back, I feel sure I lost my head over the whole affair, and – and perhaps exaggerated things. Mr Fletcher *was* using my IOUs against me, but in a playful sort of way. I expect it was only a bluff, for really he wasn't a bit like that. Only I was frightened, and behaved stupidly. I went round to his house that evening to try to persuade him to give me back my notes. Something he said made me lose my temper, and I walked out of the house in a rage. But while I was hiding behind the bush I realised that losing my temper wasn't going to help me. I thought perhaps I ought to have another shot at coaxing the notes out of Mr Fletcher, though at the same time I rather dreaded the idea of going back into that room.'

'Just a moment!' Hannasyde interrupted. 'What happened in the study while you were hiding behind the bush?'

'I don't know. You remember I told you that I thought the man I saw closed the window? Well, that was true. I only heard a confused murmur of voices. I don't think he was in the room for more than six or seven minutes. It seemed longer to me, but it can't have been, because the clock in the hall began to strike ten when I finally left the house. But I haven't got to that yet. While I was still waiting, and not knowing quite what I ought to do next, the window of the study was pushed open, and both Mr Fletcher and the other man came out. Mr Fletcher had a light, carrying voice, and I distinctly heard him say: "A little mistake on your part. Permit me to show you the way out!"'

'And the other? Did he speak?'

'Not in my hearing. Mr Fletcher said something else, but I couldn't catch what it was.'

'Did he appear to be at all put-out?'

'No, but he was the sort of man who never showed when he was annoyed. He sounded rather mocking, I thought. I don't think there can have been a quarrel, because he just strolled down the path with the other man quite casually, not hurrying, or anything. In fact, I rather thought that perhaps the man had walked in by mistake.'

'Oh! And then?'

'Well, you know that the path to the gate twists past some bushes? As soon as they had reached the bend, I slipped from behind the bush, and ran back to the study. I – I had a wild sort of hope that my notes might be in Mr Fletcher's desk, and it seemed to me that here was my chance to get hold of them. Most of the drawers were unlocked, and I didn't bother about them. But the centre drawer had its key in it, and I happened to know that Mr Fletcher used to keep it locked. I've seen him take the key out of his pocket to open it. I pulled it out, but I couldn't see my notes. Then I heard Mr Fletcher coming up the path: he was whistling. I got a sudden panic, and instead of staying where I was I shut the drawer, and whisked myself over to the door. I just had time to open it very gingerly to make sure that no one was in the hall, before escaping that way. There wasn't anyone in sight, and I slipped into the hall before Mr Fletcher had reached the study. That was when the clock began to strike. As a matter of fact, it gave me a dreadful start, because it's one of those tall-case clocks that make a whirring noise before they begin striking. I walked down the hall to the front door, let myself out as quietly as I could, and went home by way of Vale Avenue, which, I expect you know, cuts across the top of my own road.'

There was a short silence after she had finished speaking. Hannasyde moved a paper slightly on his desk. 'Mrs North, why have you told me this?' he asked.

'But – but isn't it obvious?' she said. 'I couldn't let you think that a perfectly innocent man might have murdered Mr Fletcher! You see, I *know* that Mr Fletcher was alive when that man left the house.'

'How long were you in the study, the second time?' he asked.

'I don't know, but not more than three minutes. Oh, less! I had only time to look hurriedly through that drawer before I heard Mr Fletcher coming back.'

'I see.'

Something in his voice made her stiffen. 'You don't believe me? But it's true: I can prove it's true!'

'Can you? How?'

She spread out her hands. 'I wasn't wearing gloves. My finger-prints must have been on the door. Look, I'll show you!' She got up, and moved to the door, clasping the handle in her right hand, and laying her left hand on the panel above it. 'You know how one eases a door open, if one's afraid of its making any noise? I remember putting my left hand on it, just like this.'

'Have you any objection to having your finger-prints taken, Mrs North?'

'No, none,' she answered promptly. 'I want you to have them taken. That's partly why I chose to see you here.'

'Very well, but there are one or two questions I should like to ask you first.'

She came back to her chair. 'Why, certainly!' she said.

'You have said that Mr Fletcher was using your IOUs against you. Does that mean that he was pressing for payment, or that he was threatening to lay them before you husband?'

'He did hint that my husband might be interested in them.'

'Are you on good terms with your husband, Mrs North?'

She gave an embarrassed little laugh. 'Yes, of course. Perfectly.'

'He had no cause to suspect you of any form of intimacy with Mr Fletcher?'

'No. Oh no! I have always had my own friends, and my husband never interfered.'

'He was not, then, jealous of your friendships with other men?'

'How old-fashioned of you, Superintendent! Of course not.'

'That implies great confidence in you, Mrs North.'

'Well, naturally…!'

'Yet in spite of this perfect understanding which you tell me existed between you, you were ready to steal your IOUs from Mr Fletcher rather than allow the knowledge of your gambling debts to come to your husband's ears?'

She took a moment or two to answer, but replied at length quite composedly: 'My husband very much dislikes gambling. I have always been rather extravagant, and I shrank from telling him about those debts.'

'You were afraid of the consequences?'

'In a way, yes. It was lack of moral courage, really. If I had foreseen all that was going to happen –'

'You would have told him?'

'Yes,' she said hesitantly.

'Have you told him, Mrs North?'

'No. No, I –'

'Why not?'

'But you must see!' she exclaimed. 'The whole thing has – has become so distorted! Now that Mr Fletcher is dead there would be only my word that everything happened as it did. I mean, his getting hold of my IOUs, and my not having till then the least suspicion of his – well, of his wanting me to become his mistress! I know very well how incredible it sounds, and I've no doubt I was a perfect fool, but I *didn't* guess! But anyone just hearing my account would be bound to think there must have been more between Mr Fletcher and me than there actually was. If I'd had the sense to tell my husband at once – as soon as I knew Mr Fletcher had got possession of my IOUs – But I hadn't! I tried to get them back myself, which makes it look as though I were afraid of something coming out about me and Mr Fletcher. Oh, can't you understand?'

'I think so,' he replied. 'The fact of the matter is that you were not speaking the truth when you told me that your husband did not object to your friendship with Mr Fletcher. Isn't that so?'

'You are trying to make me say that he was jealous, but he wasn't! He certainly did not like Mr Fletcher much: he thought he had rather a bad reputation with women. But –' Her throat contracted; she lifted her head and said with difficulty: 'My husband does not care enough for me to be jealous of me, Superintendent.'

His eyes dropped to the papers under his hand. He said quite gently: 'He might perhaps be jealous of your good name, Mrs North.'

'I don't know.'

'That is not consistent with the rest of your evidence,' he pointed out. 'You ask me to believe in a state of confidence existing between you and your husband that was unaccompanied by any great depth of affection, yet at the same time you wish me to believe that it is impossible for you to make a clean breast of the whole story to him.'

She swallowed and said: 'I do not wish to be dragged through the Divorce Courts, Superintendent.'

He raised his eyes. 'There is, then, so little confidence between you that you were afraid your husband might do that?'

'Yes,' she said, doggedly returning his look.

'You had no fear that he might, instead, be – very angry – with the man who had put you in this unpleasant position?'

'None,' she said flatly.

He allowed a pause to follow. When he spoke again, it was with an abruptness that startled her. 'A few minutes ago you repeated words to me which you heard Mr Fletcher utter when he passed down the garden-path with his visitor. How was it that you were able to hear these so clearly, and yet distinguish nothing that his companion said?'

'I have told you that Mr Fletcher had a light, rather high-pitched voice. If you have ever been with a deaf person you must know that such a voice has a far greater carrying power than a low one.'

Apparently he accepted this explanation, for he nodded, and got up. 'Very well, Mrs North. And now, if you are willing, your finger-prints.'

A quarter of an hour later, when Helen had left the police station, he sat down again at his desk, and meditatively studied certain notes which he had jotted down on a slip of paper.

Evidence of PC Glass: At 10.02, man seen coming out of garden-gate. Evidence of Helen North: At 9.58, approximately, unknown man escorted to garden-gate by Fletcher.

He was still looking pensively at these scribblings when PC Glass entered the office to report that no trace of any weapon had been found in the garden at Greystones.

Hannasyde gave a grunt, but said as Glass turned towards the door: 'Just a moment. Are you certain that the time when you saw a man come out of the garden-gate was two minutes after ten?'

'Yes, sir.'

'It could not, for instance, have been two or three minutes *before* ten?'

'No, sir. The time, by my watch and the clock in the room, was 10.05 p.m. when I entered the study. Therefore I am doubly certain, for to reach that room from the point where I was standing was a matter of three minutes, not of seven.'

Hannasyde nodded. 'All right; that's all. Report to Sergeant Hemingway in the morning.'

'Yes, sir,' Glass replied, but added darkly: 'He that hath a froward heart findeth no good.'

'I daresay,' said Hannasyde discouragingly.

'And he that hath a perverse tongue falleth into mischief,' said Glass with a good deal of severity.

Whether this pessimistic utterance referred to himself or to the absent Sergeant, Hannasyde did not inquire. As Glass walked towards the door, the telephone-bell rang, and the voice of the constable on duty informed the Superintendent that Sergeant Hemingway was on the line.

The Sergeant sounded less gloomy than when Hannasyde had parted from him. 'That you, sir?' he asked briskly. 'Well, I've got something, though where it's going to lead us I *don't* see. Shall I come down?'

'No, I'm coming back to town; I'll see you there. Any luck with those prints?'

'Depends what you call luck, Super. Some of 'em belong to a bloke by the name of Charlie Carpenter.'

'Carpenter?' repeated Hannasyde. 'Who the dickens is he?'

'It's a long story – what you might call highly involved,' replied the Sergeant.

'All right: reserve it. I'll be up in about half-an-hour.'

'Right you are, Chief. Give my love to Ichabod!' said the Sergeant.

Hannasyde grinned as he laid down the receiver, but refrained from delivering a message which, judging by Glass's forbidding countenance, would not be well received. He said kindly: 'Well, Glass, you've been doing a lot of work on this case. You'll be glad to hear that some of the finger-prints have been identified.'

Apparently he was wrong. 'I hear, but I behold trouble and darkness,' said Glass.

'The same might be said of all murder cases,' replied Hannasyde tartly, and closed the interview.

Six

Hannasyde found his subordinate awaiting him in a cheerful mood. 'Any luck your end, Chief?' he inquired. 'I've had a fullish sort of a day myself.'

'Yes, I got hold of a certain amount,' Hannasyde replied. 'Glass could find no trace of the weapon at Greystones, though, which is disappointing.'

'He was probably too busy holding prayer meetings with himself to have time to look for the weapon,' said the Sergeant. 'How's he doing? I can see he's going to be my cross all right.'

'As far as I can gather, you're likely to be his,' said Hannasyde, with the ghost of a smile. 'He made a somewhat obscure reference to forward hearts and perverse tongues which I took to mean you.'

'He did, did he? Ah well, the only wonder to me is he didn't call me a hissing and an abomination. I daresay he will yet. I don't mind him reciting his pieces, though it isn't strictly in accordance with discipline, as long as he doesn't take it into his silly head I've got to be saved. I've been saved once, and that's enough for me. Too much!' he added, remembering certain features of this event. 'Nasty little tracts about Lost Sheep, and the Evils of Drink,' he explained. 'It's a funny thing, but whenever you come up against any of these reforming chaps they always have it fixed in their minds you must be a walking lump of vice. You can't persuade 'em otherwise either. What you might call a Fixation.'

Hannasyde, who knew that the Sergeant's study of his favourite subject had led his adventurous feet into a strange realm of bastard words and lurid theories, intervened hastily, and asked for an account of his day's labours.

'Well, it's been interesting, but like what Glass said about me: obscure,' said the Sergeant. 'Taking our friend Abraham Budd first, we come to the first unexpected feature of the case. When I got up to Headquarters this morning, what should I find but his lordship waiting for me on the mat.'

'Budd?' said Hannasyde. 'Do you mean he came here?'

'That's right, Chief. Came along as soon as he'd read the news in the evening paper. They'll start getting the evening editions out before breakfast soon, if you ask me. Anyway, Mr Budd had his copy tucked under his arm, and was just oozing helpfulness.'

'Do get on!' said Hannasyde. 'Does he know something, or what?'

'Not so as you'd notice,' responded the Sergeant. 'According to him, he left the house by way of the garden-gate at about 9.35 p.m.'

'That tallies with Mrs North's account, at all events!' said Hannasyde.

'Oh, so you got something there, did you, Super?'

'Yes, but go on with your report. If Budd left at 9.35 he can't have seen anything, I suppose. What did he come to Scotland Yard for?'

'Funk,' said the Sergeant tersely. 'I've been reading a whole lot about causations, and that naturally made it as plain as a pikestaff to me –'

'Cut out the causations! What's Budd got to be frightened of? And don't hand me anything about Early Frustrations or Inhibitions, because I'm not interested! If you knew what you were talking about I could bear it, but you don't.'

The Sergeant, accustomed to this lack of sympathy, merely sighed, and said with unimpaired good humour: 'Well, I haven't, so far, got to the bottom of Mr Budd's trouble. He calls himself an outside broker, and, by what I can make out, the late Ernest was in the habit of using him as a kind of cover-man every time he wanted to put through any deals which, strictly speaking, he oughtn't to have put through. At least, that's the way it looked to me, putting two and two together, and making allowances for a bit of coyness on friend Budd's part.'

'I'd gathered that he was a broker. There are one or two copies of letters to him amongst Fletcher's papers, and a few of his replies. I haven't had time yet to go through them carefully. What took him down to see Fletcher at nine o'clock at night?'

'That's where the narrative got what you might call abstruse,' replied the Sergeant. 'Nor, if you was to ask me, should I say that I actually believed all that Budd told me.

Sweating very freely, he was. But then, it's been a hot day, and he's a fleshy man. However, the gist of it was that owing to the difficulty of hearing very well over the telephone there was some sort of misunderstanding about some highly confidential instructions issued by the late Ernest in – er – a still more highly confidential deal. Our Mr Budd, not wishing to entrust any more of this hush-hush business to the telephone, went off to see the late Ernest in person.'

'It sounds very fishy,' said Hannasyde.

'That's nothing to what it smelt like,' said the Sergeant. 'I had to open the window. But bearing in mind that the man we're after isn't Budd, I didn't press the matter much. What I did see fit to ask him, though, was whether the aforesaid misunderstanding had led to any unpleasantness with the late Ernest.'

Hannasyde nodded. 'Quite right. What did he say?'

'Oh, he behaved as though I was his Father Confessor!' said the Sergeant. 'That may have been on account of my nice, kind personality, or, on the other hand, it may not. But he opened right out like a poppy in the sun.'

'I can do without these poetical flights,' said Hannasyde.

'Just as you say, Chief. Anyway, he took me right to his bosom. Fairly oozed natural oil, and what I took to be highly unnatural frankness. He didn't keep a thing from me – nothing I'd already got wind of, at any rate. There was a little unpleasantness, due to the late Ernest's having assumed that certain of his instructions had been acted on, which, owing to the telephone and one thing and another, they hadn't been. However, once the late Ernest had got over his naughty temper, all became jake again, and they parted like brothers.'

'Oh!' said Hannasyde. 'Quite plausible. It might be true.'

'Yes, but I'll tell you a funny thing,' said the Sergeant. 'I've been swotting flies all day, but the whole time little Abraham was with me I never saw a fly settle on him, not once.'

'Oh!' said Hannasyde again. 'Like that, is he?'

'Yes,' replied the Sergeant. 'He is. What's more, Super, though you and I may not see eye to eye about Psychology, I know when a man's got the wind up. Little Abraham was having quite a job to keep his feet down on the ground. But I'm bound to say he did it. He answered all my questions before I'd even had time to ask them, too. Gave me a word-picture of his state of mind when he read about the late Ernest's death that was a masterpiece. First you could have knocked him down with a feather; then he thought, why, it must have happened not half-an-hour after he had left the late Ernest. After that he hoped he wouldn't get mixed up in it, and from there it was only a matter of seconds before he remembered handing the late Ernest's butler his card; and, on top of that, having Ernest address him in a loud and angry voice. Finally, it struck him like a thunder-clap that the late Ernest had shown him out by the side gate, so that no other person had witnessed his departure. Having assembled all these facts, he perceived that he was in a very compromising situation, and the only thing to be done was to come straight round to the kind police, whom he was brought up to look upon as his best friends.'

Hannasyde was frowning. 'It's almost too plausible. What did you do?'

'Gave him a piece of toffee, and sent him home to his mother,' answered the Sergeant promptly.

Hannasyde, who knew his Sergeant, apparently approved of this somewhat unorthodox conduct, for he said: 'Yes, about the best thing you could do. He'll keep. Now, what about this Charlie Carpenter you spoke of over the telephone?'

The Sergeant abandoned flippancy for the moment. 'A packet!' he said. 'That's where we come on the second unexpected feature of this case. As a matter of fact, I thought we were going to draw a blank on those fingerprints. But this is what we've got.' He picked up a folder from the desk as he spoke, and handed it to his superior. It contained a portrait of a young man, two sets of photographed finger-prints, and a brief, unsentimental record of the latter career of one Charlie Carpenter, aged twenty-nine years, measuring five feet nine inches, weighing eleven stone six pounds, having light-brown hair, grey eyes, and no distinguishing birth-marks.

Hannasyde's brows went up as he read, for the record was one of petty rogueries, culminating in a sentence of eighteen months' imprisonment for false pretences. 'This is certainly unexpected,' he said.

'Doesn't fit at all, does he?' agreed the Sergeant. 'That's what I thought.'

Hannasyde was studying the portrait. 'Flashy-looking fellow. Hair probably artificially waved. All right, Sergeant: I can see you're bursting with news. Let's have it.'

'Newton handled his case,' said the Sergeant. 'He doesn't know much about him, beyond his little lapses. Young waster with no background, and a taste for hitting the high spots. Dances and sings a bit; been on the stage, but not what you'd call noticeably; at one time did the gigolo act at a cheap dance-hall in the East End; seems to have gone pretty big with the ladies: you know the type. Not in the late Ernest's walk of life at all. In fact, I was just thinking I'd hit on the greatest discovery of the age, which was that Bertillon had made a mistake after all, when Newton said something that opened out a whole new vista before me.'

'Well?'

'He said that at the time of his arrest, which took place, as you'll notice, in November of 1934, Charlie was living with an actress – that means front row of the Beauty Chorus – of the name of Angela Angel!'

Hannasyde looked up. 'Angela Angel? Wasn't there a case about a year ago to do with a girl called Angela Angel? Suicide, wasn't it?'

'It was,' said the Sergeant. 'Sixteen months ago, to be precise.' He opened the case in which he had borne Ernest Fletcher's papers away from Greystones, and picked up a photograph that was lying on the top of a pile of documents. 'And that, Super, is Angela Angel!'

Hannasyde took the photograph, and recognised it at once as the one which had struck an elusive chord of memory in the Sergeant's brain earlier in the day.

'As soon as Newton mentioned the name, which he only did because of the girl having been a case herself, poor kid, I remembered,' said the Sergeant. 'Jimmy Gale was in charge of her little affair, which was how I came to hear a bit about it at the time. Did herself in for no particular reason that anyone ever discovered. She wasn't in trouble, she'd got a job in the chorus of the cabaret show at Duke's, and quite a bit of money put by in the bank. All the same, she stuck her head in a gas oven one night. Well, looked at as a case, there was nothing to it. But there were points which interested Gale in a mild sort of a way. For one thing, she didn't leave any letter behind, explaining why she'd done it, which, in Gale's experience, was unusual. Nine times out of ten a suicide'll leave a letter behind which'll make some poor devil feel like a murderer for the rest of his life, whether he deserves to or not. She didn't. What's more, they never found out what her real name was. She even opened her bank account under the name of Angela Angel. She didn't seem to have any relations, or if she had they never came forward to claim her; and she wasn't, by all accounts, one of those who tell their girl-friends the whole story of their lives. None of the rest of the chorus knew much about her when it came to the point. But what they did know was that about seven or eight months before she killed herself she got off with a very nice gentleman, who set her up in style in a smart flat with the usual trimmings.'

'Fletcher?'

'Taking one thing with another, and adding up a few simple figures, that's what it looks like, Chief. Not that I've got his name yet, for I haven't. There are two girls still dancing at Duke's who were there in Angela's time, but they neither of them seem to think they ever heard what her boy-friend's real name was. All they could think of was Boo-Boo, which was what she called him, but which doesn't sound to me the sort of name any self-respecting man would put up with except from a girl he happened to have gone nuts over. So that's not much help.'

'Any description?'

'Yes, he was middle-aged, dark, thin, and natty. The late Ernest to the life. A lot of other people to the life too, if you come to think of it, but it'll do to go on with. Well, as I say, he set Angela up in the best of style, and she chucked dancing for a life of gilded leisure. That was a matter of six months after friend Charlie had gone to gaol. Nothing more was heard of Angela at Duke's for the next six months, which brings us to the end of December 1935, when she turned up again, wanting her old job back.'

'Cast off?'

'That,' said the Sergeant guardedly, 'is the inference, but the fair Lily –'

'Who?'

'One of the chorus. She stated at the time, and today, when I saw her, that Angela was as close as an oyster about the whole business. Sifting the grain from the chaff, which isn't as easy as you might think when Lily starts talking, I came to the conclusion that the late Ernest (or substitute) was by way of being the great passion of Angela's life. Only he'd cooled off. But taking into account the fact that she wasn't in trouble, and had quite a bit of money put by, I'm bound to say it looks to me as though he didn't treat her so badly. However, the fair Lily sticks to it that she'd got a broken heart, and couldn't seem to fancy any of the other fellows who were floating around. After a couple of months she decided she couldn't live without the late Ernest, so she put her head in a gas oven, and that was the end of her.'

'Poor girl! The more I discover about Fletcher the less I like him.'

'Now, be fair, Chief!' begged Hemingway. 'This isn't one of your seduction rackets. If Angela didn't know what was likely to happen she ought to have. But that's neither here nor there. What I want to know is, where and how does Charlie Carpenter fit into the scenario?'

'Have you been able to discover anything about his movements since he was released from prison? When exactly was that?' He consulted the dossier on the desk. 'June 1936! A year ago, in fact. What's he been up to all this time?'

'You can search me,' said the Sergeant. 'He hasn't got pinched for anything, that's all I can tell you. Funny, isn't it? If he was out to pull a big revenge act, what's he want to wait a year for?'

Hannasyde looked at the photograph again. 'Revenge? Does he give you that impression?'

'No, he doesn't. Silly, weak kind of face, and by all accounts he was a selfish young bounder, not given to putting himself out for anyone *but* himself. No, what it looks like to me, at first glance, is an attempt to put the black on the late Ernest. Not much of an attempt either, which is about what you'd expect, judging from his record.'

'Yes,' Hannasyde agreed. 'And then we come up against the murder.'

'Slap up against it,' nodded the Sergeant. 'And it doesn't fit.'

'Several loose ends somewhere. He fits the description given by Glass and Mrs North, though – but I admit they were too vague to be of much use.'

'Oh, so Mrs North was there, was she?'

'She was there, and unless I am much mistaken she thinks it was her husband who killed Fletcher.'

The Sergeant opened his eyes at that. 'You do see life in the suburbs, don't you? Nice goings-on! Whatever does Ichabod say about it?'

'As I haven't told him anything about it, he hasn't yet favoured me with his opinion.'

'You wait till he gets wind of it. He'll learn a whole new piece to say to us. But this line on Mrs North's husband is very confusing. What's been happening your end, Chief?'

Hannasyde gave him a brief account of his two interviews with Helen North. The Sergeant listened in silence, his bright, penetrating eyes fixed on his superior's face with an expression in them of gradually deepening disgust.

'What did I tell you?' he said, when Hannasyde had finished. 'The whole stage is getting cluttered up with supers. I'll tell you something else, too; by the time we're through we shall have had just about all we can stand of this North woman. I wouldn't mind betting she thinks we've got nothing better to do than run round in circles while she gets on with this three-act problem play of hers. I'm surprised at you, Chief, letting yourself get dragged into her differences with her husband. What's more, where's the sense of her hiding all this IOU business from him? He's bound to find out in the end.'

'I daresay, but I can't see that it's any part of my job to tell him.'

The Sergeant sniffed. 'What's the husband like? Give any reason for coming home a week before he was expected?'

'None. He's a good-looking chap. Got a bit of a chin, and thinks more than he says. Determined fellow, I should imagine; not easily rattled, and by no means a fool.'

'I hope we bring it home to him,' said the Sergeant uncharitably. 'From the sound of it, he's going to be as big a nuisance as his wife. No alibi?'

'So he said. In fact, he made me a present of that piece of information.'

The Sergeant cocked an eye at him. 'He did, did he? Did it strike you he might be fancying himself in the part of a red herring?'

'It's a possibility, of course. He may suspect his wife of having killed Fletcher. It depends how much he knows about her dealings with the man.'

The Sergeant groaned. 'I get it. A nice game of battledore and shuttlecock, with you and me cast for the shuttlecocks. Of course, our heads won't really start aching till Mrs North gets on to it that the man she saw may have been Charlie Carpenter. We'll have her eating all that evidence of hers about the late Ernest showing him off the premises then. Probably boloney, anyway.'

'It may be, but she spoke the truth about her fingerprints being on the door. I verified that before I left Marley. The real discrepancy is in the time. At 9.35 p.m. Budd left Greystones by the garden-gate. I think we can take that as being true. Mrs North was walking up Maple Grove at that time, and states that she saw a fat man come out of Greystones.'

The Sergeant jotted it down on a piece of paper. 'That checks up with his own story: 9.35 p.m. Budd leaves; the North dame arrives.'

'Next we have Mrs North leaving the study at 9.45.'

'Short visit,' commented the Sergeant.

'She and Fletcher had a row. She admitted to that the second time I saw her. Also at 9.45 we have the unknown man entering the garden by the side gate.'

'X,' said the Sergeant. 'That's when Mrs North hid behind the bush?'

'Yes. X entered the study, we suppose, a minute later. That isn't important. Now, according to her first story, Mrs North then left by way of the garden-gate. According to her second version, she remained where she was, until about 9.58, when X, accompanied by Fletcher, came out of the study, and walked down the path to the gate. She then slipped back into the study to search for her IOUs, heard Fletcher returning, and escaped through the door into the hall. She was in the hall as the clock began to strike 10.00. At 10.02, Glass, on his beat, saw a man corresponding to Mrs North's description of X coming out of the garden-gate, and making off towards the Arden Road. He entered the garden and reached the study at 10.05 p.m., to find Fletcher dead, and no sign of his murderer to be seen. What do you make of it?'

'I don't,' said the Sergeant flatly. 'It's looked like a mess to me from the start. What I do say is that all this stuff of Mrs North's isn't to be trusted. In fact, there's only one thing we've got to hold on to, which is that at 10.05 p.m. Glass found the late Ernest with his head bashed in. That at least is certain, and what's more it makes Mrs North's evidence look a bit cock-eyed. Glass saw X leaving the premises at 10.02, which means that if he was the murderer he must have done Ernest in between 10.00 and 10.01, allowing him a minute to get out of the study and down the path to the gate.'

'All right: that's probably a fair estimate.'

'Well, it doesn't fit – not if you're accepting Mrs North's evidence. According to her, it was just on 10.00 when she heard Ernest coming back to the study. You think of it, Chief: Ernest has got to have time to get into his chair behind the desk again, and start to write the letter that was found under his head. It was obvious he was taken by surprise, which means that X didn't come stampeding up the path directly behind him. He waited till Ernest was in the house: it stands to reason he must have. Once Ernest has settled down he gets to work – enters, strikes Ernest with some kind of a blunt instrument, not once, mark you! but two or three times – and then makes off. Well, if you can cram all that into two minutes you're cleverer than I am, Super, that's all. Take it this way: if Ernest saw him off the premises, he pretended to walk away, didn't he?'

'You'd think so.'

'I'm dead sure of it. While Ernest is strolling back to the house, he comes back cautiously to the gate. If he'd made up his mind, as he must have, to kill Ernest, he didn't open that gate till Ernest had reached the house again, which was at 10.00 p.m. He wouldn't have run the risk of Ernest hearing him. No point in it. Does he stride up the path bold as brass, thus advertising his presence? Of course he doesn't! He creeps up, and if it takes a minute to reach the study from that gate, walking ordinarily, as we know it does, it's my belief it took X a sight longer to do it in the dark, treading warily. By the time he's in the study again it must be a couple of minutes after 10.00, at which time, mark you, Glass saw him coming out of the garden-gate.'

'I'm afraid you've got a fixation, Skipper,' said Hannasyde gently. 'We don't know that X was the murderer.'

The Sergeant swallowed this, replying with dignity: 'I was coming to that. It could have been Budd, come back secretly, and lying in wait in the garden till the coast was clear; or it could have been Mr North. But if X, whom Glass saw, was Charlie Carpenter, what was he doing while Ernest was being knocked on the head?'

'There's another possibility,' said Hannasyde. 'Suppose that North was the murderer –'

'Just a moment, Super! Is North X?' demanded Hemingway.

'Nobody is X. Assuming that North was the man Mrs North saw coming up the path, we have to consider the possibility of Fletcher's having been killed at any time between 9.45 and 10.01.'

The Sergeant blinked. 'Mrs North's revised version being so much eye-wash? Where does Carpenter come in?'

'After the murder,' replied Hannasyde.

There was a short pause. 'We've got to find Carpenter,' announced the Sergeant.

'Of course. Have you got anyone on to that?'

'I've got practically the whole Department hunting for him. But if he's kept out of trouble for the past year, it may be a bit of a job to locate him.'

'The other point that puzzles me is the weapon used. The doctors seem to be agreed that the blows were struck with a blunt instrument like a weighted stick. The skull was smashed right in, you know. Now, both Glass and Mrs North say that the man they saw was carrying nothing. You may rule Mrs North's evidence out of court if you like, but you can't rule out what Glass says. The natural thing would be for the murderer to get rid of the weapon at once, but I've had the garden searched with a toothcomb, and nothing has come to light.'

'Anything in the room? Bronze ornament, or paperweight, which could have been stuffed into the murderer's pocket?'

'The butler states that nothing is missing from the room, and although there is a heavy paper-weight there, I understand that it was produced later by your playful little friend, Neville Fletcher – about whom I'm going to make a few inquiries, by the way.'

The Sergeant sat up. 'He produced it, did he? From what I've seen of him, Chief, that's just about what he would do – if he happened to have murdered his uncle with it! It would strike him as being a really high-class bit of humour.'

'Fairly cold-blooded.'

'Don't you fret, he's cold-blooded enough! Clever enough, too. But if he did it, Mrs North must have seen him on her way out of – Oh, now we're assuming Mrs North's first story was the true one, are we?'

'If we're considering Neville Fletcher as the possible murderer, it looks as though we should have to. But that brings us up against two difficult fences. The first is that her finger-prints *were* on the panel of the door, and I don't quite see how they came there if she didn't leave the room by that way. The second is that if her original story was true we know that a man entered the study at about 9.45, and left the premises again at 10.02 – for it seems a trifle far-fetched to suppose that more than one man visited Fletcher during those seventeen minutes. That being so, when did Neville find time to murder his uncle? In between Glass's seeing X depart and himself entering the study? Stretching the bounds of probability rather far, isn't it?'

'It is,' admitted the Sergeant, caressing his chin. 'But now you come to point it out to me I don't mind owning that the absence of the weapon wants a bit of explanation. I suppose the murderer could have shoved a heavy stick down his trouser leg, but it would have made him walk with a stiff leg, which Glass would have been bound to have noticed. I'm trying to think of something he could have had in his pocket – a spanner, for instance.'

'That's assuming the murder was premeditated. One doesn't carry heavy spanners in one's pockets. Somehow it doesn't look premeditated to me. I can't bring myself to believe in a murderer who plans to kill his victim by battering his skull in, midway through the evening, in his own study.'

'No, that's true,' said the Sergeant. 'And we went over the fire-irons. It looks as though the weapon, whatever it may have been, was got rid of pretty cleverly. It might be a good thing if I had a look round the place myself. A little quiet chat with that butler wouldn't do any harm. Surprising what you can pick up from servants – if you know the way to go about it.'

'By all means go down there,' said Hannasyde. 'I want the place kept under observation. Meanwhile, I've some inquiries to make about the state of Neville Fletcher's bank balance, Mr North's movements on the night of the murder, and the expansive Mr Budd's mysterious business with Fletcher.'

'You'll have a busy morning,' prophesied the Sergeant. 'Growing, isn't it? We started off with one man, and we've now got one lady, one jealous husband, one outside broker, one dead cabaret-girl, one criminal and one suspicious-looking nephew implicated in it. And we've only been at work on it since 9.00 this morning. If it goes on at this rate, we shan't be able to move for suspects in a couple of days' time. You know, I often wonder what made me join the Force.' He began to put his papers together. 'If it weren't for the fact that murder doesn't seem to fit in with what we know of Charlie Carpenter, my money would be on him. Do you suppose he's been hunting the late Ernest down ever since he came out of gaol?'

'I don't know, but considering that not even your fair Lily knew who Angela's protector was, it seems quite possible.'

'Or,' said the Sergeant musingly, 'he found out by accident, and thought he saw his way to putting the black on the late Ernest. Come to think of it, that theory goes nicely with Mrs North's revised version – the bit about Ernest saying the man X had made a mistake. Well, one thing's certain: we've got to get hold of Carpenter.'

'The Department can look after that. I'd like you to get down to Marley first thing tomorrow, and see what you can pick up.' Hannasyde rose, adding with a twinkle: 'By the way, if you should run across a forceful young woman with a monocle, God help you! She's Mrs North's sister, and interested in crime. Writes detective stories.'

'What?' said the Sergeant. 'You mean to tell me I'm going to have an authoress tagging round after me?'

'I should think it's quite probable,' replied Hannasyde gravely.

'Well, isn't that nice?' said the Sergeant with awful sarcasm. 'You'd have thought Ichabod was a big enough cross for anyone to bear, wouldn't you? It just shows you: when Fate's got it in for you there's no limit to what you may have to put up with.'

Hannasyde laughed. 'Go home and study Havelock Ellis, or Freud, or whoever it is you do study. Perhaps that'll help you to cope with the situation.'

'Study! I won't have time,' said the Sergeant, reaching for his hat. 'I'm going to be busy this evening.'

'You'd better relax. You've had a pretty strenuous day. What *are* you going to do?'

'Mug up the Bible,' said the Sergeant bitterly.

Seven

I T WAS LATE WHEN HANNASYDE LEFT HIS ROOM AT SCOTLAND
Yard, and when at last he went home he had learnt
enough from his perusal of Ernest Fletcher's papers to make
him visit the offices of Mr Abraham Budd shortly after nine
o'clock the following morning.

Mr Budd did not keep him waiting. The typist who
had carried his card in to her employer returned almost
immediately, pop-eyed with curiosity, ready to dramatise,
as soon as a suitable audience should present itself, this
thrilling and sinister call, and invited him, in a fluttering
voice, to follow her.

Mr Budd, who rose from a swivel-chair behind his desk as
Hannasyde was ushered in, and came eagerly forward to greet
him, corresponded so exactly with Sergeant Hemingway's
description of him, that Hannasyde had to bite back a smile.
He was a short, fat man, with a certain oiliness of skin, and
an air of open affability that was almost oppressive. He shook
Hannasyde by the hand, pressed him into a chair, offered
him a cigar, and said several times that he was very glad to
see him.

'Very glad, I am, Superintendent,' he said. 'What a shocking tragedy! What a terrible affair! I have been most upset. As I told the Sergeant at Scotland Yard, it struck me all of a heap. All of a heap,' he repeated impressively. 'For I respected Mr Fletcher. Yes, sir, I respected him. He had a Brain. He had a Grasp of Finance. Over and over again I've said it: Mr Fletcher had a Flair. That's the word. And now he's gone.'

'Yes,' said Hannasyde unemotionally. 'As you say. You did a good deal of business with him, I understand?'

Mr Budd managed to convey by a glance out of his astute little eyes and a gesture of the hands which betrayed his race, an answer in which assent was mingled with deprecation.

'What kind of business?' said Hannasyde.

Mr Budd leaned forward, resting his arms upon his desk, and replied in a confidential tone: 'Strictly private, Mr Hannasyde!' He looked slyly at Hannasyde. 'You take my meaning? There isn't a soul in this world I'd discuss a client's affairs with, least of all Mr Fletcher's, but when a thing like this happens, I see it's different. I'm discreet. I have to be discreet. If I weren't, where do you think I'd be? *You* don't know; *I* don't know, but it wouldn't be where I am today. But I'm on the side of law and order. I realise it's my duty to assist the police where and how I can. My duty as a citizen. That's why I'm going to make an exception to my rule of silence. Now, you're a broad-minded man, Mr Hannasyde. You're a man of experience. You know that everything that goes on in the City doesn't get published in the *Financial News.*' He shook with amusement, and added: 'Not by a long chalk!'

'I am aware, certainly, that a not-over-scrupulous man in Mr Fletcher's position – he was upon several boards, I think? – might find it convenient to employ an agent to buy on his behalf stocks which he would not like it to be known that he had bought,' replied Hannasyde.

Mr Budd's eyes twinkled at him. 'You know everything, don't you, Mr Hannasyde? But that's it. That's it in a nutshell. *You* may not approve of it, *I* may not approve of it, but what has it to do with us, after all?'

'It has this much to do with you, that Mr Fletcher was in the habit of employing you in that manner.'

Budd nodded. 'Quite right. I don't deny it. Where would be the sense in that? My business is to obey my clients' instructions, and that's what I do, Mr Hannasyde, asking no questions.'

'Not always, I think,' said Hannasyde.

Budd looked hurt. 'Why, what do you mean? Now, that's a thing that has never been said to me yet. I don't like it, Mr Hannasyde. No, I don't like it.'

'Surely you told Sergeant Hemingway yesterday that you had failed to obey certain of Mr Fletcher's instructions?'

The smile, which had vanished from Budd's face, reappeared. He leaned back in his chair, his mind apparently relieved, and said: 'Oh now, now, now! That's an exaggeration. Oh yes, that's just a little exaggeration, I assure you! What I told the Sergeant was that there had been a misunderstanding between Mr Fletcher and me.'

'What was the misunderstanding?' asked Hannasyde.

Mr Budd looked reproachful. 'Now, Superintendent, have a heart! You don't expect a man in my position to disclose the nature of strictly confidential transactions. It wouldn't be right. It wouldn't be honourable.'

'You are mistaken: I do expect just that. We shall probably save time if I tell you at once that Mr Fletcher's private papers are at this moment in the possession of the police. Moreover, what you refuse to tell me your ledgers will no doubt show.'

The look of reproach deepened. More in sorrow than in anger, Budd said gently: 'Come, Superintendent, you know you can't act in that high-handed fashion. *You're* not a fool, *I'm* not a fool. Where's the sense in trying to get tough with me? Now, I ask you!'

'You will find that I have it in my power to get remarkably tough with you,' replied Hannasyde brutally. 'On your own showing, you visited Mr Fletcher on the night of his murder; you admit that a quarrel took place –'

'Not a quarrel, Superintendent! Not a quarrel!'

'– between you; you can bring no evidence to prove that you left the house at the time you stated. Added to these facts, there is enough documentary evidence amongst Mr Fletcher's papers to justify my applying for a warrant to search these premises.'

Budd flung up a hand. 'Don't let's have any unpleasantness! You're not treating me as you should, Superintendent. You've got nothing against me. Didn't I go round to Scotland Yard the moment I read the shocking news? Didn't I tell your Sergeant the whole truth? This isn't what I expected.

No, it certainly is not what I expected. I've never been on the wrong side of the Law, never in my life. But what reward do I get for that?'

Hannasyde listened to this plaint with an unmoved countenance. Without troubling to reply to it, he said, consulting a paper he had in his hand: 'On 10 June Mr Fletcher wrote to you, instructing you to buy ten thousand shares in Huxton Industries.'

'That's correct,' said Budd, eyeing him with a little perturbation. 'I don't deny it. Why should I?'

'It was what is known, I believe, as a dead market, was it not?'

Budd nodded.

'Did you buy those shares, Mr Budd?'

The directness of the question startled Budd. He stared at Hannasyde for a moment, then said feebly: 'That's a funny question to ask. I had my instructions, hadn't I? Perhaps I didn't approve of them; perhaps it didn't seem to me wise to invest in Huxton Industries; but was it my business to advise Mr Fletcher?'

'Did you buy those shares?'

Budd did not answer immediately, but kept his troubled gaze on Hannasyde's face. It was plain that he was at a loss, perhaps uncertain of what Fletcher's papers might have revealed. He said uneasily: 'Suppose I didn't? You know that a block like that isn't bought in the twinkling of an eye. It would look funny, wouldn't it? I know my business better than that.'

'At the time when you received Mr Fletcher's instructions to buy, Huxton Industries were not quoted?'

'Moribund company,' said Budd tersely.

'The stock was, in your opinion, worthless?'

Budd shrugged.

'You were no doubt surprised at receiving instructions to buy such a large block of shares?'

'Maybe I was. It wasn't my business to be surprised. Mr Fletcher may have had a tip.'

'But your own opinion was that Mr Fletcher had made a mistake?'

'If it was, that's neither here nor there. If Mr Fletcher wanted the shares it wasn't anything to do with me. I bought them. Why, if you know so much you'll know that there's been considerable activity in Huxton Industries. That's me.'

'Buying?'

'What else would I be doing, I should like to know?' said Budd, almost indulgently. 'Now, I'm going to be frank with you, Mr Hannasyde. There's no reason why I should be, not a ha'p'orth of reason, but I've nothing to hide, and I'm anxious to help the police in every way I can. Not that my dealings with Mr Fletcher can help you, but I'm a reasonable man, and I realise that you want to know about this little deal. The fact is, the misunderstanding that took place between Mr Fletcher and me occurred over these instructions. Now, it struck you as remarkable – I think we can say it was remarkable – that Mr Fletcher should have wanted to buy ten thousand shares in a company which was dying. It struck me that way too. It would anyone, wouldn't it? I put it to you! Well, what do I do? I ask myself if there's been a mistake in the typing. Very easy to add an extra nought, isn't it? So I ring up my client, to verify. I ask him, am I to buy a thousand shares? He says yes. He's impatient: wants to know why I need to question my instructions. I don't get a chance to tell him. While I'm explaining, he rings off. Now where's the sense in trying to pull the wool over your eyes? There's none. I know that. I slipped up. Yes, Mr Hannasyde, I slipped up. The first time in twenty years I've got to accuse myself of carelessness. I don't like admitting it. You wouldn't yourself. I ought to have got written confirmation from my client that a thousand shares was what he wanted. That's what I neglected to do. I bought a thousand shares on his behalf, in small packets. The shares rise as a result. Then I get a telephone call from my client. He's seen the record of the transactions on the ticker: he knows that's me. He rings up to know whether I've fulfilled instructions. I tell him yes. He's in a high good humour. Him and me have done business for years; I've obeyed orders, so he lets me in on the secret. That was his way: there wasn't anything mean about him. Not a thing! He tells me IPS Consolidated are taking over Huxton Industries, and if I want to buy, to buy quick, but discreetly. Get the idea? He tells me they'll go to fifteen shillings. That's the truest thing you know. Maybe they'll go higher. Then what happens? He says in his joking way, now did I think he was mad to buy ten thousand shares? Plain as I'm speaking now he said it. Ten thousand. You get it? Ten thousand, and I've got one thousand, and the shares have risen from half-a-crown to seven-and-six. They aren't going to sink again, either. No sir, Huxton Industries is on the up and up. So where am I? What am I going to do? There's only one thing to *be* done. I do it. I go down to see Mr Fletcher. He knows me; he trusts me; he'll believe what I say. Because it's the truth. Was he pleased? No, Mr Hannasyde. Would you be? But he was a gentleman. A perfect gentleman, he was. He sees it was the result of a misunderstanding. He's sore, but he's fair. We part on good terms. Forgive and forget. That's the truth in a nutshell.'

Hannasyde, on whom this frank recital did not seem to have made quite the desired impression, said dampingly: 'Not quite, surely? How was it that Mr Fletcher, who, you say, watched the records as they appeared on the ticker, failed to notice that the shares weren't rising as much as they must have done had you bought ten thousand?'

There was an uncomfortable silence. Mr Budd pulled himself together, and said glibly: 'Why, you don't suppose Mr Fletcher had nothing better to do than to watch the ticker, do you, Superintendent? No, no, the little deal I was putting through for him was nothing more than a side-line for him.'

'I should like to see your books,' said Hannasyde.

For the first time a sharp note came into Budd's rather unctuous voice: 'I don't show my books to anyone!'

Hannasyde looked at him under frowning brows. 'Is that so?' he said.

Mr Budd lost some of his colour. A rather sickly smile was brought into action. 'Now, don't get me wrong! Be fair, Mr Hannasyde! That's all I ask of you. Be fair! If it was to get about I'd shown my books to a soul outside this office I should lose half my clients.'

'It won't,' said Hannasyde.

'Ah, if I could be sure of *that*!'

'You can be.'

'Well, look here, Mr Hannasyde, I'm a reasonable man, and if you show me a warrant, I've nothing to say. But if you haven't got one, I'm not showing my books to you. Why should I? There's no reason. But the instant you walk in here with a warrant you won't find me making trouble.'

'If you're wise you won't make trouble under any circumstances,' said Hannasyde. 'I'll see your books now.'

'You can't do it,' said Budd, doggedly staring into his eyes. 'You can't come that high-handed stuff in my office. I won't put up with it.'

'Do you realise,' said Hannasyde sternly, 'The position you are in? I am giving you a chance to clear yourself of suspicion of –'

'I had nothing to do with the murder! Why, you know that, Mr Hannasyde! Didn't I come right away to Scot –'

'The fact of your having come to Scotland Yard has no bearing on the case whatsoever. You have just told me a story a child wouldn't believe, and, for reasons best known to yourself, you refuse to substantiate it by the evidence of your books. You leave me no alternative –'

'No, no!' Budd said quickly. 'Don't let's get hasty! No use getting hasty! I didn't see it like that, that's all. You'll be wasting your time if you arrest me. You don't want to do that, now do you? I'm not a violent man. You couldn't think I'd break anyone's head open! Why, I couldn't do it! Just couldn't do it! As for what I told you, well, perhaps it wasn't exactly the truth, but I swear to you –'

'Never mind about swearing to me. What was the truth?'

Mr Budd licked his lips, shifting restlessly in his chair. 'It was a miscalculation on my part. It might have happened to anyone. I never dreamed of IPS taking over Huxton Industries. It looked to me like a little flutter. A man's got to do the best he can for himself, hasn't he? You would yourself. There's nothing criminal in it.'

'Get on!' said Hannasyde. 'You thought the shares would sink back again, didn't you?'

'That's the way it was!' answered Budd eagerly. 'If Mr Fletcher had let me into the secret earlier, it needn't have happened. Wouldn't have happened.'

'Instead of buying the ten thousand shares you were told to buy, you played a little game of your own, didn't you?'

'A man's got to take a chance sometimes,' Budd pleaded. 'You know how it is! I didn't mean to do anything wrong.'

Hannasyde ignored this extremely unconvincing statement. 'Buying and then selling, and again buying and selling, with the profits finding their way into your pocket. That's what you did? The ticker recorded the transactions, but Fletcher was not to know what you were up to. Then he let you in on the secret – I believe that part of your story – and you found yourself with one thousand shares only of the ten thousand you were instructed to buy, and the market steadily rising. Is that the true story?'

'You – you ought to have been in business yourself, Mr Hannasyde,' said Budd unhappily. 'It's wonderful the way you spotted it!'

'And on the night he was murdered you had gone down to spin some kind of a yarn to Mr Fletcher to account for your being unable to deliver the correct number of shares?'

Budd nodded. 'That's the way it was. A bit of bad luck, Mr Hannasyde. I don't deny I acted foolishly, but –'

'I take it Mr Fletcher was very angry?'

'He was angry. I didn't blame him. I saw his point. But he couldn't do anything, not without coming out into the open. He wouldn't do that. See? He couldn't afford to have it known he had been buying Huxton Industries under cover. You haven't got anything on me, Mr Hannasyde. You'll only regret it if you do anything impulsive. Take my word for it!'

He looked anxiously at Hannasyde as he spoke, beads of sweat standing on his brow. When he found that he was not, apparently, to be arrested, he heaved a gusty sigh of relief, and wiped his face with a large silk handkerchief.

Hannasyde went away to promote inquiries into the state of Neville Fletcher's finances.

Meanwhile, Sergeant Hemingway, arriving betimes in Marley, found PC Glass awaiting him with his customary air of gloomy disapproval. The Sergeant was in a cheerful frame of mind, and took instant exception to his subordinate's joyless mood. 'What's the matter with you?' he demanded. 'Colic, or something?'

'Nothing is the matter with me, Sergeant,' replied Glass. 'I enjoy perfect health.'

'Well, if that's the way you look when you're enjoying yourself I hope I never see you when you're feeling a bit blue,' said the Sergeant. 'Do you ever smile? I won't say laugh, mind you! Just smile!'

'Sorrow is better than laughter,' said Glass stiffly. 'For by the sadness of the countenance the heart is made better.'

'If it's my heart you're talking about, you're wrong!' responded the Sergeant instantly.

'I see no reason for mirth,' Glass said. 'I am troubled; I am bowed down greatly; I go mourning all day long.'

'Look here, let's get this straight!' begged the Sergeant. 'Have you really got anything to mourn about, or is this just your idea of having a good time?'

'I see sin upon sin discovered by reason of one man's death. I see how abominable and filthy is man, which drinketh iniquity like water.'

'You know, when I came down here this morning,' said the Sergeant, restraining himself with a strong effort, 'I was feeling all right. Nice sunny day, birds singing, the case beginning to get interesting. But if I have to listen to much more of that kind of talk I shall have the horrors, which isn't going to help either of us. You forget about iniquity and think about this case you're supposed to be working on.'

'It is that which is in my mind,' said Glass. 'An evil man is slain, but by his death hidden sins are laid bare. There is not one implicated in the case who can say: "I am blameless; there is no spot on me."'

'Today's great thought!' said the Sergeant. 'Of course no one can say there's no spot on them! What did you expect! You know, your trouble is you take things too hard. What have other people's spots got to do with you, anyway? I may not know as much as you do about the Bible, but what about the mote in your neighbour's eye, eh?'

'It is true,' said Glass. 'You do right to reprove me. I am full of sin.'

'Well, don't take on about it,' recommended the Sergeant. 'Let's get down to business. Nothing fresh come to light, I suppose?'

'I know of nothing.'

'You'd better come along up to Greystones with me. I'm going to have a look for that blunt weapon myself.'

'It's not there.'

'That's what you think. What's all this I was hearing from the Superintendent about young Neville producing a hopeful-looking paper-weight?'

Glass's brow darkened. 'They that are of froward heart are an abomination to the Lord,' he said coldly. 'Neville Fletcher walks in vanity. He is of no account.'

'What do you know about him?' inquired the Sergeant. 'Anything, or nothing?'

'I think him an irreligious man, who despises the Word. But I know no other ill of him.'

'What about the Norths?'

'He is said to be an upright man, and such I believe him to be. She speaks with a lying tongue, but she did not strike the blow that killed Ernest Fletcher.'

'No, not unless she did it with a sledge-hammer,' agreed the Sergeant. 'It's my belief that when we find him Charlie Carpenter is going to tell us who killed Fletcher. You heard about him, didn't you?'

'I heard, but I did not understand. What is known of this Carpenter?'

'He's a small-time criminal. Done time and came out of gaol about a year ago. We found his finger-prints on the late Ernest's desk.'

Glass frowned. 'How is such an one concerned in the case? Truly, the way is dark.'

'Not as dark as you think,' replied the Sergeant. 'Carpenter was mixed up with one of the late Ernest's little bits of fluff. That crack of yours about the girl in the photograph having an end as bitter as wormwood was one of your luckier shots. That was Angela Angel, the same that committed suicide sixteen months ago. It looks as though she didn't want to go on living when the late Ernest shook her off – supposing he was the boy-friend, which it's pretty certain he was. Silly little fool, of course, but you can't help feeling sorry for the kid.'

'The soul that sinneth, it shall die,' Glass said harshly. 'Is it thought that Carpenter slew Ernest Fletcher?'

'That's what we can't make out. We shan't till we lay our hands on him. It looks a cinch, on the face of it, but somehow it doesn't fit with what we know of him. My own idea is that Charlie thought he saw his way to putting the black on the late Ernest, over Angela's death.'

'It is possible. But he would not then kill Fletcher.'

'You wouldn't think so, but when you've seen as much crime as I have, my lad, you'll know that the more improbable a thing seems to be the more likely it is it'll turn out to be a fact. But I won't deny you've made a point. What the Chief thinks is that Carpenter may have seen the real murderer.'

Glass turned his arctic gaze upon the Sergeant. 'How should that be? Why should he remain silent if it were so?'

'That's easy. He's not the sort to go running to the police. He'd have to explain why he was at Greystones, for one thing.'

'True. Is his habitation known to you?'

'If you'd talk plain English, we'd get on better,' remarked the Sergeant. 'No, it isn't known to me, but I'm hoping it soon will be. Meanwhile, we've got to see what we can find out about friend North.' He saw the question in Glass's eyes, and added: 'Oh, you don't know about that little problem play, do you? According to the Chief, Mrs North thinks North was the man she saw in the garden. So what must she do but alter her evidence to suit this new development? Lying lips about hits her off.'

'Why should she think it?'

'Because it turns out that he was sculling around without an alibi at the time. The Chief's working on him now. Then there's Budd. He's been up to no good, or I'm a Dutchman.'

They had by this time reached Greystones. As they turned in at the front gate, Glass suddenly said: 'The day cometh that shall burn them as an oven; and all the proud, yea, and all that do wickedly shall be stubble!'

'You may be right, but it won't be in your time, my lad, so don't you think it!' replied the Sergeant tartly. 'Now you can go and make yourself useful. The butler's a friend of yours, isn't he?'

'I know him. I do not call him a friend, for I have few friends.'

'You surprise me!' said the Sergeant. 'Still, if you're acquainted with him, that ought to be good enough. You go and have a chat with him – just a nice, casual chat.'

'An idle soul shall suffer hunger,' said Glass austerely.

'Not when it's idling with a butler. Or thirst either, if it comes to that,' retorted the Sergeant.

'Thy tongue deviseth mischiefs, like a sharp razor working deceitfully,' Glass told him. 'Simmons is an honest man, in the way of Light.'

'Yes, that's why I'm handing him over to you,' said the Sergeant. 'And I don't want any more backchat! You'll get that butler talking, and see what you can pick up.'

Half-an-hour later the Sergeant, standing before the wall at the end of the garden, and gazing thoughtfully at one of the espaliers growing against it, was interrupted in his cogitations by the arrival on the scene of Neville Fletcher and Miss Drew.

'Oh, here's the Sergeant!' said Neville. 'He's a nice man, Sally: you'll like him.'

The Sergeant turned, foreboding in his breast. The monocle in Miss Drew's eye confirmed his fears. He regarded her with misgiving, but, being a polite man, bade her good-morning.

'You're looking for the weapon,' said Miss Drew. 'I've given a good deal of thought to that myself.'

'So have I. I was even constructive,' said Neville. 'But Malachi told me to stand in awe, and sin not.'

The Sergeant's lips twitched, but he said dryly: 'Well, from all I hear, sir, that was about what you were asking for.'

'Yes, but he also advised me to commune with my own heart upon my bed, and be still, which I maintain was unreasonable at three in the afternoon.'

'I rather think of making a study of Malachi,' announced Miss Drew. 'He's probably a very interesting case – psychologically speaking. He ought to be psychoanalysed, I think.'

'You're right, miss; he ought,' agreed the Sergeant, regarding her with a kindlier light in his eye. 'Ten to one, it would come out that he had something happen to him when he was an infant that would account for the kink he's got now.'

'Dropped on his head?' inquired Neville.

'Oh no, it was probably some seemingly trivial episode which affected his subconscious,' said Sally.

'My precious!' said Neville, with spurious fondness. 'He hasn't got one.'

The Sergeant could not allow this assertion to pass. 'That's where you're wrong, sir. Everyone's got a subconscious.'

Neville's interest was at once aroused: 'Let us sit down, and talk this over. I can see you're going to support Miss Drew, but though I know little, if anything, about the subject I have a very agile brain, and I'm practically certain to refute all your statements. We will have a lovely argument, shall we?'

'Very nice, I'm sure, sir,' said the Sergeant, 'but I'm not here to argue with you. It would be a waste of my time.'

'It wouldn't be half such a waste of time as staring at that broken branch,' said Neville. 'Argument with me is very stimulating to the brain, and as a matter of fact that branch, which looks like a clue, is a snare for the unwary.'

The Sergeant looked at him rather narrowly. 'Is it, sir? Perhaps you can tell me how it comes to be broken?'

'I can, of course, but it isn't awfully interesting. Are you sure you wouldn't rather –'

'It might be very interesting to me,' interposed the Sergeant.

'You're wrong,' Neville said. 'It looks to you as though someone climbed over the wall, using the espalier as a foot-hold, doesn't it?'

'Yes,' replied the Sergeant. 'It looks remarkably like that to me.'

'You're jolly clever,' said Neville, 'because that's exactly what did happen.'

'It did, did it?' The Sergeant eyed him with acute suspicion. 'Are you trying to get funny with me, sir?'

'No, I wouldn't dare. You mightn't think it, but I'm frightened of you. Don't be misled by my carefree manner: it's a mask assumed to hide my inward perturbation.'

'That I might believe,' said the Sergeant grimly. 'But I'd like to hear a little more about this branch. Who climbed over the wall?'

'Oh, I did!' replied Neville, with his seraphic smile.

'When?'

'The night my uncle was murdered.' He observed the Sergeant's expression, and said: 'I can see you think there's a catch coming, and, of course, if your mind is running on the murder, there is. I climbed over the wall when everyone, including the policeman parked in the hall, thought I'd gone to bed. Oh, and I climbed out of my bedroom window as well. I'll show you.'

'Why?' demanded the Sergeant.

Neville blinked at him. 'Policeman in the hall. I didn't want him to know I was going out. It would have put unsuitable ideas into his head – same sort of ideas that you're toying with now, which all goes to show that policemen have very dirty minds. Because I'm innocent. In fact, I had to go and confer with an accomplice.'

'You…Now, look here, sir!'

Sally interrupted to say: 'I hand it to you; you're as clever as stink, Neville.'

'Don't be coarse, precious: the Sergeant isn't mealy-mouthed, but he doesn't like to hear young women being vulgar.'

'What I'd like to hear,' said the Sergeant, 'is the truth of this story you're trying to gammon me with!'

'Of course you would,' said Neville sympathetically. 'And just because I like you, I'll tell you. I went round by stealth to tell Mrs North that my uncle had been murdered.'

The Sergeant's jaw dropped. 'You went round to tell – And why, may I ask?'

'Well, obviously it was important to her to know, on account of her sordid financial transactions with Uncle Ernie,' explained Neville.

'So you knew about that, did you, sir?'

'Yes, didn't I make that clear? I was her accomplice.'

'And a damned bad one!' struck in Sally.

'She shouldn't have bullied me into it. I don't wonder you look surprised, Sergeant. You're perfectly right, it wasn't in my line at all. However, I did try to make my uncle disgorge the IOUs. That's what Simmons meant when he told you that he heard my uncle telling me to go to hell, before dinner.' He paused, watching the Sergeant through his long lashes. 'You know, you're awfully quick,' he told him. 'I can see that you've hardly finished thinking that that gives me a motive for having committed the murder, before your mind has grasped the flaw in that theory. Not, mind you, that I could have got hold of those IOUs, even if I had murdered my uncle. I haven't actually tried, but I'm pretty sure I couldn't open a safe. Miss Drew could – at least, she says she could, but I noticed that when it came to the point she went to pieces a bit. That's the worst of women: they can never carry anything in their heads. If she had had her criminal notes with her she would have made some very violent stuff which she calls soup, and blown the safe up. You mustn't think I encouraged her, because though I may look effeminate I'm not really, and the sort of primeval crudity which characterises the female mind nauseates me.'

The Sergeant, who had listened to this remarkable speech with an air of alert interest, said: 'And why, sir, did you think it was so important that Mrs North should know that your uncle was dead?'

'Well, naturally it was important,' said Neville patiently. 'You people were bound to discover the IOUs, and if you don't think that their presence in my uncle's safe was extremely incriminating, why on earth did your Superintendent go and grill the poor girl?'

The Sergeant stared at him, unable immediately to think of a suitable rejoinder. He was relieved of the necessity of answering.

'Why boasteth thou thyself in mischief, O mighty man?' demanded the condemnatory voice of PC Glass.

Eight

THE SERGEANT, WHO HAD NOT HEARD HIS SUBORDINATE'S approach across the lawn, jumped, but Neville proved himself to be Glass's equal by retorting without an instant's hesitation: 'Am I a sea or a whale that thou settest a watch over me?'

This question, delivered as it was in a tone of pained surprise, took Glass aback, and had also the effect of warming the Sergeant's heart towards Neville.

Miss Drew said dispassionately: 'The devil can quote Scripture for his own use. All the same, that's a jolly good bit. Where did you find it?'

'Job,' responded Neville. 'I found some other good bits, too, but unfortunately they aren't quite drawing-room.'

'Whoso despiseth the Word,' announced Glass, recovering from the shock of having been answered in kind, 'shall be destroyed!'

'That'll do!' intervened the Sergeant. 'You go and wait for me in the drive, Glass!' He waited until the constable had withdrawn, and then said: 'Well, sir, you've told me a very straightforward story, but what I'm asking myself is, why didn't you tell it before?'

'You didn't notice the espalier before,' said Neville.

'It might be better for you, sir, if you told the truth about your doings on the night of the murder without waiting to be questioned,' suggested the Sergeant, with a touch of severity.

'Oh no! You'd have thought it very fishy if I'd been as expansive as all that,' said Neville.

Upon reflection, the Sergeant privately agreed with him. However, all he said was that Neville would be wise not to try to be too clever with the police.

'You may be right,' answered Neville, 'but your Super-intendent said that no good would come of my taking the Press to my bosom, and lots of good came of it. I've got my picture in the papers.'

'You have?' said the Sergeant, diverted in spite of himself. 'What, you're not going to tell me they went and printed all that International spy stuff?'

'No,' replied Neville regretfully. 'Not that, but one of the eager brotherhood really thought I was the Boots.'

Sally gave a crow of mirth. 'Neville, is that what you told them? Oh, do let me see your interview!'

'I will, if the Sergeant doesn't mind putting off my arrest for ten minutes.'

The Sergeant said: 'You know very well I've got nothing to arrest you on, sir.'

'But wouldn't you love to do it?' murmured Neville.

'You get along with you, sir,' recommended the Sergeant.

To his relief, Neville obeyed his command, linking his arm in Sally's, and strolling away with her towards the house. Out of earshot, she said: 'You spilled more than I bargained for.'

'Diverting his mind.'

'I hope to God you didn't say too much.'

'Yes, so do I,' agreed Neville. 'One comfort is that we shall soon know. How's the heroine of this piece doing?'

'If you mean Helen –'

'I do, darling, and if one of your sisterly fits is coming on, go home and do not bore me with it.'

'Gosh, how I do dislike you!' exclaimed Sally.

'Well, you're not singular,' said Neville comfortingly. 'In fact, I'm getting amazingly unpopular. Aunt Lucy gets gooseflesh whenever she sets eyes on me.'

'I'm not surprised. I must say, I think –'

'What compels you?' inquired Neville.

'Oh shut up! I *will* say that I think it's fairly low of you to get yourself photographed as the Boots. Miss Fletcher's got enough to bear without your antics being added to the rest.'

'Not at all,' he replied. 'My poor aunt was becoming lachrymose, and no pleasure to herself or me. The paper that printed my story, carefully imported into the house by me, has been another of my diversions. Indignation not profitable, but better than aimless woe. How's Helen?'

'She's all right,' said Sally, a note of reserve in her voice.

A sleepy but intelligent eye was cocked at her. 'Ah, the atmosphere a trifle strained? I wondered why you came round here.'

'It wasn't that at all. I wanted to take another look at the lay-out. And I thought it might be a good thing to evaporate for a bit. John's not going up to town till after lunch.'

'Don't tell me it's a necking-party!' said Neville incredulously.

She gave a short laugh. 'No. But I'm giving it a chance to become one. If only John weren't so – so idiotically unapproachable!'

'These strong men! Oh, do tell me! If it turns out to be John who killed Ernie, do we seek to cover up the evidence of his guilt, or not?'

She did not answer, but, as they reached the drawing-room window, pulled her arm away from his, and said abruptly: 'Are you capable of speaking the truth, Neville?'

'Didn't you hear me just now, speaking the truth to the Sergeant?'

'That was different. What I want to know is this, are you in love with Helen?'

'Oh, God give me strength!' moaned Neville. 'A chair – brandy – a basin! Romance, as pictured by Sally Drew! Tell me, does anyone *really* read your works?'

'All very well,' said Sally, critically surveying him. 'But you're quite a good actor, and I can't get it out of my head that you agreed to try and wrest those IOUs from Ernie. I haven't before seen you falling over yourself to render assistance to people.'

'No, darling, and believe me, you won't see it again. Not that I did. If I fell it was because I was pushed. Don't tell me you've inserted this repulsive notion into John's head!'

'I haven't, of course, but I shouldn't be altogether surprised if it were there. I may be wrong, but one thing I do know, and that is that he's being extremely guarded – not to say frozen.'

'You'd be guarded if you looked like being pinched for murder.'

She let her monocle drop. 'Neville, do you think there's a danger of that?'

'I do, of course. What is more, I don't think that the further instalment of Helen's adventures on the fatal night are going to be as helpful to John as she no doubt felt they would be.'

'No,' said Sally bluntly. 'Nor do I. If she'd only keep her mouth shut…By the way, John doesn't know anything about her second interview with the Superintendent, so don't go and let it out!'

'How simple life would be without friends! Why, in the name of all that's feeble-minded –'

'Because he'd be bound to ask why she went back to the study, of course, and that would tear the whole thing wide open. She'd have to tell him about the IOUs.'

'Let's go and write an anonymous letter to John, divulging the whole story, shall we?' suggested Neville. 'It would be a kindness to them both, and I don't in the least mind doing people kindnesses if it doesn't cost me anything.'

Sally sighed. 'I darned nearly told him myself, when he first arrived. Only Helen was so terrified of his knowing that I didn't. And since then…Oh, I don't know! She may be right. I can't make John out. Neville, *what brought him home?*'

'Dear heart, will you purge your mind of the belief that I'm good at riddles?'

'He doesn't suspect her of having had an affair with Ernie. Apparently he told her he didn't.'

'Well, it's nice to know that he hasn't joined the great majority.'

She looked sharply at him. 'Is that what people have been thinking? Go on, tell me!'

'People are so lewd,' murmured Neville.

'Has there been talk? Much of it?'

'Oh no! Just a little light-hearted gossip to pass the time.'

She was silent for a moment, frowning. At last she said: 'That's bad. Easily discovered, and saddles John with a motive. If he got wind of that…Hang it, he wouldn't burst home just to bash Ernie on the head! It's archaic.'

Neville handed her a cigarette, and lit one himself. 'You could work that up into a plausible story if you put your mind to it,' he said. 'While in Berlin, John heard repercussions of the gossip –'

'Why in Berlin?' she interrupted.

'That I can't tell you. You'll probably be able to think out several attractive answers for yourself. He returned to remonstrate with Ernie –'

'I don't see John remonstrating.'

'No, darling; if you'd seen John remonstrating you'd be a suspect yourself.'

'What I mean is –'

'We know, we know! Have it your own way! He came home to issue an ultimatum. Ernie got under his skin, and without taking much thought he knocked him on the head.'

'Several flaws,' said Sally. 'Why did he enter by the side gate, if not with malice aforethought?'

'State entry heralded by butler leading to undesirable publicity. Gossip amongst servants, possibility of encountering Aunt Lucy. Lots of answers.'

'All right. What did he do with the weapon?'

'Not a fair question. Doesn't apply exclusively to John. Whoever killed Ernie disposed of the weapon with such skill as to provide this case with its most baffling feature.'

'Very nice,' said Sally. 'You've been reading my books. But let me tell you that I'm not a believer in these sudden flashes of brilliance on the part of murderers. When I think out a bit of dazzling ingenuity for my criminal to indulge in, it usually costs me several hours of brain-racking thought.'

'The human mind sharpened by fear –'

'Bosh!' said Sally, flicking the ash from the end of her cigarette. 'In my experience, the human mind, when under the influence of fear, rushes round in frantic circles. No, thanks: that theory doesn't go big with me at all. As I see it, there was one person who had time, motive and opportunity to kill Ernie, and lashings of time in which to dispose of the weapon.'

He met her look with a flickering smile, and lifted his hand. 'Oh, no! *This hand of mine Is yet a maiden and an innocent hand, Not painted with the crimson spots of blood.*'

'Round of applause from the gallery. But quotations prove nothing. You could have done it, Neville.'

'Oh, but why stop at me? Perhaps Aunty Lucy did it, with one of her Indian clubs. I believe she wields them with considerable vigour.'

'Don't be silly. Why should she?'

'Heaven knows. If you don't fancy her, what about Simmons?'

'Again why?'

'And again, Heaven knows. Why leave all the brain-work to me? You think.'

'Yes, well, I see very little point in thinking out fantastic motives for Miss Fletcher and Simmons while you're right under my nose, complete with a motive I don't have to hunt for.'

He looked bored. 'Well, if you're going to make me the favourite, I shall lose all interest. The crime becomes at once pedestrian and commonplace. Oh, here's my poor aunt! Come and help us to solve the mystery, Aunt Lucy. My theory is that you did it.'

Miss Fletcher, who had entered the drawing-room, came over to the window, but said in a voice of shocked indignation: 'I'm sure I don't know where you get your dreadful tongue from, Neville. It certainly wasn't from your dear father. I know it is only thoughtlessness, but the things you say are in the very worst of bad taste. And you haven't even bought an armband!'

'I know. I thought it would look like the fall from the sublime to the ridiculous if I did,' he explained, indicating with a wave of his hand her funereal attire.

'One likes to show respect for the dead,' she said. 'Oh, Miss Drew, so kind of your sister to send such beautiful flowers!' She pressed Sally's hand, and added: 'I expect you must find this all *most* interesting. I always think it so clever of you to write books. So complicated, too. Not that I've read them, of course. I find I'm too stupid to understand detective stories, but I always put them down on my library list.'

'You wouldn't be so encouraging if you knew what she's up to,' said Neville. 'She's trying to prove that I murdered Ernie.'

'Oh no, dear!' said Miss Fletcher distressfully. 'I'm afraid Neville's often very thoughtless, but he wouldn't do a thing like that.'

'Why on earth you can't keep a still tongue in your head baffles conjecture!' Sally told Neville wrathfully.

'His poor father was very talkative,' explained Miss Fletcher. 'Dear Ernie, too, was always good company. But unfortunately Neville has got into a bad habit of mumbling, which makes it very difficult to hear what he says. Neville, I have just discovered that there will have to be an inquest. Can nothing be done to stop it?'

'No. Do you mind?' he inquired.

'Well, dear, it's not very *nice*, is it? We've never had such a thing in the family. So common! I wonder if Mr Lawrence could do anything about it? I think I will go and ring him up.'

'But Miss Fletcher – !' began Sally, only to be silenced by having her foot trodden on by Neville.

Miss Fletcher, recommending Neville to take care of his guest, drifted away. Neville said softly: 'You know, you're a menace. Leave my aunt to me, will you?'

'But what's the use of letting her think there needn't be an inquest? It isn't very considerate of you to –'

'Of course it's not considerate! It wasn't considerate of me to discover that I hadn't a shirt fit to wear this morning, or a pair of socks without holes in them; and it won't be considerate of me when I think up a new annoyance, which I shall do as soon as this inquest-business begins to wear thin. You've got a disgustingly sentimental idea that bereaved persons ought to be humoured, cosseted, and given plenty of time in which to indulge their grief. I shouldn't be at all surprised to find that you're one of those paralysing monsters of unselfishness, with a bias towards self-sacrifice, and a strong yen for shouldering other people's burdens.'

Sally gave a gasp. 'Go on! It's the rankest kind of boloney, but I should be interested to know how you defend it.'

'Shouldn't place people under obligations,' said Neville briefly. 'Nearly always intolerable. Effect on your own character probably disastrous.'

'Why?'

'Spiritual conceit.'

She polished her monocle. 'There's something in what you say,' she admitted. 'Not much, but a grain of truth. Sorry I tried to butt in on your plans for Miss Fletcher's consolation. I very nearly took a hand in Helen's differences with John, too. A small, inner voice bade me hold my peace.'

'A woman's instinct!' said Neville, deeply moved. 'Not but what I sympathise with your purely rational desire to disperse the fog they grope in. But one should never forget that some people fair revel in fog.'

'Helen isn't revelling in any of this,' Sally replied. 'Married couples who can't get on rather bore me in the ordinary way, but though I think she's been cavorting around like a prize ass my withers are a trifle wrung by Helen's troubles. They really do seem to have gathered thick and fast upon her. The worst of it is, I can't be sure which way John will jump if he discovers the truth.'

'Baffling man – John,' agreed Neville.

'Well, he is. Just consider it! He arrives in England, unexpectedly, the day Ernie is murdered, and turns up here the next morning, suspecting that the footprints discovered in the garden might be Helen's.'

'Oh no, did he really? That leads us to suppose that he knew something.'

'Yes, but what? Helen says he doesn't suspect her of having had any kind of liaison with Ernie. But when he walked in on us yesterday the general impression I got was that an iceberg had drifted in. In fact, he was coldly angry, and not loving any of us very noticeably.'

'Forgive the interruption, but if he thought Helen was mixed up in a murder case, there was a certain amount of excuse for peevishness. I don't want to be old-world, but wife's admitted presence in home of noted lady-killer is enough to make most men feel a trifle out of humour.'

'I know, and if he'd raged at her I could have understood it. He was just deadly polite.'

'Obviously the moment for Helen to put over a big act as repentant wife.'

'That is what I hope she is doing, but she's so burned up over the whole thing that she seems to have lost grip. Of course, if John were to say: "Darling, tell me all," I expect she would. But he isn't that sort. They must have let themselves drift an awful way apart.'

The same thought was in Helen's mind at that moment. She had just entered the library, where her husband sat writing at his desk, and almost before she closed the door behind her she wished that she were on the other side of it.

North looked up, regarding her in a way which did not tend to put her any more at her ease. 'Do you want me, Helen?' he asked impersonally.

'I – No, not exactly. Are you busy?'

He laid down his pen. 'Not if you wish to talk to me.'

This reply, though possibly intended to be encouraging, had the effect of making Helen feel a very long way away from him. She moved across the room to a chair by the window, and sat down in it. 'It's such a long time since we talked together – really talked – that I seem to have forgotten how,' she said, trying to speak lightly.

His face hardened. 'Yes.'

She realised that hers had been an unfortunate remark. She said, not looking at him: 'We – we ought to talk this thing over, don't you think? It concerns us both, doesn't it?'

'Certainly. What do you want to say?'

She tried to formulate sentences in her brain; he neither moved nor spoke, but sat watching her. Suddenly she raised her eyes, and said abruptly: 'Why did you come home like that? So unexpectedly, and without a word to me?'

'I thought, Helen, that you already knew the answer to that question.'

'I? How could I know?'

'You informed me that you did. You said that I had come home to spy on you.'

She flushed. 'I didn't mean it. I was upset.'

'That you were upset by my arrival is not, my dear Helen, a very reassuring thought.'

'Not that! Ernie's death – that policeman asking me such ghastly questions!'

'We should get on better,' he remarked, 'if you did not lie to me. I know you rather well. You were horrified to see me.'

She looked rather hopelessly across at him. 'Oh, what's the use of talking like this? It only leads to misunderstandings, and bitterness.'

After a moment's silence, he answered levelly: 'Very well. What did you want to talk to me about? Fletcher's murder?'

She nodded. 'Yes.'

'It seems to be very much on your nerves.'

'Wouldn't it be on yours?'

'That would depend on whether I felt either grief, or fear.'

'Grief! Oh no! But I was there that evening. I don't want to be dragged into it. You must see how awful my position is!'

'Had you not better tell me exactly what happened?' he suggested.

'I did tell you. I think I've made the Superintendent realise that it would be no use asking me to identify the man I saw, but –'

'Just a moment, Helen. It is time we understood one another. Did you, in fact, recognise that man?'

'No!' she said quickly. 'I never saw his face.'

'But you have some idea, haven't you, who he was?'

She said in a low voice: 'If I had I shouldn't tell a soul. You can be sure of that.'

'In that case, there does not seem to be much point in pursuing the matter further,' he said. 'The only advice I can possibly give you, as things are, is to keep calm, and to say as little as you can.' He picked up his pen again, but after writing a couple of lines, said, without looking up: 'By the way, have you any objection to telling me why Neville Fletcher came to see you on the night of the murder?'

She gave an uncontrollable start, and faltered: 'How do you know? Who told you?'

'Baker saw him leave the premises, and mentioned it to me this morning.'

'Do you encourage the servants to report to you who visits me?'

'No,' he replied imperturbably.

'Neville came to tell me Ernie had been killed.'

He looked up at that. 'Indeed! Why?'

'He knew I was a friend of Ernie's. I suppose he thought I'd want to know. He's always doing mad things. You simply can't account for anything he says or does.'

'What does he know about this business?'

'Nothing. Only what we all know.'

'Then why did he think it necessary to visit you at midnight to tell you what you would certainly know a few hours later?'

'He'd seen my footprints,' she said desperately. 'He thought they might be mine. He came to find out.'

'If Neville leapt to the conclusion that the footprints were yours he must enjoy a greater share of your confidence than I suspected. What is there between you?'

She pressed her hands to her throbbing temples. 'Oh, my God, what do you take me for? Neville! It's – it's almost laughable!'

'You misunderstand me. I wasn't suggesting that there was any love between you. But your explanation of his visit is altogether too lame to be believed. Did he by any chance *know* that you were at Greystones that evening?'

'No, of course not! How could he? It was a guess, that's all.'

'Not even Neville Fletcher would make such a guess without having very good reason for doing so. Am I to understand that you were so much in the habit of visiting Fletcher in that – you will have to forgive me if I call it clandestine – manner, that it was a natural conclusion for Neville to arrive at?'

'Oh no! Neville knew all the time that I didn't feel about Ernie except as a friend.'

He raised his brows. 'Was your possible relationship with Fletcher of interest to Neville?'

'No. No, of course not. But I've known Neville for years.' Her voice tailed off uncertainly.

'I am quite aware of that. I too have known Neville – or shall we say, have been acquainted with him? – for years. Are you asking me to believe that that extremely detached young man asked you to explain your dealings with his uncle?'

She could not help smiling, but there was fright in her eyes. 'No. Actually, I told him.'

'You told Neville Fletcher…I see. Why?'

She muttered: 'No reason. It – sort of came out. I can't explain.'

'That at least is evident,' he said harshly.

'You don't believe anything I say.'

'Do you find that surprising?'

She was silent, staring down at her clasped hands.

'Is Neville in love with you?'

She said, with genuine surprise: 'Neville? Oh no, I'm sure he's not!'

'You must forgive me for being so ignorant,' he said. 'So little have I spied on you that I'm not at all up to date. Who, at the moment, is an enamoured swain? Is Jerry Maitland still in the running?'

'If I told you no one had ever been in the running you'd believe that as little as you believe the rest of my story.'

'As I have yet to hear the rest of your story, I can't answer that. Oh, don't insult my intelligence by telling me that I have heard it!'

Her lips were trembling. 'If you think that, is this the way to get me to tell you the whole truth? You treat me as though I were – as though I were a criminal, and not your wife!'

'My wife!' He gave a short laugh. 'Is not that a trifle farcical?'

'If it is, it's your fault!' she said in a choking voice.

'Oh, undoubtedly! I failed to satisfy you, didn't I? You wanted more excitement than was to be found in marriage with me, and one man's love was not enough for you. Tell me this, Helen; would you have married me if I had not been a rich man?'

She made a gesture, as though thrusting his words away from her, and rose jerkily to her feet, and stood with her back to him, staring out of the window. After a moment she said in a constricted tone: 'If they don't arrest me for Ernie's murder, you had better divorce me.'

'They won't arrest you. You needn't let that bugbear ride you.'

'Things look very black against me,' she said wearily. 'I don't know that I care much.'

'If things look black, you've kept something from me which must be of vital importance. Are you going to tell me what it is?'

She shook her head. 'No. When the case is over – if we come out of it intact – I'll make it possible for you to divorce me.'

'I'm not going to divorce you. Unless –' He stopped.

'Well? Unless?'

'Unless there's someone else whom you've fallen in love with enough to – But I don't believe there is. You don't fall in love, Helen. All you want is a series of flirtations. But if I am to help you now –'

'Why should you?' she interrupted.

'Because you're my wife.'

'The whole duty of a husband, in fact. Thank you, but I would prefer you to keep out of it.'

'I can't do that.'

'You were a fool to come down here!' she said.

'Possibly, but if you were to be dragged into the case there was nothing to be done.'

She turned. 'To save your own good name? Do you hate me, John?'

'No.'

'You're indifferent, in fact. We're both indifferent.' She came away from the window. 'I don't want to be divorced. I realise that all this mess – Ernie's death, the scandal, everything! – has been my fault, and I'm sorry. In future, I'll be more careful. There really isn't anything more to be said, is there?'

'If you don't trust me enough to tell me the whole truth, nothing.'

'I trust you as much as you trust me!' she said fiercely. 'You know how much that is! Now, if you please, let's banish the whole subject. Do you mean to come home to dinner tonight?'

He was looking rather narrowly at her, and did not answer. She repeated the question; he replied in his usual cold way: 'No, I shall dine in town. I may be late back. Expect me when you see me.'

Nine

SERGEANT HEMINGWAY LEFT GREYSTONES IN A THOUGHTFUL mood. An exhaustive search had failed to discover the hiding-place of any weapon, but one fact had emerged with which he seemed to be rather pleased.

'Though why I should be I can't tell you,' he said to Glass. 'It makes the whole business look more screwy than ever. But in my experience that's very often the way. You start on a case which looks as though it's going to be child's play, and you don't seem to get any further with it. By the time you've been at work on it a couple of days you've collected enough evidence to prove that there couldn't have been a murder at all. Then something breaks, and there you are.'

'Do you say that the more difficult a case becomes the easier it is to solve?' asked Glass painstakingly.

'That's about the size of it,' admitted the Sergeant. 'When it's got so gummed up that each new fact you pick up contradicts the last I begin to feel cheerful.'

'I do not understand. I see around me only folly and sin and vanity. Shall these things make a righteous man glad?'

'Not being a righteous man, I can't say. Speaking as a humble flatfoot, if it weren't for folly and sin and vanity I wouldn't be where I am now, and nor would you, my lad. And if you'd stop wasting your time learning bits of the Bible to fire off at me – which in itself is highly insubordinate conduct, let me tell you – and take a bit of wholesome interest in this problem, you'd probably do yourself a lot of good. You might even get promoted.'

'I set no store by worldly honours,' said Glass gloomily. 'Man being in honour abideth not: he is like the beasts that perish.'

'What you do want,' declared the Sergeant with asperity, 'is a course of Bile Beans! I've met some killjoys in my time, but you fairly take the cake. What did you get out of your friend the butler?'

'He knows nothing.'

'Don't you believe it! Butlers always know something.'

'It is not so. He knows only that harsh words passed between the dead man and his nephew on the evening of the murder.'

'Young Neville explained that,' said the Sergeant musingly. 'Not that I set much store by what he says. Pack of lies, I daresay.'

'A lying tongue is but for the moment,' observed Glass, with melancholy satisfaction.

'You can't have been about the world much if that's what you think. Do you still hold to it that the man you saw on the night of the murder wasn't carrying anything?'

'You would have me change my evidence,' said Glass, fixing him with an accusing glare, 'but I tell you that a man that beareth false witness is a maul, and a sword, and a sharp arrow!'

'No one wants you to bear false witness,' said the Sergeant irritably. 'And as far as I'm concerned, you're a sharp arrow already, and probably a maul as well, if a maul means what I think it does. I've had to tell you off once already for giving me lip, and I've had about enough of it. Wait a bit!' He stopped short in the middle of the pavement and pulled out his notebook, and hastily thumbed over the leaves. 'You wait!' he said darkly. 'I've got something here that I copied out specially. I knew it would come in useful. Yes, here we are! *He that being often reproved hardeneth his neck, shall suddenly be destroyed.*' He looked up to see how this counter-blast was being received, and added with profound satisfaction: '*And that without remedy!*'

Glass compressed his lips, but said after a moment's inward struggle: 'Pride goeth before destruction, and an haughty spirit before a fall. I will declare my iniquity, I will be sorry for my sin.'

'All right,' said the Sergeant, returning his notebook to his pocket. 'We'll carry on from there.'

A heavy sigh broke from Glass. 'Mine iniquities have gone over my head; as an heavy burden they are too heavy for me,' he said in a brooding tone.

'There's no need to take on about it,' said the Sergeant, mollified. 'It's just got to be a bad habit with you, which you ought to break yourself of. I'm sorry if I told you off a bit roughly. Forget it!'

'Open rebuke,' said Glass with unabated gloom, 'is better than secret love.'

The Sergeant fought for words. As he could think of none that were not profane, and felt morally certain that Glass would, without hesitation, condemn those with Biblical aphorisms, he controlled himself, and strode on in fulminating silence.

Glass walked beside him, apparently unaware of having said anything to enrage him. As they turned into the road where the police station was situated, he said: 'You found no weapon. I told you you would not.'

'You're right,' said the Sergeant. 'I found no weapon, but I found out something you'd have found out two days ago if you'd had the brains of a louse.'

'He that refraineth his lips is wise,' remarked Glass. 'What did I overlook?'

'Well, I don't know that it was any business of yours, strictly speaking,' said the Sergeant, always fair-minded. 'But the grandfather clock in the hall is a minute slow by the one in the late Ernest's study, which synchronised with your watch. What's more, I found out from Miss Fletcher that it's been like that for some time.'

'Is it important to the case?' asked Glass.

'Of course it's important. I don't say it makes it any easier, because it doesn't, but that's what I told you: in cases like this you're always coming up against new bits of evidence which go and upset any theory you may have been working on. On the face of it, it looks as though the man you saw – we'll assume it was Carpenter – did the murder, doesn't it?'

'That is so,' agreed Glass.

'Well, the fact of that hall clock's being a minute slow throws a spanner in the works,' said the Sergeant. 'In the second act of her highly talented performance, Mrs North stated that that clock struck the hour, which was 10 p.m., while she was in the hall, on her way to the front door. You saw Carpenter making his getaway at 10.02. That gave him a couple of minutes in which to have killed the late Ernie, disposed of the weapon, and reached the gate. It's my opinion it couldn't have been done, but at least there was an outside chance. Now I discover that when Mrs North left the study it wasn't 10.00, but 10.01, and that's properly upset things. It begins to look as though Carpenter wasn't in on the murder at all, but simply went down to try his luck at putting the black on the late Ernie, and was shown off the premises as described by Mrs North. In fact, it wouldn't surprise me if Carpenter turns out to be one of those highly irrelevant things that seem to crop up just to make life harder. The real murderer must have been hiding in the garden, waiting for his opportunity, and while you were taking notice of Carpenter, and deciding to go and investigate, he was doing the job.'

Glass considered this for a moment. 'It is possible, but how did he make his escape? I saw no one in the garden.'

'I daresay you didn't see anyone, but you didn't go looking behind every bush, did you? You flashed your torch round, and *thought* there was no one in the garden. There might have been, and what was to stop him making his getaway while you were in the study?'

They had reached the police station by this time. Glass paused on the steps, and said slowly: 'It does not seem to me that it can have happened like that. I do not say it was impossible, but you would have me believe that between 10.01, when Mrs North left the house, and 10.05, when I discovered the body, a man had time to come forth from his hiding-place, enter the study, slay Ernest Fletcher, and return to his hiding-place. It is true that I myself did not enter the study until 10.05, but as I came up the path must I not have seen a man escaping thence?'

'You know, when you keep your mind on the job you're not so dumb,' said the Sergeant encouragingly. 'All the same, I've got an answer to that one. Who says the murderer escaped by way of the side gate? What was to stop him letting himself out the same way Mrs North did – by the front door?'

Glass looked incredulous. 'He must be a madman who would do so! Would he run the risk of being seen by a member of the household, perhaps by Mrs North, who had only a minute or two before passed through the study door into the hall, as he must have known, had he been lying in wait as you suggest?'

'Heard you coming up the path, and had to take a chance,' said the Sergeant.

'Folly is joy to him that is destitute of wisdom!' said Glass scornfully.

'Well, for all you know he was destitute of wisdom,' replied the Sergeant. 'You go and get your dinner, and report here when you've had it.'

He went up the steps, and into the building. It was not until he had passed out of Glass's sight that it occurred to him that the constable's last remark might not have been directed at the unknown murderer. A wrathful exclamation rose to his lips; he half turned, as though to go after Glass; but thought better of it. Encountering the Station Sergeant's eye, he said: 'Somebody here must have had a grudge against me when they saddled me with that pain in the neck.'

'Glass?' inquired Sergeant Cross sympathetically. 'Chronic, isn't he? Mind you, he isn't usually as bad as he's been over this case. Well, it stands to reason, doesn't it? His sort has to have a bit of sin in front of them to get properly wound up, as you might say. Do you want him taken off?'

'Oh no!' said the Sergeant, with bitter irony. 'I like being told-off by constables. Makes a nice change.'

'We'll take him off the job,' offered Cross. 'He's not used to murder-cases, that's what it is. It's gone to his head.'

The Sergeant relented. 'No, I'll put up with him. At least he's a conscientious chap, and apart from this nasty habit he's got of reciting Scripture I haven't anything against him. I daresay he's got a fixation, poor fellow.'

An hour later, mellowed by food, he was propounding this theory to Superintendent Hannasyde, who arrived at the police station just as his subordinate came back from a leisurely dinner.

'You never know,' he said. 'We shall quite likely find that he had some shocking experience when he was a child, which would account for it.'

'As I have no intention of wasting my time – or letting you waste yours – in probing into Glass's past, I should think there is nothing more unlikely,' replied Hannasyde somewhat shortly.

The Sergeant cast him a shrewd glance, and said: 'I told you this wasn't going to be such a whale of a case, Chief. Said so at the start. Bad morning?'

'No, merely inconclusive. Budd had been double-crossing Fletcher; Neville Fletcher seems to be up to his eyes in debt; and North did not spend the evening of the 17th at his flat.'

'Well, isn't that nice?' said the Sergeant. 'Stage all littered up with suspects, just like I said it would be! Tell me more about friend Budd.'

Hannasyde gave him a brief account of the broker's exploits. The Sergeant scratched his chin, remarking at the end of the tale: 'I don't like it. Not a bit. You can say, of course, that if he had to hand over nine thousand shares which he hadn't got, and couldn't get without pretty well ruining himself, he had a motive for murdering the late Ernest. On the other hand, what he said to you about Ernest's not being able to come out into the open to prosecute him rings very true. Very true indeed. He's not my fancy at all. What about North?'

'North, unless I'm much mistaken, is playing a deep game. He told me that after dinner at his club he returned to his flat, and went early to bed. What actually happened was that he returned to his flat shortly after 8.30 p.m., and went out again just before 9.00. He came back finally at 11.45.'

'Well, well, well!' said the Sergeant. 'No deception? All quite open and above-board?'

'Apparently. He paused to exchange a word with the hall porter on his way in at 8.30; when he went out the porter offered to call a taxi, and he refused, saying he would walk.'

'Who saw him come in later, Chief?'

'The night porter. He says that he caught sight of North stepping into the lift.'

'Well, for a man who impressed you as having a head on his shoulders he doesn't seem to me to be doing so very well,' said the Sergeant. 'What was the use of his telling you he'd spent the evening at his flat when he must have known you could bust the story wide open at the first blow?'

'I don't know,' Hannasyde replied. 'Had it been Budd, I should have thought that he had got into a panic, and lost his head. But North wasn't in a panic, and I'm quite sure he didn't lose his head. What I do suspect is that for some reason, best known to himself, he was stalling me.'

The Sergeant thought it over. 'Stalling you till he could have a word with his wife. I get it. I'd call it a risky game to play, myself.'

'I don't know that I think that would worry him much.'

'Oh, that sort, is he?' said the Sergeant. 'A little course of Ichabod wouldn't do him any harm, by the sound of it.'

Hannasyde smiled, but rather absently. 'He wasn't at his office this morning, and as his secretary didn't seem to think he was going there today, I came down to see him here. But he's going to be difficult, just because he doesn't say a word more than he need.'

'So is young Neville going to be difficult,' said the Sergeant. 'But not, believe me, for the same reason. That bird talks so much you have a job to keep up with him. What do you make of him having the nerve to tell me he climbed out of his bedroom window, and over the garden wall, the night the late Ernest was murdered, just to go and tell Mrs North all about it? Said he was her accomplice over the business of those IOUs of hers.'

Hannasyde frowned. 'Cool hand. It might be true.'

'Cool! I believe you! Brass isn't the word for what he's got. However, I'm bound to admit I've got a soft corner for him. He laid old Ichabod out with the neatest right counter you ever saw.'

'What?'

'Figure of speech,' explained the Sergeant. 'He landed a Biblical text which Ichabod wasn't expecting, and which pretty well crumpled him up. But that's nothing to go on. I wouldn't put it above him to bump his uncle off, if it happened to suit his book. Though, now I come to think of it,' he added reflectively, 'it would be more in his line to have stuck a knife in his ribs. No; if it weren't for the fact that there's no trace of the weapon, and not one hiding-place that I could spot, I wouldn't fancy him at all for the role of murderer. Which brings me to the only bit of useful evidence I picked up. The hall clock is a minute slow, Chief.'

Hannasyde looked at him. 'If that is so,' he said slowly, 'it makes Mrs North's evidence practically valueless.'

'The second batch, you mean? It does look like it, doesn't it? Not that I ever set much store by it myself, from what you told me of her. Mind you, I don't say the murder couldn't still have happened but what I do say is that the man Glass saw – call him Charlie Carpenter – couldn't have done it. It must have been Budd, which I *don't* think, young Neville, North, or the dizzy blonde herself.'

Hannasyde shook his head. 'I can't swallow that, Hemingway. If we are to assume that Mrs North's evidence was true, it means that Fletcher did not re-enter the study until 10.01. You yourself put the time it would take him to sit down at his desk again and start to write his letters at two minutes at the least. That leaves two minutes for the murderer to walk in, kill him, and get away again. Less, for though Glass didn't actually enter the study until 10.05, he must have had the window in view for quite a minute, on his way up the path.'

'Yes, that's what he said,' replied the Sergeant. 'I admit it would be cutting it a bit fine. What's your idea, Chief? Think Mrs North's first story was the true one?'

'No,' said Hannasyde, after a pause. 'I think she did go back into the study. If she didn't let herself out of it as she described, I don't see how her finger-prints came to be on the panel. But the fact of the hall clock's being slow points to a discrepancy somewhere in her story. She stated that the man X left the study with Ernest at 9.58, that she went back into it, and left it as the hall clock struck 10.00. Now, the only times we *know* to be correct are 10.02, when Glass saw X making off; and 10.05, when he discovered Fletcher's body. That left us with a difference of four minutes, between the time Mrs North said X left and the time Glass actually saw him leave. We could just, and only just, account for that by assuming that X doubled back to the study, murdered Fletcher, and again made off. But if Fletcher returned to the study not at 10.00, but at 10.01, then there is no possibility of X's having returned, committed the murder, and reached the gate again. So either X left by the side gate at 9.58, to be followed in four minutes by a second man – Y, if you like; or the first man, X, was a pure fabrication of Mrs North's.'

'Hold on, Super! I'll have to see it on paper,' said the Sergeant. He wrote for a moment or two, and regarded the result with disgust. 'Yes, that is a hopeful-looking mess,' he remarked. 'All right – X is out. So what? We know the North dame hid in the garden, because we found her footprints. Yes, I get it. Y, who is obviously North, was with the late Ernest; she recognised his voice – or maybe she didn't: I haven't worked that bit out. Anyway, Y killed Ernest while Mrs North was in the garden, and bunked. Mrs North then entered the study to have a look-see, and – for reasons which I won't attempt to fathom – made off by way of the front door. You can make the times fit if you juggle with them. Someone may have passed down Maple Grove when Y reached the gate, which would mean that he'd have to wait till whoever it was had cleared off before making his getaway. Or, if you prefer it, Mrs North didn't leave at 10.01, but later. Though why she should make that bit up, I don't quite see. That eliminates X, and fits the only facts we know to be certain.'

'You can eliminate X if you like,' interposed Hannasyde, 'but you can't eliminate Charlie Carpenter. Where does he fit into this otherwise plausible story?'

The Sergeant sighed. 'That's true. If we've got to have him in, then he's Y, and North is X – eliminated. Yes, that's all right. Mrs North didn't recognise his voice, but she caught a glimpse of him, and thought he might be her husband. Hence her erroneous evidence. How's that?'

'Not bad,' conceded Hannasyde. 'But if North is eliminated, will you tell me why he stated that he spent the evening in his flat, when in actual fact he did nothing of the kind?'

'I give it up,' said the Sergeant despairingly. 'There isn't an answer.'

Hannasyde smiled. 'There might be. It's just possible that North had nothing to do with the murder, but suspects that his wife had.'

The Sergeant stared at him. 'What, and deliberately chucked his own alibi – if any – overboard, so as to be all set to leap in and take the rap for his wife? Go on, Super! You don't believe that!'

'I don't know. He might. Rather that type of man.'

'Regular film star, he sounds to me,' said the Sergeant, revolted. 'Red blood, and hair on his chest, too, I should think.' He turned his head, as the door opened, and encountered the solemn stare of PC Glass. 'Oh, so you're back, are you? Well, if you're working on this case, I suppose you'd better come in. I daresay I'll be able to think up a job for you.'

Hannasyde nodded. 'Yes, come in, Glass. I want you to cast your mind back to the night of the murder. When you were walking along Vale Avenue, on your beat, do you remember seeing anyone, beyond the man who came out of the side gate of Greystones? Anyone who might, at about 10.00 p.m., have been passing the front entrance to Greystones?'

Glass thought deeply for a moment, and then pronounced: 'No, I remember no one. Why am I asked this question?'

'Because I have reason to doubt the truth of Mrs North's statement, that she left Greystones by the front door, at a minute after 10.00. What I want is a possible passer-by, who may or may not have seen her.'

'If that is so, the matter is simple,' said Glass. 'There is a pillar-box at the corner of Vale Avenue and Glynne Road, where she dwells, which is cleared at 10.00 p.m. each night. I do not doubt that the postman saw her, if she was indeed upon her way home at that hour.'

'Nice work, Ichabod!' exclaimed the Sergeant. 'You'll end up in the CID yet.'

A cold eye was turned upon him. 'A man that flattereth his neighbour spreadeth a net for his feet,' said Glass, adding, since the Sergeant seemed unimpressed: 'Even the eyes of his child shall fail.'

'Well, don't sound so cocky about it,' said the Sergeant. 'And as it happens I haven't got any children, so now where are you?'

'We won't discuss the matter,' interposed Hannasyde in a chilling tone. 'You will please remember, Glass, that you are talking to your superior officer.'

'To have respect of persons is not good,' said Glass seriously. 'For, for a piece of bread that man will transgress.'

'Oh, will he?' said the indignant Sergeant. 'Well, he won't – not for fifty pieces of bread! What next!'

'That'll do,' said Hannasyde, a tremor in his voice. 'Get hold of that postman, Glass, and discover at what time he cleared the box, whether he saw Mrs North, and if so, whether she was carrying anything. Got that?'

'Yes, sir.'

'All right, that's all. Report here to me.'

Glass withdrew. As the door closed behind him, Hannasyde said: 'Why do you encourage him, Skipper?'

'Me? Me encourage him?'

'Yes, you.'

The Sergeant said: 'Well, if you call it encouraging him to tell him where he gets off –'

'I believe you enjoy him,' said Hannasyde accusingly.

The Sergeant grinned. 'Well, I've got to admit it adds a bit of interest to the case, waiting for him to run dry. You'd think he must have got pretty well all he's learnt off his chest by now, wouldn't you? He hasn't, though. I certainly have to hand it to him: he hasn't repeated himself once so far. Where do we go from here?'

'To North's house,' replied Hannasyde. 'I must see if I can get out of him what he was doing on the night of the murder. You, I think, might put in a little good work in the servants' hall.'

But when he arrived at the Chestnuts Hannasyde was met by the intelligence that North had left the house immediately after lunch. The butler was unable to state his master's destination, but did not think, since he was driving himself in his touring car, that he was bound for his City office.

After a moment's consideration, Hannasyde asked to have his card taken to Mrs North. The butler accepted it, remarking repressively that he would see whether it were convenient for his mistress to receive him, and ushered him into the library.

Here he was presently joined by Miss Drew, who came in with her monocle screwed firmly into her eye, and a cigarette stuck into a long amber holder. 'My sister's resting, but she'll be down in a moment,' she informed him. 'What do you want to see her about?'

'I'll tell her, when she comes,' he replied politely.

She grinned. 'All right: I can take a snub. But if it's about that epic story Neville Fletcher burbled into your Sergeant's ears, I can tell you now you're wasting your time. It leads nowhere.'

'Epic story? Oh, you mean his adventures on the night of his uncle's death! No, I haven't come about that.'

'I quite thought you might have. I shouldn't have been altogether surprised had you asked to see me.'

'No? Are you concerned in those adventures?'

'Actually, I'm not, but Neville, who, you may have noticed, is rather reptilian, told the Sergeant, in his artless way, that I had plans for opening Ernie Fletcher's safe.'

'And had you?'

'Well, yes and no,' said Sally guardedly. 'If I'd had my criminal notebook with me, and time to think it out, I believe I could have had a stab at it. But one very valuable thing this case has taught me is that in real life one just doesn't have time. Of course, if I'd been writing this story, I should have thought up a perfectly plausible reason for the fictitious me to have had the means at hand of concocting the stuff you call soup. I should have turned myself into a scientist's assistant, with the run of his laboratory, or something like that. However, I'm nothing of the sort, so that wasn't much good.'

Hannasyde looked at her with a good deal of interest. 'Mr Fletcher's story was true, then, and not an attempt to keep the police amused?'

'You seem to have weighed him up pretty accurately,' commented Sally. 'But, as it happens, he really did come here to tell Helen (a) that his uncle had been murdered, and (b) that he hadn't managed to get hold of her IOUs. That, naturally, looked very bad to me. Of course, it was idiotic of my sister to co-opt Neville in the first place: she'd have done better to have put me on to it. You won't misunderstand me when I tell you that I was all for abstracting those IOUs from the safe before you could get your hands on them. Unfortunately, there was a policeman mounting guard over the study, which completely cramped my style.'

'I quite see your point,' said Hannasyde. 'But if you've made a study of crime you must know that it would have been quite culpable of you to have abstracted anything at all from the murdered man's safe.'

'Theoretically, yes; in practice, no,' responded Sally coolly. 'I knew that the IOUs had nothing whatsoever to do with the case. Naturally you can't be expected to know that, and just look at the trouble they're causing you! Not to mention the waste of time.'

'I appreciate your point of view, Miss Drew, but, as you have already realised, I don't share it. It seems to me that the IOUs may have a very direct bearing on the case.'

She gave a chuckle. 'Yes, wouldn't you love me to pour my girlish confidences into your ears? It's all right: I'm going to. If you're toying with the notion that my sister may have been the murderess, I can put you right straight away. Setting aside the fairly evident fact that she simply hasn't got it in her to smash anyone's head in, there wasn't a trace of blood on her frock or her cloak when she came home that night. If you want me to believe that she could have done the deed, and not got one drop of blood on her, you'll have to hypnotise me. Of course, I don't expect you to pay much heed to what I say, because I'm bound to stand by my sister, but you can interrogate her personal maid, can't you? She'll tell you that none of my sister's clothes have disappeared, or have been sent to the cleaners' during the past week.' She paused, extracted the end of her cigarette from the holder, and stubbed it out. 'But, as I see it, you don't really think she did it. The man you suspect is my brother-in-law, and I'm sure I don't blame you. Only there again I may be able to help you. You can take it from me that he doesn't know of the existence of those IOUs. I've no doubt that sounds a trifle fatuous to you, but it happens to be true. And – just in case you haven't grasped this one – he doesn't suspect my sister of having had any what-you-might-call improper dealings with Ernest Fletcher.' She stopped, and looked critically at him. 'I'm not making a hit with you at all. Why not? Don't you believe me?'

'Yes, I believe you're telling me what *you* believe to be the truth,' he answered. 'But it is just possible that you don't know the whole truth. If – for the sake of argument – your brother-in-law is the man I'm looking for, it must be obvious to you that he wouldn't give anything away, even to you.'

'That's perfectly true,' conceded Sally fair-mindedly. 'But there's one other point: my brother-in-law's no fool. If he'd done it, he'd have taken darned good care to have covered up his tracks.' She frowned suddenly, and began to fit another cigarette into her holder. 'Yes, I see there's a snag there. You think that he meant to, but that Helen's getting mixed up in it gummed up the works. You may be right, but if I were you I wouldn't bank on it.'

'At my job,' said Hannasyde, 'one learns not to bank on anything.'

He turned, for the door had opened, and Helen had come into the room. She looked tired, and rather strained, but greeted him quite calmly. 'Good-afternoon. I'm sorry to have kept you waiting. I was lying down.'

'I'm sorry to be obliged to disturb you, Mrs North,' he replied, 'but there are one or two points in your evidence which I want to go over with you again.'

She moved to a chair by the fireplace. 'Please sit down. I can't tell you anything more than I have, but, of course, I'll answer any questions you want to ask me.'

He took a seat beside a table near her, and laid on it his notebook. 'I am going to be perfectly frank with you, Mrs North, for I think it will save a great deal of time and misunderstanding if you know what facts are in my possession.

Now, the first thing I am going to tell you is that I have proof that a certain man, who need not concern you much, since it is in the highest degree unlikely that you have ever heard of him, visited Ernest Fletcher at some time during the evening on which he was murdered.'

Her eyes were fixed upon his face with an expression in them of painful anxiety, but she merely said in a low voice: 'No doubt he was the man I saw. Go on, please.'

He opened his notebook. 'I am going to read to you, Mrs North, the sequence of events, between the hours of 9.35 and 10.05, according to your own evidence, and to that of the Constable who discovered Fletcher's body. If I have got any of the times wrong, you must stop me. To begin with, at 9.35 you arrived at the side entrance of Greystones. You noticed a short, stout man come out of the gate, just before you reached it, and walk away towards Vale Avenue.'

She was clasping the arms of her chair rather tensely, but when he paused, and looked inquiringly at her, she replied with composure. 'Yes, that is correct.'

'You entered the garden of Greystones, walked up the path, and found Ernest Fletcher alone in his study.'

'Yes.'

'At 9.45, after a short dispute with Fletcher, you left the study, by the way you had entered, unattended, and were about to go home, when you heard footsteps approaching up the path. You then concealed yourself behind a bush a few feet from the path.'

'Yes. I've already told you all this.'

'Just a moment, please. You were able to see that this new visitor was a man of medium height and build, wearing a light Homburg hat, and carrying no stick in his hand; but you were not able to recognise him.'

She said nervously: 'I thought he seemed to be quite an ordinary-looking person, but I only caught a glimpse of him, and the light had practically gone. I couldn't *swear* to anything about him.'

'We won't go into that at present. This man entered the study through the window, closing it behind him, and remained there until approximately 9.58. At 9.58, he came out of the study, followed by Fletcher, who escorted him in a leisurely fashion to the gate. As soon as both men were out of sight round the bend in the path, you went back into the study to search in the desk for your IOUs. You heard Fletcher returning to the house, and you escaped from the study before he reached it, passing through the door into the hall. While you were in the hall, the tall-case clock there struck the hour of 10.00. But I must tell you, Mrs North, that the clock was a minute slower than the one in the study, so that the time was actually one minute past ten.'

'I don't see –'

'I think you will, for I am coming now to the evidence of the Constable. At 10.02 he observed, from the point where Maple Grove runs into Vale Avenue, a man coming out of the side gate of Greystones, and making off towards the Arden Road. Thinking the circumstance suspicious, he made his way down Maple Grove, entered the garden of Greystones by the side gate, and walked up the path to the study window. There he discovered the body of Ernest Fletcher, lying across the desk, with his head smashed. The time then, Mrs North, was 10.05 p.m.'

She faltered: 'I don't think I understand.'

'If you think it over, I feel sure you will,' he suggested. 'If your evidence is true, Fletcher was alive at one minute past ten.'

'Yes,' she said hesitantly. 'Yes, of course he must have been.'

'Yet at 10.02 the Constable saw an unknown man coming out of the garden-gate; and by 10.05 Fletcher was dead, and there was no trace to be found of his murderer.'

'You mean it couldn't have happened?'

'Consider it for yourself, Mrs North. If you say that the man you saw left at 9.58, who was the man the Constable saw?'

'How can I possibly tell?'

'Can you suggest any reason to account for his presence in the garden?'

'No, of course I can't. Unless he murdered Ernie.'

'In considerably less than a minute?'

She stared at him uncomprehendingly. 'I suppose not. I don't know. Are you – are you accusing *me* of having murdered Ernie Fletcher?'

'No, Mrs North. But I am suggesting that you have falsified your evidence.'

'It's not true! I did see Ernie taking that man to the gate! If there was another man in the garden, I knew nothing of it. You've no right to say I falsified my evidence! Why should I?'

'If, Mrs North, you did, in point of fact, recognise the man who entered the garden, that in itself might constitute a very good reason for falsifying your evidence.'

Sally's hand descended on her sister's shoulder, and gripped it. 'Quiet. You're not obliged to answer.'

'But I didn't! What I told you was true! I know nothing about the second man, and since I heard Ernie whistling just before I went into the hall I presume he was alive at a minute past ten. You want me to say he didn't see that man out, but you won't succeed! He *did*!'

'That's enough,' said Sally. She looked across at Hannasyde. 'My sister is entitled to see her solicitor before she answers any questions, I think. Well, she isn't going to say any more now. You've heard her evidence: if you can't make it fit with your constable's evidence, that's your look out, not hers.'

She spoke with considerable pugnacity, but Hannasyde replied without any apparent loss of temper: 'Certainly she may consult her solicitor before answering me. I think she would be wise to. But perhaps she will be good enough to tell me where I may find Mr John North?'

'I don't know!' Helen said sharply. 'He didn't tell me where he was going. All I can tell you is that he isn't coming back to dinner, and may be late home.'

'Thank you,' said Hannasyde, rising to his feet. 'Then I won't detain you any longer, Mrs North.'

Helen stretched her hand towards the bell, but Sally said curtly: 'I'll see him out,' and strode to the door and opened it.

When she returned to the library she found her sister pacing up and down, a twisted handkerchief being jerked between her hands. She looked at her under frowning brows, and inquired: 'So now what?'

'What am I going to do?'

'Search me. Do you feel inclined to tell me the truth?'

'What I have already said is the truth, and nothing will make me go back on it!' Helen said, holding Sally's eyes with her own.

There was a slight pause. 'All right,' Sally said. 'I don't know that I blame you.'

Ten

J OINING HIS SUPERIOR OUTSIDE THE GATE, SERGEANT
Hemingway said: 'Nothing much to be made of it my end.
Did you shake the fair Helen?'

'No. She's sticking to it that her story's true. She's bound
to, of course. I didn't expect her to go back on it. What I did
want to do – and what I rather fancy I succeeded in doing – was
to frighten her. Did you get anything out of the servants?'

'Precious little. The butler saw young Neville walking off
down the drive at about 12.30 that night, which makes it look
as though what he told me was true. Otherwise, I wasted my
time. Old-fashioned sort of servants: been employed there
several years, seem to be fond of both master and mistress,
and aren't talking. Come to think of it, it's a pity there aren't
more like them – though not from our point of view. Did
you get the impression Mrs North was working in cahoots
with her husband, or what?'

'I don't know. Her sister warned her not to answer me
until she'd seen her solicitor, so I didn't press the matter.'

'Just about what that dame with the eyeglass would do!'
remarked the Sergeant disapprovingly. 'In my young days

women didn't know anything about such things. I don't believe in all this emancipation. It isn't natural. What are we going to do now? Get after young Neville?'

'No. I'm going back to the police station. It's no use my tackling Neville. I haven't anything against him, except the state of his bank overdraft, and he knows it. I'm hoping Glass may have managed to make contact with that postman. As far as I can see, the two people we've got to get hold of are North and Carpenter. I'll put a call through to North's office, and find out if he's there, or has been there. With any luck Jevons has been able to ferret out some more information about Angela Angel. I put him on to that first thing this morning. Which reminds me that there's one thing I want to pick up, and that's a photograph of Fletcher. We'll call in at Greystones on our way, and borrow one from his sister. I take it no photograph was found amongst Angela Angel's possessions?'

'Only a few of stage pals, and one of Charlie Carpenter. I asked Jimmy Gale particularly, but he was positive there wasn't one of the man who'd been keeping her. Few flies on the late Ernest. Think Angela's an important factor, Chief?'

Hannasyde did not answer for a moment. As they turned in at the front gate of Greystones, he said: 'I hardly know. If North's our man, I should say not. But in some way or other she seems to be linked up with the case. It won't do any harm to see what we can find out about her.'

He rang the front-door bell, and in a few minutes the door was opened by Simmons, who, however, told them that his mistress had gone out. Hannasyde was about to ask him if he could produce a photograph of his master when Neville strayed into the hall from a room overlooking the drive, and said with his shy, slow smile: 'How lovely for me! I was getting so tired of my own company, and I daren't go out in case you're having me watched. My aunt wouldn't like it if I became conspicuous. But where's the Comic Strip? You don't mean to tell me you haven't brought him?'

The Sergeant put up a hand to his mouth. Neville's large eyes reproached him. 'You can't like me as much as I thought you did,' he said, softly slurring his words. 'I've learnt two new bits to say to him, and I'm sure I shan't be able to carry them in my head much longer.'

The Sergeant had to fight against a desire to ask what the new bits might be. He said: 'Ah, I daresay, sir!' in a non-committal tone.

Young Mr Fletcher, who seemed to have an uncanny knack of reading people's thoughts, said confidentially: 'I know you want me to tell you what they are. I would – though you oughtn't to try and pick my brains, you know – if it weren't for the Superintendent's being with you. You understand what I mean: they're awfully broad – not to say vulgar.'

The Sergeant cast an imploring glance at his superior, who said with an unmoved countenance: 'You can tell the Sergeant some other time, Mr Fletcher. I called in the hope of seeing your aunt, but perhaps you can help me in her stead. Have you a photograph of your uncle which you could let me borrow for a few days?'

'Oh no!' said Neville. 'I mean, I haven't. But if I had I wouldn't lend it to you: I'd give it to you.'

'Extremely kind of you, but –'

'Well, it isn't really,' Neville explained, 'because I hate photographs. I'll tell you what I'll do: I'll give you the one that stands on a table all to itself in the drawing-room. As a matter of fact, I was wondering what next I could do to annoy my aunt.'

'I have no wish to annoy Miss Fletcher. Isn't there some other –'

'No, but I have,' said Neville in his gentle way. 'I shan't tell her I gave it to you, and then she'll organise a search for it. That will be uncomfortable, of course, but since I started to do good turns I've found that they invariably entail a certain amount of self-immolation, which has a very degrading effect on the character.' Talking all the time, he had led the way into the drawing-room, where, as he had described, a large studio portrait of his uncle stood in solitary state upon an incidental table. He stopped in front of it, and murmured: 'Isn't it a treat?'

'I don't want to borrow a photograph which Miss Fletcher obviously values,' said Hannasyde somewhat testily. 'Surely there must be another somewhere.'

'Oh, there is, beside my aunt's bed! But I shan't let you have that, because it wouldn't suit my book. There's an almost indistinguishable but certainly existent line drawn between the counter and the added irritant.'

'I'm bothered if I know what you're talking about, sir!' said the Sergeant, unable to contain himself. 'Nice way to treat your poor aunt!'

The flickering gaze rested on his face for an instant. 'Yes, isn't it? Will you have it with or without frame, Superintendent?'

'Without, please,' Hannasyde replied, looking at him a little curiously. 'I think I understand. Your methods are slightly original, aren't they?'

'I'm so glad you didn't say eccentric,' said Neville, extracting the portrait from its frame. 'I hate being called eccentric. Term employed by mediocre minds to describe pure rationalism. Now I will hide the frame, and bribe Simmons to keep his mouth shut. Practically the only advantage I have yet discovered in inheriting a fortune is the ability it confers on one to exercise the unholy power of bribery.'

'And then I suppose you'll join in the search for it?' said the Sergeant, torn between disapproval and amusement.

'No, that would savour strongly of hypocrisy,' answered Neville serenely. 'There you are, Superintendent. I shan't invite you to stay and have tea, because my aunt might come back.'

Once outside the house, the Sergeant said: 'Came over me in a flash! Do you know what that silly smile of his makes me think of, Super?'

'No, what?'

'That picture people make such a fuss about, though why I've never been able to make out. Pie-faced creature, with a nasty, sly smile.'

'The Mona Lisa!' Hannasyde laughed suddenly. 'Yes, I see what you mean. Odd young man. I can't make up my mind about him at all.'

'There are times,' said the Sergeant, 'when I'd ask nothing better than to be able to pin this murder on to him.

However, I'm bound to say it isn't, to my way of thinking, arty enough for him. My lord would go all out for something pretty subtle, if you ask me.'

'I shouldn't be at all surprised if you're right,' said Hannasyde.

In another few minutes they boarded an omnibus which set them down within a stone's throw of the police station. PC Glass had not returned from his quest, and Hannasyde, having ascertained over the telephone that North was not at his office, put through a call to Scotland Yard, and asked whether Inspector Jevons had come in. He was soon connected with the Inspector, who had, however, little to report. He had discovered the block of flats in which her unknown protector had installed Angela Angel, but her apartment had been rented by a man calling himself Smith. The hall porter was sure he would recognise the gentleman if he saw him again, and described him as being slim, dark, and very well dressed.

Hannasyde glanced at his watch, and decided to return to London, leaving the Sergeant to pick up any information that Glass might bring in. He appointed a meeting-time at Head-quarters, and went off, bearing the portrait of Fletcher with him.

It was some little while before Glass presented himself, and when he did arrive he appeared to be suffering from strong indignation. He no sooner set eyes on the Sergeant than he said sternly: 'Whoso causeth the righteous to go astray in an evil way, he shall fall himself into his own pit!'

'What on earth's the matter with you?' said the Sergeant. 'You can't have been on the jag, because the pubs aren't open yet.'

'Let them be ashamed and confounded together that seek after my soul to destroy it! I will turn away mine eyes from beholding vanity; I am like a green olive tree in the house of the Lord.'

'Look here, what the devil have you been up to?' demanded the Sergeant.

Glass fixed him with a sombre glare. 'Mine eyes have beheld lewdness, and a Babylonish woman!' he announced.

'Where?' asked the Sergeant, suddenly interested.

'In a glittering house of corruption I have seen these things. I have escaped from an horrible pit.'

'If you mean what I think you do, all I can say is that I'm ashamed of you,' said the Sergeant severely. 'What were you doing in that kind of a house, I'd like to know? The Chief told you to find the postman; instead of obeying orders you go and –'

'I have done as I was bidden. I have found him though my feet were led in the path of destruction.'

'Now, look here, my lad, that's quite enough. There's no need to go nuts over the postman's morals. It doesn't matter to you where you found him, as long as you did find him – though I must say I'd no idea postmen got up to those kinds of larks in the suburbs. Did you get his evidence?'

'I summoned him forth from that place of sin, yes, and his wife also –'

'What?' exclaimed the Sergeant. 'Here, where *was* the poor fellow?'

'In a playhouse, which is an habitation of the devil.'

'Do you mean to tell me all this song and dance is because the postman took his wife to the pictures in his off-time?'

gasped the Sergeant. 'It's my belief you're crazy! Now, cut it out, and let's get down to brass tacks! Did he see Mrs North on the night of the murder, or did he not?'

'I have roared by reason of the disquietness of my heart,' apologised Glass, with a groan. 'But I will make my report.' He produced a notebook, and with a bewilderingly sudden change from zeal to officialdom, read in a toneless voice: 'On the night of 17 June, having cleared the box at the corner of Glynne Road at 10.00 p.m. precisely, the postman, by name Horace Smart, of 14 Astley Villas, Marley, mounted his bicycle, and proceeded in an easterly direction, passing the gates of Greystones. Smart states he saw a woman walking down the drive.'

'Did he notice whether she was carrying anything?'

'He states that she carried nothing, that when he saw her she had one hand raised to hold her hair against the breeze. With the other she held up the skirts of her dress.'

'Did he recognise –' The Sergeant broke off to answer the telephone, which at that moment interrupted him. 'Scotland Yard? Right! Put 'em through...Hullo? Hemingway speaking.'

'We've got Carpenter for you,' announced a voice at the other end of the line.

'You have?' said the Sergeant incredulously. 'Nice work! Where is he?'

'We don't know that, but we can tell you where he will be this evening. Got it through Light-Fingered Alec, who says Carpenter's hanging out in a basement room at 43 Barnsley Street, W. That's –'

'Half a shake!' said the Sergeant, reaching for a pencil. '43 Barnsley Street, W. – basement room. Where is Barnsley Street?'

'I'm telling you. You know the Glassmere Road? Well, Barnsley Street leads out of it into Letchley Gardens.'

'Letchley Gardens? Classy address for friend Carpenter.'

'It would be if he lived there, but he doesn't. Barnsley Street's not so hot. No. 43 looks like a lodging-house. Do you want Carpenter pulled in?'

'I thought you said you didn't know where he was?'

'We don't, but his landlady might.'

The Sergeant thought for a moment, and then said: 'No. You never know, and we don't want to give him warning we're on to him. He'll keep till he gets home. I'm meeting the Superintendent at the Yard when I get through here. We'll go along to this Barnsley Street then, and catch his lordship unawares.'

'Well, from what Light-Fingered Alec told Fenton, you won't find him till latish. He's got a job in some restaurant. Anything else we can do for you?'

'Not that I know of. If he's working in a restaurant, the Chief may decide to pick him up in the morning. Anyway, I'll be seeing you. So long!' He replaced the receiver, and said with satisfaction: 'Well, now we are getting on, and no mistake!' He found that Glass was still waiting, open note-book in hand, and his eyes fixed on his face, and said: 'Oh yes, you! What was I saying?'

'You were about to ask me whether the man Smart recognised the woman he saw. And I answer you, No. He rode upon the other side of the road, and saw but the figure of a female, her robe caught up in one hand, the other smoothing her hair, which the breeze ruffled.'

'Oh well, there doesn't seem to be much doubt it was Mrs North, anyway!' said the Sergeant. He collected his papers together and got up. The Constable was apparently still brooding over the experience through which he had passed, for he said with a shudder: 'The lamp of the wicked shall be put out: but the tabernacle of the righteous shall flourish.'

'I daresay,' agreed the Sergeant, bestowing his papers in his case. 'But if the picture you saw was wicked enough to set you off like this, all I can say is I wish I'd seen it. I've never struck a really hot one in my life – not what I call hot, that is.'

'How long shall thy vain thoughts lodge within thee?' demanded Glass. 'I tell you, when the wicked perish there is shouting!'

'You go off home, and treat yourself to a nice aspirin,' recommended the Sergeant. 'I've had enough of you for one day.'

'I will go,' Glass replied, restoring his notebook to his pocket. 'I am tossed up and down as the locust.'

The Sergeant deigned no reply, but walked out of the office. Later, when he met Superintendent Hannasyde in his room at Scotland Yard, he said: 'You've properly put your foot into it now, Chief. Turned poor old Glass into a locust, that's what you've done. You never heard such a commotion in your life!'

'What on earth – ?'

'Led his feet into a horrible pit,' said the Sergeant with unction. 'I've sent him off duty to get over it.'

'What are you talking about?' said Hannasyde impatiently. 'If you'd forget Glass and attend to this case –'

'Forget him! I wish I could! Thanks to you, he's been to the pictures, and what he's got to say about it would make your hair stand on end. However, he found the postman, and Mrs North *was* seen about ten o'clock – though not recognised – and she was not carrying anything. So at any rate she was speaking the truth about the time she left Greystones. You heard about Carpenter?'

'Yes, I've been talking to Fenton about that. From what he could pick up from this Light-Fingered Alec of his, it looks as though we ought to find Carpenter at home any time after 9.30 p.m. We'll drop round to see him, Skipper.'

The Sergeant nodded. 'Right you are. What time?'

'Oh! Give him half-an-hour's law, just to be sure of catching him. I'll meet you at the corner of Glassmere Road and Barnsley Street at 10.00 p.m. Meanwhile, you'll like to hear that the hall porter at Chumley Mansions recognised Fletcher's photograph as soon as I showed it to him. He was "Smith" all right.'

'Well, we never had much doubt, did we?' said the Sergeant. 'Was he able to tell you anything more?'

'Nothing of much use to us. Like everyone else who came into contact with Fletcher, he seems to have found him invariably pleasant. He knows nothing more about the girl than he told Gale at the time of her death.'

'I must say it looks as though Angela Angel's suicide and the late Ernest's murder do hang together,' pondered the

Sergeant. 'But I'm damned if I see where North fits into it, if they do.'

'We shall probably know more when we've heard what Carpenter has to say,' replied Hannasyde.

'What you might call the key to the whole mystery,' agreed the Sergeant.

He arrived a little before ten o'clock at the appointed rendezvous that evening, and found Barnsley Street to be a drab road connecting the main thoroughfare of Glassmere Road with the prim respectability of Letchley Gardens. Glassmere Road, which the Sergeant knew well, was a busy street, and at the corner of Barosley Street, close to an omnibus stopping-place, was a coffee-stall. The Sergeant bought himself a cup of coffee, and entered into idle chat with the proprietor. He was soon joined by Hannasyde, who came walking along the Glassmere Road from an Underground Railway Station a few hundred yards distant.

'Evening,' Hannasyde said, nodding to the coffee-stall proprietor. 'Not much of a pitch, this, is it?'

'Not bad,' replied the man. He jerked his thumb over his shoulder. 'I get folks coming out of the Regal Cinema later on. Of course, it's quiet now, but then, it's early. Can't complain.'

The Sergeant pushed his empty cup and saucer across the counter, bade the man a cheerful good-night, and strolled away with his superior.

The sky was overcast, and although the daylight had not yet failed entirely, it was growing dark. Barnsley Street, curling round in a half-circle towards Letchley Gardens, was ill lit, a depressing street lined with thin, drab houses. No. 43 was discovered midway down it. A card in the window on the ground-floor advertised Apartments, and a shallow flight of six steps led up to the front door. A light was burning at the top of the house, but the basement was in darkness. 'Looks as though we're too early,' remarked the Sergeant, pulling the bell-knob. 'Of course, if he's got a job at a really swell restaurant, it isn't likely he'd be back yet.'

'We can but try,' Hannasyde replied.

After an interval, the Sergeant pulled the bell again. He was about to pull it a third time when a light appeared in the fanlight over the door, and slip-shod feet were heard approaching inside the house.

The door was opened by a stout lady of disagreeable aspect, who held it slightly ajar, and said pugnaciously: 'Well? What do you want? If you've come about lodgings, I'm full up.'

'If I had, that would break my heart,' said the Sergeant instantly. 'I don't know when I've taken such a fancy to anyone as I have to you. Came over me the instant I laid eyes on you.'

'I don't want none of your sauce,' responded the lady, eyeing him with acute dislike.

'Well, tell me this: is Mr Carpenter in?'

'If it's him you want, why don't you go down the area steps? Pealing the bell, and having me down from the top of the house, as though I'd nothing better to do than run up and down stairs the whole evening!'

'Run?' said the Sergeant. 'Go on! You couldn't! Now, put a sock in it, and let's have a real heart to heart. Is Charlie Carpenter in?'

She said grudgingly: 'Yes, he's in. If you want him, you can go down and knock on his door.'

'Thank you for nothing,' said the Sergeant. 'You let me see this running act of yours. You and me will trip downstairs, and you'll do the knocking, after which you'll tell Mr Charlie Carpenter to shut his eyes and open the door, and see what the fairies have brought him.'

'Oh, I will, will I?' said the lady, bristling. 'And who says so?'

The Sergeant produced his card, and showed it to her. 'That's the name, Clara, but if you like you can call me Willy, seeing that you're so stuck on me. Come on, now, get a move on!'

She read the card painstakingly, and seemed to feel an increased aversion from him. 'I'm a respectable woman, and I don't want any busies nosing round my house, nor there's no reason why I should have them what's more. If that young fellow's been up to any tricks, it's no business of mine, and so I'll have you know!'

'Well, now that I know it, let's get going,' said the Sergeant.

She led the way, grumbling under her breath, to the top of the basement stairs. Hannasyde nodded to the Sergeant, and himself remained on the doorstep, keeping a strategic eye on the area.

No reply was made to the landlady's imperative knock on the door of the basement room, nor was any sound audible.

'Funny. He don't generally go to bed early,' remarked the landlady, renewing her assault upon the door. 'I daresay he's gone out again. Well, I hope you're satisfied, that's all.'

'Just a moment, sister!' said the Sergeant, pushing her aside. 'No objection to my having a look round, have you?'

He turned the handle as he spoke. The door opened, and he groped for the light-switch. 'Looks as though you're right,' he remarked, stepping into the room.

But the landlady was not right. Charlie Carpenter had not gone out. He was lying fully dressed across the bed that was pushed against the wall opposite the door, and he was, as the Sergeant saw at a glance, dead.

The landlady, peeping over the Sergeant's shoulder, gave a piercing shriek, and cowered away from the door into the gloom of the passage.

'Shut up!' said the Sergeant curtly. He walked across the room, and bent over the tumbled body, feeling its hands. They were quite warm.

Hannasyde's voice sounded on the stairs. 'Anything wrong, Hemingway?' he called.

The Sergeant went to the door. 'We're just a bit too late, Chief, that's what's wrong,' he said. 'You come and see.'

Hannasyde descended the stairs, cast one shrewd glance at the landlady's pallid countenance, and strode into the front room.

The Sergeant was standing beside the bed, his bright eyes dispassionately surveying the dead man. At Hannasyde's involuntary exclamation, he looked up. 'Something we *weren't* expecting,' he remarked.

Hannasyde bent over the body, his face very grim. Carpenter had been killed as Ernest Fletcher had been killed, but whereas Fletcher had apparently been taken unawares, some struggle had taken place in this dingy basement room. A chair had been overturned, a mat rucked up, and above the dead man's crumpled collar a bruise on his throat showed dark on the white skin.

'Same method – probably the same weapon. But this man knew what to expect,' Hannasyde muttered. He glanced over his shoulder. 'Get on to the Department, Hemingway. And get rid of that woman. Tell her she'll have to answer questions. Not that she's likely to know anything.'

The Sergeant nodded, and went out. Left alone in the room, Hannasyde turned his attention from the body to his surroundings. These told him little enough. The room was sparsely furnished, but had been embellished by a number of photographs and coloured pictures, some framed, some pinned on the wall, or stuck into the frame of the spotted mirror over the fireplace. A curtain, drawn across one corner of the room, concealed from view several cheap suits, and a few pairs of shoes. On the dressing-table before the window were ranged bottles of hair oil, shaving lotion, nail varnish, and scent. Hannasyde grimaced at them, and taking out his handkerchief, covered his hand with it, and pulled open the two top drawers of the table. A motley-coloured collection of socks and handkerchiefs was all that one contained, but in the other, under a pile of ties, were scattered a number of letters, old programmes, playbills, and Press cuttings.

Hannasyde had gathered all these together into a heap by the time the Sergeant returned, and was standing looking at a photograph, cut from a picture paper, which he held in his hand. He looked round as the Sergeant entered the room, and held the cutting out to him without comment.

The Sergeant took it, and read out: '*Snapped at the Races, the Hon. Mrs Donne, Miss Claudine Swithin, and Mr Ernest Fletcher.* You don't say! Well, X has been eliminated all right, hasn't he, Chief? Find anything else?'

'Not yet. I'll wait till the room's been gone over for possible finger-prints.' Still with his hand wrapped up, he extracted the key from the door, fitted it in again on the outside, and went out.

The Sergeant followed him, watched him lock the door and pocket the key, and said: 'The old girl's in the kitchen. What do you want me to do?'

'Find out if the man at the coffee-stall saw anyone passing down this road about half-an-hour ago. Wait, I'll try and get out of the landlady exactly when Carpenter came home.'

He walked down the passage to the kitchen at the back of the house, where he found the landlady fortifying herself with gin. She whisked the bottle out of sight when he appeared, and broke at once into a torrent of words. She knew nothing; and her poor husband, whom the shock would kill, was upstairs in bed with the influenza, and she had been with him for the past hour. All she could take her oath to was that Carpenter was alive at 9.30, because he had shouted up the stairs to her, wanting to know if a parcel of shoes hadn't come for him from the cobbler, as though she wouldn't have put it in his room if it had, as she told him, pretty straight.

'Steady! Could anyone have entered the house without your knowing it?' Hannasyde asked.

'They did, that's all I know,' she said sullenly. 'If someone got in, it must have been by the area door, and it isn't my blame. Carpenter, he ought to have bolted it when he come in. 'Tisn't the first time he's been too lazy to put the chain up. The key's lost. I've been meaning to get a new one made.'

'Did he use that door?'

'Yes, he did. Saved trouble, see?'

'Who else is in the house?'

'Me and my 'usband, and my gal, Gladys, and the first-floor front.'

'Who is that?'

'A very nice lady. Stage, but she's resting.'

'Who is on the ground-floor?'

'No one. He's away. His name's Barnes. He travels in soap.'

'How long has Carpenter lodged here?'

'Six months. He was a nice young fellow. Smart, too.'

'Were you friendly with him? Did he tell you anything about himself?'

'No. Ask no questions and you'll be told no lies, is what I say. As long as he paid his rent, nothing else didn't matter to me. I guessed he'd had his bit of trouble, but I'm not one for poking my nose into what don't concern me. Live and let live's my motto.'

'All right, that's all for the present.' Hannasyde left her, and went along the passage to the door that gave on to the area. The bolts were drawn back, and the chain hung loose beside the wall.

A few minutes later the police ambulance drew up outside the house. The divisional surgeon, the photographer, and the finger-print expert were soon busy in the basement room, and a fresh-faced young sergeant was dispatched to assist Hemingway in his search for possible witnesses.

Sergeant Hemingway returned just after Carpenter's body had been removed, and joined Hannasyde in the basement room, where he was engaged, with the help of an inspector, in searching through the dead man's possessions.

'Well?' Hannasyde said.

'Yes, I got something,' the Sergeant answered. 'The coffee-merchant only arrived at his pitch at 9.30, since when, Chief, the only person he's seen come down the road, setting aside you, me and the Constable on his beat, was a medium-sized man in evening dress, who walked quickly down the other side of the street, making for the taxi-rank in Glassmere Road. And what do you make of that?'

'Any description?'

'No. He didn't notice him particularly. Says it was too dark to see his face. But what he does say, Super, is that he wasn't wearing an overcoat, and he wasn't carrying anything in his hands. Talk about history repeating itself! I don't need to ask if you've found the weapon here. I wouldn't believe you if you said you had.'

'I haven't. Did you find anyone to corroborate the coffee-stall owner's evidence?'

'If you can call it corroboration,' said the Sergeant with a sniff. 'There's a couple propping the wall up at the other end of the street. You know the style: kissing and canoodling for the past hour. I wouldn't set much store by what they say, but for what it's worth the girl seems to think she saw a gentleman in evening dress and an opera hat pass by about half-an-hour ago. Not what you'd call a lot of traffic on this road. I've put Lyne on to the houses opposite, on the chance someone may have been looking out of a window.'

'Did the couple at the other end of the street notice whether the man in evening dress was carrying a stick?'

'Not they. First thing they said was they hadn't noticed anyone at all. I had to press them a bit before they came out of the ether, so to speak. Then the girl remembered seeing a man with a white shirt-front on the other side of the road, and the boy-friend says after thinking hard, yes, he believes he did see someone, only he didn't look at him particularly, and whether it was before or after the Constable passed them, he wouldn't like to say. Actually, it was just before, if the coffee-merchant is to be believed, which I think he is. What's more, they were going opposite ways, and there's an outside chance they may have passed each other. Shall I get hold of the chap who has this beat?'

'Yes, as soon as possible. Obviously he saw nothing suspicious, but if he did meet the man in evening dress he may be able to describe him.'

'Not much doubt who he was, if you ask me,' said the Sergeant. 'It's North all right. But what he does with his weapon has me fairly beat. Sleight-of-hand isn't in it with that chap. You got any ideas, Chief?'

'No. Nor have I any idea why, if it was he, he had to kill Carpenter.'

The Sergeant stared at him. 'Well, but it's plain enough, isn't it, Chief? Carpenter must have seen the murder of the late Ernest. My own hunch is that he was trying his hand at blackmailing North for a change.'

'Look here, Hemingway, if Carpenter was shown off the premises at 9.58 by Fletcher, how can he have seen the murder?'

'Perhaps he wasn't shown off the premises,' said the Sergeant slowly. 'Perhaps Mrs North made that up.' He paused, and scratched his chin. 'Yes, I see what you mean. Getting what you might call involved, isn't it? It looks to me as though Charlie Carpenter knew a sight more about this business than we gave him credit for.'

Eleven

THE AMOROUS COUPLE, INTERROGATED AT THE POLICE station by Hannasyde, were eager to be of assistance, but as their evidence was vague, and often contradictory, it was not felt that either could be considered a valuable witness. The girl, who was an under-housemaid enjoying her evening out, no sooner discovered that the fact of her having seen a man in evening dress was considered important by the police than she at once began to imagine that she had noticed more than she had at first admitted.

'I thought he looked queer,' she informed Hannasyde. 'Oo, I thought, you do look queer! You know: funny.'

'In what way funny?' asked Hannasyde.

'Oh, I don't know! I mean, I can't say exactly, but there was something about him, the way he was walking – awfully fast, you know. He looked like a gangster to me.'

At this point her swain intervened. 'Go on!' he said. 'You never!'

'Oh, I did, Syd, honest, I did!'

'You never said nothing to me about it.'

'No, but I got a *feeling*,' said Miss Jenkins mysteriously.

'You and your feelings!'

'Tell me this,' interposed Hannasyde. 'Was the man dark or fair?'

But Miss Jenkins refused to commit herself on this point. Pressed, she said that it was too dark to see. Mr Sydney Potter said indulgently: 'You never sor a thing. It was this way, sir: me and my young lady were having what you might call a chat. We didn't notice no one particularly. What I mean is, not to be sure of them.'

'Did you see the man in evening dress?'

Mr Potter said cautiously: 'Not to remember, I didn't. There was two or three people passed, but I didn't take no notice. It's like this: I do seem to think there was a toff walking down the other side of the road, but I wouldn't like to swear to it.'

'Yes, and he must have met the policeman, what's more,' put in Miss Jenkins. 'It was just a minute after he went by that I saw the policeman. Fancy if he done it under the policeman's nose, as you might say. Oo, some people haven't half got a nerve! I sort of *know* it was a gangster.'

'You're barmy! The policeman came by ages before,' said Mr Potter fondly. 'Go on, put a sock in it! You don't remember nothing.'

This opinion was shared by Sergeant Hemingway, who said disgustedly as soon as the couple had departed: 'Nice pair of witnesses, I *don't* think! If they were carrying on the whole evening like they were when I found them, it's a wonder to me they saw anyone. Proper necking-party. I'm bothered if I know how people keep it up for the hours they do. The girl wants to see her picture in the papers, I've met her sort before. Potter's not much better, either. In fact, they're neither of them any good.'

'Except that the girl did see a man in evening dress, which corroborates the coffee-stall proprietor's story. We'll see what the policeman has to say. If the girl was speaking the truth about his having passed just after she saw the man in evening dress, we may get somewhere.'

But when Constable Mather, a freckle-faced and serious young man, came in, he said regretfully that when he passed up Barnsley Street he had seen nothing of any man in evening dress.

'There you are!' said Hemingway, exasperated. 'What did I tell you? Just making up a good tale, that's all the silly little fool was doing.'

Hannasyde addressed the young policeman. 'When you passed, did you happen to notice whether the light was on in the basement of No. 43?'

'That's Mrs Prim's,' said Mather. 'If you'll excuse me, I'll have to think a minute, sir.'

The Sergeant regarded him with bird-like curiosity, and said: 'Either you know or you don't.'

The grave grey eyes came to rest on his face. 'Not till I've walked up the road, sir. I'm doing that now – if you wouldn't mind waiting a minute. I find I can think back if I do that.'

'Carry on,' said Hannasyde, quelling the sceptical Sergeant with a frown.

There was a pause, during which PC Mather apparently projected his spirit back to Barnsley Street. At last he said with decision: 'Yes, sir, it was. No. 39 – that's Mrs Dugdale's – had a window open, but she's got bars up, so it didn't matter. Then the next house, which is No. 41, was all dark, and after that there was one with the basement light on. That was No. 43.'

'I see,' Hannasyde said. 'You feel sure of that?'

'Yes, sir.'

'You didn't hear any sounds coming from that basement room, or notice anything wrong?'

'No, sir. The blind was drawn down, and I didn't hear anything.'

'If the light was on, the murderer may have been there,' said the Sergeant. 'In fact, it looks to me as though he was there, having done in Carpenter, waiting till you'd passed to make his escape.'

The Constable looked distressed. 'Yes, sir. I'm sure I'm very sorry.'

'Not your fault,' said Hannasyde, and dismissed him.

'Nice case, isn't it?' said the Sergeant. 'Now we only want to find that the taxi-driver didn't happen to notice what his face looked like, and we'll be sitting pretty.'

He was not destined to be disappointed. Some time later, when he and Hannasyde were back at Scotland Yard, a message was received to the effect that one Henry Smith, taxi-driver, while waiting in the rank in Glassmere Road, had been engaged by a gentleman in evening dress, and directed to drive to the Piccadilly Hotel. Whether his fare had actually entered the hotel, he was unable to say. He had not inspected the gentleman closely, but retained an impression of a man of medium height and build. He did not recall the man's face particularly; he was just an ordinary, nice-looking chap.

'Well, at any rate it can't have been Budd,' remarked the Sergeant. 'No one in their senses would call him nice-looking. We've drawn a blank on the finger-prints, Chief. Whoever did this job wore gloves.'

'And no trace of the weapon,' Hannasyde said, frowning. 'A heavy, blunt instrument, wielded with considerable strength. In fact, exactly the same instrument that was used to kill Fletcher.'

'It's nice to think we didn't overlook it at Greystones, at all events,' said the Sergeant cheerfully. 'The murderer must have walked off with it under his hat. Have you got anything out of Carpenter's papers?'

'Nothing that looks like being of much assistance. There's this.'

The Sergeant took a limp, folded letter from him, and spread it open. A glance at the signature made him exclaim: 'Angela! Well, well, well!'

The letter, which was undated, was not a long one. Written in a round, unformed hand, it began abruptly: *Charlie – By the time you get this I won't be at our old address any more. I don't think you really care, but I wouldn't want to do it without telling you, because in spite of everything, and the wrong you have fallen into, dear Charlie, and the evil companions, and everything, I don't ever forget the old times. But I know now it wasn't the real thing, because I have found the real thing, and I see everything differently. I shan't tell you his name, because I know you, Charlie, you are without truth and would make trouble if you could. Don't think it is because of the disgrace you have got into that I am leaving you, because I know now that love is as strong as death, and if it had been the real thing I would have stuck to you, because many waters cannot quench love, neither can the floods drown it. They used to teach us that that bit and all the rest was about the Church, but I know better now.*

The Sergeant read this missive, remarking as he gave it back to Hannasyde: 'She *had* got it bad, hadn't she? Fancy anyone feeling that way about the late Ernest! Looks as though she must have written it when Charlie was in jug. What you might call corroborative evidence only. She probably did do herself in for love of the late Ernest, and Charlie *was* the sort of dirty little squirt who'd put the black on anyone if he saw his way to it. And where are we now? Do you take it that Carpenter saw the late Ernest murdered?'

'If he did, it raises one or two questions,' replied Hannasyde. 'Did the murderer not only see Carpenter, but also recognise him? Or did Carpenter recognise the murderer, and attempt to blackmail him?'

'Look here, Chief, are we casting North for the part, or are we assuming the murderer is an entirely new and unsuspected character, whom we haven't even laid eyes on?'

'How do I know? I admit, nearly everything points to North. Not quite, though. In favour of that theory, we have North's unexpected return to England, his unexplained movements on the night of the murder, Mrs North's peculiar behaviour, and the presence of a man in Barnsley Street tonight who corresponds vaguely with his description.

Against it, I think we ought to set North's character first. I have his sister-in-law's word for it that he's no fool, and I believe it. But what could be more blundering and foolish than to murder a second man in precisely the same way as he murdered the first?'

'I don't know so much,' interrupted the Sergeant. 'Come to think of it, it's worrying us a bit, isn't it? If he's the smart Alec you say he is, it might strike him as a pretty fruity idea to do in his victims as clumsily as he could. Moreover, it's not as dumb as it looks. He doesn't leave his finger-prints behind him, and he's got some trick of concealing his weapon which a conjurer couldn't better.'

'Yes, I've thought of that,' admitted Hannasyde. 'But there are other points. Where and when did a man in his position come into contact with Carpenter?'

'At Greystones, on the night of the late Ernest's murder,' replied the Sergeant promptly. 'Look, Super! Supposing you forget Mrs North's second instalment for the moment. Take it that Carpenter was hiding in the garden all the time she was with the late Ernest –'

'What the devil would he be hiding for, if he had come to blackmail Fletcher?'

The Sergeant thought for a moment. 'How about his having hidden for exactly the same reason Mrs North did? He may have been walking up the path when he heard her open the gate behind him –'

'Impossible. If that were so, he must have met Budd, and he didn't.'

'All right,' said the Sergeant, in long-suffering accents.

'We'll take it he was there all the time. Came in while Budd was with the late Ernest. Instead of hopping out of his hiding-place the instant Budd left, he waited a moment to be sure the coast was clear. Then Mrs North came into the garden, and he continued to lie low. When she left the late Ernest, North had just arrived. She hid, just as she told us, recognised her husband, and bunked – No, she didn't, though! The postman saw her leaving by the front entrance just after 10.00! Wait a bit! Yes, I've got it. North killed the late Ernest somewhere between 9.45 and 10.00, and left by way of the garden-gate, watched by Mrs North, and our friend Charlie. Not knowing of Charlie's presence, Mrs North slipped into the study, just to see what kind of fun and games had been going on, found the late Ernest, got into a panic, and bunked through the house. Carpenter, meanwhile, made his exit by way of the garden-gate – time 10.02 – was seen by Ichabod, and bolted in the same direction that North had taken. He came in sight of North, followed him –'

'Followed him where?'

'Back to town, I suppose. He must have tracked him to his flat to have found out who he was. After that he tried his blackmailing game on North, and North naturally had to eliminate him. How do you like that?'

'Not much,' said Hannasyde.

'Well, if it comes to that I don't fancy it a lot myself,' confessed the Sergeant. 'The trouble is that whichever way you look at it that North dame's story gums up the works. We've got to believe she hid behind the bush at some time or other, because we found her footprints. Similarly we've got to believe she went back into the house, because of the postman's evidence.'

'Exactly,' said Hannasyde. 'And, according to your latest theory, she went back into the study when Fletcher was dead. Now, you've seen the photographs. Do you seriously think that a rather highly strung woman, seeing what she must have seen from the window, deliberately went into the study?'

'You never know what women will do when they want something badly, Chief. She wanted her IOUs.'

'That won't do, Hemingway. She could not have opened the desk drawer without moving Fletcher's body. She must have known that before she set foot in the room. We can take it she didn't go in to try and render first aid, because if she had she'd have called for help, not stolen out of the house without saying a word to anyone.'

'She might have done that if she knew the murderer was her husband.'

'If she knew that I can't think she'd have gone into the study at all. Unless she and he are working together, which hypothesis is against all the evidence we have, I don't believe she saw the murder done.'

'Wait, Super! I've got it!' the Sergeant said. 'She couldn't see into the study from behind the bush, could she?'

'No.'

'Right! North leaves at 10.02. He's the man Ichabod saw. Mrs North, not knowing what's been happening, creeps up to the study window to see. That's reasonable, isn't it?'

'So far,' agreed Hannasyde. 'Where's Carpenter? Still in ambush?'

'That's right. Now, you say Mrs North wouldn't have gone through the study. She had to!'

'Why?'

'Ichabod!' said the Sergeant triumphantly. 'By the time she was all set to do a disappearing act down the path, he must have reached the gate. She wouldn't risk hiding in the garden with the late Ernest lying dead in the study. She had to get clear somehow, and her best chance was through the house.'

Hannasyde looked up with an arrested expression in his eyes, 'Good Lord, Skipper, you may be right! But what happened to Carpenter?'

'If he was hidden behind one of the bushes by the path he could have sneaked back to the gate as soon as Ichabod passed him on his way to the study. Must have done.'

'Yes, possibly, but bearing in mind the fact that the other man left the garden at 10.02, and made off as fast as he could walk towards the Arden Road, and was seen by Glass to turn the corner into it, how did Carpenter manage (*a*) to guess in which direction he'd gone, and (*b*) to catch up with him?'

'There you have me,' owned the Sergeant. 'Either he had a lot of luck, or it didn't happen.'

'Then how do you account for his having known who North was? The Norths have been kept out of the papers so far.' He paused, tapping his pencil lightly on the desk. 'We've missed something, Hemingway,' he said at last.

'If we have, I'd like to know what it is!' replied the Sergeant.

'We've got to know what it is. I may find it out from North, of course, but somehow I don't think I shall. He's more likely to stand pat, and say nothing.'

'He'll have to account for his movements last night, and the night of the late Ernest's murder.'

'Yes. But if he gives me an alibi he can't substantiate and I can't check up on, I shall be no better off than I am now. Unless I can trace the connection between him and Carpenter, or prove he was in Barnsley Street last night, I haven't any sort of case against him. Unless I can rattle his wife into talking – or him, through her,' he added.

'I suppose it's just possible North may have had a meal at that restaurant friend Charlie was working at,' suggested the Sergeant doubtfully.

'I should think it in the highest degree unlikely,' replied Hannasyde. 'North's a man of considerable means, and if you can tell me what should take him to a fly-blown restaurant off the Fulham Road I shall be grateful to you. You were with me when I visited the place: can you picture North there?'

'No, but no more I can at any of those joints in Soho,' said the Sergeant. 'But it's a safe bet he's dined at most of those.'

'Soho's different.' Hannasyde collected the scattered documents before him, and put them away in his desk. 'Time we both went home, Skipper. There's nothing more to be done till we've seen North. I propose to pay him a visit first thing in the morning – before he's had time to leave the house, in fact. I'll leave you to look after this end of the business. No need for you to attend the inquest. See what you can dig out of Carpenter's past history. I'll take Glass along with me to the Norths', just in case I need a man.'

'He'll brighten things up for you, anyway,' remarked the Sergeant. 'I'm sorry I shan't be there to hear him give his evidence at the inquest. I bet it's a good turn.'

Superintendent Hannasyde reached Marley at half-past eight on the following morning, but he was not the first visitor to the Chestnuts. At twenty minutes to nine, as Miss Drew sat down to a solitary breakfast, a slender figure in disreputable grey flannel trousers, a leather-patched tweed coat, and a flowing tie, was ushered into the room by the slightly affronted butler.

'Hullo!' said Sally. 'What do you want?'

'Breakfast. At least, I've come to see if you've got anything better than we have. If you have, I shall stay. If not, not. Kedgeree at home. On this morning of all mornings!'

'Are you going to the inquest?' asked Sally, watching Neville inspect the contents of the dishes on the hotplate.

'No, darling, but I'm sure you are. Herrings, and kidneys and bacon, and a ham as well! You do do yourselves proud. I shall start at the beginning and go on to the end. Do you mind? Something rather nauseating in the sight of persons eating hearty breakfasts, don't you think?'

'I am what is known as a good trencher-woman,' replied Sally. 'Roll, or toast? And do you want tea or coffee, or would you like a nice cup of chocolate to go with all that food?'

'How idly rich!' sighed Neville, drifting back to the table. 'Just coffee, darling.'

'You're one of the idle rich yourself now,' Sally reminded him. 'Rich enough to buy yourself a decent suit, and to have your hair cut as well.'

'I think I shall get married,' said Neville meditatively.

'Get married?' exclaimed Sally. 'Why?'

'Aunt says I need someone to look after me.'

'You need someone to furbish you up,' replied Sally, 'but as for looking after you, I've a shrewd notion that in your backboneless way, Mr Neville Fletcher, you have the whole art of managing your own life weighed up.'

He looked up from his plate with his shy, slow smile. 'Art of living. No management. Is Helen a witness?'

She was momentarily at a loss. 'Oh, the inquest! No, she hasn't been subpœnaed so far. Which means, of course, that the police are going to ask for an adjournment.'

'I expect she's glad,' said Neville. 'But it's a great disappointment to me. One of life's mysteries still unsolved. Which story would she have told?'

'I don't know, but I wish to God she'd tell the true story to John, and be done with it. You've no idea of the atmosphere of cabal and mystery we live in. I have to think before I speak every time I wish to make an observation.'

'That must come hard on you,' said Neville. 'Where are they, by the way?'

'In bed, I should think. John didn't get in till very late last night, and Helen hardly ever appears till after breakfast. I suppose Miss Fletcher's going to the inquest?'

'Then you suppose wrong, sweetheart.'

'Really? Very sensible of her, but I made sure she'd insist on going.'

'I expect she would if she happened to know it was being held today,' he agreed.

She regarded him curiously. 'Do you mean you've managed to keep it from her?'

'No difficulty,' he answered. 'Entrancingly womanly woman, my aunt. Believes what the male tells her.'

'But the papers! Doesn't she read them?'

'Oh yes! Front and middle page of *The Times*. All cheaper rags confiscated by adroit nephew, and put to ignoble uses.'

'I hand it to you, Neville,' said Sally bluntly. 'You've been a brick to Miss Fletcher.'

He gave an anguished sound. 'I haven't! I wouldn't know how! You shan't tack any of your revolting labels on to me!'

At that moment Helen came into the room. Her eyes looked a little heavy, as though from lack of sleep, and the start she gave on seeing Neville betrayed the frayed state of her nerves. 'Oh! You!' she gasped.

'I never know the answer to that one,' remarked Neville. 'I expect it's similarly dramatic, but I can't be dramatic at breakfast. Do sit down!'

'What are you doing here?' Helen asked.

'Eating,' replied Neville. 'I wish you hadn't come down. I can see you're going to disturb the holy calm which should accompany the first meal of the day.'

'Well, it's my house, isn't it?' said Helen indignantly.

Sally, who had risen, and walked over to the side-table, came back with a cup and saucer, which she handed to her sister. 'You look pretty rotten,' she said. 'Why did you get up?'

'I can't rest!' Helen said with suppressed vehemence.

'Night starvation,' sighed Neville.

Helen cast an exasperated glance at him, but before she could retort, the butler came into the room, and said austerely: 'I beg your pardon, madam, but Superintendent Hannasyde has called, and wishes to see the master. I have informed him that Mr North is not yet down. Would you have me wake the master, or shall I request the Superintendent to wait?'

'The Superintendent?' she said numbly. 'Yes. Yes, you must tell the master, of course. Show the Superintendent into the library. I'll come.'

'What for?' asked Sally, when the butler had withdrawn. 'He didn't ask for you.'

'It doesn't matter. I must see him. I must find out what he wants. Oh dear, if only I could *think*!'

'Can't you?' asked Neville solicitously. 'Not at all?'

'For the Lord's sake, drink your tea, and don't agitate!' said Sally. 'If I were you I'd let John play his own hand.'

Helen set her cup and saucer down with a jar. 'John is not your husband!' she said fiercely, and walked out of the room.

'Now we can resume the even tenor of our way,' said Neville, with a sigh of relief.

'I can't,' replied Sally, finishing her coffee in a hurry. 'I must go with her, and try to stop her doing anything silly.'

'I love people who go all out for lost causes,' said Neville. 'Are you a member of the White Rose League too?'

Sally did not trouble to reply to this, but went purposefully out of the room. Her arrival in the library coincided with that of the butler, who informed Hannasyde that Mr North was shaving, but would be down in a few minutes.

Helen looked at her sister, with a frown in her eyes. 'It's all right, Sally. I don't need you.'

'That's what you think,' said Sally. ''Morning, Superintendent. Why, if it isn't Malachi! Well, that is nice! Now we only want a harmonium.'

'A froward heart,' said Glass forbiddingly, 'shall depart from me. I will not know a wicked person.'

Helen, who had not previously encountered the Constable, was a little startled, but Sally responded cheerfully: 'Quite right. Evil associations corrupt good manners.'

'Be quiet, Glass!' said Hannasyde authoritatively. 'You have asked me, Mrs North, why I wish to see your husband, and I will tell you quite frankly that I wish to ask him to explain his movements on the night of Ernest Fletcher's death.'

'And what could be fairer than that?' said Sally.

'But my husband told you! You must remember. Surely you remember! He spent the evening at the flat.'

'That's what he told me, Mrs North, but it was unfortunately not true.'

Sally had been engaged in the task of polishing her monocle, but this remark, dropped like a stone into a mill pond, made her look up quickly. 'Good bluff,' she remarked. 'Try again.'

'I'm not bluffing, Miss Drew. I have proof that between the hours of 9.00 p.m. and 11.45 p.m. Mr North was not at his flat.'

Helen moistened her lips. 'That's absurd. Of course he was. He can have had no possible reason for having said so if it weren't true.'

Hannasyde said quietly: 'You don't expect me to believe that, do you, Mrs North?'

Sally stretched out her hand for the cigarette-box. 'Obviously not. According to your idea, my brother-in-law may have been at Greystones.'

'Precisely,' nodded Hannasyde.

A flash of anger made Helen's eyes sparkle. 'Be quiet, Sally! How dare you suggest such a thing?'

'Keep cool. I haven't suggested anything that wasn't already in the Superintendent's mind. Let's look at things sanely, shall we?'

'I wish you'd go away! I told you I didn't need you!'

'I know you wish I'd go away,' replied Sally imperturbably. 'The Superintendent wishes it too. It stands out a mile that his game is to frighten you into talking. If you've a grain of sense you'll keep your mouth shut, and let John do his own talking.'

'Very perspicacious, Miss Drew,' struck in Hannasyde. 'But your words imply that there would be danger in your sister's being frank with me.'

Sally lit her cigarette, inhaled deeply, and expelled the smoke down her nostrils. 'Quite a good point. But I'm nearly as much in the dark as you are. Not entirely, because

I have the advantage of knowing my sister and her husband pretty well. Do let's be honest! It must be evident to a child that things look rather black against my brother-in-law. He apparently had a motive for killing Ernest Fletcher; his sudden return from Berlin was unexpected and suspicious, and now you seem to have collected proof that the alibi he gave you for 17 June was false. My advice to my sister is to keep her mouth shut. If her solicitor were here I fancy he would echo me. Because, Mr Superintendent Hannasyde, you are trying to put over one big bluff. If you'd any real evidence against my brother-in-law you wouldn't be wasting your time talking to my sister now.'

'Very acute of you, Miss Drew; but aren't you leaving one thing out of account?'

'I don't think so. What is it?'

'You are preoccupied with the idea of Mr North's possible guilt. It is quite natural that you should not consider the extremely equivocal position of your sister.'

She gave a scornful laugh. 'You don't think she had anything to do with it!'

'Perhaps I don't. But I may think that she knows much more than she has told me. You wish me to be frank, so I will tell you that Mrs North's evidence does not tally with those facts which I know to be true.'

Helen came forward, throwing up a hand to silence her sister. 'Yes, you told me that the last time you were here. I agree with what Miss Drew says; it is time to be frank, Superintendent. You believe that the man I saw was my husband, and that I recognised him. Is not that so?'

'Let us say, Mrs North, that I consider it a possibility.'

'And I tell you that it is not so!'

'That is what I propose to find out,' said Hannasyde. 'You yourself have given me two separate accounts of your movements on the night of the 17th. The first was before your husband arrived here on the morning after the murder; the second, which was apparently designed to convince me, first, that the mysterious man seen by you was shown off the premises by Fletcher himself; and, second, that Fletcher was alive at 10.00 p.m., you told me after the arrival of your husband. You will admit that this gives me food for very serious thought. Added to this, I have discovered that Mr North left his flat at 9.00 p.m. on the evening of the 17th, and only returned to it at 11.45.'

Helen was white under her delicate make-up, but she said perfectly calmly: 'I appreciate your position, Super-intendent. But you are wrong in assuming that my husband was implicated in the murder. If you have proof that he was not in the flat on the evening of the 17th, no doubt you are right. I know nothing of that. What I do know is that he had no hand in the murder of Ernie Fletcher.'

'Yes, Mrs North? Shall we wait to hear what he himself may have to say about that?'

'It would be useless. As far as I know, he was nowhere near Greystones on the night of the 17th. It is quite possible that he may try to convince you that he was, for – for he is the sort of man, Superintendent, who would protect his wife, no matter how – how bad a wife she had been to him.'

Her voice quivered a little, but her face was rigid. Sally caught her breath on a lungful of smoke, and broke into help-less coughing. Hannasyde said quite gently: 'Yes, Mrs North?'

'Yes.' Helen's eyes stared into his. 'You see, I did it.'

Hannasyde said nothing. Glass, who had been watching Helen, said deeply: 'It is written, speak ye every man the truth to his neighbour. Surely the net is spread in vain in the sight of any bird!'

'Not this bird!' choked Sally. 'Helen, don't be a fool! Don't lose your head!'

A faint smile just curved Helen's lips. She said, still with her gaze fixed on Hannasyde's face: 'My evidence was true as far as it went. Ernie Fletcher did show the stranger off the premises, and I did return to the study to search for my IOUs. What was untrue was my story that I got out of the room before he returned to it. I didn't. He found me there. He sat down at his desk. He laughed at me. Taunted me. I saw it was no use trying to plead with him. I – I suppose I must have been mad. I killed him.'

Sally, who had by this time recovered from her coughing fit, said witheringly: 'With your little hatchet. Don't you realise that this isn't a gun-pulling affair, you cuckoo? Whoever killed Ernie did it by violence. If you'd tried to bat him on the head I don't say you wouldn't have hurt him, but you haven't the necessary strength to smash his skull.'

'I caught him unawares. I think I must have stunned him. At that moment, I was so – so angry I wanted to kill him. I hit him again and again…' Her voice failed; a shudder shook her, and she raised her handkerchief to her lips.

'A highly unconvincing narrative,' said Sally. 'You know, if you make up much more of this gruesome story you'll be sick. I can just see you beating someone's head in!'

'Oh don't, don't!' whispered Helen. 'I tell you I wasn't myself!'

'Mrs North,' interposed Hannasyde, 'I think I ought to inform you that it is not enough merely to say that you murdered a man. You must prove that you did so, if you wish me to believe you.'

'Isn't that for you to do?' she said. 'Why should I convict myself?'

'Don't be silly!' said Sally. 'You've confessed to a murder, so presumably you want to be convicted. All right, let's hear some more! How did you do it? Why weren't there any bloodstains on your frock? I should have thought you must have been splashed with blood.'

Helen turned a ghastly colour and groped her way to a chair. 'For God's sake, be quiet! I can't stand this!'

Glass, standing by the wall like a statue of disapproval, suddenly exclaimed: 'Woman, thou shalt not raise a false report!'

'Be quiet!' snapped Hannasyde.

The Constable's glacial blue eyes seemed to scorn him, and turned towards Helen, who had raised her head, and was staring at him in fright and doubt. He said to her in a milder tone: 'Deceit is in the heart of them that imagine evil. The fear of man bringeth a snare: but whoso putteth his trust in the Lord shall be safe.'

Hannasyde said angrily: 'Another word from you, and –'

'Hold on!' interrupted Sally. 'He has my vote. What he says is absolutely right.'

'That is as may be,' responded Hannasyde. 'But he will nevertheless hold his tongue! Mrs North, if you killed Ernest Fletcher, perhaps you will tell me what was the implement you used, and what you did with it?'

There was a brief silence. Helen's eyes travelled from one sceptical face to another. An interruption occurred, in the shape of Mr Neville Fletcher who at that moment appeared at the open window, a cup and saucer in one hand, and a slice of toast in the other. 'Don't mind me,' he said, with his sweet smile. 'I heard your last pregnant words, Superintendent, and I'm all agog to hear the answer. Why, there's Malachi!' He waved the piece of toast to the unresponsive Constable, and seated himself on the low window-sill. 'Do go on!' he said invitingly to Helen.

Hannasyde looked consideringly at him for an instant, and then turned back to Helen. 'Yes, go on, Mrs North. What was the implement, and what did you do with it?'

'I'll tell you,' Helen said breathlessly. 'You've seen the – the implement. A heavy bronze paper-weight surmounted by a statuette. It was on Mr Fletcher's desk. I caught it up, and struck him with it, several times. Then I escaped by way of the front door, as I told you. I hid the paper-weight under my cloak. When I reached home I – washed it, and later, when – when Mr Neville Fletcher visited me, I – I gave it to him, and he restored it, as you know!'

Her eyes were fixed imploringly on Neville, who was staring at her with his mouth open. He blinked, shut his mouth, swallowed, and said faintly: 'Oh, give Malachi permission to speak! He'll say it all so much better than I can. Something about one's sins finding one out. Now I don't fancy this piece of toast any more. God give me strength!'

Sally found her tongue, 'Helen! You can't do that! Good Lord, you're trying to make Neville an accessary after the fact! It's too thick!'

'Thank you, darling!' said Neville brokenly. 'Take this cup and saucer away from me. My hand shakes like a reed. Women!'

'Well, Mr Fletcher?' said Hannasyde. 'What have you to say to Mrs North's accusation?'

'Don't worry!' said Neville. 'Chivalry has practically no appeal for me whatsoever. It's a wicked lie. I produced the paper-weight to create a little diversion. I suppose Miss Drew told her sister about it. That's all.'

'Yes, I did,' admitted Sally. 'And I'm very sorry, Neville. I never dreamed Helen would use the story like this!'

'The ruthlessness of the so-called gentle sex!' he said. 'But I can disprove it. The paper-weight was never on Ernie's desk. It came from the billiard-room. Ask any of the servants. You might even ask my aunt.'

'It's true!' Helen said, in a strained, unnatural voice. 'Neville had nothing to do with the murder, but he replaced the paper-weight for me. Neville, it isn't as though anyone suspects you of killing Ernie! Just – just to have put a paper-weight back isn't such an awful thing to admit to!'

'Nothing doing!' said Neville firmly. 'I've no doubt you think I should look noble as a sacrifice, but I've never wanted to look noble, and I won't be made to.'

'Neville –'

'Now, don't waste your breath in arguing with me!' he begged. 'I know I ought to be falling over myself with desire to save your husband from arrest, but, strange as it may seem to you, I'm not. In fact, if it's to be his arrest for murder, or mine for being an accessary, I'd a lot rather it was his.'

'You are hardly to be blamed,' said a cool voice from the doorway. 'But may I know upon what grounds I am to be arrested for murder?'

Twelve

A T THE SOUND OF HER HUSBAND'S VOICE, HELEN HAD
started to her feet, turning an anguished face of warning
towards him. He looked at her, slightly frowning, then with
deliberation shut the door and came forward into the room.

'You've timed your entry excellently, John,' said Sally.

'So it seems,' he replied. His glance took in Glass, and
Hannasyde, and Neville. 'Perhaps you will tell me why my
house has been invaded at this singularly inappropriate hour
of the day?'

'John!' The faint cry came from Helen. 'I'll tell you.
Don't ask them! Oh, won't you let me speak to him alone?
Superintendent, I beg of you – you must realise – give me
five minutes, only five minutes!'

'No, Mrs North.'

'You're inhuman! You can't expect me to break such news
to him in public – like this! I can't do it! I won't do it!'

'If your sister and Mr Fletcher choose to withdraw they
may do so,' said Hannasyde.

'You too! Oh, please! I won't run away! You can guard the
door and the window!'

'No, Mrs North.'

'Gently, Helen.' North walked across the room to where she was standing, and held out his hand. 'You needn't be afraid to tell me,' he said. 'Come, what is it?'

She clasped his hand with both of hers, looking up into his face with dilated eyes full of entreaty. 'No. I'm not afraid. Only of what you'll think! Don't say anything! Please don't say anything! You see, I've just confessed to the Superintendent that it was I – that it was I who killed Ernie Fletcher!'

A silence succeeded her words. North's hold on her hand tightened a little; he was looking down at her, his own face rather pale, and set in grim lines. 'No,' he said suddenly. 'It's not true!'

Her fingers dug into his hand. 'It is true. You don't know. You weren't there. You *couldn't* know! I struck him with a heavy paper-weight that stood on his desk. There was a reason –'

His free hand came up quickly to cover her mouth. 'Be quiet!' he said harshly. 'You're demented! Helen, I order you to *be quiet*!' He turned his head towards Hannasyde. 'My wife doesn't know what she's saying! There's not a word of truth in her story!'

'I need more than your assurance to convince me of that, Mr North,' replied Hannasyde, watching him.

'If you think she did it you must be insane!' North said. 'What evidence have you? What possible grounds for suspecting her?'

'Your wife, Mr North, was the last person to see Ernest Fletcher alive.'

'Nonsense! My wife left the garden of Greystones while an unknown man was in Fletcher's study with him.'

'I'm afraid you are labouring under a misapprehension,' said Hannasyde. 'Mrs North, on her own confession, did not leave the garden while that man was with Ernest Fletcher.'

North's eyelids flickered. 'On her own confession!' he repeated. He glanced down at Helen, but her head was bowed. He led her to a chair, and pressed her gently down into it, himself taking up a position behind her, with one hand on her shoulder. 'Just keep quiet, Helen. I should like the facts, please, Superintendent.'

'Yes, Mr North. But I, too, should like some facts. At my previous interview with you, you informed me that you spent the evening of the 17th at your flat. I have discovered this to have been untrue. Where were you between the hours of 9.00 p.m. and 11.45 p.m.?'

'I must decline to answer that question, Superintendent.'

Hannasyde nodded, as though he had been expecting this response. 'And yesterday evening, Mr North? Where were you between the hours of 9.15 and 10.00?'

North was regarding him watchfully. 'What is the purpose of that question?'

'Never mind the purpose,' said Hannasyde. 'Do you choose to answer me?'

'Certainly, if you insist. I was in Oxford.'

'Can you prove that, Mr North?'

'Are my whereabouts last night of such paramount importance? Haven't we wandered a little from the point? I've asked you for the facts of the case against my wife. You seem curiously disinclined to state them.'

Sally, who had retreated to the big bay window, and was listening intently, became aware of Neville's soft voice at her elbow. 'What a lovely situation! Shall you use it?'

Hannasyde took a minute to reply to North. When he at last spoke it was in his most expressionless voice. 'I think perhaps it would be as well if you were put in possession of the facts, Mr North. Your wife has stated that at 9.58, on the night of the murder, Ernest Fletcher escorted this unknown visitor to the garden-gate. While he was doing this Mrs North re-entered the study, with the object of obtaining possession of certain IOUs of hers which were in Fletcher's possession. According to her story, Fletcher returned to find her there. A quarrel took place, which terminated in Mrs North's striking Fletcher with the paper-weight which, she informs me, stood upon the desk. She then escaped from the study by the door that leads into the hall, leaving her finger-prints on one of the panels. The time was then one minute past ten. At five minutes past ten Constable Glass here discovered the body of Ernest Fletcher.'

From the window, Sally spoke swiftly. 'Leaving out something, aren't you? What about the man whom Glass saw leaving the garden at 10.02?'

'I have not forgotten him, Miss Drew. But if either of your sister's stories is to be believed he can hardly have had anything to do with Fletcher's murder.'

'Either?' protested Neville. 'You've lost count. She's told three to date.'

'I think we need not consider Mrs North's first story. If her second story, that she left the study at 10.01, just before Fletcher returned to it, was correct, the man seen by the Constable cannot have had time to commit the murder. If, on the other hand, it is true that she herself killed Fletcher –'

Helen raised her head. 'It's true. Must you go on? Why don't you arrest me?'

'I warn you, I shall strenuously deny my alleged part in your unprincipled story,' said Neville.

'I never suggested that you were my – my accomplice!' Helen said. 'You didn't know why I wanted you to take the paper-weight back!'

'Oh no, and I wouldn't guess, would I?' said Neville. 'And to think that in a misguided moment I told the Sergeant I was your accomplice! I can almost feel the cruel prison bars closing round me. Sally, I appeal to you! Did your unspeakable sister give me a paper-weight on that memorable night?'

'Not in my presence,' replied Sally.

'She would hardly have done so in your presence, Miss Drew,' said Hannasyde.

'Good God, you don't believe that story?' Sally exclaimed. 'Are you suggesting that Mr Fletcher was in it too? Next you'll think I had a hand in it! Is no one immune from these idiotic suspicions of yours?'

'No one who was in any way concerned in the case,' he replied calmly. 'You must know that.'

'How true! how very true!' said Neville. 'There isn't one of us who doesn't suspect another of us. Isn't that delight-fully succinct?'

'It is so!' Glass, who had been silently listening and watching, spoke in a voice of righteous wrath. 'I have held my peace, reading the thoughts you harbour! How long will ye imagine mischief against a man? Ye shall be slain, all of you: as a bowing wall shall ye be, as a tottering fence!'

'I'm like a tottering fence already,' said Neville. 'But as for you, you're like an overflowing scourge. Isaiah, 28,15. Why isn't the Sergeant here?'

'Oh, for God's sake – !' Helen cried out. 'I've told you what happened, Superintendent! Can't you put an end to this?'

'Yes, I think so,' he said.

'Just a moment!' North interposed. 'Before you take a step which you will regret, Superintendent, had you not better inquire a little more fully into one thing which seems to have been left out of your calculations?'

'And what is that, Mr North?'

'*My* movements on the night of Fletcher's murder,' said North.

Helen twisted round in her chair. 'No, John! No! You shan't, you shan't! I *beg* of you, don't say it! John, you don't want to break my heart!' Her voice broke piteously; she caught at his hands, and gripped them hard in hers, tears pouring down her face.

'Now look what you've done!' said Neville. 'You know, this will have to go down in the annals of my life as a truly memorable morning.'

'Helen!' North said, in a curious voice. 'Helen, my dear!'

'What *were* your movements on the night of the 17th, Mr North?'

'Does it matter? I killed Fletcher. That's all you want to know, isn't it?'

'No!' panted Helen. 'He's only saying it to save me! You can see for yourself he is! Don't listen to him!'

Hannasyde said: 'It is by no means all I want to know, Mr North. At what hour did you arrive at Greystones?'

'I can't tell you. I didn't consult my watch.'

'Will you tell me just what you did?'

'I walked up the path to the study, entered it, told Fletcher why I had come –'

'Why had you come, Mr North?'

'That I do not propose to tell you. I then killed Fletcher.'

'With what?'

'With the poker,' said North.

'Indeed? Yet no finger-prints or bloodstains were discovered upon the poker.'

'I wiped it, of course.'

'And then?'

'Then I left the premises.'

'How?'

'By the way I came.'

'Did you see anyone in the garden, or the road?'

'No.'

'What took you to Oxford yesterday?'

'A business conference.'

'A business conference of which your secretary knew nothing?'

'Certainly. A very confidential conference.'

'Did anyone besides yourself know that you were going to Oxford?'

'Both my partners.'

'What proof can you give me that you actually were in Oxford last night?'

'What the devil has my visit to Oxford got to do with Fletcher's murder?' North demanded. 'Of course I can bring proof! I dined at my college, if you must know, and spent the evening with my old tutor.'

'When did you leave your tutor?'

'Just before midnight. Anything else you'd like to know?'

'Nothing else, thank you. I shall ask you presently to give me the name and address of your tutor, so that I can just check up on your story.'

Helen got up jerkily. 'You don't believe all he's told you! It isn't true! I swear it isn't!'

'No, I only believe that your husband was in Oxford yesterday evening, Mrs North. But I think you had better not swear to anything more. You have already done your best to obstruct the course of justice, which is quite a serious offence, you know. As for you, Mr North, I'm afraid your account of the murder of Fletcher doesn't fit the facts. If I am to believe that you killed him, I must also believe the story your wife told me at the police station on the day I first interviewed you both. Your wife did leave Greystones by way of the front drive just after ten o'clock, for she was seen. That means that you murdered Fletcher, cleaned the poker with such scrupulous care as to defy even the microscope, and reached the side gate all within the space of one minute. I sympathise with the motive that prompted you to concoct your fairy story, but I must request you to stop trying to hinder me.'

'What, didn't he do it after all?' said Neville. 'You don't mean to tell me we're right back at the beginning again? How inartistic! How tedious! I can't go on being interested; it's time we reached a thrilling climax.'

'There's a catch in it somewhere, and I can't spot it,' said Sally, frowning at Hannasyde. 'What makes you so sure my brother-in-law's innocent?'

'The fact that he was not in London last night, Miss Drew.'

Helen put out a wavering hand and grasped a chair-back. 'He didn't do it?' she said, as though she hardly understood. 'Are you trying to trick me into saying something – something –'

'No,' Hannasyde replied. 'When Mr North has told me just where he really was on the evening of the 17th I shall be satisfied that neither of you murdered Ernest Fletcher. You, at least, could never have done so.'

She gave a queer little sigh, and crumpled up in a dead faint.

'Oh, damn you, Superintendent!' exclaimed Sally, and went quickly forward.

She was thrust somewhat unceremoniously out of the way. North went down on his knee, gathered Helen into his arms, and rose with her. 'Open the door!' he ordered curtly. Over his shoulder he said: 'I went to see a friend of mine on the evening of the 17th. You can verify that. Peter Mallard, 17 Crombie Street. Thanks, Sally: I shan't need your assistance.'

The next instant he was gone, leaving his sister-in-law meekly to shut the door behind him.

Neville covered his eyes with his hand. 'Drama in the home! Oh, my God, can you beat it? He thought she did it, and she thought he did it, in the best Lyceum tradition. And they performed their excruciating antics on empty stomachs!'

'Trouble and anguish have taken hold on me!' suddenly announced Glass. 'They will deceive every one his neighbour, and will not speak the truth: they have taught their tongue to speak lies!'

'You know, I won't say that I don't appreciate Malachi,' remarked Neville critically, 'but you must admit that he has a paralysing effect on conversation.'

Hannasyde said briefly: 'You can wait in the hall, Glass.'

'Rebellion,' said Glass, 'is as the sin of witchcraft, and stubbornness is an iniquity and idolatry. Therefore I will depart as I am bidden.'

Hannasyde refused to be drawn into any sort of retort, merely waiting in cold silence until Glass had left the room. Neville said: 'I wish you'd brought the Sergeant. You don't understand how to play up to Malachi a bit.'

'I have no wish to play up to him,' replied Hannasyde. 'Miss Drew, when your sister feels well enough to see me, I want to have a short talk with her.'

'All right,' said Sally, lighting another cigarette.

He looked at her. 'I wonder if you would perhaps go and find out when I may see her?'

'Don't leave me, Sally, don't leave me!' begged Neville. 'My hand must be held. Suspicion has veered in my direction. Oh, I do wish John had done it!'

'I'm not going,' replied Sally. 'For one thing, I wouldn't be so tactless; for another, this problem is just beginning to get interesting. You needn't mind me, Superintendent: carry on!'

'I know what's coming,' said Neville. 'Who were you with last night?'

'Precisely, Mr Fletcher.'

'But it's very awkward: you've no idea how awkward!' said Neville earnestly. 'I can see that you're asking a very pregnant question, of course. But it would make things much easier for me if you'd tell me what the secret of last night is.'

'Why?' said Hannasyde. 'All I wish you to do is to tell me where you were yesterday evening. Either you know why I'm asking this, or you don't – in which case you can have no possible objection to answering the question.'

'You know, that sounds very specious to me,' said Neville. 'I can see myself falling headlong into a trap. How terribly right Malachi always is! He warned me against deceit repeatedly.'

'Am I to understand that you have been practising deceit?'

'Oh yes! I lied to my aunt,' said Neville. 'That's what makes it all so awkward. I told her I was coming here last night, to see Miss Drew. I can't but see that that is going to cast an extremely bilious hue over my whole story.'

'You didn't come here, in fact?'

'No,' said Neville unhappily.

'Where did you go?'

'I'd better tell the truth, hadn't I?' Neville asked Sally. 'One is at such a disadvantage with the police: they always know more than they say. On the other hand, if I tell the truth now I may find it awfully hard to lie afterwards.'

'Mr Fletcher, this sort of thing no doubt amuses you, but it fails entirely to amuse me!' said Hannasyde.

'You must think I've got a perverted sense of humour!' said Neville. 'I haven't; I'm not in the least abnormal: it's only other people's troubles that amuse me. I'm wriggling in the toils.'

'I am still waiting for an answer to my question, Mr Fletcher.'

'If I had my way you'd wait for ever,' said Neville frankly. 'Oh God, why didn't I go to Oxford, and call on *my* tutor? He'd have been very glad to see me, too. You mightn't think it, but they all hoped for great things of me at Oxford. You know: Fellowships, and what-nots. I was thought to have an intellect.'

'That doesn't surprise me at all,' said Hannasyde dryly.

'Yes, but doesn't it all go to show that a classical education is so much dross? Double firsts – yes, I did really! – are of no practical use whatsoever. Oh, let us end this ghastly suspense! I was in London last night.'

'Intrigue!' said Sally, her eyes dancing. 'He lied to his aunt, and went to the great, wicked city! Spill it, Neville! What haunt of vice did you visit?'

'I didn't. I wish I had. All I sought was rational companionship.'

'Beast! You could have found that here!'

'Oh no, darling! No, really! Not with Helen in the offing!'

'Where did you find this rational companionship?' interrupted Hannasyde.

'I didn't. I went to call upon one Philip Agnew, who lives in Queen's Gate, and pursues a delightfully scholarly and ineffective career at the South Kensington Museum. But he was out.'

'Indeed? So what did you do?'

'I wandered lonely as a cloud, trying to think of anyone besides Philip whom I could bear to consort with. But I couldn't, so I came home, and went to bed.'

'Thank you. At what hour did you leave Greystones?'

'Oh, but I don't know! After dinner. I expect it was somewhere between half-past eight and nine.'

'How were you dressed?'

'God, I can see the pit yawning at my feet! You could get the answer to that one out of my aunt, or Simmons, couldn't you? Black tie, Superintendent. Rather a nice one, too. Even my aunt was pleased.'

'Did you wear an overcoat?'

'What, in the middle of June? No, of course not.'

'Hat?'

'Yes.'

'What sort of a hat?'

'A black felt hat.'

'What, that thing?' exclaimed Sally.

'It's a very good hat. Besides, I haven't got another.'

'Forgive the interruption,' said Sally to Hannasyde, 'but if you are trying, as I gather you are, to convict Mr Fletcher of having murdered his uncle, do you mind telling me how you account for the man Malachi saw leaving Greystones at 10.02?'

'I have an idea, Miss Drew,' replied Hannasyde deliberately, 'That that man is dead.'

Neville blinked at him. 'Did – did I kill him?' he asked in an anxious voice.

'Someone killed him,' said Hannasyde, looking searchingly at him.

'Who was he?' Sally demanded.

'His name was Charles Carpenter. He was present at Greystones on the night of the murder, and was murdered yesterday evening between the hours of 9.30 and 10.00.'

'How do you know he was present at Greystones?'

'His finger-prints were discovered, Miss Drew.'

'Oh! Known to the police, was he?'

'How acute!' said Neville admiringly. 'I should never have thought of that.'

'Yes, he was known to the police,' said Hannasyde. 'But before the police could interrogate him he was killed – as Ernest Fletcher was killed.'

'Can't we pretend he murdered my uncle?' begged Neville.

'No, Mr Fletcher, we can not.'

'Killed because he knew too much,' said Sally, getting up, and beginning to walk up and down the room. 'Yes, I see. Not Neville, though. Any weapon discovered?'

'No,' said Hannasyde. 'In both cases, the murderer contrived to conceal his weapon with – let us say – extraordinary ingenuity.'

'Oh!' Sally threw him a somewhat scornful smile. 'You think that points to Mr Fletcher, do you? There's a difference,

Superintendent, between ingenuity of mind and practical cleverness. Neville – practically speaking – is half-witted.'

'I suppose I ought to be grateful,' murmured Neville. 'What was my weapon, by the way? You know, I don't want to upset the only theory left to you, but I doubt very much if I could nerve myself to commit an act of such repulsive violence – let alone two of them.'

'Just a moment!' Sally intervened. 'My sister's evidence now becomes of vital importance. I'd better go and see if she's fit enough to see you, Superintendent.'

'I should be very grateful to you if you would,' said Hannasyde.

'I will, but I don't suppose I shall be frightfully popular,' said Sally, going to the door.

'Tell her a man's life is at stake,' recommended Neville, swinging his legs over the window-sill, and stepping into the room. 'That'll appeal to her morbid mind.'

Sally went upstairs to her sister's bedroom. She entered to find that Helen, having recovered consciousness, was indulging in a comfortable fit of weeping on her husband's shoulder, gasping at intervals: 'You didn't do it! You didn't do it!'

'No, darling, of course I didn't do it. If you'd only told me!'

Sally paused for a moment in the doorway, and then came in and shut it behind her. 'Delicately nurtured female suffering from a fit of strong hysterics?' she inquired. 'Come on, Helen. Snap out of it! You're wanted downstairs.' She walked into the adjoining bathroom, discovered a bottle of sal volatile in the medicine-chest, mixed a ruthless dose of it, and returned to the bedroom, and put the glass into North's hand. 'Push that down her throat,' she said.

'Come, Helen! Drink this!' North commanded.

Helen gulped some of the mixture and choked. 'Oh! Filthy stuff! I'm all right; really I am! Oh, John, tell me it's true, and I'm not dreaming? It wasn't you I saw that awful night?'

'Of course it wasn't. Is that what you have been thinking all this time?'

'I've been so much afraid! Then that ghastly Superintendent told me you weren't in your flat that evening, and it seemed to make it quite certain. I hoped you'd get away while I talked to the police. That's why I sent Baker up to tell you. I hoped you'd understand it was a warning.'

'Was that why you told the Superintendent you had committed the murder?' he asked.

'Yes, of course. I couldn't think of anything else to do. I was too unhappy to mind what happened to me. It didn't matter.'

He took her hands, and held them. 'You cared as much as that, Helen?'

'John, John, I've always cared! You thought I didn't, and I know I behaved like a beast, but I never meant to let this awful gulf grow between us!'

'It was my fault. I didn't try to understand. I even made you afraid to turn to me when you were in a mess. But, Helen, believe me, I never meant to lose your trust like that! I would have got you out of it, no matter what it cost me!'

'Oh, no, no, it was all my utter folly! Oh, John, forgive me!'

Sally polished her monocle. 'Don't mind me!' she said.

North raised his head. 'Oh, Sally, do go away!'

'I would if I could. Don't think it's any pleasure to me to watch a couple of born idiots dripping all over one another,' said Miss Drew with brutal frankness. 'I'm here on a mission. The Superintendent wants to see Helen. Do you think you could pull yourself together, sister?'

Helen sighed, still clinging to North's hand. 'I never want to set eyes on the Superintendent again.'

'I daresay, but you happen to be an important witness. Now that you aren't labouring under the delusion that John's a murderer, the police would like to hear your evidence all over again. Take another swig of sal volatile! Tell me, John: why *did* you come back from Berlin in such a hurry?'

'It doesn't matter any longer,' he said.

Sally opened her eyes at that. 'What a lurid thrill! Did you get an anonymous letter about Helen's goings-on?'

'No. Not anonymous.'

Helen swallowed some more sal volatile. 'Who?' she asked, flushing.

'Never mind. It wasn't what your somewhat vulgar sister thinks. In fact, it was a metaphorical kick in the pants for me. So I came home.'

'And very helpful you were,' said Sally. 'You spread such a blight all over everywhere that even I began to think Helen might be wise not to tell you all.'

'It was – a little difficult,' he replied. 'Helen was so obviously dismayed at seeing me, and so obviously afraid of my finding out the nature of her dealings with Fletcher –'

'That,' said Sally, 'was your cue, and you missed it. If you'd gone the right way to work, she would have told you the whole story.'

'Yes,' said North. 'But I wasn't sure that I wanted to hear it.'

'An ostrich act? You? Well, I wouldn't have thought it of you,' said Sally.

Helen pulled his hand to her cheek. 'And thinking that, you – you tried to get yourself arrested to save me! Oh, John!'

'I'm sorry, Helen. We seemed to have lost one another.'

Sally took the empty glass away from her sister. 'Look here, do you mind postponing all this? You've got to come down and tell the Superintendent exactly what did happen on the fatal evening. At the moment he looks like pinching Neville for the murder, which I'm not at all in favour of. I don't know whether your evidence will be any good to him, but it might be. Shove some powder on your nose, and come downstairs.'

Helen got up and went rather wearily to her dressing-table. 'All right, if I must. Though why you should care, I don't know. I thought you had no use for Neville.'

'I have never,' said Miss Drew, inaccurately, but with dignity, 'allowed vulgar prejudice to influence my judgment. Moreover, I don't share your conviction that as long as John isn't pinched for the murder it doesn't matter who is. Are you ready?'

Helen passed a comb through her hair, patted the waves into place, critically surveyed her profile with the aid of a hand-mirror, and admitted that she was ready.

Hannasyde was awaiting them in the library still with Neville. North said to him, with a slight, rueful smile: 'We owe you an apology, Superintendent. I rather think we've rendered ourselves liable to criminal prosecution.'

'Yes, you've been thoroughly obstructive,' replied Hannasyde, but with a twinkle. 'Now, Mrs North, will you please tell me exactly what did happen while you were at Greystones on the 17th?'

'I did tell you,' she said, raising her eyes to his face. 'It was quite true, my story. Really, it was!'

'Which one?' inquired Neville.

'The one I told the Superintendent at the police station that day. I did hide behind the bush, and I did go back into the study to look for my IOUs.'

'And the man you saw enter the study? You're quite sure that Fletcher saw him off the premises before 10.00 p.m.?'

'Yes, absolutely.'

'And you heard Fletcher returning towards the house just before you left the study?'

She nodded. 'Yes, and he was whistling. I heard his step on the gravel path. He was strolling, I think, not hurrying at all.'

'I see. Thank you.'

Sally saw that he was frowning a little, and said shrewdly: 'You don't like my sister's evidence, Superintendent?'

'I wouldn't say that,' he answered evasively.

'Just a moment,' said Neville, who had been jotting some notes down on the back of an envelope. 'Do you think I could have done this? 10.01, my uncle alive and kicking; 10.02, man seen making off down Maple Grove; 10.05, my uncle discovered dead. Who was the mysterious second man? Did he do it? Was I he? And if so, why? Actions strange and apparently senseless. I shall resist arrest.'

'No question of arrest,' announced Sally. 'There's no case against you. If you did it, what was your weapon?'

Neville pointed a long finger at Hannasyde. 'The answer is in the Superintendent's face, loved one. The paper-weight! The paper-weight which I myself introduced into the plot.'

Hannasyde remained silent. Sally replied: 'Yes, I see that. But if you had murdered Ernie, it would have taken some nerve to make the police a present of your weapon.'

'Yes, wouldn't it?' he agreed. 'I should have stuttered with fright. Besides, I don't see the point. What would I do it for?'

'Oh, the overweening conceit of the murderer!' said Sally. 'That's a well-known feature of the homicidal mind, isn't it, Superintendent?'

'You have made a study of the subject, Miss Drew,' he answered non-committally.

'Of course I have. But my own opinion is that Neville doesn't suffer from that kind of conceit. You can say it was a piece of diabolical cunning, if you like, but there again there's an objection. There was no reason why you should suspect the paper-weight more than any other of the weapons there must be at Greystones. So why should he have brought it to your notice?'

'Perverted sense of humour,' supplied Neville. 'The murderer's freakish turn of mind. I shall soon begin to believe I'm guilty. Oh, but just think of me murdering a man for his millions! No, I won't subscribe to it: it's a repulsive solution to an otherwise recherché crime.'

'Yet it is, I believe, a fact that your financial condition, at the time of your uncle's death, was extremely precarious?' said Hannasyde.

North, who had been standing behind his wife's chair in silence, intervened at this, saying in his even way: 'That question, Superintendent, should surely not be put to Mr Fletcher in public?'

Neville blinked. 'Oh, isn't that sweet of John? And I quite thought he didn't like me!'

Hannasyde said, with something of a snap: 'Quite right, Mr North. But as, at the outset of this interview, I made it plain that I wished to interrogate him in private, and he refused to allow Miss Drew to leave the room, you will agree that discretion on my part would be quite superfluous. I am, however, still prepared to see Mr Fletcher alone, if he wishes it.'

'But I don't, I don't!' said Neville. 'I should dither with fright if closeted with you alone. Besides, Miss Drew is acting as my solicitor. I shouldn't dare to open my mouth if she weren't here to check my irresponsible utterances.'

'Then perhaps you will tell me whether I am correct in saying that you were very awkwardly placed, as regards finance, at the time of your uncle's death?'

'Well, no,' answered Neville diffidently. 'I didn't find anything awkward about it.'

'Indeed! Are you prepared to state that you had a credit balance at your bank?'

'Oh, I shouldn't think so!' said Neville. 'I never have at the end of the quarter.'

'Were you not, in fact, very much overdrawn?'

'I don't know. Was I?'

'Isn't this a little unworthy of you, Mr Fletcher? Did you not receive a communication from your bank, on the 14th of the month, informing you of the state of your overdraft?'

'Ah, I thought that was what it was about!' said Neville. 'It generally is. Though not always, mind you. The bank once wrote to me about some securities, or something, of mine, and it led to quite a lot of trouble, on account of their stamping the name of the bank on the envelope. Because, of course, when I saw that I put the letter into the waste-paper basket. I mean, wouldn't you?'

'Are you asking me to believe that you did not open the bank's letter?'

'Well, it'll make things much easier for you if you do believe it,' said Neville engagingly.

Hannasyde looked a little non-plussed, but said: 'You did not, then, apply to your uncle for funds to meet your liabilities?'

'Oh no!'

'Did you perhaps know that it would be useless?'

'But it wouldn't have been,' objected Neville.

'Your uncle had not warned you that he would not be responsible for your debts?'

Neville reflected. 'I don't think so. But I do remember that he was most annoyed about an episode in my career that happened in Budapest. It was all about a Russian woman, and I didn't really want Ernie to interfere. But he had a lot of hidebound ideas about the honour of the name, and prison being the final disgrace, and he would insist on buying me out. He didn't like me being County Courted either. I've always thought it would probably save a lot of bother to be declared bankrupt, but Ernie couldn't see it in that light at all. However, I don't want to speak ill of the dead, and I expect he meant well.'

'Unpaid bills do not worry you, Mr Fletcher?'

'Oh, no! One can always fly the country,' said Neville, with one of his sleepy smiles.

Hannasyde looked rather searchingly at him. 'I see. A novel point of view.'

'Is it? I wouldn't know,' said Neville innocently.

Helen, who had been leaning back in her chair, as though exhausted, suddenly said: 'But I don't see how it could have been Neville. It isn't a bit like him, and anyway, how could he have done it in the time? He wasn't anywhere in sight when I left the house.'

'Peeping at you over the banisters, darling,' explained Neville. 'When you think that Helen was in the study at 10.00 p.m., and my dear friend Malachi at 10.05, I had a lot of luck, hadn't I? What do you think, Superintendent?'

'I think,' said Hannasyde, 'That you had better consider your position very carefully, Mr Fletcher.'

Thirteen

'WHAT DO YOU SUPPOSE HE MEANT BY THAT?' ASKED
Neville, as the door closed behind Baker, ushering
Superintendent Hannasyde out.

'Trying to rattle you,' replied Sally briefly.

'Well, he's succeeded,' said Neville. 'I'm glad I ate that
handsome breakfast before he came, for I certainly couldn't
face up to it now.'

'Talking of breakfast –' began North.

'How insensate of you, if you are!' said Neville. 'Helen,
darling, you have such a fertile imagination: are you quite
sure you really saw Ernie showing his strange visitor out?'

'Of course I'm sure! What would be the point of making
up such a tale?'

'If it comes to that, what was the point of deceiving John
all this time?' said Neville reasonably. 'Irrational lunacy –
that's tautology, but let it stand – peculiar to females.'

She smiled, but replied defensively: 'It wasn't irrational. I
know now it was silly, but I – I had a definite reason.'

'It would be nice to know what that was,' he remarked. 'Or
no, on second thoughts, it would probably tax my belief too

far. Only inference left to John was that you had committed what the legal profession so coyly calls misconduct with Ernie. Sally and I nearly wrote him an anonymous letter, divulging the whole truth.'

'In some ways, I wish you had,' said North. 'If you will allow me to say so, it would have been far more helpful than your efforts to get your uncle to give back those IOUs. I've no doubt your spirit was willing, but –'

'Then you know very little about me,' interrupted Neville. 'My spirit was not in the least willing. I was hounded into it, and just look at the result! Being regarded as a sort of good Samaritan, which in itself is likely to lead to hideous consequences, is the least of the ills likely to befall me.'

'I'm terribly sorry,' sighed Helen, 'but even though you didn't get my notes back, and we did land ourselves in a mess, my bringing you into it did lead to good. If I hadn't, John and I might never have come together again.'

Neville closed his eyes, an expression on his face of acute anguish. 'What a thought! How beautifully put! I shall not have died in vain. Ought I to be glad?'

'Look here!' Sally interposed. 'It's no use regretting what you've done. You've got to think about what you're going to do next. It's obvious that the police suspect you pretty hotly. On the other hand, it's equally obvious that they haven't got enough evidence against you to allow of their applying for a warrant for your arrest. The question is: can they collect that evidence?'

Neville opened his eyes, and looked at her in undisguised horror. 'Oh, my God, the girl thinks I did it!'

'No, I don't, I've got an open mind on the subject,' said Sally bluntly. 'If you did it, you must have had a darned good reason, and you have my vote.'

'Have I?' Neville said, awed. 'And what about my second victim?'

'As I see it,' replied Sally, 'The second victim – we won't call him yours just yet – knew too much about the first murder, and had to be disposed of. Unfortunate, of course, but, given the first murder, I quite see it was inevitable.'

Neville drew a deep breath. 'The weaker sex!' he said. 'When I recall the rubbish that has been written about women all through the ages, it makes me feel physically unwell. Relentless, primitive savagery! Inability to embrace abstract ideas of right and wrong utterly disruptive to society. Preoccupation with human passions nauseating and terrifying.'

Sally replied calmly: 'I think you're probably right. When it comes to the point we chuck all the rules overboard. Abstractions don't appeal to us much. We're more practical than you, and – yes, I suppose more ruthless. I don't mean that I *approve* of murder, and I daresay if I read about these two in the papers I should have thought them a trifle thick. But it makes a difference when you know the possible murderer. You'd think me pretty rotten if I shunned you just because you'd killed one man I loathed, and another whom I didn't even know existed.'

'I'm afraid, Sally, you're proving Neville's point for him,' said North, faintly smiling. 'The fact that he is a friend of yours should not influence your judgment.'

'Oh, that's absolute rot!' said Sally. 'You might just as well expect Helen to have hated you when she thought you were the murderer.'

'So I might,' he agreed, apparently still more amused.

'Well, we've wandered from the point, anyway,' she said. 'I want to know whether the police can possibly discover more evidence against you, Neville.'

'There isn't any evidence! I keep on telling you I had nothing to do with it!' he said.

'Who had, then?' she demanded. 'Who *could* have had?'

'Oh, the mystery man!' he said airily.

'With what motive?'

'Same as John's. *Crime passionnel.*'

'What, *more* IOUs?'

'No. Jealousy. Revenge. All the hall-marks of a passionate murder, don't you think?'

'It's an idea,' she said, knitting her brows. 'Do you happen to know if he'd done the dirty on anyone?'

'Naturally I don't. I should have spilt the whole story, dear idiot. But lots of pretty ladies in Ernie's life.'

'You think some unknown man murdered him because of a woman? It sounds quite plausible, but how on earth did he manage to do it in the time?'

'Not having been there, I can't say. You work it out.'

'The point is, will the Superintendent be able to work it out?' she said.

'A much more important point to me is, will he be able to work out how I could have committed both murders?' retorted Neville.

Both points were exercising the Superintendent's mind at that moment. Having told PC Glass in a few well-chosen words what he thought of his conduct in condemning the morals of his betters, he set off with him towards the police station.

'The Lord,' announced Glass severely, 'said unto Moses, say unto the children of Israel, Ye are a stiff-necked people: I will come up into the midst of thee in a moment, and consume thee.'

'Very possibly,' replied Hannasyde. 'But you are not Moses, neither are these people the children of Israel.'

'Nevertheless, the haughtiness of men shall be bowed down. They are sinners before the Lord.'

'That again is possible, but it is no concern of yours,' said Hannasyde. 'If you would pay more attention to this case, and less to other people's shortcomings, I should be the better pleased.'

Glass sighed. 'I have thought deeply. All is vanity and vexation of the spirit.'

'There I agree with you,' said Hannasyde tartly. 'With the elimination of both Mr and Mrs North, nearly everything points now to Neville Fletcher. And yet – and yet I don't like it.'

'He is not guilty,' Glass said positively.

'I wonder? How do you arrive at that conclusion?'

'He has not seen the light; he has a naughty tongue, and by his scorning will bring a city into a snare; yet I do not think him a man of violence.'

'No, he doesn't give me that impression either, but I've been wrong in my summing up of men too often to set much store by that. But whoever murdered Fletcher must also have murdered Carpenter. Perhaps it was young Fletcher – but I'd give a year's pension to know what he did with the weapon!'

'Is it so certain that the same weapon was used?' asked Glass in his painstaking way.

'It seems extremely probable, from the surgeon's reports on the injuries in each case.'

'What of the man whom I saw? He was not Neville Fletcher.'

'Perhaps Carpenter.'

Glass frowned. 'Who then was the man seen by Mrs North?'

'I can't tell you, unless again it was Carpenter.'

'You would say that he returned, having been sent away? For what purpose?'

'Only he could have answered that, I'm afraid.'

'But it seems to me that the matter is thus made darker. Why should he return, unless to do Fletcher a mischief? Yet, since he himself is dead, that was not so. I think the man Fletcher had many enemies.'

'That theory is not borne out by what we know of him. There was always the possibility that North might have been the murderer, but no one else, except Budd, who does not correspond with the description of the man in evening dress seen last night, has come into the case. And we've been into Fletcher's past fairly thoroughly. A nasty case. The Sergeant said so at the start.'

'The unholy,' said Glass, his eye kindling, 'are like the chaff which the wind driveth away!'

'That'll do,' said Hannasyde coldly, terminating the conversation.

When the Sergeant heard, later, that North's innocence was established, he spoke bitterly of resigning from the Force. 'The hottest suspect we had, and he must needs go and clear himself!' he said. 'I suppose there's no chance his alibis were faked?'

'I'm afraid not, Skipper. They're sound enough. I've been into them. We seem to be left with Neville Fletcher only. He has no alibi for last night. He admits, in fact, that he was in London.'

'Well,' said the Sergeant judicially, 'if it weren't for his work on Ichabod, I'd as soon pinch him as anybody.'

'I know you would, but unfortunately there's a snag – two snags. He stated, quite frankly, that he was wearing a dinner-jacket suit last night. But he also said that his hat was a black felt. The man we want wore an opera hat.'

'That's nothing,' said the Sergeant. 'He probably made that up.'

'I don't think so. No flies on that young man. He said it was the only hat he possessed. I could so easily disprove that, if it weren't true, that I haven't even tried to. What is more, he is either a magnificent actor, or he really didn't know what I was driving at when I questioned him on his movements last night.'

'All the same,' said the Sergeant, 'if North's out, young Neville's the only one who could have done it in the time.'

'What time?'

The Sergeant answered with a touch of impatience: 'Why, between Mrs North's leaving and Ichabod's arrival, Chief!'

'Less time than that,' corrected Hannasyde. 'The murder must have been committed after 10.01 and before 10.02.'

'Well, if that's so there hasn't been a murder,' said the Sergeant despairingly. 'It isn't possible.'

'But there has been a murder. Two of them.'

The Sergeant scratched his chin. 'It's my belief Carpenter didn't see it done. If he left at 10.02, he couldn't have. Stands to reason.'

'Then why was he killed too?'

'That's what I haven't worked out yet,' admitted the Sergeant. 'But it seems to me as though he knew something which would have told him who must have committed the murder. Wonder if Angela Angel had any other boy-friends?' He paused, his intelligent eyes more bird-like than ever. 'Suppose he was shown out at 9.58? And suppose, when he was walking off, he caught sight of a chap he knew, sneaking in at that side gate? Think that might put ideas into his head? Seems to me he'd add two and two together and make 'em four when he read about the late Ernie's being found with his head bashed in.'

'Yes, quite reasonable except for one detail you've forgotten. You're assuming that the man Glass saw at 10.02 was not Carpenter, but the murderer, and we're agreed that whenever that man may have entered the garden he cannot have murdered Fletcher until after 10.01. And that won't do.'

'Nor it will,' said the Sergeant, discomfited. After a moment's thought, he perked up again. 'All right! Say Carpenter went back, to see what this other chap was up to.

He saw the murder done, and he legged it for the gate as hard as he could.'

'And the other man?'

'Like I said before. He heard Ichabod's fairy footfall, and hid himself in the garden, and slipped out as soon as Ichabod reached the study. The more I think of it, Chief, the more I see it must have been like that.'

'It does sound plausible,' Hannasyde conceded. 'What was the unknown man's motive? Angela?'

'Yes, I think we'll have to say it was Angela, on account of Charlie's being linked up with him.'

'Yet her friend – what was her name? Lily! – whom you questioned didn't mention any man but Carpenter and Fletcher in connection with Angela, did she?'

'Not what you might call specifically. She said there were plenty hanging round the poor girl.'

'Doesn't seem likely that an apparently unsuccessful admirer would go to the lengths of killing Fletcher, does it?'

'If it comes to that, nothing seems likely about this case, except that we'll never get to the bottom of it!' said the Sergeant crossly.

Hannasyde smiled. 'Cheer up! We've not done with it yet. What did you manage to find out today?'

'Nothing that looks like being of any use,' the Sergeant replied. 'We've got hold of one of Carpenter's relations, but he couldn't tell us much. Wait a bit: I've got it all here, for what it's worth.' He picked up a folder, and opened it. 'Carpenter, Alfred. Occupation, Clerk. Aged

34 years. Brother to the deceased. Has not set eyes on deceased since 1935.'

'Did he know anything about Angela Angel?'

'No, only hearsay. According to him, Charlie was never what you'd call the hope of the family. Sort of kid who pinched the other kids' belongings at school. He started life in the drapery business, and got the sack for putting the petty cash in the wrong place. No prosecution; old Carpenter – he's dead now – paid up. After that, our hero joined a concert-party. Seems he could sing a bit, as well as look pansy. He stuck to that for a bit, and then he got a job on the stage proper – male chorus. By that time what with one thing and another, his family had got a bit tired of him, and they gave him order of the boot from home, and no mistake. Then he went and got married to an actress. Name of Peggy Robinson. The next thing the family knew was that he'd waltzed off into the blue, and his wife was on their doorstep, calling out for his blood. Alfred didn't take to her. Said that was one thing he didn't blame brother Charlie for, leaving a wife that was more like a raging tigress than a decent woman. They managed to get rid of her, but not for long. Oh no!! She went off on tour, and though Alfred says they had news that she was properly off with another fellow, that didn't stop her coming back to tell Charlie's people how she'd heard that he was in town again, and living with a girl he'd picked up somewhere in the Midlands. Seems he'd been on tour likewise. What the rights of it was I don't know, and nor does Alfred, but there doesn't seem to be much doubt about it that the girl was none other than Angela Angel.'

'Where is the wife now?' interrupted Hannasyde.

'Pushing up daisies,' replied the Sergeant. 'Died of pneumonia following influenza, a couple of years ago. Alfred knew Charlie had been to gaol, but he hadn't had word of him since he came out, and didn't want to. He never saw Angela, but he says he was pretty sure she wasn't on the stage when Charlie picked her up. From what the wife told him, he gathered it was a regular village-maiden story. You know the sort of thing. Romantic girl, brought up very strict, falls for wavy-haired tenor, and elopes with him. Well, poor soul, she paid for it in the end, didn't she?'

'Did Alfred Carpenter remember what her real name was?'

'No, because he never knew it. But taking one thing with another, it looks to me as though one mystery's solved at least, which is why no one ever turned up to claim Angela when she did herself in. If she came from a strait-laced sort of home you may bet your life she was cast off, same as Charlie was. I've known people like that.'

Hannasyde nodded. 'Yes, but it doesn't help us much. Did you dig anything out of Carpenter's landlady, or the proprietor of the restaurant he worked at?'

'What I dug out of Giuseppe,' replied the Sergeant acidly, 'was a highly talented performance, but no good to me. How these foreigners can keep it up and not get tired out beats me! He put on a one-man show all for my benefit, hair-tearing, dio-mios, corpo-di-baccos, and the rest of it. I had to buy myself a drink to help me get over it, but he was as fresh as a daisy when he got through, and starting a row with his wife. At least, that's the way it looked to me, but I daresay it was only his way of carrying on a quiet chat. Anyhow, he doesn't know anything about Charlie.'

'And the landlady?'

'She doesn't know anything either. Says she's one for keeping herself to herself. That doesn't surprise me, either. She's not my idea of a comfortable body anyone would confide in. And there we are. It's Neville or no one, Chief. And if you want to know what he did with his weapon, how about him having slid a stout stick up his sleeve?'

'Have you ever tried sliding a club up your sleeve?' inquired Hannasyde.

'Not a club. Call it a malacca cane.'

'A malacca cane would not have caused those head injuries. The weapon was heavy, if a stick a very thick one, more like a cudgel.'

The Sergeant pursed his lips. 'If it's Neville we don't have to worry about the weapon he used to do in his uncle. He had plenty of time to get rid of that, or clean it, or whatever he did do with it. As far as the second murder's concerned – I suppose he couldn't have got that paper-weight into his pocket, could he?'

'Not without its being very noticeable. The head of the statue on top must have stuck out.'

'Might not have been noticed in the bad light. I'll get on to Brown again – he's the chap with the coffee-wagon – and that taxi-driver. Not but what I'm bound to say we questioned them pretty closely before. Still, you never know.'

'And the hat?'

'The hat's a nuisance,' declared the Sergeant. 'If he hasn't got an opera hat, perhaps he borrowed the late Ernie's, just because he knew no one would expect him to wear one. He could have carried it shut up under his arm without the butler's noticing it when he left the house. When he changed hats, he must have stuffed his own into his pocket.'

'Two bulging pockets now,' observed Hannasyde dryly. 'Yet two witnesses – we won't commit the girl; she was too vague – said there was nothing out of the ordinary about him. And that raises another point. The taxi-driver, who seemed to me quite an intelligent chap, described his fare's appearance as that of an ordinary, nice-looking man. He didn't think he would know him again if confronted with him. When pressed, he could only repeat that he looked like dozens of other men of between thirty and forty. Now, if you met Neville Fletcher, do you think you'd recognise him again?'

'Yes,' said the Sergeant reluctantly. 'I would. No mistaking him. For one thing he's darker than most, and not what I'd call a usual type. He's got those silly long eyelashes too, and that smile which gets my goat. No: no one in their senses would say he's like dozens of others. Besides, he's younger than thirty, and looks it. Well, what do we do now?'

Hannasyde drummed his fingers lightly on the desk, considering. The Sergeant watched him sympathetically. Presently he said in his decided way: 'Angela Angel. It comes back to her. It may sound far-fetched to you, Skipper, but I have an odd conviction that if only we knew more about her we should see what is so obstinately hidden now.'

The Sergeant nodded. 'Sort of a hunch. I'm a great believer in hunches myself. What'll we do? Advertise?'

Hannasyde thought it over. 'No. Better not.'

'I must say, I'm not keen on that method. What's more, if her people didn't come forward at the time of her death it isn't likely they will now.'

'I don't want to precipitate another tragedy,' Hannasyde said grimly.

The Sergeant sat up with a jerk. 'What, more head-bashings? You don't think that, do you?'

'I don't know. Someone is pretty determined that we shan't penetrate this fog we're groping in. Everything about the two murders suggests a very ruthless brain at work.'

'Maniacal, I call it,' said the Sergeant. 'I mean, just think of it! You can understand a chap cracking open another chap's head if he was worked up into a white-hot rage. At the same time you'd expect him to feel a bit jolted by what he'd done, wouldn't you? I don't reckon to be squeamish, but I wouldn't like to have done the job myself, no, nor to have seen it done. Nasty, messy murder, I call it. But our bird isn't upset. Not he! He waltzes off and repeats the act – in cold blood, mind you! Think that's sane? I'm damned if I do!'

'All the more reason for being careful not to hand him a motive for killing someone else.'

'That's true enough. But if we are dealing with a lunatic, Super, it's worse than I thought. You can catch up on a sane man. His mind works reasonably, same as your own; and, what's more important, he always has a motive for having committed his murder, which again is helpful. But when you come to a madman's brain you're properly in the soup, because you can't follow the way it works. And ten to one he hasn't got a motive for murder – not what a sane person would consider a motive, that is.'

'Yes, there's a lot in what you say, but I don't think our man's as mad as that. We've a shrewd idea of what his motive was for killing Carpenter, and presumably he had one for killing Fletcher.'

The Sergeant hunted amongst the papers before him on the desk, and selected one covered with his own handwriting. 'Well, Super, I don't mind telling you that I've had a shot at working the thing out for myself. And the only conclusion I've come to is that the whole thing's impossible from start to finish. Once you start putting all the evidence down on paper you can't help but see that the late Ernest wasn't murdered at all. Couldn't have been.'

'Oh don't be absurd!' said Hannasyde rather impatiently.

'I'm not being absurd, Chief. If you could chuck Mrs North's evidence overboard, all well and good. But, setting aside the fact that she's got no reason to tell lies now she knows that precious husband of hers isn't implicated in the crime, we have the postman's word for it that a woman dressed like her came out of Greystones at just after 10.00 p.m. on the 17th. So that fixes her. If it weren't for his having compared his watch with the clock in the late Ernest's study, I'd say old Ichabod was mistaken in the time he saw a chap coming out of the side gate. But he's a conscientious, painstaking officer, is Ichabod, and he's not the sort to state positively that it was 10.02 if it wasn't. I mean to say, you ought to hear him on the subject of false witnesses. Ticked me off properly, when I tried to shake his evidence a bit. But if you can make his evidence fit Mrs North's, all I can say is you're cleverer than I am. It wasn't so bad when the only fixed times we had were 10.02, when Ichabod saw the unknown, and 10.05 when he discovered the body of the late Ernest. But the moment we began to collect more fixed times the whole case got so cock-eyed there was no doing anything with it. We're now faced with four highly incompatible times, unless you assume young Neville murdered his uncle, and Carpenter saw it, and bolted for his life. We've got 9.58, or thereabouts, when Ernest saw Mrs North's man off; 10.01, when Mrs North left; 10.02 when Ichabod's man left by the side gate; and 10.05 when Ernest was found dead. Well, it just doesn't add up, and that's all there is to it. Unless you think Neville did it, and Mrs North's covering him up?'

'No, not a chance. Mrs North isn't interested in anyone except her husband. But I think the man she saw and the man Glass saw were one and the same. It's by no means conclusive, but we did find a pale grey felt hat amongst Carpenter's belongings.'

'All right, we'll say they were the same. Now, we don't know what Carpenter went back for, having been shown out, but there might be scores of reasons, setting aside any violent ones. Suppose he saw young Neville in the study with his uncle, and decided it was no use waiting? Quite reasonable, isn't it? Well, he goes off. The fact that he hurried away doesn't prove a thing. He wasn't up to any good anyway, and he naturally wouldn't want to be questioned by a policeman. All this time Carpenter doesn't know Neville from Adam. But here's where we have the brainwave of the century, Chief! Do you remember young Neville getting his photo in one of the daily picture papers?'

'I do – as the Boots, and under the name of Samuel Crippen,' said Hannasyde grimly.

'That wouldn't matter. Suppose Carpenter saw the paper? Stands to reason he'd be following the case fairly closely. He'd recognise Neville straight off. And if he'd seen him in evening dress on the night of the murder he'd know there was something phoney about that story of Neville's being employed as the Boots. My idea is that he saw his way to make a bit of easy money, and sneaked down to make a contact with Neville. No difficulty about that. Only Neville's too sharp to allow anyone to share a secret that would put a rope round his neck, and he proceeded to eliminate Carpenter double-quick. How's that?'

'It's perfectly plausible up to a point, Skipper. But it falls down as soon as it reaches the time of Carpenter's death, for reasons already stated.'

'Then Carpenter was murdered by someone else altogether,' said the Sergeant despairingly.

'Where's the data you collected about that murder?' Hannasyde asked suddenly. 'Let me have a look at it.'

The Sergeant handed him some typewritten notes. 'Not that you'll be able to make much of it,' he remarked pessimistically.

Hannasyde ran his eye down the notes. 'Yes, I thought so.

Landlady stated Carpenter was alive at 9.30. Dora Jenkins said that the man in evening dress passed by on the other side of the road just before the policeman appeared, coming from the other direction.'

'Yes, and if you read on a bit further you'll see that her boy-friend said the policeman came by ages before the man in evening dress. Of the two, I'd sooner believe him. She was simply trying to spin a good tale.'

'She was, but surely – yes, I thought so. Brown put the time he saw the policeman at about 9.40, and stated that as far as he could remember the man in evening dress passed a minute or two later. That seems to tally more or less with the girl's story. Did we ascertain from the Constable what time it was when he entered Barnsley Street?'

'No,' admitted the Sergeant. 'As he didn't see any man in evening dress, or notice anything wrong at No. 43, I didn't think that it was important.'

'I wonder?' Hannasyde was frowning at the opposite wall.

'Got an idea, Chief?' the Sergeant asked, his interest reviving.

Hannasyde glanced at him. 'No. But I think we'll find out just when the Constable did pass up the street.'

The Sergeant said briefly: 'Sorry, Chief!' and picked up the telephone-receiver.

'My own fault. I didn't see that it might be important either. It may not be. Can but try.'

While the Sergeant waited to be connected with the Glassmere Road Police Station, Hannasyde sat reading the notes on both cases, his brows knit. The Sergeant, having exchanged a few words with the official on duty at the police station, lowered the receiver, and said: 'Just come on duty, Super. Will you speak to him?'

'Yes, tell them to bring him to the phone,' said Hannasyde absently.

The Sergeant relayed this message, and while Constable Mather was being summoned, sat watching his superior with a puzzled but alert expression on his face. A voice speaking in his ear distracted his attention. 'Hullo! Is that Mather? Hold on! Detective-Superintendent Hannasyde wants a word with you. Here you are, Chief.'

Hannasyde took the instrument from him. 'Hullo! This is with reference to last night, Mather. I want you to clear up a point which seems to have been left in the air.'

'Yes, sir,' said PC Mather dutifully.

'Do you remember at what hour you reached Barnsley Street on your beat?'

There was a slight pause; then the Constable said rather anxiously: 'I don't know to the minute, sir.'

'No, never mind that. As near as possible, please.'

'Well, sir, when I passed the post office in Glassmere Road the clock there said 9.10, so by my reckoning it would be just about 9.15 when I got to Barnsley Street.'

'What?' Hannasyde said. 'Did you say 9.15?'

'Yes, sir. But I wouldn't want to mislead you. It might have been a minute or so more or less.'

'Are you quite certain that it wasn't after 9.30?'

'Yes, sir. Quite. It wouldn't take me all that time to get to Barnsley Street from the post office. There's another thing, too, sir. Brown – the man with the coffee-stall – hadn't taken up his pitch when I passed.'

'But Brown stated when questioned that he had seen you shortly after he arrived at 9.30!'

'Said he saw me last night?' repeated Mather.

'Yes, quite definitely.'

'Well, sir,' said Mather, in a voice of slowly kindling suspicion, 'I don't know what little game he thinks he's playing, but if he says he saw me last night he's made a mistake. If I may say what I think, sir –'

'Yes, go on!'

'Well, sir, I suppose for a matter of six or seven days he *has* seen me, for I've been down Barnsley Street, sometimes at one time, and sometimes at another, each evening, but always after 9.30. Only, as it so happens, I took Barnsley Street and Letchley Gardens early last night. It seems to me Brown was making that up, sir, kind of banking on what he thought probably did happen. If I may say so.'

'All right: thanks! That's all.'

Hannasyde replaced the instrument on its rest, and turned to find the Sergeant regarding him with newly awakened interest.

'You needn't tell me, Super! I gathered it all right. Mather passed up the street at 9.15, and Brown never saw him at all. Well, well, well! Now we do look like getting somewhere, *don't* we? What you might call opening up a new avenue. Who is Mr Brown, and what has he got to do with the case? Come to think of it, he did answer me remarkably pat. But what he's playing at – unless he killed Carpenter – I don't see.'

'Alfred Carpenter,' said Hannasyde, disregarding these remarks. 'What's his address? I want the name of that travelling company Carpenter joined.'

'Back on to Angela?' said the Sergeant, handing over Alfred Carpenter's deposition. 'She wasn't one of the members of the company, if that's what you're thinking.'

'No, I'm not thinking that. What I want is a list of the towns visited by that company.'

'Holy Moses!' gasped the Sergeant. 'You're never going to comb the Midlands for a girl whose name you don't even know?'

Hannasyde looked up, a sudden twinkle in his deep-set eyes. 'No, I'm not as insane as that – quite.'

The Sergeant said suspiciously, 'What do you mean by that, Chief? Pulling my leg?'

'No. And if the notion that has occurred to me turns out to be as far-fetched as I fear it is, I'm not going to give you a chance to pull mine either,' replied Hannasyde. 'Yes, I see Alfred Carpenter's on the telephone. Get his house, will you, and ask if he knows the name of that company or, failing that, a possible agent's name. He ought to be home by now.'

The Sergeant shook his head in a somewhat dubious manner, but once more picked up the telephone. After a few minutes, he was able to inform his superior that Mr Carpenter, denying all knowledge of the companies his brother had toured with, did seem to remember hearing him speak of an agent.

'It might have been Johnson, or Jackson, or even Jamieson,' said the Sergeant sarcastically. 'Anyway, he feels sure the name began with a J. Isn't that nice?'

'Good enough,' Hannasyde replied. 'I'll go into that in the morning.'

'And what do you want me to do?' the Sergeant inquired. 'Ask Mr Brown a few searching questions?'

'Yes, by all means. Get hold of the girl again as well, and see if she sticks to her original story. And look here, Hemingway! Don't mention any of this to anyone at all. When you've interviewed Brown and Dora Jenkins, go down to Marley. I'll either join you there, or send a message through to you.'

'What do I do there?' asked the Sergeant, staring. 'Hold a prayer meeting with Ichabod?'

'You can check up on your own theory about Neville Fletcher's hat. You can take another careful look at the paper-weight, too.'

'Oh, so now we go all out for young Neville, do we?' said the Sergeant, his gaze fixed on the Superintendent's face. 'Are you trying to link *him* up with Angela, Chief? What have you suddenly spotted, if I may make so bold as to ask? Twenty minutes ago we had two highly insoluble murder cases in front of us. It doesn't seem to me as though you're particularly interested in Brown, so what is it you're after?'

'The common factor,' answered Hannasyde. 'It only dawned on me twenty minutes ago, and may very possibly be a mare's nest.'

'Common factor?' repeated the Sergeant. 'Well, that's the weapon, and I thought we'd been after that ever since the start.'

'I wasn't thinking of that,' said Hannasyde, and left him gaping.

Fourteen

T HE FOLLOWING MORNING WAS CONSIDERABLY ADVANCED
when Sergeant Hemingway was at last free to journey
down on the Underground Railway to Marley. His two interviews had not been very successful. Miss Jenkins, vacillating
between instinctive fear of the police and a delightful feeling
of importance, screwed the corner of her apron into a knot,
giggled, patted her frizzy curls, and didn't know what to say,
she was sure. She hoped no one thought she had had anything
to do with the murder, because you could have knocked her
down with a feather when she read about it in the paper, and
realised why she had been questioned. Under the Sergeant's
expert handling she gradually abandoned her ejaculatory and
evasive method of conversation, and reiterated her conviction
that the gentleman in evening dress had passed only a minute
or two before the policeman, and had certainly been wearing
an opera hat, ever so smart.

From what he had seen of the erratic young man, Sergeant
could not believe that this rider could be applied with any
degree of appositeness to Neville Fletcher. He left Miss
Jenkins, and went in search of Mr Brown.

This quest led him to Balham, where Brown lived, and was peacefully sleeping after his night's work. His wife, alarmed, like Miss Jenkins, by the sight of the Sergeant's official card, volunteered to go and waken him at once, and in due course Mr Brown came downstairs, bleary-eyed and morose. He looked the Sergeant over with acute dislike, and demanded to know why a man was never allowed to have his sleep out in peace. The Sergeant, who felt a certain amount of sympathy for him, disregarded this question, and propounded a counter one. But Mr Brown replied testily that if the police thought they could wake a working-man up just to ask him what he'd already told them they were wrong. What he had said he was prepared to stand by. Confronted with PC Mather's own statement, he stared, yawned, shrugged, and said: 'All right: have it your own way. It's all the same to me.'

'So you didn't see the Constable, eh?' said the Sergeant.

'No,' retorted Mr Brown. 'The street's haunted. What I saw was a ghost.'

'Don't try and get funny with me, my lad!' the Sergeant warned him. 'What were you doing at 9.40?'

'Cutting sandwiches. What else would I be doing?'

'That's for you to say. Ever met a chap called Charlie Carpenter?'

Mr Brown, recognising the name, turned a dark beetroot colour, and invited the Sergeant to get out before he was put out. Rebuked, he defied the whole of Scotland Yard to prove he had ever laid eyes on Carpenter, or had left his coffee-stall for as much as a minute the whole evening.

There was little more to be elicited from him. The Sergeant presently departed, and made his way down to Marley. Finding Glass awaiting his orders at the police station, he said somewhat snappishly that he wondered he could find nothing better to do than hang about looking like something out of a bad dream.

Glass replied stiffly: 'He that uttereth slander is a fool. I have held myself in readiness to do the bidding of those set over me. Wherein I have erred?'

'Oh, all right, let it go!' said the exasperated Sergeant. 'You haven't erred.'

'I thank you. I see that your spirit is troubled and ill at ease. Are you no nearer the end of your labour on this case?'

'No, I'm not. It's a mess,' said the Sergeant. 'When I've had my lunch, I'm going up to make a few inquiries about Master Neville's doings. He's about the only candidate for the central role we've got left. I don't say it was easy when North was a hot favourite, but what I do say is that it's a lot worse now he's out of it. When I think of the way he and that silly wife of his have been playing us up, I'd as soon arrest him for the murders as not.'

'They have told lies, and it is true that lying lips are an abomination to the Lord, but it is also written that love covereth all sins.'

The Sergeant was quite surprised. 'Whatever's come over you?' he demanded. 'You'd better be careful: if you go on like that you'll find yourself growing into a human being.'

'I, too, am troubled and sore-broken. But if you go to seek out that froward young man, Neville Fletcher, you will waste your time. He is a scorner, caring for nothing, neither persons nor worldly goods. Why, then, should he slay a man?'

'There's a lot in what you say,' agreed the Sergeant. 'But, all the same, his latest story will bear sifting. You go and get your dinner: I shan't be wanting you up at Greystones.'

An hour later he presented himself at the back door of Greystones, and after an exchange of compliments with Mrs Simmons, a plump lady who begged him to get along, do, retired with her somewhat disapproving husband into the butler's pantry.

'Tell me this, now!' he said. 'How many hats has young Fletcher got?'

'I beg pardon?' said Simmons blankly.

The Sergeant repeated his question.

'I regret to say, Sergeant, that Mr Neville possesses only one hat.'

'Is that so? And not much of a hat either, from the look on your face.'

'It is shabbier than one cares to see upon a gentleman's head,' replied Simmons, but added rather hastily: 'For man looketh on the outward appearance, but the Lord looketh on the heart.'

'Here!' said the Sergeant dangerously. 'You can drop that right away! I hear quite enough of that sort of talk from your friend Glass. Let's stick to hats. I suppose your late master had any number of them?'

'Mr Fletcher was always very well dressed.'

'What's been done with his hats? Packed up, or given away, or something?'

'No,' replied Simmons, staring. 'They are in his dressing-room.'

'Under lock and key?'

'No, indeed. There is no need to lock things up in *this* house, Sergeant!'

'All right,' said the Sergeant. 'Just take me along to the billiard-room, will you?'

The butler looked a little mystified, but raised no objection, merely opening the pantry door for the Sergeant to pass through into the passage.

A writing-table set in one of the windows in the billiard-room bore upon it a leather blotter, a cut-glass inkstand, and a bronze paper-weight, surmounted by the nude figure of a woman. The Sergeant had seen the paper-weight before, but he picked it up now, and inspected it with more interest than he had displayed when Neville Fletcher had first handed it to him.

The butler coughed. 'Mr Neville will have his joke, Sergeant.'

'Oh, so you heard about that joke, did you?'

'Yes, Sergeant. Very remiss of Mr Neville. He is a light-hearted gentleman, I am afraid.'

The Sergeant grunted, and began to coax the paperweight into his pocket. He was interrupted in his somewhat difficult task by a soft, slurred voice from the window, which said: 'But you mustn't play with that, you know. Now they'll find nothing but your finger-prints on it, and that might turn out to be very awkward for you.'

The Sergeant jumped, and turned to find Neville Fletcher lounging outside one of the open windows, and regarding him with the smile he so much disliked.

'Oh!' said the Sergeant. 'So it's you, is it, sir?'

Neville stepped over the low window-sill into the room. 'Oh, didn't you want it to be? Are you looking for incriminating evidence?'

'The Sergeant, sir,' said Simmons woodenly, 'wishes to know whether the master's hats are kept under lock and key.'

'What funny things policemen are interested in,' remarked Neville. 'Are they, Simmons?'

'No, sir – as I informed the Sergeant.'

'I don't immediately see why, but I daresay you have put a rope round my neck,' said Neville. 'Do go away, Simmons! I'll take care of the Sergeant. I like him.'

The Sergeant felt quite uncomfortable. He did not demur at being left with his persecutor, but said defensively: 'Soft soap's no good to me, sir.'

'Oh, I wouldn't dare! Malachi told me what happens to flatterers. I do wish you had been here yesterday. I found such a good bit in Isaiah, all about Malachi.'

'What was that?' asked the Sergeant, diverted in spite of himself.

'Overflowing scourge. I do think the Superintendent ought to have told you.'

The Sergeant thought so too, but remarked repressively that the Superintendent had something better to think about.

'Not something better. His mind was preoccupied with my possible but improbable guilt. I think yours is too, which upsets me rather, because I thought we were practically blood-brothers. On account of Malachi. Why hats?' His sleepy eyes scanned the Sergeant's face. 'Tell me when I'm getting warm. My ill-fated journey to London. Black felt. And Ernie's collection. Oh, did I borrow one of Ernie's hats?'

The Sergeant thought it best to meet frankness with frankness. 'Well, did you, sir?'

Neville gave a joyous gurgle, and took the Sergeant by the hand. 'Come with me. Do policemen lead drab lives? I will lighten yours, at least.'

'Here, sir, what's all this about?' protested the Sergeant, dragged irresistibly to the door.

'Establishing my innocence. You may not want me to, but you oughtn't to let that appear.'

'It's a great mistake to get any silly idea into your head that the police want to arrest an innocent man,' said the Sergeant severely. He found himself being conducted up the shallow stairs, and protested: 'I don't know what you're playing at, but you might remember I've got work to do, sir.'

Neville opened the door into an apartment furnished in heavy mahogany. 'My uncle's dressing-room. Not, so far, haunted, so don't be frightened.'

'To my way of thinking,' said the Sergeant, 'The things you say aren't decent.'

Neville opened a large wardrobe, disclosing a view of a shelf of hats, ranged neatly in a line. 'Very often not,' he agreed. 'These are my uncle's hats. Theoretically, do you feel that private possession is all wrong? What sort of a hat was I wearing?'

'According to you, sir, you were wearing a black felt.'

'Oh, don't let's be realistic! Realism has been the curse of art. That's what upset the Superintendent. He is very orthodox, and he felt my hat was an anachronism. Of course, I must have been wearing one of those that go pop. Irresistible to children, and other creatures of simple intellect, but too reminiscent of patent cigarette-boxes, and other vulgarities. Now tell me, Sergeant, do you think I borrowed my uncle's hat?'

The Sergeant, gazing at the spectacle of Mr Neville Fletcher in an opera hat quite three sizes too small for him, fought with himself for a moment, and replied in choked accents: 'No sir, I'm bound to say I do not. You'd – you'd have to have a nerve to go about in that!'

'Yes, that's what I thought,' said Neville. 'I like comedy, but not farce – I can see by your disgruntled expression that the hat lets me out. I hope it never again falls to my lot to be suspected of murder. Nerve-racking, and rather distasteful.'

'I hope so too, sir,' replied the Sergeant. 'But if I were you I wouldn't jump to conclusions too hastily.'

'You're bound to say that, of course,' said Neville, returning his uncle's hat to its place on the shelf. 'You can't imagine who the murderer can be if not me.'

'Well, since you put it like that, who can it be?' demanded the Sergeant.

'I don't know, but as I don't care either, it doesn't worry me nearly as much as it worries you.'

'Mr Fletcher was your uncle, sir.'

'He was, and if I'd been asked I should have voted against his death. But I wasn't, and if there's one occupation that seems more maudlin to me than any other it's crying over spilt milk. Besides, you can have too much of a good thing. I'd had enough of this mystery after the second day. Interest – but painful – revived when I stepped into the rôle of chief suspect. I must celebrate my reprieve from the gallows. How do you ask a girl if she'd like to marry you?'

'How do you do what?' repeated the Sergeant, faint but pursuing.

'Don't you know? I made sure you would.'

'Are you – are you thinking of getting married, sir?' asked the Sergeant, amazed.

'Yes, but don't tell me I'm making a mistake, because I know that already. I expect it will ruin my entire life.'

'Then what are you going to do it for?' said the Sergeant reasonably.

Neville made one of his vague gestures. 'My changed circumstances. I shall be hunted for my money. Besides, I can't think of any other way to get rid of it.'

'Well,' said the Sergeant dryly, 'you won't find any difficulty about that if you *do* get married, that's one thing.'

'Oh, do you really think so? Then I'll go and propose at once, before I have time to think better of it. Goodbye!'

The Sergeant called after him: 'Here, sir, don't you run away with the idea I said you were cleared of suspicion, because I didn't say any such thing!'

Neville waved an airy farewell, and disappeared down the stairs. Ten minutes later he entered the drawing-room of the Norths' house through the long window. Helen was writing a letter at her desk, and her sister was sitting on the floor, correcting four typescripts at once.

'Hullo!' she said, glancing up. 'You still at large?'

'Oh, I'm practically cleared! I say, will you come to Bulgaria with me?'

Sally groped for her monocle, screwed it into her eye, and looked at him. Then she put down the typescript she was holding, and replied matter-of-factly: 'Yes, rather. When?'

'Oh, as soon as possible, don't you think?'

Helen twisted round in her chair. 'Sally, what on earth do you mean? You can't possibly go away with Neville like that!'

'Why not?' asked Neville interestedly.

'Don't be absurd! You know perfectly well it wouldn't be proper.'

'Oh no, it probably won't. That's the charm of travel in the Balkans. But she's very broadminded, really.'

'But –'

'Wake up, darling!' advised Sally. 'You don't seem to realise that I've just received a proposal of marriage.'

'A…?' Helen sprang up. 'You mean to tell me that was a proposal?'

'Oh, I do hate pure women: they have the filthiest minds!' said Neville.

'Sally, you're *not* going to marry a – a hopeless creature like Neville?'

'Yes, I am. Look at the wealth he's rolling in! I'd be a fool if I turned him down.'

'*Sally!*'

'Besides, he's not bossy, which is more than can be said for most men.'

'You don't love him!'

'Who says I don't?' retorted Sally, blushing faintly.

Helen looked helplessly from one to the other. 'Well, all I can say is I think you're mad.'

'Oh, I am glad!' said Neville. 'I was beginning to feel frightfully embarrassed. If you haven't got anything more to say it would be rather nice if you went away.'

Helen walked to the door, remarking, as she opened it: 'You might have waited till I'd gone before you proposed – if that extraordinary invitation was really a proposal.'

'But you showed no signs of going, and it would have made me feel very self-conscious to have said: "Oh, Helen, do you mind going, because I want to propose to Sally?"'

'You're both mad!' declared Helen, and went out.

Sally rose to her feet. 'Neville, are you sure you won't regret this?' she asked anxiously.

He put his arms round her. 'No, of course I'm not: are you?'

She gave one of her sudden smiles. 'Well, yes – pretty sure!'

'Darling, that's handsome of you, but deluded. *I'm* only sure that I shall regret it awfully if I don't take this plunge. I think it must be your nose. Are your eyes blue or grey?'

She looked up. He kissed her promptly; she felt his arms harden round her, and emerged from this unexpectedly rough embrace gasping for breath, and considerably shaken.

'Ruse,' said Neville. 'Grey with yellow flecks. I knew it all along.'

She put her head on his shoulder. 'Gosh, Neville, I – I wasn't sure – you really meant it till now! I say, is it going to be a walking tour, or something equally uncomfortable?'

'Oh no! But I thought we might do some canal work, and we're practically bound to spend a good many nights in peasants' huts. Can you eat goat?'

'Yes,' said Sally. 'What's it like?'

'Rather foul. Are you busy this week, or can you spare the time to get married?'

'Oh, I should think so, but it'll mean a special licence, and you can't touch Ernie's money till you've got probate.'

'Can't I? I shall have to borrow some, then.'

'You'd better leave it to me,' said Sally, her natural competence asserting itself. 'You'd come back with a dog-licence, or something. By the way, are you certain you won't be arrested for these tiresome murders?'

'Oh yes, because Ernie's hat doesn't fit!' he replied.

'I suppose that's a good reason?'

'Yes, even the Sergeant thought so,' he said happily.

The Sergeant did think so, but being unwilling to let his last suspect go, he kept his conviction to himself. On his way downstairs from Ernest Fletcher's dressing-room, he encountered Miss Fletcher, who looked surprised to see him, but accepted quite placidly his explanation that Neville had invited him. She said vaguely: 'Dear boy! So thoughtless! But men very often are, aren't they? I hope you don't think he had anything to do with this dreadful tragedy, because I'm sure he would never do anything really wicked. One always knows, doesn't one?'

The Sergeant made a non-committal sound.

'Yes, exactly,' said Miss Fletcher. 'Now, what can have become of Neville? He ought not to have left you alone upstairs. Not that I mean – because, of course, that would be absurd.'

'Well, madam,' said the Sergeant. 'I don't know whether I'm supposed to mention it, but I fancy Mr Fletcher has gone off to get engaged to be married.'

'Oh, I'm so glad!' she said, a beaming smile sweeping over her face. 'I feel he ought to be married, don't you?'

'Well, I'm bound to say it looks to me as though he needs someone to keep him in order,' replied the Sergeant.

'You're so sensible,' she told him. 'But how remiss of me! Would you care for some tea? Such a dusty walk from the police station!'

He declined the offer, and succeeded bit by bit in escaping from her. He walked back to the police station in a mood of profound gloom, which was not alleviated, on his arrival there, by the sight of Constable Glass, still awaiting his pleasure. He went into a small private office, and once more spread his notes on the case before him, and cudgelled his brain over them.

Glass, following him, closed the door, and regarded him in a melancholy fashion, saying presently: 'Fret not thyself because of evil-doers. They shall soon be cut down like the grass, and wither as the green herb.'

'A fat lot of withering they'll do if I *don't* fret over them!' said the Sergeant crossly.

'Thou shalt grope at noonday as the blind gropeth in the darkness.'

'I wish you'd shut up!' snapped the Sergeant, exasperated by the truth of this observation.

The cold blue eyes flashed. 'I am full of the fury of the Lord,' announced Glass. 'I am weary of holding-in!'

'I haven't noticed you doing much holding-in so far, my lad. You go and spout your recitations somewhere else. If I have to see much more of you I'll end up a downright atheist.'

'I will not go. I have communed with my own soul. There is a way which seemeth right to a man, but the end thereof are the ways of death.'

The Sergeant turned over a page of his typescript. 'Well, there's no need to get worked up about it,' he said. 'If you take sin as hard as all that, you'll never do for a policeman. And if you're going to stay here, for goodness' sake sit down, and don't stand there staring at me!'

Glass moved to a chair, but still kept his stern gaze upon the Sergeant's face. 'What said Neville Fletcher?' he asked.

'He talked me nearly as silly as you do.'

'He is not the man.'

'Well, if he isn't he may have a bit of a job proving it, that's all I can say,' retorted the Sergeant. 'Hat or no hat, he was in London the night Carpenter was done in, and he was the only one of the whole boiling who had motive *and* opportunity to kill the late Ernest. I grant you, he isn't the sort you'd expect to go around murdering people, but you've got to remember he's no fool, and is very likely taking us all in. I don't know whether he did in Carpenter, but the more I look at the evidence, the more I'm convinced he's the one man who *could* have done his uncle in.'

'Yet he is not arrested.'

'No, he's not, but it's my belief that when the Superintendent thinks it over he will be.'

'The Superintendent is a just man, according to his lights. Where is he?'

'I don't know. He'll be down here soon, I daresay.'

'There shall be no more persecution of those that are innocent. My soul is tossed with a tempest, but it is written, yea, and in letters of fire! Whoso sheddeth a man's blood by man shall his blood be shed!'

'That's the idea,' agreed the Sergeant. 'But as for persecuting the innocent –'

'Forsake the foolish and live!' Glass interrupted, a grim, mirthless smile twisting his lips. 'Woe to them that are wise in their own eyes! Know that judgments are prepared for scorners, and stripes for the back of fools!'

'All right!' said the Sergeant, nettled. 'If you're so clever, perhaps you know who really is the murderer?'

Glass's eyes stared into his, queerly glowing. 'I alone know who is the murderer!'

The Sergeant blinked at him. Neither he nor Glass had noticed the opening of the door. Hannasyde's quiet voice made them both jump. 'No, Glass. Not you alone,' he said.

Fifteen

THE SERGEANT, WHO HAD BEEN LOOKING AT GLASS IN utter incredulity, glanced quickly towards the door and got up. 'What the – What is all this, Chief?' he demanded.

Glass turned his head, regarding Hannasyde sombrely. 'Is the truth known, then, to you?' he asked. 'If it be so, I am content, for my soul is weary of my life. I am as Job; my days are swifter than a post: they flee away, they see no good.'

'Good Lord, he's mad!' exclaimed the Sergeant.

Glass smiled contemptuously. 'The foolishness of fools is folly. I am not mad. To me belongeth vengeance and recompense. I tell you, the wicked shall be turned into hell!'

'Yes, all right!' said the Sergeant, keeping a wary eye on him. 'Don't let's have a song and dance about it!'

'That'll do, Hemingway,' said Hannasyde. 'You were wrong, Glass. You know that you were wrong.'

'Though hand join in hand the wicked shall not be unpunished!'

'No. But it was not for you to punish.'

Glass gave a sigh like a groan. 'I know not. Yet the thoughts of the righteous are right. I was filled with the fury of the Lord.'

The Sergeant grasped the edge of the desk for support. 'Holy Moses, you're not going to tell me *Ichabod* did it?' he gasped.

'Yes, Glass killed both Fletcher and Carpenter,' replied Hannasyde.

Glass looked at him with a kind of impersonal interest. 'Do you know all, then?'

'Not all, no. Was Angela Angel your sister?'

Glass stiffened, and said in a hard voice: 'I had a sister once who was named Rachel. But she is dead, yea, and to the godly dead long before her sinful spirit left her body! I will not speak of her. But to him who led her into evil, and to him who caused her to slay herself I will be as a glittering sword that shall devour flesh!'

'Oh, my God!' muttered the Sergeant.

The blazing eyes swept his face. 'Who are you to call upon God, who mock at righteousness? Take up that pencil, and write what I shall tell you, that all may be in order. Do you think I fear you? I do not, nor all the might of man's law! I have chosen the way of truth.'

The Sergeant sank back into his chair, and picked up the pencil. 'All right,' he said somewhat thickly. 'Go on.'

Glass addressed Hannasyde. 'Is it not enough that I say it was by my hand that these men died?'

'No. You know that's not enough. You must tell the whole truth.' Hannasyde scanned the Constable's face, and added: 'I don't think your sister's name need be made public, Glass. But I must know all the facts. She met Carpenter when he was touring the Midlands, and played for a week at Leicester, didn't she?'

'It is so. He seduced her with fair words and a liar's tongue. But she was a wanton at heart. She went willingly with that man of Belial, giving herself to a life of sin. From that day she was as one dead to us, her own people. Even her name shall be forgotten, for it is written that the wicked shall be silent in darkness. When she slew herself I rejoiced, for the flesh is weak, and the thought of her, yea, and her image, was as a sharp thorn.'

'Yes,' Hannasyde said gently. 'Did you know that Fletcher was the man she loved?'

'No. I knew nothing. The Lord sent me to his place where he dwelt. And still I did not know.' His hands clenched on his knees till the fingers whitened. 'When I have met him he has smiled upon me, with his false lips, and has bidden me good-evening. And I have answered him civilly!'

The Sergeant gave an involuntary shiver. Hannasyde said: 'When did you discover the truth?'

'Is it not plain to you? Upon the night that I killed him! When I told you that at 10.02 I saw the figure of a man coming from the side gate at Greystones I lied.' His lip curled scornfully; he said: 'The simple believeth every word: but the prudent man looketh well to his going.'

'You were an officer of the Law,' Hannasyde said sternly. 'Your word was considered to be above suspicion.'

'It is so, and in that I acknowledge that I sinned. Yet what I did was laid upon me to do, for none other might wreak vengeance upon Ernest Fletcher. My sister took her own life, but I tell you he was stained with her blood! Would the Law have avenged her? He knew himself to be safe from the Law, but me he did not know!'

'We won't argue about that,' Hannasyde said. 'What happened on the evening of the 17th?'

'Not at 10.02, but some minutes earlier did I see Carpenter. At the corner of Maple Grove did I encounter him, face to face.'

'Carpenter was the man Mrs North saw?'

'Yes. She was not lying when she told of his visit to Fletcher, for he recounted all to me, while my hand was still upon his throat.'

'What was his object in going to see Fletcher? Blackmail?'

'Even so. He too had been in ignorance, but once, before he served his time, he saw Fletcher at that gilded den of iniquity where my sister displayed her limbs to all men's gaze, in lewd dancing. And when he was released from prison, and my sister was dead, there was none to tell him who her lover was, except only one girl who recalled to his memory the man he had once seen. He remembered, but he could not discover the man's name until he saw a portrait of him one day in a newspaper. Then, finding that Ernest Fletcher was rich in this world's goods, he planned in his evil brain to extort money from him by threats of scandal and exposure. To this end, he came to Marley, not once but several times, at first seeking to enter by the front door, but being repulsed by Joseph Simmons who, when he would not state his business with Fletcher, shut the door upon him. It was for that reason that he entered by the side gate on the night of the 17th. But Fletcher laughed at him, and mocked him for a fool, and took him to the gate, and drove him forth. He went away, not towards the Arden Road, but to Vale Avenue. And there I met him.'

He paused. Hannasyde said: 'You recognised him?'

'I recognised him. But he knew not me until my hand was at his throat, and I spake my name in his ear. I would have slain him then, so great was the just rage consuming me, but he gasped to me to stay my hand, for my sister's death lay not at his door. I would not heed, but in his terror he cried out, choking, that he could divulge the name of the guilty man. I hearkened to him. Still holding him, I bade him tell what he knew. He was afraid with the fear of death. He confessed everything, even his own evil designs. When I knew the name of the man who had caused my sister's death, and remembered his false smile and his pleasant words to me, a greater rage entered into my soul, so that it shook. I let Carpenter go. My hand fell from his throat, for I was amazed. He vanished swiftly, I knew not whither. I cared nothing for him, for at that moment I knew what I must do. There was none to see. My mind, which had been set whirling, grew calm, yea, calm with the knowledge of righteousness! I went to that gate, and up the path to the open window that led into Fletcher's study. He sat at his desk, writing. When my shadow fell across the floor, he looked up. He was not afraid; he saw only an officer of the Law before him. He was surprised, but even as he spoke to me the smile was on his lips. Through a mist of red I saw that smile, and I struck him with my truncheon so that he died.'

The Sergeant looked up from his shorthand notes. 'Your truncheon!' he ejaculated. 'Oh, my Lord!'

'The time?' Hannasyde asked.

'When I looked at the clock, the hands stood at seven minutes past ten. I thought what I should do, and it seemed to me that I saw my path clear before me. I picked up the telephone that stood upon the desk, and reported the death to my sergeant. But that which is crooked cannot be made straight. I was a false witness that speaketh lies, and through my testimony came darkness and perplexity, and the innocent was brought into tribulation. Yea, though they are enclosed in their own fat, though they are sinners in the sight of the Lord, every one, it was not just that they should suffer for my deed. I was troubled, and sore-broken, and my heart misgave me. Yet it seemed to me that all might remain hidden, for you who sought to unravel the mystery were astonished, and knew not which way to turn. But when the finger-prints were discovered to be those of Carpenter's hand, I saw that my feet had been led into a deep pit from which there could be no escape. When it was divulged to the Sergeant where Carpenter abode, I was standing at his elbow. I heard all, even that he dwelt in a basement room, and was become a waiter in an eating-house. The Sergeant gave me leave to go off duty, and I departed, wrestling with my own soul. I hearkened to the voice of the tempter, but a man shall not be established by wickedness. Carpenter was evil, but though he deserved to die, it was not for that reason that I killed him.'

'You were the Constable the coffee-stall owner saw!' the Sergeant said.

'There was such a stall; I doubt not that the man saw me. I passed him as though upon my beat; I came to the house wherein Carpenter dwelt; I saw the light shining through the blind in the basement. I went down the area steps. The door at the bottom was not locked. I entered softly. When I walked into his room Carpenter was standing with his back to me. He turned, but he had no time to utter the scream I saw rising to his lips. Yet again I had his throat in my hands, and he could not prevail against me. I slew him as I slew Fletcher, and departed as I had come. But Fletcher I slew righteously. When I killed Carpenter I knew that I had committed the sin of murder, and my heart was heavy in me. Now you would arrest Neville Fletcher in my stead, but he is innocent, and it is time that the lip of truth be established.' He turned towards the Sergeant, saying harshly: 'Have you set down faithfully what I have recounted? Let it be copied out, and I will set my name to it.'

'Yes, that will be done,' Hannasyde said. 'Meanwhile, Glass, you are under arrest.'

He stepped back a pace to the door, and opened it. 'All right, Inspector.'

'Do you think I fear you?' Glass said, standing up. 'You are puny men, both. I could slay you as I slew the others. I will not do it, for I have no quarrel with you, but set no handcuffs about my wrists! I will be free.'

A couple of men who had come in at Hannasyde's call took him firmly by the arms. 'You come along quiet, Glass,' said Sergeant Cross gruffly. 'Take it easy now!'

Sergeant Hemingway watched Glass go out between the two policemen, heard him begin to declaim from the Old Testament in a fanatical sing-song, and mopped his brow with his handkerchief, bereft for once of all power of speech.

'Mad,' Hannasyde said briefly. 'I thought he was verging on it.'

The Sergeant found his voice. 'Mad? A raving homicidal lunatic, and I've been trotting around with him as trusting as you please! My God, it gave me gooseflesh just to sit there listening to him telling his story!'

'Poor devil!'

'Well, that's one way of looking at it,' said the Sergeant. 'What about the late Ernest and Charlie Carpenter? Seems to me they got a pretty raw deal. And all for what? Just because a silly bit of fluff who was no better than she should be ran off with one of them, and was fool enough to kill herself because of the other! I don't see what you've got to pity Ichabod for. All that'll happen to him is that he'll be sent to Broadmoor, an expense to everybody, and have a high old time preaching death and destruction to the other loonies.'

'And you call yourself a psychologist!' said Hannasyde.

'I call myself a flatfoot with a sense of justice, Super,' replied the Sergeant firmly. 'When I think of the trouble we've been put to, and that maniac ticking us off right and left for being ungodly – well, I daren't let myself think of it for fear I'll go and burst a blood-vessel. What was it first put you on to it?'

'Constable Mather's saying that Brown hadn't taken up his pitch when he passed up Barnsley Street. That, coupled with the conflicting evidence of the pair at the other end of the street, made me suddenly suspicious. The presence of a policeman on the occasions of both murders was the common factor I spoke of. But I admit it did seem to me in the wildest degree improbable. Which is why I didn't tell you anything about it until I'd worked it out a bit more thoroughly. As soon as I began to think it over, all sorts of little points cropped up. For instance, there was the letter from Angela Angel which we found in Carpenter's room. Do you remember the quotations from the Bible in it? Do you remember when we discovered Angela's photograph in Fletcher's drawer that Glass wouldn't look at it, but said something in rather an agitated way about her end being as bitter as wormwood? The more I thought about it the more certain I felt that I'd hit on the solution. When I traced Carpenter's old agent this morning, and got a list of the towns Carpenter visited on that tour his brother spoke of, all I did was to inquire of the police at each one whether a family of the name of Glass lived, or had ever lived, there. As soon as I discovered some Glasses living at Leicester, and heard from the local Superintendent that there had been a girl attached to the family who had run off with an actor some years ago, I knew I was right on to it. All things considered, I thought it wisest to come straight down here and confront Glass with what I knew – before he took it into his head to murder you,' he added, twinkling.

'Well, that *was* nice of you, Chief,' said the Sergeant, with exaggerated gratitude. 'And what about me getting myself disliked by Brown, and wasting my time watching young Neville try on his uncle's hats?'

'Sorry, but I didn't dare let Glass suspect I might be getting on to his trail. I must notify Neville Fletcher that the mystery is cleared up.'

'You needn't bother,' replied the Sergeant. 'He's lost interest in it.'

Hannasyde smiled, but said: 'All the same, he must be told what's happened.'

'I wouldn't mind betting he'll think it's a funny story. He hasn't got any decency at all, let alone proper feelings. However, I won't deny he dealt with Ichabod better than any of us. You tell him I'm expecting a bit of wedding-cake.'

'Whose wedding-cake?' demanded Hannasyde. 'Not his own?'

'Yes,' said the Sergeant. 'Unless that girl with the eyeglass has got more sense than I give her credit for.'

He was interrupted by the entrance into the room of the Constable on duty, who announced that Mr Neville Fletcher wanted to speak to him.

'Talk of the devil!' exclaimed the Sergeant.

'Show him in,' said Hannasyde.

'He's on the phone, sir.'

'All right, put the call through.'

The Constable withdrew, Hannasyde picked up the receiver, and waited. In a few moments Neville's voice was wafted to him. 'Is that Superintendent Hannasyde? How lovely! Where can I buy a special licence? Have you got any?'

'No,' replied Hannasyde. 'Not our department. I was just coming up to see you, Mr Fletcher.'

'What, again? But I can't be bothered with murder cases now. I'm going to get married.'

'You aren't going to be bothered any more. The case is over, Mr Fletcher.'

'Oh, that's a good thing! We've really had quite enough of it. Where did you say I can buy a special licence?'

'I didn't. Do you want to know who murdered your uncle?'

'No, I want to know who keeps special licences!'

'The Archbishop of Canterbury.'

'No, does he really? What fun for me! Thanks so much! Goodbye!'

Hannasyde laid down the instrument, a laugh in his eyes.

'Well?' demanded the Sergeant.

'Not interested,' Hannasyde replied.

About the Author

Georgette Heyer wrote over fifty books, including Regency romances, mysteries, and historical fiction. Her barrister husband, Ronald Rougier, provided many of the plots for her detective novels, which are classic English country house mysteries reminiscent of Agatha Christie. Heyer was legendary for her research, historical accuracy, and her inventive plots and sparkling characterization.

Georgette Heyer Mysteries now available from Sourcebooks:

Behold, Here's Poison

It's no ordinary morning at the Poplars—the master is found dead in his bed and it turns out that his high blood pressure was not the culprit. From the dotty Zoe Matthews to her wonderfully malicious nephew Randall, every single member of the quarrelsome Matthews family has a motive and none, of course, has an alibi. The suspects maneuver, mislead, quibble and prevaricate as the amiable Detective Inspector Hannasyde sifts through the evidence trying to discover the murderer before the next victim succumbs. Heyer's dialogue is a master class in British wit, sarcasm and the intricacies of life above and below stairs. A truly fiendish plot tests the ingenuity of the quietly resourceful Inspector Hannasyde and leads to a clever and unpredictable conclusion.

The Unfinished Clue

At first glance, it should have been a lovely English country-house weekend party. But it's the guest list from hell and the host, Sir Arthur Billington-Smith, is an abusive wretch who everyone at the party turns out to have a reason to hate. When he's found in his study, stabbed to death and clutching a torn check in his hand, the unhappy guests and estranged family find themselves under the scrutiny of Scotland Yard's cool-headed Inspector Harding. The unlikely cast of characters is sketched with Georgette Heyer's usual brilliant wit and insight into human nature. Inspector Harding emerges as an unlikely hero, following red herring after red herring and finding his own happiness in the process.

Why Shoot a Butler?

In a classic English country-house murder mystery with a twist, it's the butler who's the victim of murder. When local barrister Frank Amberley stumbles upon the scene of the crime, on impulse he protects the young woman he catches there. In the course of ferreting out the real killer, Amberley's disdain for the bumbling police adds comic relief, and he displays true brilliance at solving a crime in which every clue complicates the puzzle, and the police are typically baffled. The conclusion will come as a surprise and delight to Heyer afficionados and general mystery lovers alike.

No Wind of Blame

Wally Carter's murder seems impossible—no one was near the murder weapon at the time the shot was fired. In typical Heyer fashion, everyone on the scene seems to have a motive, not to mention the wherewithal to commit murder, and alibis that simply don't hold up. The superlatively analytical Inspector Hemingway is confronted by a neglected widow, the neighbor who's in love with her, her resentful daughter, a patently phony Russian prince, and a case of blackmail that may—or may not—be at the heart of the case...

Death in the Stocks

A bobby on his night rounds discovers a corpse in evening dress locked in the stocks on the village green. Superintendent Hannasyde is called in, but sorting out the suspects proves a challenge. Everyone in the eccentric, exceedingly uncooperative Vereker family had motive and means to kill the unpopular Andrew Vereker. One cousin allies himself with the inspector, while the victim's half-brother and sister, each of whom suspects the other, markedly try to set him off the scent. To readers' delight, the killer is so cunning that his (or her) identity remains a mystery until the very end...

More of your favorite

GEORGETTE HEYER

titles are available wherever books are sold, or order them directly from Sourcebooks!

Title	ISBN	Price
☐ *An Infamous Army*	978-1-4022-1007-5	$14.95 U.S./$19.95 CAN
☐ *Cotillion*	978-1-4022-1008-2	$13.95 U.S./$16.95 CAN
☐ *Royal Escape*	978-1-4022-1076-1	$14.95 U.S./$17.95 CAN
☐ *Friday's Child*	978-1-4022-1079-2	$12.95 U.S./$15.50 CAN
☐ *False Colours*	978-1-4022-1075-4	$12.95 U.S./$15.50 CAN
☐ *Lady of Quality*	978-1-4022-1077-8	$13.95 U.S./$16.95 CAN
☐ *Black Sheep*	978-1-4022-1078-5	$13.95 U.S./$16.95 CAN
☐ *The Spanish Bride*	978-1-4022-1113-3	$14.95 U.S./$17.95 CAN
☐ *Regency Buck*	978-1-4022-1349-6	$13.95 U.S./$14.99 CAN
☐ *Charity Girl*	978-1-4022-1350-2	$13.95 U.S./$14.99 CAN
☐ *The Reluctant Widow*	978-1-4022-1351-9	$13.95 U.S./$14.99 CAN
☐ *Faro's Daughter*	978-1-4022-1352-6	$13.95 U.S./$14.99 CAN
☐ *Simon the Coldheart*	978-1-4022-1354-0	$14.95 U.S./$15.99 CAN
☐ *The Conqueror*	978-1-4022-1355-7	$14.95 U.S./$15.99 CAN
☐ *Frederica*	978-1-4022-1476-9	$13.95 U.S./$14.99 CAN

Send this form, along with your name, mailing address and payment to:

Sourcebooks   Fax (630) 961-2168
1935 Brookdale Rd, Suite 139
Naperville, IL 60563

☐ I've included a check payable to Sourcebooks

Charge my ☐ MasterCard   _____   _____
       ☐ Visa   Card Number   Expiration Date

Contact us at (630) 961-3900 or email info@sourcebooks.com

Prices and availability subject to change without notice, allow 2–4 weeks for delivery
OTHER TITLES AVAILABLE AT: WWW.SOURCEBOOKS.COM

BACH FLOWER REMEDIES TO THE RESCUE

Gregory Vlamis

Foreword by Dr. Charles K. Elliot
Former Physician to Her Majesty the Queen

Healing Arts Press
Rochester, Vermont

Healing Arts Press
One Park Street
Rochester, Vermont 05767

Copyright © 1986, 1988, 1990 Gregory Vlamis

All rights reserved. No part of this book may be reproduced or utilized in any
form or by any means, electronic or mechanical, including photocopying,
recording, or by any information storage and retrieval system, without
permission in writing from the publisher.

*Note to the reader: This book is intended as an informational guide. The
remedies, approaches, and techniques described herein are meant to
supplement, and not to be a substitute for, professional medical care or
treatment. They should not be used to treat a serious ailment without prior
consultation with a qualified healthcare professional.*

Library of Congress Cataloging-in-Publication Data
Vlamis, Gregory.
Bach flower remedies to the rescue / Gregory Vlamis.
p.   cm.
Rev. ed. of: Flowers to the rescue. c1988.
Includes bibliographical references.
ISBN 0-89281-378-4
1. Bach, Edward, 1886–1936.   2. Flowers—Therapeutic use.
3. Flowers—Therapeutic use—Case studies.   I. Vlamis, Gregory.
Flowers to the rescue.   II. Title
RX615.F55V55   1990
615'.321—dc20   90-30311
CIP

Printed and bound in the United States

10 9 8 7 6 5 4 3

Healing Arts Press is a division of Inner Traditions International, Ltd.

Distributed to the book trade in the United States by American International
Distribution Corporation (AIDC)

Distributed to the book trade in Canada by Publishers Group West (PGW),
Montreal West, Quebec

Distributed to the health food trade in Canada by Alive Books, Toronto
and Vancouver

'Gregory Vlamis has made a fine contribution to the understanding of the Bach Flower Remedies and one which will greatly increase our awareness of these wonderful healing agents. His account of their development by Edward Bach, supplemented by very practical descriptions of their use, forms a valuable treatise for which we are grateful.' — *Maesimund Panos, MD, DHt, former President, National Center for Homeopathy, Washington, D.C.; co-author of 'Homeopathic Medicine at Home' (Tarcher).*

'I am glad that Gregory Vlamis has taken the trouble to collect all these testimonies to the Bach Flower Remedies. Medical research into them is long overdue.' — *Alec Forbes, MA, DM, FRCP, formerly member Expert Advisory Panel on Traditional Medicine, World Health Organization; medical director Bristol Cancer Help Centre, and author of 'The Bristol Diet: a Get Well and Stay Well Eating Plan' (Century).*

'An outstanding reference work, *Bach Flower Remedies to the Rescue* is both a reference tool and reader for all those interested in the Bach Flower Remedies and especially Dr. Bach's combination formula Rescue Remedy. Mr. Vlamis has excelled in bringing together numerous case studies on the current use of Rescue Remedy, many by top physicians in the field. Additionally, the inclusion of two out-of-print philosophical works by Dr. Edward Bach makes this book a *must* for all those interested in whole person healing.'—*Leslie J. Kaslof, author of 'Wholistic Dimensions in Healing' (Doubleday) and President of the Dr. Edward Bach Healing Society, North America.*

'...a valuable record of how Dr. Bach's work has continued in the 50 years since his death. It is a well organized book of impressive and thorough research.'—*Julian Barnard, author of 'A Guide to the Bach Flower Remedies' (C. W. Daniel).*

'*Bach Flower Remedies to the Rescue* shows us the impressive range of experience from health professionals and consumers with the Bach Flower Remedies. This book provides strong testimony to the value of these flower remedies and encourages us all to use them for the various trials and tribulations of modern life.'—*Dana Ullman, MPH, co-author of 'Everybody's Guide to Homeopathic Medicines' (Tarcher), and Director of Homeopathic Educational Services, Berkeley, California.*

'This book will be of great interest to many veterinarians. The wonderful accounts of the efficacy of Rescue Remedy in animals is particularly fascinating'. — *Richard H. Pitcairn, DVM, PhD, author of 'Dr. Pitcairn's Complete Guide to Natural Health for Dogs and Cats' (Rodale Press).*

DEDICATION

To those who suffer and are in distress; to Dr. Edward Bach, and to his spirit; to the Bach Centre for carrying on his good work; to my daughter, Roxanne Vlamis; to my father, Constantine Vlamis, and especially to my mother, Roxanne Vlamis Santos—for her tremendous caring and support.

Contents

Contents

Acknowledgements

A great many people helped to put this book together. I am especially indebted to:

Nickie Murray and John Ramsell, current curators of the Dr. Edward Bach Centre, for their co-operation, general support and permission to use case studies from their files, and the right to reproduce *Ye Suffer From Yourselves* and *Free Thyself* by Dr. Edward Bach.

Leslie Kaslof for his wisdom, advice, encouragement, and pioneering of the Bach Flower Remedies in North America.

Ralph Kaslof for his commitment to the work.

Mary Hayden, Dr. Bach's sister and Evelyn Varney, his daughter, for sharing their memories and photographs.

Dr. Charles K. Elliott for his kind comments and foreword.

Dr. J. Herbert Fill for the introduction.

Andrewjohn and Eleni Clarke for their hospitality in the United Kingdom.

Deborah Mills for her meticulous typing.

I wish to deeply thank the many who responded to my letters and questionnaires, as well as those hundreds of people throughout the world who provided case studies, kind words and encouragement for the completion of this work.

The following, whom I warmly thank, have contributed in one way or another:

Anne Catherine, Didier and Georgette Basilios, Mark Blumenthal, Michael Bookbinder, Bruce Borland, Thomas Boyce, Mary Carter, Robert and Sharon Corr, Marsha DeMunnik, Sonny Delmonico, Leonard and Nilda Durany, Ron Eager, Gloria Early, Marilyn Preston Evans, Professor Norman R. Farnsworth, Marie Firestone, Demos Fotopoulos, Dr. Benjamin G. Girlando, Fred Hahn, Yvonne Hillman, Judy Howard, Celia Hunting, Jeanne Janssen, Margie Kuyper, Stewart Lawson, Dr. Robert Leichtman,

Acknowledgements

Sanna Longden, Linda Nardi, Robert Krell, Nancy Madsen, Marilyn Marcus, Dick and Rita Marsh, Molly Morgan, Malcolm Murray, Beverly Oldroyd, Ann Parker, Dr. Richard Pitcairn, Katherine Prezas, Victoria Pryor, Melanie Reinhart, Mary Rita, John-Roger, the Royal London Homoeopathic Hospital, London, England, Vera Rugg, George Santos, Sue Smith, Mrs. Spalding, Robert Stevens, Serita Stevens, the University College Hospital Medical School, London, England, Ginny Weissman, Bette, Eileen and Francis Wheeler, Ingrid Williams, and Jennifer Wright.

A special thank you to Bonnie Corso, Elinore Detiger, Faye Waisbrot Honor, Jack Honor, Bobbie Philip, and Lisa Sperling.

Most of all an exceptional acknowledgement to Sharon Steffensen for being the inspiration for this work.

Preface

During the past fifty years, many prominent medical doctors, homoeopaths,[1] and other health care professionals have reported the successful treatment of adult patients, children, and animals with the thirty-eight flower remedies discovered by the late Dr. Edward Bach.

Prepared from the flowers of wild plants, bushes, and trees, the Bach Flower Remedies do not directly treat physical disease, but help stabilize the emotional and psychological stresses reflecting the root cause. The stress factors include such things as fear, loneliness, worry, jealousy, and insecurity. Carried to the extreme, these emotions lower the body's natural resistance to disease. By assisting the integration of emotional, psychological, and physiological patterns, the remedies produce a soothing, calming effect, thereby allowing the body to heal itself.

These flower remedies are simple to use, and relatively inexpensive; moreover, they have reportedly been shown to be consistently effective when chosen correctly.

All thirty-eight of the Bach Flower Remedies have been included in the *Supplement to the Eighth Edition of the Homoeopathic Pharmacopeia of the United States*[2], and are officially recognized as homoeopathic drugs. This was primarily due to the efforts of Leslie J. Kaslof, author, researcher, and pioneer in the field of holistic health.

---

1. For editorial consistency the traditional spelling "homoeopathy" has been used wherever the word appears except when "homeopathy" (a more contemporary spelling) is used in a book's title.

2. Official compendium of homoeopathic drugs.

Most widely known of all the Bach remedies is the Rescue Remedy, a combination of five of the Bach flowers. Rescue Remedy is the emergency first aid remedy. It is extremely useful in many situations and generally works very quickly.

I first observed the effects of Rescue Remedy on a friend who was grieving over his father's death. So dramatic was his relief that I felt compelled to explore Bach's discoveries in more depth. Eventually, this led me on a four-month journey through the United Kingdom, where I came upon rare photographs, unpublished writings and letters of Dr. Bach's, all kindly supplied to me by his relatives and close friends.

I have been most impressed by the consistent reports of success in the use of Rescue Remedy, both in simple and complicated circumstances. These reports justify further investigation and controlled studies.

Though Rescue Remedy is called for in diverse circumstances, it is not a panacea or a replacement for orthodox medical care. It is used during minor stressful periods to develop emotional and psychological equilibrium, and during crisis situations, to ease emotional and psychological stress before and during emergency medical treatment. Many medical doctors, homoeopaths, other physicians and health care professionals throughout the world, carry the Rescue Remedy in their emergency kits or on their person for use in such circumstances.

The case studies contained in this book are authentic and based on extensive research and personal interviews. They illustrate, however, only a small part of the Rescue Remedy's versatility.

If only a few people obtain relief from their suffering and distress through the use of the Rescue Remedy, the purpose of this work will have been accomplished.

Gregory Vlamis
Chicago, Illinois
25 January 1986

Foreword

Dr. Edward Bach's (1886-1936) contribution to medicine—his system and philosophy known as the Bach Flower Remedies—provides us with an ideal of health beyond the absence of symptoms. True well-being comes from within. Like Hippocrates, Paracelsus, and Hahnemann, Bach knew that good health depended on spiritual, mental, and emotional factors being in harmony.

The effects of disharmony are shown by negative moods and thoughts that assail each of us at times. Bach understood that these, in turn, can affect the body, depleting it of strength and vitality by blocking the life force necessary to our existence at all levels. True healing—restoring harmony —opens up the channel for this vital flow of life.

Dr. Bach astutely noted that illness is ultimately beneficial and constitutes a period of true refinement and purification.

Heal Thyself, Bach's brilliant essay, published by C. W. Daniel, 1931, should be mandatory for every student of health. In it Bach states: "There is a factor which science is unable to explain on physical grounds, and that is why some people become affected by disease whilst others escape, although both classes may be open to the same possibility of infection. Materialism forgets that there is a factor above the physical plane which in the ordinary course of life protects or renders susceptible any particular individual with regard to disease, of whatever nature it may be."

Devoted and inspired research, coupled with Bach's unique background as a physician, pathologist, immunologist, and bacteriologist, led him to create one of the most comprehensive state-of-the-art systems of healing known, a gentle, simple system that works and is available to all.

Foreword

The Bach Flower Remedies can be used with orthodox or complementary, alternative systems of medicine. Nature's wisdom is always added to any treatment employed. In ancient wisdom, medicine existed in closest communion with spiritual vision. Today, Dr. Edward Bach's holistic system embodies this ancient ideal.

Current scientific research is proving that a person's mental and emotional state can influence, positively or negatively, ills ranging from the common cold to cancer.

This new field of research, psychoneuroimmunology, is rapidly gaining the respect of the medical establishment. Mental states and emotions are now seriously considered in the total treatment of most illness.

I hope that progressive scientists examine the varied merits of the Bach Flower Remedies. Bach's philosophy of health offers us inner peace, harmony, and hope for the future.

Charles K. Elliott, MB, BCh,
MFHom, MRCGP, MLCO, AFOM RCP,
London; Former Physician to
Her Majesty Queen Elizabeth II;
co-editor of *Classical Homoeopathy* (Beaconsfield,
England: Beaconsfield Publishers Ltd., 1986)

Introduction

I have been using the Bach Flower Remedies in my practice for over ten years and have found them, including the Rescue Remedy, invaluable when used correctly. I use them almost exclusively instead of tranquilizers and psychotropics, and in many cases they alleviate the problem when all else has failed. The Bach Flower Remedies are extremely sophisticated in their alleviation of specific moods, gentle and yet potent in balancing the body's subtle energy fields. Though subtle in their action, the Bach Flower Remedies are not placebos.

The Bach Flower Rescue Remedy deserves its special place in the Bach literature. Its action is unique, as the reader will discover in the subsequent pages. Until this present work, little has been made available on this subject.

In writing this book, Gregory Vlamis has produced a well-written summary for the professional as well as the general public. The reader is given practical information on how to use the Bach Flower Rescue Remedy in dealing with the crises of everyday life, from acute to chronic. *Bach Flower Remedies to the Rescue* is easily readable and abundantly filled with case accounts, illustrating the great variety of applications of this amazing gift of nature. As a psychiatrist, I distinctly appreciate the preventive value of the Bach Flower Remedies and Rescue Remedy as a powerful and safe alternative to tranquilizers without their characteristic side effects.

It is my sincere wish that all, especially my colleagues and medical students, become aware of the Bach Flower Rescue Remedy and Bach's work in order to experience the remedy's efficacy and to confirm the insights of a modern medical genius.

With many people now losing faith in modern medicine, this is the right era for us to learn about this time-honored method of healing that uses preparations obtained from English wildflowers.

Thanks to the author, we have been given a valuable opportunity to become aware of a most precious adjunct to medicine. This book and the Bach Flower Rescue Remedy should be in every health care professional's armamentarium, in every home, vehicle, and first aid kit.

J. Herbert Fill, MD, psychiatrist;
former New York City Commissioner
of Mental Health; author of
The Mental Breakdown of a Nation
(New York: Franklin Watts, 1974)

PART I

"Everyone of us is a healer, because every one of us at heart has a love for something, for our fellow-man, for animals, for nature, for beauty in some form. And we every one of us wish to protect and help it to increase. Everyone of us also has sympathy with those in distress, and naturally so because we have all been in distress ourselves at some time in our lives.

"We are all healers, and with love and sympathy in our natures we are also able to help anyone who really desires health. Seek for the outstanding mental conflict in the patient, give him the remedy that will assist him to overcome that particular fault, and all the encouragement and hope you can, and then the healing virtue within him will of itself do all the rest."

Dr. Edward Bach

Dr. Edward Bach: Healing Pioneer

The spirit of Edward Bach lives in the lush green country-side of England—in the trees, plants, and flowers he used for his remedies.

Born on September 24, 1886, at Moseley, outside Birmingham, he was the eldest of three children.

Independent in outlook, even from his earliest years, Bach had a great sense of humor, which sustained him through many trials. As a child, he loved to meditate, and he often roamed the countryside alone, pausing just to sit and to contemplate the beauty of nature. As he grew, his love for nature and life developed into a great compassion for all living things, especially those in pain or distress. His overwhelming desire to help the suffering compelled him to become a physician.

Even before he began his medical studies, Bach observed that standard medical treatment was often more palliative than curative. He became convinced that there had to exist a simpler method of healing, one that could be applied to all diseases, including those regarded as chronic or incurable. He decided that he would search out those long-forgotten truths of the healing arts.

To accomplish this he sought medical training. In 1912, Bach obtained the Conjoint Diploma of MRCS, LRCP, and in 1913 he received his MB and BS[1] degrees from the Univer-

---

1. MRCS—Member Royal College of Surgeons; LRCP—Licentiate of the Royal College of Physicians; MB—Bachelor of Medicine; BS—Bachelor of Surgery.

Dr. Edward Bach, 1921. (Courtesy E. Varney)

sity College Hospital Medical School, London. In 1914, he received the Diploma of Public Health from Cambridge.

Though occasionally referred to as batch; his family, close friends and colleagues called him bache as in the letter H, meaning little one, petite, or dear. Today, most people, unaware of this specific pronunciation, commonly pronounce Bach as they would the name of the well-known musical composer.

In the early years of his practice, Bach became a respected pathologist, immunologist, and bacteriologist. Still, he was never satisfied with the results of orthodox medical treatment. Bach observed that although pills, drugs, and surgery were helpful in relieving specific symptoms, they did little to fight long-term and chronic disease. At this time, Bach set out to find and develop a treatment for the relief of chronic illness. In 1915 he accepted a position at University College Hospital as assistant bacteriologist. There he discovered that certain strains of intestinal bacteria had a specific relationship to the cause of chronic disorders. He began preparing vaccines from these bacteria. The results of his research exceeded all expectations.

Complaints such as arthritis and severe headaches were alleviated, and patients began to report remarkable improvements in their general health.

Pleased with these results but not with the side effects of vaccination, Bach searched for a method of treatment that would be gentle yet effective.

In 1919, after taking a position at London Homoeopathic Hospital, he discovered the works of Dr. Samuel Hahnemann, the founder of homoeopathy.[2] Bach found much of Hahnemann's philosophy similar to his own. It was similar to the same principles and philosophy which had inspired him from the beginning of his medical career. Hahnemann's concept—"treat the patient and not the disease"—was to become the basis of Bach's system of healing, a system he was to discover many years later.

Bach began preparing his bacterial vaccines homoeopathically and administered them orally. These oral vaccines, or nosodes, as they are called, seemed to fulfill all his

2. A system based on the theory and practice that disease is cured by remedies which produce in a healthy person effects similar to symptoms in the patient. The remedies are normally administered in minute or even infinitesimal doses, thus minimizing the potential for toxic side effects often found with the use of most allopathic drugs.

expectations.. Hundreds of chronic cases were treated, yielding exceptional results.

Welcomed enthusiastically by the medical profession, these vaccines became widely used, and they are still used today by homoeopaths and medical doctors in England, America, and Germany. Bach's works on intestinal toxemia appeared in the *Proceedings of the Royal Society of Medicine*,[3] 1919-1920, and in 1920-1921 additional works appeared in the *British Homoeopathic Journal*.[4] During his career, Bach contributed many other original articles to the British medical and homoeopathic journals. Of particular acclaim was his book *Chronic Disease: A Working Hypothesis* (London: H.K. Lewis & Co., Ltd., 1925), co-authored with Dr. C.W. Wheeler, his highly respected homoeopathic colleague.

Despite these successes, Bach was still not satisfied. He felt that by treating only physical disorders, he was overlooking the real issues of health and the cure of disease.

Disease, he concluded, was the result of disharmony between a person's physical and mental state; illness, the physical manifestation of negative states of mind. Bach noted that deep disharmony within the sufferer, such as worry, anxiety, and impatience, so depleted the individual's vitality that the body lost its natural resistance and became vulnerable to infection and other illnesses. Though Bach came to this understanding in his own right, it had been propounded in the past by such noted individuals as Hippocrates, Maimonides, and Paracelsus, and more recently substantiated by the research of Drs. Hans Selye, O. Carl Simonton, and many others working in the field of stress-related disorders. In light of the tranquillity and inner har-

---

3. "The Nature of Serum Antitrypsin and Its Relation to Autolysis and the Formation of Toxins," and "The Relation of the Autotryptic Titre of Blood to Bacteria Infection and Anaphylaxis," Teale, F.H. and Bach, E. *Proc. of the Royal Society of Medicine*, (13) December 2, 1919, pp. 5, 43, respectively.

4. "The Relation of Vaccine Therapy to Homoeopathy," and "A Clinical Comparison Between the Actions of Vaccines and Homoeopathic Remedies," *British Homoeopathic Journal*, 10:2 April 1920 p. 6, 11:1 January 1921 p. 21, respectively.

mony Bach always experienced when out in nature, he felt that the solution to disease-causing states was to be found among the plants, trees, and herbs of the field.

Obeying his intuition, which had proved successful in his earlier experiments, Bach decided to visit Wales in 1928. There, by a mountain stream, he gathered the flowers of Impatiens (*Impatiens glandulifera*) and Mimulus (*Mimulus guttatus*). Later that year, he discovered the wild Clematis (*Clematis vitalba*). Preparations of these flowers were later administered to his patients, producing immediate and noteworthy results.

At this time, Dr. Edward Bach was at the height of his medical career. But in 1930, again following his inner conviction, Bach courageously closed his laboratory, left his London home, and spent his remaining years traveling throughout Wales and Southern England, perfecting his new system of medicine. Walking hundreds of miles in his search for curative plants, he discovered thirty-eight remedies—all, with one exception, derived from flowering plants and trees he found in the English countryside.

As his work progressed, he realized that his own senses were becoming more refined. For several days before he found a remedy, he would intensely experience the physical and mental symptoms of the disease that this remedy was to cure. Then he would go into the fields and find the appropriate healing flower. He could place a petal or flower in his palm or on his tongue and experience the effects of the plant on his mind and body. Coupled with extensive research and application, the newly found remedies proved extremely successful.

Bach immediately published his discoveries in the leading homoeopathic journals of the day. It was also his intention that this new system be made available to the lay person as well as to the professional community. Bach described his system of medicine in inexpensive booklets, the first three entitled *Heal Thyself*, *Free Thyself*, and the *Twelve Healers*. (See page 159 for references.)

Dr. F.J. Wheeler, a close friend and colleague, verified

Bach's findings by using many of the flower remedies in his own practice. He gave Bach valuable feedback and encouraged him to continue his research.

Bach treated many patients, particularly during the winter months, with his new remedies and his unique system of diagnosis. He developed a special love for the people of Cromer (Norfolk, East Anglia, England), where he settled and took up practice, feeling especially close to the fishermen and lifeboat men. What Bach most admired about these men was their 'down-to-earth' lives. Not caring for money, Bach often received gifts of fish, eggs, or vegetables in payment for his medical services.

It was at Cromer, during a terrible storm, that Bach first used three of the flowers found in the Rescue Remedy to aid an ailing crew member of a ship wrecked in the storm. Unconscious, foaming at the mouth, and almost frozen, the

The Bach Centre, Mount Vernon. (Courtesy Here's Health)

man seemed beyond hope. At repeated intervals, Dr. Bach moistened the patient's lips with the remedies as the unconscious fisherman was being carried up the beach to a nearby house. Within minutes, the patient regained consciousness.

Bach continued with his work in this small community until 1934 when, at Sotwell near Wallingford, Oxfordshire, England, he located a small house named Mount Vernon. Here he was to spend the final two years of his life.

Bach's humanity, as much as his genius, drew people to him. Believing that anyone who needed help or sought it for others should be given the tools for healing, he advertised his remedies in local newspapers. As a result, in 1936 the General Medical Council threatened to remove him from its register. In his reply, Dr. Bach wrote, "I consider it the duty and privilege of any physician to teach the sick and others how to help themselves.... My advertisements were for the public good, which, I take it, is the work of our profession." Reconsidering its charge, the General Medical Council never did remove Dr. Bach's name from its register, and to this day Bach's work has been a major source of inspiration to doctors and the general public worldwide.

For further information on Dr. Bach's life, the reader is encouraged to consult *The Medical Discoveries of Edward Bach, Physician*, by Nora Weeks (London: C.W. Daniel, 1940), published in the United States by Keats, New Canaan, Connecticut, 1979.

The Work of Bach Continues

Following Dr. Bach's passing in 1936, Victor Bullen and Nora Weeks carried on his work at Mount Vernon. Nora, who during her years as trustee of the Bach Centre at Mount Vernon wrote *The Medical Discoveries of Edward Bach, Physician* was, along with Victor Bullen, mainly responsible for the growth of Bach's work until their respective deaths in 1978 and 1975.

Victor Bullen and Nora Weeks worked with Dr. Bach, carrying on his work at Mount Vernon, after Bach's passing in 1936. (Courtesy Bach Centre)

Nickie Murray and John Ramsell worked together at the Bach Centre with Nora Weeks, till her passing in 1978. From that time to the present they carried on Bach's work, and are the current curators of the Bach Centre. (Courtesy Bach Centre)

In the early 1960s, Nickie Murray and then her brother, John Ramsell, joined the Bach Centre, and after Nora's and Victor's passing continued on as trustees with the same devotion and commitment as their predecessors.

During their walks about the country, Bach had taught Victor and Nora the names of every wildflower and every tree, saying, "You must recognize them by the leaves of their seedlings so that you can know them and make friends with them from their very beginning."

To this day, the Bach Flower Remedies are prepared exactly as Dr. Bach had done, taken from Bach's original wildflower locations. In addition to preparing the Bach remedies and overseeing appointed distributors in many parts of the world, the Dr. Edward Bach Centre answers inquiries from around the world and publishes *The Bach Remedy News Letter.*

Mount Vernon will always be the center of Dr. Bach's work. Before Bach departed, he made it a point to emphasize: "Though the work will ever increase, keep your life and the little house as it is, for simplicity is the keyword to this system of healing."

Dr. Edward Bach, c.1931-32. (Courtesy Bach Centre)

The Philosophy of Bach on Health and Disease

For many years, since he had come upon the works of Samuel Hahnemann, Bach had concentrated on "treating the patient, not the disease." His personal philosophy on health and disease was an important element in his discovery and development of the flower remedies.

Bach himself was deeply religious, believing all mankind was created in a state of perpetual Unity with God. Man's Soul—the real Self—is most directly connected to the Creator and ever leads man to a higher good. Although the physical body is temporary, the soul is everlasting. Moreover, the soul infuses and guides the personality, comprising the mind and the body as a whole.

Dr. Bach also believed that each person has a mission in life. He wrote:

"...this divine mission means no sacrifice, no retiring from the world, no rejecting of the joys and beauty of nature; on the contrary, it means a fuller and greater enjoyment of all things; it means doing the work we love to do with all our heart and soul whether it be housekeeping, farming, painting, acting or serving our fellow-man in shops or houses. This work, whatever it may be, if we love it above all else, is the definite command of our soul."

Taking this idea a step further, Bach defined health as perfect harmony between the soul, mind, and body. Disease, then, results from a lack of harmony between these elements.

When we do not follow the dictates of our soul by following our intuition—our knowledge of "good"—disease develops in our body as a result of our resistance. This resistance occurs, "when we allow others to interfere with our purpose in life, and implant in our minds doubt, or fear, or indifference." Emotions such as fear and anger, as well as cruelty and rigidity of thought, surface when we are diverted from the soul's purpose, and, consequently, from the personality's true development.

But disease, according to Bach, is paradoxically a healing process because it warns us against carrying our wrong actions too far. Once disease has manifested itself, we must modify our erring mental state and bring it back into line with the convictions of our soul, if we are to be healed. When this realignment begins, so does the physical healing; and both will continue until mind and soul are again in tune and the body is well.

Thus, Bach argued that disease is not an evil, but a blessing in disguise whose purpose is "solely and purely corrective." Indeed, the area where we have physical difficulties is a mirror of our mental difficulties. Bach wrote:

> "If you suffer from stiffness of joint or limb, you can be equally certain that there is stiffness in your mind; that you are rigidly holding on to some idea...which you should not have. If you suffer from asthma, you are in someway stifling another personality; or from lack of courage to do right, smothering yourself....The body will reflect the true cause of disease such as fear, indecision, doubt—in the disarrangement of its systems and tissues."

Complete healing Bach said, depended on four factors:

● The realization of the Divinity within us, and our consequent knowledge that we have the ability to overcome all harm.

● The knowledge that disease is due to disharmony between our personality and our soul.

- Our desire and ability to discover the fault that is causing the conflict.

- The removal of that fault by our developing the opposing virtue.

Over and over again, Bach emphasized that if we want to return to health, we must expect change. Disease was not to be conquered by direct fighting, since "darkness is removed by light, not by greater darkness." To help us make the necessary changes in our personalities, he urged that we learn to replace our weaknesses with strengths, such as substituting acceptance for intolerance.

Bach realized, of course, that "certain maladies may be caused by direct physical means, such as those associated with some poisons, accidents, and injuries, and gross excesses; but disease in general is due to some basic error in our constitution—the conflict of personality and soul…"we have so long blamed the germ, the weather, the food we eat as the causes of disease; but many of us are immune in an influenza epidemic; many love the exhilaration of a cold wind and many can eat cheese and drink black coffee late at night with no ill effects. Nothing in nature can hurt us when we are happy and in harmony."

Believing that physical disease manifested as a result of negative mental and emotional states, Bach opposed those aspects of modern medicine that directed efforts only toward the healing of the physical. He felt that drugs were often counter-productive because the temporary relief they produced in many instances suggested a complete return to health while negative mental and emotional patterns continued unchecked. True healing was postponed, and the inevitable result was more serious illness later on.

When Bach developed his flower remedies, his aim was to effect a healing on a much deeper level than just the physical. Bach, referring to the remedies once wrote:

"they are able…to raise our very natures, and bring us nearer to our Souls.…They cure, not by attacking disease, but by flooding our bodies with the beautiful vibrations of our Higher Nature in the presence of which disease melts as snow in the sunshine."

As a physician, Bach believed that doctors should play the part of adviser and counselor to a patient, providing guidance and insight. The patient must come to realize that he has responsibility for his own healing. He must be prepared to face the truth that his illness was caused by faults that lie within himself, and he must have the desire to rid himself of those faults.

One of the unique advantages of the Bach Flower Remedies is that they can be applied before the first signs of physical illness, thereby preventing disease before it takes hold in the body. Bach noted that "before almost all [serious] complaints there is usually a time of not being quite fit, or a bit run down; that is the time to treat our conditions, get fit and stop things going further." Even a temporary state of conflict between the personality and soul may render the body susceptible to infectious agents that are ready to attack when the body's normal defenses are weak.

A more in-depth explanation on Dr. Bach's Philosophy can be found in *Heal Thyself,* by Edward Bach (London: C.W. Daniel, 1931), and in *The Bach Flower Remedies,* by Drs. Edward Bach and F.J. Wheeler (New Canaan, Connecticut: Keats, 1977). Previously unavailable philosophical writings, *Ye Suffer From Yourselves* and *Free Thyself* are included in appendices A & B.

The Thirty-eight Bach Flower Remedies

The following chapter provides an overview of the various conditions and situations to which all thirty-eight of the Bach Flower Remedies apply.

Additional information on the use of the entire thirty-eight remedies, may also be found, either in *The Twelve Healers and Other Remedies*, by Edward Bach (London: C.W. Daniel, 1933) or in *The Bach Flower Remedies* (New Canaan, Connecticut: Keats, 1977).

Since 1936, the thirty-eight flower remedies discovered by Dr. Bach have been used to restore emotional and psychological equilibrium to individuals during periods of both mild and intense stress. Within his system, Bach classified the following seven major emotional and psychological states:

- **FEAR**
- **UNCERTAINTY**
- **INSUFFICIENT INTEREST IN PRESENT CIRCUMSTANCES**
- **LONELINESS**
- **OVERSENSITIVE TO INFLUENCES AND IDEAS**
- **DESPONDENCY OR DESPAIR**
- **OVERCARE FOR THE WELFARE OF OTHERS.**

Within every classification, he described their variations.

The following is a brief summary of all the thirty-eight Bach Flower Remedies and their uses. These are listed within their appropriate categories. This list is not intended as a definitive explanation of all the Bach remedies and their uses. For further information consult the references listed above.

1. FEAR

Rock Rose (*Helianthemum nummularium*) for extreme terror, panic, hysteria, fright, and nightmares.

Mimulus (*Mimulus guttatus*) for known fears; for example, fear of heights, pain, darkness, poverty, death, being alone, of other people, etc. Also for timidity and shyness.

Cherry Plum (*Prunus cerasifera*) for fear of losing mental and physical control; inclination to uncontrollable rages and impulses, with fear of causing harm to oneself or others, for example suicidal tendencies,** or losing one's temper.

Aspen (*Populus tremula*) for vague fears and anxieties of unknown origin, a sense of foreboding, apprehension, or impending disaster.

Red Chestnut (*Aesculus carnea*) for excessive fear or over-concern for others—especially loved ones, for example; overconcern during their illness, automobile trips, etc., always anticipating that something unfortunate may happen to them.

2. UNCERTAINTY

Cerato (*Ceratostigma willmottianum*) for those who doubt their own ability to judge and make decisions. They are constantly seeking others advice and are often misguided.

---

*One of the original twelve healers.

**The Bach Flower Remedies and Rescue Remedy are not meant to take the place of emergency medical treatment. In all cases requiring psychiatric or medical attention, a licensed physician should be called immediately.

*Scleranthus (*Scleranthus annuus*) for those who are indecisive, being unable to decide between two choices, first one seeming right then the other. They may also be subject to energy or mood swings.

*Gentian (*Gentianella amarella*) for those easily discouraged, in whom even small delays may cause hesitation, despondency and self-doubt.

Gorse (*Ulex europaeus*) for feelings of despair, hopelessness, and futility.

Hornbeam (*Carpinus betulus*) for that Monday-morning feeling of not being able to face the day; for tiredness and a tendency towards procrastination; for those who feel that some part of their bodies or minds need strengthening.

Wild Oat (*Bromus ramosus*) for those dissatisfied in their current career or life style, their difficulty however, is in determining exactly what career to follow.

3. **INSUFFICIENT INTEREST IN PRESENT CIRCUMSTANCES**

*Clematis (*Clematis vitalba*) for those who tend toward escapism living more in the future than in the present; for lack of concentration, daydreaming, lack of interest in present circumstances, and spaciness.

Honeysuckle (*Lonicera caprifolium*) for those dwelling too much in the past, reminiscing about the "good old days;" nostalgia, and homesickness.

Wild Rose (*Rosa canina*) for those who are apathetic and have resigned themselves to their circumstances, making little effort to improve things or to find joy.

Olive (*Olea europaea*) for total mental and physical exhaustion and weariness; for sapped vitality from a long illness or personal ordeal.

White Chestnut (*Aesculus hippocastanum*) for persistent, unwanted thoughts, mental arguments, or preoccupation with some worry or episode.

Mustard (*Sinapis arvensis*) for deep gloom that comes on for no apparent reason, bringing sudden melancholy and heavy sadness.

Chestnut Bud (*Aesculus hippocastanum*) for those who fail to learn from experience, continually repeating the same patterns and mistakes.

4. LONELINESS

*__Water Violet__ (*Hottonia palustris*) for those whose preference is to be alone; seemingly aloof, proud, reserved, self-reliant, sometimes 'superior' in attitude. Capable and reliable they will advise, but not get 'personally' involved in others affairs.

*__Impatiens__ (*Impatiens glandulifera*) for those quick in thought and action but often impatient, especially with those who are slower than they; for those who show irritability through lack of patience.

Heather (*Calluna vulgaris*) for those talkative persons who constantly seek the companionship of anyone who will listen to their troubles. They are self-absorbed, generally poor listeners, and have difficulty being alone for any length of time.

5. OVERSENSITIVITY TO INFLUENCES AND IDEAS

*__Agrimony__ (*Agrimonia eupatoria*) for those not wishing to burden others with their troubles, covering up their suffering with a cheerful facade; they often seek escape from pain and worry through the use of drugs or alcohol.

*__Centaury__ (*Centaurium umbellatum*) for those who have difficulty in saying no, often becoming subservient in their desire to serve others; anxious to please they can be easily exploited, neglecting their own interests.

Walnut (*Juglans regia*) for stabilizing emotions during periods of transition, such as teething, puberty, adolescence, and menopause; for breaking past links and adjusting to new beginnings, such as new jobs, adjusting to new residence, cultures, or even relationships.

Holly (*Ilex aquifolium*) for negative feelings such as envy, jealousy, suspicion, revenge, and hatred; for all states showing a need for more love.

6. DESPONDENCY OR DESPAIR

Larch (*Larix decidua*) for those who, despite being capable, lack self-confidence. Anticipating failure, they often do not make a real effort to succeed.

Pine (*Pinus sylvestris*) for those not satisfied with their own efforts, who are self-reproachful and suffer much from guilt and the faults they attach to themselves, feeling they should or could have done better. They are often quick to blame themselves for the mistakes of others.

Elm (*Ulmus procera*) for those who over extend themselves and become overwhelmed and burdened by their responsibilities.

Sweet Chestnut (*Castanea sativa*) for those who feel they have reached the limits of their endurance; for dark despair, when the anguish seems to be unbearable.

Star of Bethlehem (*Ornithogalum umbellatum*) for mental and emotional stress during and following such traumatic experiences as grief, loss and accidents.

Willow (*Salix vitellina*) for those who have suffered from some misfortune or circumstance they feel was unjust or unfair. As a result, they become resentful and bitter toward others.

Oak (*Quercus robur*) for those who despite illness and adversity never give up. They are brave and determined to overcome all obstacles in order to reach their intended goal.

Crab Apple (*Malus pumila*) for feelings of shame, uncleanliness, or fear of contamination; for poor self-image, particularly as it relates to parts of or growths on the body. Will assist in detoxification and the cleansing of wounds, both internal and external.

7. OVERCARE FOR WELFARE OF OTHERS

*Chicory (*Cichorium intybus*) for those who are overfull of care and possessive of those close to them; they can be demanding and self-pitying, with a need for others to conform to their ideals.

*Vervain (*Verbena officinalis*) for those who have strong opinions, always teaching and philosophizing. They are easily incensed by injustices, and when taken to the extreme can be overenthusiastic, argumentative, and overbearing.

Vine (*Vitis vinifera*) for those who are strong-willed leaders in their own right. However, when carried to extremes, they can become autocratic, dictatorial, ruthless, and dominating.

Beech (*Fagus sylvatica*) for those who, while desiring perfection, easily find fault with people and things. Critical and intolerant at times, they may fail to see the good within others, overreacting to small annoyances or other people's idiosyncrasies.

Rock Water (*Aqua petra*) for those who are strict and rigid with themselves in their daily living. They are hard masters to themselves, struggling toward some ideal or to set an example for others. This would include strict adherence to a life style or to religious, personal, or social disciplines.

PART II

The cure of the part should not be attempted without treatment of the whole. No attempt should be made to cure the body without the soul, and, if the head and the body are to be healthy, you must begin by curing the mind....For this is the great error of our day in the treatment of the human body, that physicians first separate the soul from the body.

Plato (427-347 B.C.) *Charmides*

Rescue Remedy:
Bach's Emergency Medicine

R escue Remedy was named by Dr. Bach for its calming and stabilizing effect on the emotions during a crisis.

The following chapter describes the composition of Rescue Remedy, its historical origin, its scope of application, and use.

Rescue Remedy is made up of the following five Bach Flower Remedies.

*Impatiens (*Impatiens glandulifera*) for the impatience, irritability, and agitation often accompanying stress. This may sometimes result in muscle tension and pain.

*Clematis (*Clematis vitalba*) for unconsciousness, spaciness, faintness, and out-of-the-body sensations, which often accompany trauma.

*Rock Rose (*Helianthemum nummularium*) for terror, panic, hysteria, and great fear.

Cherry Plum (*Prunus cerasifera*) for fear of losing mental or physical control.

Star of Bethlehem (*Ornithogalum umbellatum*) for trauma, both mental and physical.

Dr. Bach first used three (Rock Rose, Clematis and Impatiens) of the five ingredients in the Rescue Remedy with two men shipwrecked in a gale off the beach at Cromer on

---

*One of the original twelve healers.

the Norfolk coast of England, where Bach did much of his work. The men had lashed themselves to the mast of their wrecked barge and survived for five hours in a howling gale before a lifeboat could reach them. The younger man was almost frozen, delirious, and foaming at the mouth. Dr. Bach ran into the water, meeting the rescuers, and began to apply these remedies to the man's lips. Even before the sailor could be stripped of his wet clothes and wrapped in a blanket, his relief became apparent as he sat up and began conversing. After a few days of hospital rest, he had recovered completely. Bach later combined the remedies Cherry Plum and Star of Bethlehem, for their particular virtues, to the first three remedies, thereby completing the formula we know today as the Rescue Remedy.

Using the Rescue Remedy

Rescue Remedy is available in both liquid concentrate and cream form. It can be used alone or in combination with any other of the Bach Flower Remedies. In addition, it has been deemed effective when used with other remedial agents and various therapeutic modalities such as chiropractic, dentistry, and massage. As reported in the case studies, Rescue Remedy has been shown to be non-toxic, non-habit-forming, and free from side effects. However, it should be noted that **Rescue Remedy is not meant to be a panacea or a substitute for emergency medical treatment.** In serious situations such as accidents, a doctor or ambulance should be called immediately. Many times during emergencies, however, before qualified medical assistance can arrive, the sufferer may experience a variety of emotional and psychological disturbances. These can include fear, panic, severe mental stress, and tension. Rescue Remedy used during this critical period, has been reported to significantly assist in stabilizing the victim emotionally until help arrives.

Additionally, Rescue Remedy is reported to have a positive calming and stabilizing effect in a broad range of stressful situations including nervousness, anxiety, and the stress arising from bereavement, great fright, hysteria, anguish, and desperation.

Even minor incidents that cause stress, such as arguments, exams, speeches, and job interviews, are made easier with Rescue Remedy.

Application

1. Place four drops of Rescue Remedy concentrate into a quarter glass of liquid.

2. Sip every three to five minutes or as often as necessary. Hold in mouth a moment before swallowing.

If water or other beverages are not available:

1. Rescue Remedy may be taken directly from the concentrate bottle (dilute if alcohol-sensitive) by placing four drops under the tongue. Drops may also be added to a spoonful of water if desired.

2. Hold liquid in mouth a moment before swallowing.

For those unable to drink:

• Rub the remedy directly from the concentrate bottle on the lips, behind the ears, or on the wrists.

NOTE: Rescue Remedy, as with all Bach Flower Remedies, assists in restoring emotional balance. Once balance is achieved, the need for and the effect of the remedy diminishes. Therefore, no discernible effect will be noticed if a person takes Rescue Remedy when he is not distressed.

External Use

Rescue Remedy cream is prepared in a neutral, homoeopathic, non-allergenic and non-abrasive cream base. It has been reported extremely effective when applied to bruises, bumps, sprains, scratches, hemorrhoids, minor burns, insect bites, and minor inflammations. It has also been reported useful in healing minor cuts when applied directly. Using the liquid Rescue Remedy orally, in conjunction with Rescue Remedy cream, will help ease emotional upset associated with any of the above conditions. **If Rescue Remedy cream is unavailable the liquid may also be applied externally with equal effectiveness, especially for painful blows, minor burns, sprains, etc.** In addition, the cream rubbed on is said to be effective in reducing acute muscle stiffness. To use:

- Apply by smoothing gently into the affected area, or by applying on a piece of gauze to wounds or abrasions. Use as often as required, continuing applications for a short time even after the condition has improved.

Veterinary Use

Mix four drops of Rescue Remedy in an animal's drinking water or food. In the case of large animals such as cows and horses, ten drops to a bucket of water have been reported to be greatly beneficial in those conditions calling for the use of Rescue Remedy. Examples include accidents, pre- and postsurgical conditions, and birthings. If an animal is traumatized or unconscious, Rescue Remedy may be used directly from the concentrate bottle or diluted in a small glass of water and rubbed on and in the mouth or beak, behind the ears, or on other soft points of the body.

Plant Use

Researchers, such as Cleve Backster, as reported in the book *The Secret Life of Plants,* by Peter Tompkins and Christopher Bird (New York: Harper & Row, 1973), have shown plants to be affected by environmental stimuli, as well as interrelations between them and other forms of life. It comes as no surprise, then, that the Rescue Remedy has also been used to ease trauma in transplanted botanicals, drooping flowers, and injured trees. Ten drops in a watering can or sprayer, applied regularly for a day or two, will help reduce the very real shock that plants can experience and help revitalize them. In the vegetable garden, the addition of five to ten drops in the water at planting time or at any other point in the growing season has been reported of benefit to crops.

Case Studies: Professional and Consumer Use

The following case studies have been meticulously compiled and researched by the author over a three-year period. Because of the highly personal and sensitive nature of these accounts, measures were taken to protect the privacy of individual contributors using the Rescue Remedy at home. This was accomplished by listing only their city, state, or country in place of personal names. Additionally, personal consumer reports were edited when necessary, for grammatical consistency and clarity; still remaining true to the intent and experience originally described. Subsequently, quotation marks have not been included in any of the personal consumer case reports.

Wherever cases involving the professional use of Rescue Remedy appear, names of the contributing doctors or health care professionals are included, along with the names of their cities, states, or countries reported to us at the time.

All professional testimonies and case studies appear here with the full knowledge and written consent of the contributing doctors and health practitioners. Except for minor grammatical changes, indicated by editors brackets[ ] these testimonies and case studies appear verbatim.

All case studies included in this book were obtained through personal interviews, questionnaires, and letters from contributors in the United States and abroad. In addition, the Bach Centre's newsletter files were consulted and used.

NOTE: Rescue Remedy is not meant to take the place of emergency medical treatment. In all instances requiring proper medical attention, a competent physician should be notified at once.

Cases where only the name of a country was available, were primarily extracted from published Bach Centre newsletters.

It should be noted that while many of the case studies included here are impressive, they are meant only to serve as a reference—not to sensationalize or make unfounded claims of efficacy for the Rescue Remedy.

From the hundreds of reports available, every effort was made to present the reader a balanced representation of cases. Though great attention was paid to categorizing these case studies, some overlapping occurs.

Professional Testimonies

The following is a compilation of professional reports on the use of Rescue Remedy both in the United States and abroad. Highly valued, Rescue Remedy is clearly an important healing tool, used by physicians as well as by many other health care professionals worldwide.

All testimonies, as well as professional case studies and consumer reports appear in arbitrary order in their respective sections and categories.

Professional use and reports on Rescue Remedy are prolific; though seeming extensive, the statements presented here represent only a fraction of its overall use.

Physicians practicing in the United Kingdom often have numerous titles and credentials; wherever these references appear in the text, the style of the British Medical Journal was followed, whereby only the two highest medical degrees are listed. While there are many medical doctors (MD's) practicing in the United Kingdom, many British physicians have distinguishing credentials other than MD. Ninety-eight percent of the British testimonials and case studies included in this book were written by practicing physicians of one degree or another. Since all professional credentials are abbreviated, the following glossary has been included to clarify their meaning.

AFOM	—Associate Faculty Occupational Medicine (UK)
BAc	—Bachelor of Acupuncture (UK)
BAO	—Bachelor of the Art of Obstetrics (UK)
BCh	—Bachelor of Surgery (UK)
BChir	—Bachelor of Surgery (UK)
BS	—Bachelor of Surgery (UK)
BVetMed	—Bachelor of Veterinary Medicine (UK)
CA	—Certified Acupuncturist (USA)
ChB	—Bachelor of Surgery (UK)
DC	—Doctor of Chiropractic (USA & UK)
DCH	—Diploma in Child Health (UK)
DDS	—Doctor of Dental Surgery (USA & UK)
DM	—Doctor of Medicine (same as MD) (UK)
DN	—Doctor of Naprapathy (USA)
DPH	—Diploma in Public Health (UK)
DO	—Doctor of Osteopathy (Different Lic.Requirements in USA & UK)
DObst RCOG	—Diploma Royal College Obstetricians and Gynaecologists (UK)
DVM	—Doctor of Veterinary Medicine (USA)
DVSM	—Doctor of Veterinary Surgery and Medicine (UK)
FRCP	—Fellow Royal College of Physicians (UK)
LRCP	—Licentiate Royal College of Physicians (UK)
LRCS	—Licentiate Royal College of Surgeons (UK)
MB	—Bachelor of Medicine (UK)
MD	—Medical Doctor (USA & UK)
MFHom	—Member Faculty of Homoeopathy (UK)
MLCO	—Member London College of Osteopathy (UK)
MRCP	—Member Royal College of Physicians (UK)
MRCGP	—Member Royal College of General Practitioners (UK)
MRCS	—Member Royal College of Surgeons (UK)
MRCVS	—Member Royal College of Veterinary Surgeons (UK)
ND	—Naturopathic Doctor (USA & UK)
PhD	—Doctor of Philosophy (USA & UK)
(UK)	—United Kingdom
(USA)	—United States of America

"As a healer I choose to use only those systems of healing that prove themselves to be effective in my work. It is well known by all people of knowledge that disease begins on a much deeper level than the physical. This, great men have taught for thousands of years. One such man in our time was the English physician and scientist Dr. Edward Bach, who not only taught this truth but became a great herbalist, discovering those special plants and healing waters which work on this deepest of levels. His system is respected and known as the Bach Flower Remedies.

"I have used these Bach remedies and the combination Rescue Remedy for over eight years and have found them to be gentle but powerful healing medicines. Emotional upsets ranging from the deepest fear to pride and jealousy are gently resolved within and scattered like the dust in a wind. We would not want to be without the Rescue Remedy for emergencies. Hysteria and grief, or the trauma resulting from accidents, are quickly stabilized by the oral administration of Rescue Remedy and, when required, the topical use of the cream. It will even soothe the minor upsets of the child who is crying and irritable.

"Though there are many healing tools for good, Dr. Bach's combination, Rescue Remedy, is one of the finest for emergencies and trauma. I strongly encourage all people, those who have pets and range animals, and especially those with children, to keep the Rescue Remedy at home or on their person, for emergencies happen when they are least expected."

Sun Bear, medicine chief,
Bear Tribe, Spokane, Washington

"I use the Bach remedies extensively in my practice. They have proven very helpful with patients wishing to clarify issues in their minds, develop their potential, and see the positive qualities within themselves.

"Rescue Remedy is very useful in calming children who are having temper tantrums, and it alleviates their apprehension when they have to get shots. I also use it with good results for the fears and anxieties that patients experience in my office.

"I keep Rescue Remedy in my car, in my house, and in every room of my office. I even take it myself when I have a hard schedule."

G.S. Khalsa, MD,
Lathrup Village, Michigan

"The Bach Flower Remedies are underused in practice and are long overdue to be researched. I have found them extremely useful in a large number of cases. I would use Rescue Remedy without hesitation in any acute situation in addition to any other appropriate measure indicated by the circumstance."

Julian Kenyon, MD, director,
Center for Alternative Therapies,
Southampton, England

"In my experiences at the Old London Homoeopathic Hospital, now the Royal London Homoeopathic Hospital, I have found Rescue Remedy and the Bach Flower Remedy, Star of Bethlehem to be of great value."

Margery G. Blackie, MD,
former Physician to
Her Majesty Queen Elizabeth II;
author of *The Patient: Not the Cure*
(London: Macdonald & Janes, 1979;
also published in the USA by
Woodbridge Press, 1978)

"In my practice, I treat the whole person but specialize in skin and allergic diseases. I have seen many older, despondent patients sit around and scratch themselves almost raw. With kindness, patience, and the use of the Bach remedies, especially Rescue Remedy, many of these people have been remarkably helped without the use of lotions and drugs."

James Q. Gant Jr., MD,
Washington, D.C.

"I always carry Rescue Remedy in my purse. You never know when an emergency may arise and you will need it."

Maesimund Panos, MD,
Tipp City, Ohio;
former president, National Center for
Homeopathy, Washington, D.C.;
co-author of *Homeopathic Medicine at Home*
(Los Angeles, California: Tarcher, 1981)

"I have used the Bach Flower Remedies for over thirty years and have found them, especially the Rescue Remedy, to be of great value in my practice. I recommend that everybody carry the Rescue Remedy, as one never knows when it may be needed in an emergency. Dr. Bach made a great contribution to the world; he was indeed an absolute medical genius. The Bach Flower Remedies are a missing key to the new medicine of the future."

Aubrey Westlake, MB, BChir,
Fordingbridge, Hampshire, England;
president of The Psionic Medicine Society;
author of *The Pattern of Health*
(London: Shambhala Press, 1961)

"The Rescue Remedy is a very useful first aid remedy when used for acute crises, anxieties, and fears. I have often been surprised at the good results it has achieved when other measures have failed. I consider the Bach Flower Remedies a major contribution to medicine."

Robin G. Gibson, FRCP, DCH,
consultant physician to the
Glasgow Homoeopathic Hospital,
Glasgow, Scotland

"I have used the Rescue Remedy for myself and my family, as I prefer this type of 'trial' prior to deciding if a treatment is appropriate for my professional use. I have found Rescue Remedy extremely effective in relieving a wide variety of acute emotional stresses. I have also found the Rescue Remedy cream equally valuable when applied topically to bruises, bumps, sprains, swellings, etc."

Richard E. Behymer, MD,
Camptonville, California

"I would like to say how marvelous the Rescue Remedy is, both in cream and liquid form. I always carry them both with me. It never ceases to amaze me how well they work. I recommend it to many of my patients and am always hearing of its good results."

Nicola M. Hall, principal,
The Bayly School of Reflexology,
Worcester, England

"I have had amazing results, both with the individual Bach Flower Remedies and especially with Rescue Remedy. I've seen the Rescue Remedy used on people who have had accidents as well as other traumatic experiences. It works almost instantly to calm them down, and when either the Rescue Remedy liquid or cream is applied directly on the affected area, it quickly reduces any swelling or trauma there."

Eugene C. Watkins, ND,
Southfield, Michigan

"I find the Bach Flower Remedies very effective in treating anxiety, depression, mental upsets, and emotional problems. I use them in combination with other homoeopathic medicines and dietary modifications when called for, especially in cases of hyperactivity in children."

S.J.L. Mount, MB, MRCP,
former consultant to the
Royal London Homoeopathic Hospital,
London, England; medical consultant to the
London Natural Health Clinic, London, England;
author of *The Food and Health of Western Man*
(New York: John Wiley and Son, 1971)

"In my practice I often use a technique that treats imbalances of the temporal mandibular joint in the jaw. With most people, there is usually tremendous emotional tension stored in this area, and during treatment a patient may bring emotions to a conscious level. One dose of Rescue Remedy usually has an immediate and profound calming effect on them."

Gerald Brady, DC,
St. Paul, Minnesota

"I use the Rescue Remedy frequently, particularly for acute wounds such as cuts, bruises, swellings, etc. It works almost immediately to calm the system and take away nausea, faintness, or hysteria. It is also very useful during acute asthma attacks. The remedy quiets the patient almost immediately. I have also used it for morning sickness in pregnant women and in many cases of animal injury, especially with birds that fly into glass doors or windows. However, it should not be counted on as the only means of treatment, but as an aid to remove panic and trauma, giving the physician time to prepare for more specific procedures."

James E. Williams, CA,
DelMar, California

"I use quite a lot of Rescue Remedy for myself and my patients. Anyone who uses it while under pressure and stress will find that it works far better than any tranquillizer."

Elizabeth Ogden, LRCPI, LRCSI,
Dublin, Ireland

"In my experience I have seen positive results from the use of the Bach Flower Remedies, including Rescue Remedy, and feel that they definitely merit further investigation."

Jonathan Shore, MD,
Mill Valley, California

"We use a great deal of Rescue Remedy, both the liquid and cream, and find that the liquid, taken internally, helps to reduce emotional upsets, while the cream hastens the healing of conditions ranging from cuts to scalds; we also massage the cream into painful joints to alleviate discomfort. We find all the Bach remedies, especially the Rescue Remedy, to be invaluable in our work here, and would not want to be without them."

Beryl James, physical therapist,
The Roy Morris Clinic,
Oswestry and Wigan, England

"I am a volunteer in a local hospice program [a place where terminally ill people can go to spend their last days, without the use of life-support systems], and Rescue Remedy really comes in handy for the families I deal with. I give it to people who are going through emotional or physical difficulties, and it always makes them feel better."

B.J.D.,
San Antonio, Texas

"I use the Bach Flower Remedies quite extensively in my practice. Most patients tell me that within the first few days of taking the remedies they feel a greater sense of emotional balance. I find the Rescue Remedy as useful with my own family as with my patients. Any time there is a trauma, it will often calm a person down to the point where nothing else is needed. Rescue Remedy liquid is also extremely useful in dealing with grief, emotional upset, or when one is nervous or off-center.

"I have also used the Rescue Remedy cream for sprains, muscle strains, bruises, bumps, and minor burns and find it to be remarkably effective in reducing the pain, swelling, and inflammation of these conditions. I recommend that Rescue Remedy be in everyone's first aid kit. It's easy to use, inexpensive and produces no toxic side effects."

Kirby Hotchner, DO,
Des Moines, Iowa

"The most useful treatment for trauma that I know is Dr. Bach's Rescue Remedy. It is [an] invaluable first aid (along with proper medical treatment) for the victims of accidents, [and for] injuries [and] fright—especially in children—or [in] sudden bad news. The liquid comes in a handy little dropper bottle which [practically] lives in my bag. I also keep a bottle in my car [for similar situations]."

Barbara Griggs, London, England;
author of *The Home Herbal: A Handbook of Simple Remedies* (London: Pan, 1983; originally published by Jill Norman & Hobhouse, Ltd., 1982); and *Green Pharmacy: A History of Herbal Medicine* (London: Jill Norman & Hobhouse Ltd., 1981; also published by Viking Press, New York, 1981)

"I recommend that Rescue Remedy be kept on hand especially during childbirth, both for the mother and those attending. I have found it extremely valuable for relieving tension in a crisis. Rescue Remedy is an absolute must, used in childbirth, especially if there's a long labour or if forceps are used. In addition, Rescue Remedy can also be used for the newborn to assist with the trauma of the birth experience. It can be rubbed on the wrists, temples, scalp, or navel area."

Lorraine Taylor, BAc,
Oxford,England

"I use the Rescue Remedy as an alternative to prescribing Valium. It sometimes proves to be of invaluable assistance."

D. McGavin, MRCGP, DCH,
Maidstone, Kent, England

"Of the various remedies and techniques used in this office, none are more valued and respected than the Bach remedies."

Nicholas Ashfield, DC,
Toronto, Canada

45

"I find the Rescue Remedy very useful in calming and assisting patients, particularly during the transitional effects of strong treatment procedures. We often use Rescue Remedy during extensive cranial work and in other mechanical adjustments.

"I feel that Rescue Remedy helps to minimize the physiological, mental, and emotional stress that often accompanies manipulative procedures. It is an important adjunct for the doctor as well as facilitating the patient's healing response."

Joseph Unger Jr., DC,
St. Louis, Missouri

"I use Rescue Remedy with elderly patients who live alone; it seems to assist them in handling their lives more effectively. When these patients face a task they must struggle with, Rescue Remedy calms and stabilizes them quite effectively. I recommend Rescue Remedy for use in the later years and to calm and stabilize in all forms of stress."

Hilda Saenz de Deas, BAc,
Oxford, England

"I have used the Bach Flower Remedies in my clinical practice for over twenty-five years and have had very good results, especially in conjunction with other modalities. In raising my own family of four boys, my wife and I found that certain remedies were very helpful indeed."

Brian K. Youngs, ND, DO,
Harrow, England

"I have used the Bach remedies regularly for over ten years, both personally and with patients. They have certainly proven their healing powers in accidents and for functional ailments and skin conditions."

K.J. Noblett, MB, ChB,
Blackpool, England

"I have used Rescue Remedy extensively in my chiropractic work, especially with patients in acute pain as a result of emotional distress. It helps amazingly in enabling patients to focus, listen to instructions, and relax— allowing the healing process to evolve. I have used [Rescue Remedy] personally in times of emotional crisis and have given it to my dog when she has been sick, always with positive results. It definitely allows for a calming and recentering, and I would be lost without it.

"Rescue Remedy cream has also been quite helpful in speeding the healing of abrasions and contusions as well as in relieving the joint pain of arthritis and bursitis in the acute phases. I use it automatically with my other modalities, like ultrasound and galvanic currents, in order to work it into the deeper tissues."

Barbara Dorf, DC,
Culver City, California

"I have been using the Bach Flower Remedies, including Rescue Remedy, for quite some years. I find them to be of remarkable service in stabilizing emotional upset during most traumatic situations. In our applied kinesiological testing, we have found the remedies to correct not just one, but three muscles (our criteria for their use), allowing a person to be more relaxed and receptive to other corrective procedures."

George Goodheart, DC,
Detroit, Michigan;
pioneer and developer of applied kinesiology;
author of numerous articles and text books
in the field of applied kinesiology

"I have used the Bach Flower Remedies, and the Rescue Remedy, [for] over thirty years, mostly for stress and emotional problems, with excellent results. A high percentage of patients, once they return to the office, report they are able to handle stress with much greater ease."

Harold J. Wilson, MD,
Columbus, Ohio

47

"In approximately ninety percent of the patients I've used the Bach Flower Remedies with, there has been a dramatic shift within a month in their basic attitudes toward themselves and others. This [shift] has resulted in greater self-acceptance and the realization that they are responsible for, and have control over, their own lives.

"I always use the Rescue Remedy when there's been any kind of accident that has resulted in emotional, psychological, or physical trauma. Following this, my patients have found that within a few hours, and most always within a few days, they have begun shaking off the effects of the accident."

Jeff Migdow, MD,
Kripalu Center, Lenox, Massachusetts

"The Bach Flower Remedies have been an integral part of my practice for the last two years, and the clinical results I have seen range from good to remarkable."

Louis I. Berlin, DC,
Atlanta, Georgia

"If I had to pick only one set of remedies of all the many systems of healing in the world, I would choose the Bach Flower Remedies alone. I believe these remedies to be many decades ahead of their time, and I am sure we will see a much more extensive use of them by doctors and the public alike. They have in some way a subtle effect on the inner self, often evinced quickly, whereas psychotherapy would have taken years, if ever, to achieve the same positive change."

C.K. Munro, MB, BAO,
Londonderry, Northern Ireland

"In my experience, the Bach Flower Remedies [chosen for the underlying emotional stress] have been helpful in classroom phobia, agoraphobia, sexual phobia, and premature ejaculation. The Rescue Remedy is good to start with for any anxiety, acute stress, and acute mental states. I've also seen Rescue Remedy alleviate tension in youngsters, especially before they take driving and classroom exams.

"I regard the Bach medicines as an essential extension of homoeopathic practice. One reason for this is that, unlike other homoeopathic medicines, they may be repeated, if necessary, with impunity. I highly recommend that every family have a bottle of Rescue Remedy, one for the home and another to be carried in their automobile for road emergencies."

Anthony D. Fox, MRCGP, DCH
Barton-on-Sea, England

"...I have used Rescue Remedy in many childbirth cases, always with satisfactory results. In some cases, I have recommended Rescue Remedy to women who were very nervous and uneasy about having natural childbirth. I suggested that they take it whenever they felt anxious during the days approaching delivery. Many did this and later shared with me how remarkably easy the births were. It is the single most important tool I carry in my treatment bag."

Marsha Woolf, ND,
Newton Corner, Massachusetts and
Providence, Rhode Island

"I have been using the Bach Flower Remedies for about seven years now and cannot imagine practicing without them. They continue to play an important and growing role, and sometimes their effects are astounding. Many patients tell me how remarkably positive their changes are after they begin using the remedies.

"I constantly use the Rescue Remedy in situations ranging from simple emotional upsets to heavy emotional trauma, with remarkable results. I also use the Rescue Remedy cream to massage onto bruises, bumps, tension headaches, and acute muscle and spinal pains with equally exceptional results."

Mark Smith, DC,
Vienna, Virginia

"I have had positive experiences with the Bach Flower Remedies. For example, I've treated a number of patients who have had a variety of gastrointestinal disorders, many of them long- standing. These individuals were helped dramatically by the Bach Flower Remedies. Though the remedies are not used specifically for physical ailments, in most cases where there is an underlying emotional problem, as there is in most [simple] gastrointestinal dysfunctions, we generally get excellent results."

Catherine Smith, MD,
Abingdon, Virginia

"I use the Bach Flower Remedies and Rescue Remedy in ninety percent of my practice, both before and after most dental procedures. I especially find them effective after surgery and reconstructive work and in easing the patients' trauma and stabilizing their condition.

"I find the Bach remedies and Rescue Remedy to be excellent for alleviating apprehension, both in adults and children, and especially for those suffering from temporal mandibular joint (TMJ) dysfunction. Many TMJ conditions are related to emotional imbalance, with fear a key element. There is not an emotionally based condition I have come across in my practice that the Bach Flower Remedies have not in some way been able to help. I wish that more dentists knew about the gentle yet consistently positive effects that the Bach remedies and Rescue Remedy have proven in my practice. If they did, they would not hesitate to use them themselves."

Maurice Tischler, DDS,
Woodstock, New York

"I have been using the Bach Flower Remedies for ten years as a part of my general medical practice. I have prescribed these remedies to well over two thousand patients and have found them to be of immense help in overcoming the negative emotional and mental states that seem to afflict us all.

"There is no doubt that the Bach remedies are capable of restoring the patient to emotional balance. The remedies, particularly the Rescue Remedy, are excellent in relieving acute states of distress resulting from sudden changes or catastrophes. The remedies also remove fear and anger and assist one in developing a more positive direction in life.

"I personally carry a bottle of Rescue Remedy with me at all times, and have used it during numerous emergencies, with immediate results. When grief occurs in the home, as from the loss of a dear one, there is no need for a potent sedative. Even here, Rescue Remedy proves extremely safe and effective.

"As a concerned physician, it is my hope that one day the Bach remedies will be a part of every doctor's healing practice."

Abram Ber, MD,
Phoenix, Arizona

"I have used the Bach remedies for nearly twenty years and have taken hundreds of patients off drugs (antidepressants, sedatives, tranquillizers) through their use. I use the remedies regularly at the Cancer Help Centre in Bristol, England, and find them to be most helpful in alleviating the emotional and psychological stress many of these patients experience. The remedies have also helped me personally through many family crisis situations as well. They are therapeutic agents I would never be without."

Alec Forbes, MD, FRCP,
formerly member, Expert Advisory Panel on
Traditional Medicine, World Health
Organization; medical director, Bristol Cancer
Help Centre, Bristol, England; author of
The Bristol Diet: Get Well and Eating Plan
(London: Century, 1984)

"I use the Rescue Remedy liquid concentrate internally, for calming emotional upset; and the liquid concentrate or cream externally, applied to lacerations or cuts, [this] seems to speed up the healing process. Often these wounds do not need to be sutured. A few drops of the remedy or application of the cream is all it takes. I find Rescue Remedy to be a very effective and powerful healing tool."

Joe D. Goldstrich, MD,
former medical director,
Pritikin Longevity Center,
Santa Monica, California;
author of *The Best Chance Diet*
(Atlanta: Humanics, 1982)

"In my former capacity as Dr. Margery Blackie's assistant [former physician to Her Majesty Queen Elizabeth II], both Dr. Blackie and I used the Rescue Remedy with very good results to treat people under stress. I have found it quite effective, without a doubt."

Charles K. Elliott, MB, BCh,
MFHom, MRCGP, MLCO, AFOM RCP,
London: Former Physician to Her Majesty Queen Elizabeth II;
co-editor of *Classical Homoeopathy* (Beaconsfield:
Beaconsfield Publishers Ltd., 1986)

"I have been using the Bach Flower Remedies primarily for insomnia, depression, and other nervous disorders and have found them to be extremely effective. I have found the Bach remedies, especially Rescue Remedy, to be valuable adjuncts to my homoeopathic practice."

Andrew H. Lockie, MRCGP, DObst RCOG,
Guildford, England

"I always keep a bottle of Rescue Remedy in my desk drawer for personal use and for friends and office staff, whenever there is any traumatic emotional or physical incident."

Richard Crews, MD, president,
Columbia Pacific University,
Mill Valley, California

"The Bach Flower Remedies are extremely sophisticated in their action. They are unusually gentle yet at the same time profoundly potent.... I use the Bach Flower Remedies almost exclusively instead of tranquilizers and psychotropics, and I get excellent results. In many cases, they alleviate the problem when all else has failed."

J. Herbert Fill, MD, psychiatrist,
New York City, New York; former
New York City Commissioner of Mental Health;
author of *Mental Breakdown of a Nation*
(New York: Franklin Watts, 1974)

Emergencies: Professional and Consumer Use

The following section consists of emergency cases involving the professional and consumer use of Rescue Remedy. Emergencies are those situations that generally require immediate first aid or assistance.

Rescue Remedy is not meant to be a panacea or a substitute for emergency medical treatment. In all emergencies requiring medical attention, an ambulance or licensed physician should be called immediately.

Emergencies: Professional Use

"Recently, while traveling on a ship, I was called to treat a woman who wouldn't come out of her cabin. She was having an emotional crisis and was depressed and crying, saying she just couldn't face things. I administered a dose of Rescue Remedy and was then called away. One hour later, the woman approached me on deck, explaining how remarkably effective the remedy was in helping her overcome her terrible ordeal."

Alec Forbes, MD, FRCP,
Bristol, England

"We had just given a local anesthetic injection to a patient who told us that he didn't like Novocaine. Within a minute he began to shake and turn pale, apprehensive, and sweaty; he looked as though he were going to faint. I reached for the oxygen mask and the ammonia, but before I could get them to the patient my assistant had put four drops of Rescue Remedy liquid into the patient's half-open mouth. Instantly, he stopped shaking, his color returned, and he opened his eyes. He was completely recovered! Nothing but Rescue Remedy was used."

Steve Ross, DDS,
Wappinger Falls, New York

"A dentist friend and I were hiking in the woods when he was bitten by close to a hundred fire ants, over his arm and hands. These are extremely painful, itchy bites for most people, and my friend had been suffering for forty-five minutes before we were able to return to our cabin where I had some Rescue Remedy. If I had had the Rescue Remedy cream I would have used it, but since I didn't, I placed about ten to fifteen drops of Rescue Remedy liquid into a cup of spring water and applied this mixture to the bitten areas. Fire ant bites usually cause irritation to people for one to three days, or more. To our amazement, within a short time almost all itching, swelling, and inflammation ceased."

J. Hunter Lilly, ND, PhD,
Winter Haven, Florida

"During the first five days of an ocean voyage to Saudi Arabia, I was informed that a woman passenger was suffering from seasickness. I suggested to her husband that Rescue Remedy would be helpful for her. I gave him a bottle, instructing him to administer a dose under his wife's tongue every five minutes. Within the hour there was a marked improvement, and the next morning the woman was up and about, walking on deck. She had no recurrence of seasickness during the rest of the journey."

Ahmaed bin Embun, health practitioner,
Singapore, Malaysia

"I do chiropractic work with brain-damaged children, and many have responded well to Rescue Remedy. In several instances, these children were screaming and out of control when they came in for treatment. I administered a few drops of Rescue Remedy under their tongues, and their behavior improved immediately, like throwing a switch. It is quite amazing to watch."

Terry Franks, DC,
Burnsville, Minnesota

"One day, one of my patients who suffers from bouts of alcoholism came to see me. She was shaking, delirious, and completely out of control. During our two-hour session, I gave her repeated doses of liquid Rescue Remedy directly under her tongue. After the second dose, her tremors stopped, [and] she became increasingly coherent and able to function during the remaining part of the session. I gave her the rest of the bottle to take daily, which she did. Later that week at our next appointment, she said she felt better, and indeed she looked brighter than I had seen her look in a long time."

Joe Ann Cain, psychotherapist,
Encino, California

Emergencies: Consumer Use

I am a member of the Sri Chinmoy Marathon Team. After sixteen miles into a marathon, I usually become tired, irritable, and lightheaded. In my squirt bottle I carry a dilution of Rescue Remedy and water, which I usually drink during the last ten miles. It gives me energy and alleviates mental weariness and depression.

While running, I also apply Rescue Remedy cream to my knees to alleviate recurring pain, and I rub it on my calf muscles and ham strings, to relieve the muscle tightness I experience during the course of the race.

During my last race, I gave some Rescue Remedy cream to a friend who was also having knee pain midway through the race. A month before, he had had the same pain, and it had forced him to quit. This time, a few minutes after using the cream, he said his knee was fine. Following the race, he said he never would have finished if he hadn't used the Rescue Remedy.

Jamaica, New York

One day my sister and her son were digging a hole for a fence post. Accidentally she caught her leg in the equipment and ended up with a compound fracture. She quickly called out to her other son to bring the Rescue Remedy which was kept for emergencies. During the next five minutes, she promptly took repeated doses. The remedy immediately alleviated the worst effects of the trauma so that my sister was able to calmly organize her trip to the hospital.

Loudonville, New York

My oldest son cut his left thumb severely. Shortly after he became pale, dizzy, and nauseated, I gave him Rescue Remedy liquid orally and also applied it to the thumb fullstrength and wrapped the finger with gauze. Within a short time my son's color returned, and he felt fine. No stitches were needed. He even complained afterwards about not having a scar to show for the cut.

Montgomery, Texas

I find the Rescue Remedy cream invaluable here in the tropical climate of Singapore, since cuts, wounds, or bruises sometimes take months to heal. The cream clears up a cut or bruise in one to two days.

Singapore, Malaysia

I used Rescue Remedy to counter my reaction to a skin cream, which had caused my eyes to become puffy and my face to become swollen and discolored. Hoping for relief, I first tried using a cold washcloth over my face; I also spent a lot of time in bed, dozing. In a couple of days, the redness and swelling abated, but my skin was scaly and itchy, as if I had a bad sunburn.

Then someone gave me some liquid Rescue Remedy, which I applied to my face several times. By evening I noticed a visible improvement, although I was still very anxious. The next morning, the improvement was more pronounced. I continued to apply the remedy every half-hour; at the end of the day not only was my anxiety gone, but I could see that my face was going to be all right.

Los Angeles, California

My mother recently slipped on a patch of ice in a parking lot, striking her head just above the temple, against the corner of a car. She blacked out completely for several seconds, then seemed to regain consciousness but was unable to say her name or respond in any way. She was very pale, as though in shock. I got her into the car, covered her with a blanket, and then gave her several drops of Rescue Remedy liquid which I always carry.

The effect was immediate. She became more conscious and asked for another dose. She was able to respond to questions, and although she still felt cold, her condition began to stabilize. Not surprisingly, she had a very bad headache. Seeing that she was okay, I took her home, where she soaked in a hot bath laced with a dropper full of Rescue Remedy. The next day her headache was almost gone, and she was able to go to work. Besides a chiropractic adjustment, no further treatment was needed.*

Ballston Lake, New York

---

*Blows to the head may result in a fracture or other complications, in all conditions requiring medical attention a physician should be consulted immediately.

One month ago, after carelessly touching a hot oven and burning myself, I immediately plunged my scorched hand into a jar of Rescue Remedy cream. Additionally, I took the liquid remedy as I massaged the cream onto the burned area. The next day I put in a twelve-hour shift at the hospital where I work as a nurse. My hands were constantly in and out of water, but there was no tenderness, just a slight redness. I continued to apply Rescue Remedy to the burned spot, and within one week I could not even see where the burn had been.

Kansas City, Missouri

Quite recently, while doing some work in my home, I hit my thumb with a hammer. The pain was very bad, and a throbbing sensation quickly developed in the thumb. My wife applied Rescue Remedy cream, and within moments the pain and throbbing were almost gone. It was quite remarkable.

We also use the Rescue Remedy with our children; it always seems to bring relief and comfort to them following their usual mishaps.

Kent, England

Our six-month-old baby had an injury on the foreskin of his penis—a painful place! He cried every time he urinated. We decided to try the Rescue Remedy and gave him four drops in some water orally, at the same time applying the Rescue Remedy cream to the injury. Our son fell into a sound and peaceful sleep almost immediately. After a few more applications over the next two days, the injury healed completely.

East Hampton, New York

When my four-year-old grandchild was bitten behind the ear by a dog, I immediately gave the child and his mother some Rescue Remedy, since they were both badly shaken. They became visibly calm within moments as preparations for emergency care were being made.

Tipp City, Ohio

Last summer, I was cutting hedges when a large branch flew up in my face, pushing my upper tooth through a half-inch of my lower lip, which started bleeding quite a bit. I held open the wound while my husband put two drops of full-strength Rescue Remedy on it. The bleeding slowed, and after several repeated doses over the next ten minutes it stopped completely. The wound healed in one week. Although I still have a knot in my lip, there is no scar at all.

Hull, Georgia

Preparing for extensive dental surgery, my wife put twenty drops of Rescue Remedy into a glass of water, which she sipped throughout the day before and after her surgery. She did not feel any pain on the day of surgery or on the days following it, nor did she have to take any codeine or aspirin. Sleep came naturally and easily without medication that first night and on the following nights as well. My wife visited the dental surgeon two days after the surgery, and he was astounded at how quickly she had healed.

California

We couldn't get through a summer without the Rescue Remedy ointment. It instantly relieves all types of insect stings.

Washington, D.C.

One night my husband began hemorrhaging. The amount of blood he was vomiting terrified both of us. I gave him some Rescue Remedy as soon as he could keep it down, and he was soon able to walk calmly out of the bathroom. I'm a nurse, so I know that in a situation like this it is imperative that the patient be calmed. I also took a dose of Rescue Remedy myself every ten or fifteen minutes so that I, too, could stay calm. It helped us both very much; I was easily able to get my husband to the emergency room without either of us panicking.

Salisbury, North Carolina

My husband and I went for a long drive last week and were badly shaken up by a near-accident. The car ahead of us stopped very suddenly, and my husband jammed on the brakes just in time. We were very shaken, but we put some drops of the Rescue Remedy on our tongues and were genuinely surprised at the speed which it worked and with which our nervousness disappeared.

California

My friend and I used Rescue Remedy to help ourselves get through a rough climb up Mount Cruach Ardrain, in Scotland. About halfway up, it began to get very cold, and we became extremely exhausted. But we knew we had to continue if we were going to complete the climb. I took a sip from the small bottle of Rescue Remedy that I had in my coat and told my companion that he must take some if we were to make it through the climb. After remaining motionless for a few minutes, we felt sufficiently recovered to complete a final patch, returning safely, in a time that was something of a record. I am quite certain that we would not have completed that climb had it not been for the Rescue Remedy.

Scotland

One of the students in my cooking class cut her finger quite badly. Despite our prompting she refused to go to a doctor, and rather than argue with her, I gave her several drops from my Rescue Remedy bottle. I also had her lie down, and packed her finger with Rescue Remedy cream. This dressing I changed every few hours. The next day, the wound was still open but looking pink and alive. I put on a new dressing and told my student to change it every day. When she showed it to me four days later, I couldn't believe my eyes. The skin had completely healed; there wasn't even a line where it had been cut. Except for the fact that my student's nail was partially gone, there was no sign of the wound.

Amsterdam, Holland

My five-year-old niece fell off her bicycle, tearing skin off her nose, bruising both lips badly, and leaving a front tooth dangling. She screamed with pain as we squirted some Rescue Remedy straight into her mouth and headed for the nearest hospital. The remedy didn't seem to have any effect on her. We gave her a few more doses while waiting for the doctor, but that didn't help. Then it dawned on me that she was spitting blood—and the Rescue Remedy along with it. I immediately started applying the drops behind her ears, and the result was almost instantaneous; my niece stopped screaming and became very cooperative. The look of disbelief on the nurse's face was an absolute study.

In another incident: I gashed my left hand with a can opener, near the joint between the thumb and index finger. The cut was deep and half an inch long. I applied Rescue Remedy cream immediately and then covered my hand with a Band-Aid. Three days later, I found that the cut was healing. I took off the covering on the fifth day, and all that was left was a little scar. This surprised me greatly, since other cuts I've had have always healed extremely slowly.

Victoria, Australia

I burned the inside of my mouth with some very hot food. I have done this before and usually it means agony for at least two days and discomfort for another week or two. This time I rubbed some Rescue Remedy liquid on the burned spot and got relief within seconds. I applied a few more doses; before the day was over, the pain was gone.

London, England

I am physically handicapped from polio and have to walk with crutches. One day, while reaching for a jar on a high shelf, I stretched too far and felt a sudden, violent pain in my middle finger and my wrist. My hand became swollen and remained painful for the next ten days; gradually, it started to become numb.

On the tenth day I saw my doctor, who became concerned because the finger was not only swollen but was starting to curve in. An X-ray, however, showed nothing wrong. Ten days later—my hand still hurting—a friend suggested that I try my Rescue Remedy. I immediately put the cream on the finger, and in about two hours the pain was virtually gone. At this time I again applied more cream, and the next morning the pain and swelling were all but gone. I was able to stretch my hand and fingers normally. It was miraculous. Neither the pain nor the swelling has returned since then.

Herefordshire, England

A young girl of seven with a history of travel sickness was due to go on a holiday to Spain. Her parents, who were worried that they had to journey for three hours in a bus before they reached their destination, had asked if I had any ideas which might help. I suggested the girl use the Rescue Remedy, which I knew to be somewhat effective in these circumstances, along with the Bach remedy Scleranthus. After obtaining a mixture, the mother later told me that she had administered it frequently, both before and during the trip, which proceeded without any mishap whatsoever.

Pinner, England

Whenever I go to San Francisco, I spend half my time soaking my hot, swollen feet, which can't seem to take the constant trudging up and down the steep hills. Last time, however, I obtained and smoothed on the Rescue Remedy cream. The relief was immediate. The heat left my feet at once, and the swelling was reduced shortly thereafter. I continued to use the Rescue Remedy during the rest of my trip and was not bothered with foot problems for the remainder of my stay.

Everett, Washington

After a recent operation, I found it difficult to sleep. I would jerk and toss continuously. My various surgical wounds hurt me, and my brain seemed to be on fire. At one point, my wife gave me a dose of Rescue Remedy; within minutes I quieted down, shortly afterwards falling into a peaceful sleep. It was miraculous.

For two days and nights I was able to lie still. I was so tranquil that the bed clothes were left undisturbed. My mind was at peace, and I lay contentedly, not reading and rarely speaking, just enjoying the peace. By the third day, I was feeling much better and more relaxed. The Bach remedies have helped me tremendously.

USA

I was working on a fluorescent fixture and did not know that someone had forgotten to turn off the power. After grabbing the exposed wires, I got an intense electrical shock. Quite shaken up, I located my bottle of Rescue Remedy and immediately took four drops under my tongue, and several more within the next half-hour. The effects of the shock disappeared within minutes; in a half-hour, I was fine.

Philadelphia, Pennsylvania

Emotional and Psychological Stress: Professional and Consumer Use

The following section consists of cases specifically involving the use of Rescue Remedy for acute emotional and psychological stress.

Emotional and psychological stress includes, but is not limited to anxiety, nervousness, panic, and non-clinical depression. The stress may result from everyday situations, such as visiting a dentist, taking an exam, receiving bad news, or as a result of accidents.

Emotional and Psychological Stress: Professional Use

"I have my patients sip Rescue Remedy in warm water, and it always seems to calm them. One very disturbed patient, who had been on numerous tranquilizers with poor results, described to me his experience with the Rescue Remedy. He stated that Rescue Remedy assisted him in feeling calm and natural, and that it has helped him more than anything else he has ever tried for his nervous condition."

Catherine R. Smith, MD,
Abingdon, Virginia

"I prescribe Rescue Remedy liquid for the sense of internal panic brought on by the diagnosis of cancer. It helps both the patient and family cope more easily with the situation. In the acute phase of bereavement, Rescue Remedy is of definite value. One man whose thirty-two-year-old wife had suddenly died used Rescue Remedy as often as every two hours for many weeks and reported that it always eased his panic and tears.

"Rescue Remedy is excellent as a convalescent tonic, when given [four] drops four times daily, especially for the elderly."

D.T.H. Williams, MB, DObst RCOG,
Chiddingfold, Surrey, England

"Recently, a thirty-seven-year-old woman who was attempting to reduce a sixteen-year dependency on Valium came to see me. Withdrawal was causing her extreme pain in her muscles and joints, and feelings of suffocation. She had already seen several physicians who offered her no relief. I suggested that she try the Bach Rescue Remedy. After five to six doses at fifteen-minute intervals before bedtime, she would sleep quite well. After taking Rescue Remedy for two months, along with counseling during the crisis periods, she has considerably reduced her Valium intake, along with her extreme tension and worry. Now, after further Bach remedies, and counseling, she has been off Valium for over a year."

Doug Lancaster, health practitioner,
Kingston, Ontario, Canada

"An extremely depressed thirty-eight-year-old man came to me for treatment; he was nervous, exhausted, unclean, and was exacerbating his problems by smoking two to three packs of cigarettes a day. He had very low self-esteem worsened by his feeling that he lacked sufficient will-power to control his smoking.

"I gave him one dose of the Rescue Remedy at the beginning of our session, and he sat for three hours without reaching for a cigarette. He said it was the first time in years he hadn't felt like smoking.... [Following our session he later reported] that after taking the Rescue Remedy for just a short time he had begun to develop a much deeper level of self-respect and a greater sense of well-being."

Loretta Hilsher, PhD, DN,
president and founder of
Hyperactive Children's Institute,
Chicago, Illinois

"In our office we have a dropper bottle of Rescue Remedy by each chair. Before any injection or stressful treatment, we give the patient a few drops of the remedy. We explain to the patient that the Rescue Remedy is a helpful, herbal remedy without side effects. We find that the Rescue Remedy helps raise a patient's resistance to stress while at the same time having a great calming influence. We have also adopted a policy of offering a bottle of Rescue Remedy to any patient we refer to an oral surgeon or endodontist."

Jerry Mittelman, DDS,
New York City, New York

"I treated a violinist who had severe stage fright before a performance, feeling that she could not go on. I gave her some Rescue Remedy to take before going on stage, and now she says she actually enjoys performing.

"Another musician, who plays the flute, said she would be tense for two weeks before a performance. For a while, regular doses of Rescue Remedy during the days before a concert made her performances better, her experiences exciting and enjoyable. Now she finds she feels this way with only a few doses prior to a performance."

Jeff Migdow, MD,
Kripalu Center, Lenox, Massachusetts

"A forty-nine-year-old client went through a traumatic divorce, lost his medical practice, and had an emotional and physical breakdown. Though various kinds of treatments have helped him, he still has occasional periods of great emotional agitation. During these episodes, Rescue Remedy improves his ability to function and to continue his work day."

David Winston, nutritional consultant,
Franklin Park, New Jersey

Emotional and Psychological Stress: Consumer Use

A month ago my sister rammed into a Coca-Cola truck with her new VW. I received a call from the hospital and got very nervous and shaky. Immediately I took four drops of Rescue Remedy; very quickly I stopped shaking and was able to turn my attention to my sister's well-being.

Upon my arrival at the hospital I found that my sister had only minor cuts and bruises, but she was emotionally out of control. She was crying and hysterical, worried about our parents' reproaches and her unpaid-for car. I gave her a dose of Rescue Remedy, and she immediately stopped crying. With a deep breath, she relaxed and closed her eyes. Fifteen minutes later, she was anxious again, so I repeated the dose. We continued in this way for an hour and a half.

My sister was released from the hospital, laughing and back to her old self. There was no further need for the remedy after that, and within a week the cuts and bruises were completely healed.

New Mexico

The local bakery burned down a few weeks ago. When my friend, who lives next door to the baker, went in to see if she could help, she found the baker's wife completely traumatized. My friend immediately gave her two or three doses of Rescue Remedy; within a short time, the woman was back to her normal self. Her colour had completely returned, and she has not shown any signs of disturbance since then.

Ascot, England

A Japanese passenger sitting alongside us on a recent airplane trip was obviously terrified. His body was doubled up, his head buried in his hands, his meal untouched. We gave him a few drops of Rescue Remedy in water, and he became relaxed almost immediately; he soon fell asleep. He awoke quite a long time afterwards and ate the next meal quite well. Since he spoke no English, he passed on his grateful thanks for the special 'medicine' via a bilingual hostess.

Australia

I am a registered nurse working in an in-patient mental health facility. I began using Rescue Remedy regularly in February 1981, when I was a medical staff nurse under a great deal of stress. At the time, I was close to a nervous breakdown, suffering from what was eventually diagnosed as adrenal exhaustion and hypoglycemia. For several months, in addition to experiencing insomnia and depression, I would feel extremely anxious and panic-stricken whenever my blood sugar fluctuated. I used the Rescue Remedy many times throughout this period to alleviate my feelings of panic and acute anxiety. It seemed to help stabilize both my mind and my body.

Moreover, I feel that the Rescue Remedy has been invaluable to my personal growth and transformation, helping me gain a greater sense of understanding and self-awareness throughout some rough periods in my life.

Fort Wayne, Indiana

My youngest son, now six-years-old, used to be a thin, emotional child, at times very sweet and reasonable, at other times a holy terror. Touchy and sensitive, he would sometimes have a screaming tantrum over nothing. I ordered some Rescue Remedy liquid, and during the next emotional outburst I gave him four drops. Within five minutes, right before our eyes, he calmed down; his face softened and became rounded, and his demeanor changed so much that my fourteen-year-old son exclaimed, 'If it will do that for him, fix me some.'

Montgomery, Texas

Recently, my three-year-old daughter had to have a front tooth refilled. We gave her a dose of Rescue Remedy just before going to the dentist. Both my wife and the doctor were amazed at how thoroughly calm and cooperative she was throughout the process. Even while the dentist used his drill, my daughter never once winced or cried.

Mount Shasta, California

Recently, two of my friends were in similar situations of breaking up with their mates and experiencing severe emotional trauma. I gave each of them a bottle of Rescue Remedy and told them to take doses daily. Afterwards, they both reported feeling much calmer and told me how the remedy helped them through their difficult periods.

San Diego, California

Some friends of mine made the difficult decision to divorce. When they told their twelve-year-old son, he became extremely upset and frightened. He paced around, shouting and crying, hitting the walls and furniture. His mother gave him several doses of Rescue Remedy, and within twenty minutes he calmed down and was able to discuss the situation rationally.

Albuquerque, New Mexico

A young Indian girl, frightened by her first menstrual period, became deeply disturbed after a friend laughed at her and told her that she should be ashamed of herself for bleeding. For two weeks, the girl sat in a dark corner, crying and refusing to speak to anyone, even her mother. Doctors were treating the girl with vitamins and tranquilizers, but to no avail.

Fortunately, when I arrived on the scene, I had my little bottle of Rescue Remedy, and since the mother had lost faith in the treatment applied so far, she agreed to put the remedy to the test. After the first day, the girl started to speak. On the fourth day after her treatment with Rescue Remedy, the girl was completely well; she did not cry, and she said she no longer felt afraid.

Honduras

Recently, I moved from suburbia to my dream house in the mountains. While moving, I experienced total physical exhaustion, financial disaster, confusion, burnout, and sheer terror, along with an indescribable feeling of elation and joy. Close to a complete nervous breakdown, I began taking Rescue Remedy every five minutes. Within a short time, I noticed a core of strength that I had never realized before. My emotions evened out, and I felt an inner calm and a renewed self-control emerging.

Santa Barbara, California

While I was going through an intensive, five-day personal-growth training program, I began to feel a great deal of stress. Also, since the sessions lasted from early in the morning to late at night, I was getting very little sleep. I decided to try the Rescue Remedy, and after taking regular doses for about three days, I noticed a sense of well-being that surprised me. The remedy definitely helped stabilize my emotions during a particularly rough period in my personal life.

Philadelphia, Pennsylvania

As a rule, I am terribly nervous when I have to speak in public. However, the last lecture I gave was a wonderful experience. I took a dose of the Rescue Remedy upon waking that day, another at midday, and one just before I went on the platform. To my surprise and delight, I had no dry lips or butterflies in my stomach and not a twinge of fear.

Sussex, England

My whole family took Rescue Remedy every day during the first month of mourning after my mother died. It didn't change the quality of our grief, but we were able to deal with it and accept what had happened more easily.

Newton Corner, Massachusetts

Rescue Remedy has come to my rescue many times. However, my favorite Rescue Remedy story happened when my new car was stolen. I was at a gas station, paying for my gas, when two boys jumped into my car and drove off. My purse, along with my Rescue Remedy, was on the front seat. Standing there, feeling shocked and confused, I became outraged when I realized that they had stolen my Rescue Remedy, and I needed it!

Miami, Florida

In addition to being a nutritionist, I'm an actress working on a show right now. I have a highly emotional presentation at the end of scene two, which is immediately followed by a scene showing me four days later, happy and carefree. Rescue Remedy is the only thing that calms me down during the transition between scenes. I exit from one side of the stage, shaking and crying, walk around the other side of the theater, pass my dressing room, take my Rescue Remedy and three deep breaths, and go on in the next scene, relaxed and happy.

New York City, New York

My flatmate and I are both policewomen. We once interviewed a rape victim who had great difficulty recalling specific details of her recent ordeal. My partner gave the woman a dose of Rescue Remedy, and the change was almost immediate. The sequence of events became coherent, an excellent statement was obtained, and the victim's very accurate description of the offender led to his arrest a short time later.

Victoria, Australia

One of my twelve-year-old pupils played the goal position on our school football team. Before each game he would become quite upset and nervous, since the boys would tease him if he let the ball through the goal. Though skeptical, he finally agreed to sip some Rescue Remedy two hours before our next game. The following day I was thrilled when this very skeptical child, grinning from ear to ear, stated before the class, 'Your magic stuff is great; I wasn't nervous at all, even when I did let the ball go through.'

London, England

My children take Rescue Remedy before their college tests and just before their on-stage performances in order to offset anxiety. I take it before I meditate; it helps me to release my stress, relax, and enhance my experience.

New York City, New York

At the hotel where I was staying in Iona, I had great success with the Bach Flower Remedies, particularly the Rescue Remedy. Four visitors arrived, disoriented and suffering from exposure after the engine of their boat had broken down during a storm. I was able to give two of them the Rescue Remedy, and their recovery was amazing. They were calm within a matter of hours, while the other two poor souls had to be confined for two to three days.

Isle of Iona, Scotland

Two children had lost their mother to cancer. The youngest was four, the oldest eight. After the funeral, their father complained that the older girl was suddenly afraid of the dark and could not sleep through the night without wetting her bed, an unusual habit for her. She had nightmares three or four times a week and thus continued to worry her father. Her younger sister also cried incessantly and had nightmares. I gave both children Rescue Remedy.

Additionally, I suggested that their father give them both four drops of the Rescue Remedy each time they woke during the night and before meals during the day. Within three nights the bed-wetting stopped, and both children slept peacefully.

Sante Fe, New Mexico

During a meeting at our Urban Health Center, seven or eight children, all strangers to one another, began to fight and cry, and the mothers responded with angry slaps and reprimands. To try and settle the furor, I gave everyone a dose of liquid Rescue Remedy. Within just a few minutes, peace and harmony were restored.

Chicago, Illinois

I noticed a woman waiting outside the intensive care unit where her mother was dying. She was in semi-shock, quite anxious and very cold. I handed her a small bottle of Rescue Remedy and told her how to use it. She began taking the liquid, and it seemed to relax her very soon after; she seemed able to accept the situation a little more calmly.

Salisbury, North Carolina

I took the Rescue Remedy before taking an exam and found it extremely helpful. I normally waste a lot of time deciding which questions to answer and what to write. But this time, I was able to write quickly, and I felt quite alert and tranquil.

England

Some severe personal problems caused me to have acute anxiety attacks nearly every day. These attacks were no doubt aggravated by my quitting smoking. To control the anxiety, I started taking tranquilizers on and off for a year. Also, for two previous years I'd had dizzy spells whose cause no doctor could find. The day I took my first dose of Rescue Remedy was the last day I needed a tranquilizer. As I continued to take the Rescue Remedy, my anxiety attacks slowly abated, then disappeared, as did my dizzy spells.

New York City, New York

Pregnancy and Childbirth: Professional and Consumer Use

The Bach Flower Remedies can be particularly helpful before and throughout pregnancy, as well as during childbirth, when a prospective mother's moods fluctuate more than usual. Since the moods are distinctly defined, they can be treated by the mother-to-be herself or by her adviser. A quiet, happy frame of mind is one of the greatest contributors to a painless and easy birth. In addition to being taken internally, Rescue Remedy can be applied externally to the wrist, temples, and navel of the newborn, when and as needed.

The Bach Flower Remedies, as well as Rescue Remedy, have also been shown to be especially valuable in dealing with children's emotional difficulties—for example, fear and restlessness—before more complex patterns have a chance to develop.

In addition, Dr. John Diamond, a psychiatrist and well-known author, in his introduction to *Handbook of the Bach Flower Remedies*, by Philip Chancellor (New Canaan: Keats, 1980), states: "The Bach remedies have tremendous power for good and are completely free of any harmful effects." This is especially important, because many substances commonly used today for most emotional difficulties have warnings about repetition and dosage.

Because of recent FDA regulations, most over-the-counter drugs require a warning for pregnant women regardless of the drug's toxicity. *It is important to check with your physician before taking any form of medication during pregnancy.* However no known side effects have been attributed to the Bach Flower Remedies or to Rescue Remedy in over fifty years of use.

Pregnancy and Childbirth: Professional Use

"Our hospital's doctor, not able to find the cause of the illness, had done all he could for a six-week-old baby who was failing quickly. Based on my experience in emergency situations, I decided to start the infant on Bach Rescue Remedy; the effect was profound. From that point on, her condition took a dramatic shift in a positive direction. The doctor could hardly believe it when a week later, the baby's condition appeared to be stabilized."

Sister Natalie, superintendent,
St. John's Hospital, Poona, India

"While I was attending a thirty-four-year-old woman who was in the second stage of labour, she was having extreme contractions. The fetal heart monitor indicated that the fetus was in distress. The patient was getting hysterical, and we were considering a Caesarean section. I applied Rescue Remedy to her lips from a cloth three times within a fifteen-minute period. The fetal heartbeat evened out, the contractions were much milder, and the whole labour process stopped for about two hours. The woman calmed down and actually slept. When she awoke, labour began again, and there was a normal delivery, with no further complications or distress."

In another case: "I was in attendance when a child was born at home, the umbilical cord twisted twice around his neck. Since the cord was too tight, it was necessary to cut and clamp it immediately. The child was not breathing, his vital signs were low, and he displayed a poor colour. We rubbed Rescue Remedy all over his face. Within a short period, though it seemed forever, he started breathing, and his normal responses quickly picked up."

Gretchen Lawlor, ND,
Tunbridge Wells, England

"Recently, I was called to the hospital where one of my maternity patients had a series of minor convulsions directly preceding her labour. When I arrived, I immediately swabbed her tongue and inside her lips with Rescue Remedy. The convulsions ceased, and I left her drinking water 'doctored' with the Rescue Remedy. I continued this treatment throughout the next day and the following morning. Later that day, my patient delivered the child, with no discomfort."

Dr. T. L.
Northampton, England

"A fifteen-month-old-girl running a high fever was recently brought to me. I applied Rescue Remedy cream to various parts of her body, and within half an hour she was fast asleep, and her fever dropped. Two days later, she had fully recovered. I've used Rescue Remedy cream and drops in similar cases of fever in children, always with good results."

Ahmaed bin Embun, health practitioner,
Singapore, Malaysia

"I recently attended a twenty-one-year-old woman who was in labour at West London Hospital with her first child. Since she was quite agitated, I administered a dose of Rescue Remedy to calm her during the second stage and especially during the transition period of labour. She had a unusually easy birth without any complications, which I attributed to the Rescue Remedy."

Sarah Moon, BAc,
London, England

"Very shortly after her daughter was born, my patient nearly passed out. Since there were complications and a lot of bleeding, I gave her a dose of Rescue Remedy, which, within moments, brought her back to clarity. The rapidity of recovery was quite amazing to witness."

G. S. Khalsa, MD,
Lathrup Village, Michigan

"A thirty-one-year-old woman patient of mine had wanted natural childbirth but was two weeks past her delivery date. She was taken to the hospital to have labour induced. This upset her. She had lower back pain; she was apprehensive, and she felt a sense of failure at not having a home birth.

"I gave her five drops of Rescue Remedy in warm water. There was an immediate dramatic change, and she said, 'I'm going to really cope with this.' She was suddenly clear and had her first baby in three hours."

Lorraine Taylor, BAc,
Oxford, England

"Recently, I gave Rescue Remedy to a young woman in the early stages of labour. She was highly nervous, but after a few sips of the remedy in water she calmed down considerably. After ten minutes, her contractions regulated and labour progressed beautifully. She gave birth within two hours in a relaxed and normal manner. Also, as a preventative to postnatal depression, there is nothing equal to Rescue Remedy."

E. Eckstein, RMH*,
England

Pregnancy and Childbirth: Consumer Use

The following letter was written to John Ramsell who, with his sister, Nickie Murray, carries on Dr. Bach's work as the current curators of the Bach Centre in England. The letter eventually appeared in *Mothering* magazine, Spring 1983, and is printed here with permission from the

---

* Registered Medical Herbalist

writer. An extremely moving account of one woman's coura-
geous battle to save her child, the letter is included here so
that the reader may share in the woman's experience. **No
medical claims are implied or made here for the Bach remedies or Rescue Remedy, in Down's Syndrome, or any other
serious medical disorder by either the author or the publisher.**

Dear John,

I knew I would have a story to tell, but I had no idea it
would be so dramatic. You might just want to put your feet
up in one of those wonderful wooden chairs Dr. Edward
Bach built, to read this one.

I had made about eight one-ounce dropper bottles full of
my favorite Bach flowers—Rescue Remedy, Walnut, Mimulus, and Oak—the day my labor began. I took them regularly on my tongue, and put four or five drops on the crown
of my head to even out the rough edges. I was 9¾ cm. dilated when my labor stopped...thirty-six long, long hours
later.

Since I had planned a home delivery, I did my laboring at
home to the hour. Soon, I figured the son within me was not
safe in his own right; otherwise, he would have been born by
then. I got my bag, and off to the hospital I went with my
husband, my midwives, my remedies, and the baby still
within. I slipped a bottle of comfrey and chlorophyll into my
medicine pouch and thought I was ready.

When I arrived at the hospital, I had a heavy contraction
at the front desk, and the woman there screamed, "Are you
going to have your baby right here? Right now? Get into a
wheelchair and use the service elevator—it's faster!"

A fetal monitor determined that baby Anton was in distress—imagine having one's head caught in the cervix for
thirty-six hours—and we opted for a Caesarean section. It
was performed at 9 p.m.—eight long hours later.

The remedy I continued to take every three minutes in
front of all the attending doctors and nurses kept them very

curious. When asked by my doctor what I was so faithfully taking, I told him it was a remedy for impatience. He laughed, and admitted that he, too, could probably use some, although he never asked to try any.

Baby Anton was born in distress. He had no lung capacity and swallowed meconium (baby's first elimination) after my waters broke early in the morning. The heart had enlarged to keep the baby alive. He was put on 100% oxygen immediately, and he looked as if he wanted to go back to the garden.

About ten minutes out of recovery, our pediatrician told us our son was born with Down's Syndrome. In addition, he had many problems and had about two hours to live. Did we want to see him? Yes, Did we make funeral arrangements at the pediatricians suggestion? Yes, we did that too. We cried mostly; this was a little much to bear, even with the remedies. I asked my husband to return home and bring back the entire set of thirty-eight remedies. I added the Bach flower Gorse...[for hopelessness] to our remedy, and we took it continually. Soon, we calmed down.

I was wheeled into Infant Intensive Care where I could not reach my son's head after my own abdominal surgery. I asked my husband to put Oak, Walnut, and Rescue Remedy on his (the baby's) knees, feet, and chest—between the EKG and catheter wires. If our son was going to die, I wanted his transition to be a peaceful one. I knew the flower Walnut would aid his transition. We told the nurses it was holy water. Even though they were incredible women, I figured the chances of their knowing about the Bach flowers were ten to one. I felt too weak to explain.

The pediatricians said they would transport baby Anton to a large city hospital sixty miles away. They would be "better equipped" there to save his life, if in fact it could be saved. Heart surgery would probably also be necessary. Jack and I said no, no, no to both.... If baby Anton was to live, he would have to pull through where he was born, here in the mountains of this small city.

That night, I stayed with him in intensive care and reached into his oxygen tent, scared to death he might die if I opened it up. I fed him my remedy, now his, through an eyedropper. He was so dehydrated he slurped it up with all the enthusiasm he could gather. Every ten minutes I gave him his remedy: on the knees, his mouth, and on the crown of his badly misshapen head. I did this for twenty-four hours. The Newborn Nursery nurses kept him warm and dry and untangled from all those wires. Then I went to bed.

When I woke the next day, eight hours later, I slightly remember the doctor saying the crisis seemed to be over. We then administered an intense stimulation program. Soon, I could hold my son with blow-by oxygen in between the wires. He had a strong suck, and breast-fed in six or seven days. Little by little, over a ten-day period in intensive care, we used six ounces of remedy. The oxygen supply was decreased from 100% eventually to room air. I added tincture of comfrey and chlorophyll to my milk. Baby's skin was rubbed down with the gel from live Aloe Vera plants three or four times every twelve hours. He was three weeks overdue, and he looked as if he had spent that time in a bathtub. His head shaped up. His skin is beautiful. We have a baby boy.

We continue our daily use of the Bach flowers. Thanks again for carrying on Bach's work. In the eight years I have used these remedies, I have never been so appreciative that Bach discovered them. With my thanks, please expect a package of herbal teas for you and all your staff, and your guests from the world over.

Most sincerely,

Alexandra Kolkmeyer
Author of *A Modern Woman's Herbal*
(Santa Fe, New Mexico: Insight Press, 1976)

Since the birth of my first child eleven years ago was such a painful and frightening experience, I grew quite terrified as the time came closer for my second child to be born. However, following sound advice, I took Rescue Remedy during labour, and the delivery was quick and easy. I became quite relaxed both during and after the birth.

Isles of Scilly, England

When the third member of our family arrived early this summer, it became evident to me that the Rescue Remedy was also the baby's remedy. I found it a wonderful and almost instantaneous cure for colic.

Three drops in a tablespoon of warm boiled water worked like magic.

Selsdon, England

Before delivering her baby, my daughter regularly took Rescue Remedy, and her labour only lasted an hour and a half. The nurses said they had never seen such a quick and easy delivery, and called her son Speedy Gonzales. She is continuing with the remedy and is so relieved that this baby, as opposed to her first, sleeps peacefully through the night.

Devon, England

I began taking Rescue Remedy with the onset of labour contractions while on the way to the hospital. The contractions started coming every three minutes, and by the time I arrived I was fully dilated and ready to push. In the delivery room my husband gave me water with the Bach Flower Rescue Remedy added. Between each contraction, I was fully aware of all that was going on. Even through the powerful contractions I had no need for painkillers and after an hour gave birth to twin boys.

I took Rescue Remedy throughout my six days in the hospital by putting a few drops in my bedside water. This helped me to cope with the overwhelming task of breast-feeding two hungry babies. I attributed the calmness and inner strength I felt throughout this intense experience to Dr. Bach's Rescue Remedy.

Derbyshire, England

"My first birth was a nightmare. There's no other word for it. Even the midwife, who attended as one of my coaches, admitted that it was 'one of the more difficult' she had seen. ...No, I was not medicated, and yes, I was a 'prepared' woman. But prepared for what? After twenty-four hours of excruciating back labor, with little or no dilation, no breathing technique could alleviate the pain and exhaustion I was suffering....

"Sensing my panic, my coach pulled a small bottle of Rescue Remedy, a Bach flower extract, from her pocket and dripped three or four drops of the dew-like liquid into my mouth....Soon after that, an unexpected surge of energy and concentration came over me. After three long pushes, my baby girl emerged in one sudden, hot, wet 'plop.'...

"...When things got bad [during my second birth], I asked my other coach for the Rescue Remedy."

Olympia, Washington (Extracted from *Mothering* magazine, Spring 1984)

Recently, I suggested Rescue Remedy to a young woman in the early stages of labour. She was highly nervous, but after a few sips of the remedy in water she calmed down considerably. After ten minutes, her contractions regulated and labor progressed beautifully. She gave birth within two hours in a relaxed and normal manner. Also, as a preventive to postnatal depression, there is nothing equal to Rescue Remedy.

England

I was ten weeks pregnant when I started to miscarry. I began to bleed so profusely that I almost passed out. All I had time to say was, 'Get the Rescue Remedy off the shelf!' I took it every few moments until I regained my strength and was able to get medical assistance. The bleeding lessened a bit, and I was able to get to the hospital in a stable condition. Rescue Remedy will always be on hand in my home for any emergency.

New South Wales, Australia

Following a loss in the family, my stress was compounded by an ectopic pregnancy [in the Fallopian tube], which had aborted. This was followed by surgical removal of the damaged tube and ovary as well. During this period, Rescue Remedy was the only thing that kept me [emotionally] stable. Shortly after my return from the hospital, my marriage began to break up, and once again Rescue Remedy proved invaluable in helping me through this time.

I have used all the Bach remedies, and they have played an important role in helping me cope with the changes I've experienced in my life. They have allowed me to change my negative thoughts and thus develop more fully as a human being. I cannot speak highly enough of Dr. Bach and his remedies.

Lancashire, England

After much debating, we took our two-month-old daughter to receive her first immunization vaccine. The after effects of this shot were dreadful. The poor little baby ran a high fever and went into a frenzy, screaming for hours. Before her second shot, we rubbed Rescue Remedy cream on the spot where the needle would go in, and she didn't feel a thing. For the rest of the day, we gave her Rescue Remedy orally, and this time she had no after effects whatsoever. We dealt with the third shot the same way, and our daughter actually seemed to enjoy her visit with the doctor.

USA

Acute and Chronic: Professional and Consumer Use

The following section consists of cases involving the professional and consumer use of Rescue Remedy for acute and chronic conditions. Acute conditions are defined here as those conditions that appear suddenly but do not require emergency assistance. Chronic conditions are those a person has lived with over a long period of time.

Acute and Chronic: Professional Use

"One of my patients was a thirty-six-year-old woman who was a heavy drinker and' smoker with a history of chronic depression. I suggested that she take the Bach Flower Rescue Remedy, which she did. The next day, she reported that she had slept for the first time in two weeks and felt a sense of relief from her problems. She continued to take the remedy and after two or three weeks was able to stabilize her condition. She now takes the remedy intermittently."

Jeffrey Fine, ND, PhD,
Palm Beach Shores, Florida

"J.T. is a sixty-five-year-old ex-weight-lifter who had been having attacks of 'wooziness' and lightheadedness for the last year and a half. They would occur if he sat still for more than a half-hour or if he drove a car for over an hour and then stood up. He would then feel weak and tired for a few hours after the attack. When he came to my office, he had been seen by his family doctor, given tranquilizers and told 'to take it easy.'

"After talking with him and examining him, I suggested he take Rescue Remedy daily when these attacks occur. I also prescribed some vitamin supplements for stress. When I saw him next, he reported only two episodes in the intervening six weeks (he had been having them daily). At the beginning of both episodes, he had taken three drops of Rescue Remedy. He told me these drops seemed to clear up the wooziness quickly, and a full-blown attack never materialized.

"Additionally, he said that he knew things had changed when, during a recent bridge game, he got up to go to the kitchen after sitting for over two hours, (this normally would have created a problem for him) and became really excited when he realized that he had not been weak or woozy for weeks."

Ronald Dushkin, MD,
Kripalu Center, Lenox, Massachusetts

"A patient of mine was diagnosed as being severely hypoglycemic as well as having severe allergic responses to all kinds of foods and foreign proteins. The Rescue Remedy liquid has proven significant in terms of providing stress relief during the acute episodes, especially after [the patient takes] any offending substances."

Jim Said, DC, ND
Grants Pass, Oregon

Acute and Chronic:
Consumer Use

I have suffered from head noises for forty years, and all the doctor and ear specialists I have seen have been of little help. Two nights ago, I awoke at 3 a.m.. The noises were so terrible that I felt I couldn't take anymore and rose with the intention of trying to 'end it all.' Stepping out of bed, I noticed the little bottle of Rescue Remedy that I keep on my bedside table for emergencies. Unbelievable as this may sound, I took three small sips from the bottle, and in less than a minute my panic had subsided, allowing me to fall asleep peacefully.

Stirling, Scotland

I get a powerful allergic reaction to a combination of pollution and cats. My eyes itch; I get a rash on the back of my knees and around my eyes; I sneeze; and, if I stay in that environment, I have coughing and retching spasms. The only thing that alleviates my distress is Rescue Remedy.

East Hampton, New York

During a bout of sinusitis with associated congestion and pain, I poured a diluted dose of Rescue Remedy in my palm and sniffed it up each nostril; it was not pleasant, but it was most effective. I patted the rest of the dose over my sinuses, and the relief was almost instantaneous. I have shared this knowledge with several other folks who also report excellent results.*

Christchurch, New Zealand

---

*Rescue Remedy cream can be used here in the same way.

I began to prepare for a difficult heart operation by taking the Rescue Remedy each day. I took it full strength right before the operation, a double-bypass and mitral valve replacement, and then again each hour afterwards in the intensive care unit.

Following my operation, I had an unusually rapid recovery. This surprised the doctors, who felt it would be at least six months before I could do much of anything. I continued to take the remedy and was back at work before three months were up. Even now, during my checkups, the doctors are amazed at how swift my recovery was.

United States

A friend of mine who is an accomplished runner took regular doses of Rescue Remedy while running a thirty-one-mile marathon. After his seven-and-a-half-hour run, he had no soreness or significant exhaustion; he said he felt better than he did after any previous run.

In another incident: A thirty-eight year-old acquaintance of mine who was not used to strenuous exercise took a three-hour hike over snow, ice, and rocks, while wearing only soft moccasins. After his walk he took a hot shower, then applied the Rescue Remedy cream to his calves and to the soles of his feet. Shortly thereafter, he reported happily that there was no muscle soreness or swelling in his feet or legs.

New Mexico

My lips were chapped to the point where I could not smile, eat, or talk. My lower lip was also split about one-eighth of an inch. I applied Rescue Remedy cream to my lips, and within minutes I felt a great deal of relief from the pain—I could even smile again. I applied the cream several times that day and the next, and on the third day, I found I didn't need it any more. The split had come together, and my lips had completely healed.

New York City, New York

Years ago, my fingernails began to crack, flake, peel and split, and I tried every sort of cream and nail-hardener on the market—calcium tablets, cod liver oil, iodine, biochemic remedies. All proved ineffective. Finally, I bought a set of false nails, which I wore on social occasions. Five weeks ago, as I was rubbing Rescue Remedy cream into a bad bruise on my hand, I absent-mindedly smoothed it on my nails and cuticles. It worked! Now I am showing everyone my really lovely, healthy, strong, long fingernails. I am absolutely thrilled.

Plymouth, England

One of my co-workers was in pain during her menstrual cycle. She was sitting with her head on her desk, almost fainting. I squeezed a few drops of Rescue Remedy into a glass of water and urged her to drink it. She did, and to her great surprise, the pain diminished, then stopped almost immediately. Afterwards, she was able to finish her day's work without a recurrence of the pains or cramps.

Berkshire, England

Not getting consistent results from the various steroid creams I had been taking, I followed the suggestion of a homoeopathic physician and used the Rescue Remedy cream for an irritating eczema on my arms. I applied it two or three times a day, and after several weeks, the area improved greatly. Since last year, there have been very few recurrences, and those few promptly disappear when I apply a little Rescue Remedy cream.

Los Angeles, California

Rescue Remedy helped my wife deal with her emotional stress throughout the most severe and fearsome period of continuous illness that she has ever had. I believe that Rescue Remedy, which she took frequently during this period, stabilized her to the point that she was able to cope with her situation in a way that saved her life.

Arizona

Animals: Professional and Consumer Use

Out of thousands of case studies, some of the most extraordinary and dramatic reports have been those involving the use of the Bach Flower Remedies and Rescue Remedy with animals. The following is a compilation of cases from veterinarians and other professionals working with animals, as well as from individual consumers and pet owners.

Many veterinarians, using the Rescue Remedy as a last resort after standard procedures had failed, reported remarkable results.

It should be noted however, that the cases outlined here represent the use of Rescue Remedy with animals; and is not meant to imply its use or effectiveness for similar situations or conditions in humans.

Although the exact way in which the Bach remedies and the Rescue Remedy work is not yet known, the many animal reports outlined here strongly indicate that the remedies are not placebos. In light of this, the importance of further controlled studies cannot be emphasized enough.

Animals: Professional Testimonies

"I strongly encourage all my fellow veterinarians to use Rescue Remedy. I have used it, especially with dogs, in cases of shock, accidents, injuries, presurgical work, and tooth extractions. It does make a difference in reducing anxiety and calming the animals down so they are less susceptible to stress. In addition, it generally makes the anaesthetic procedure go a lot smoother. I believe the Rescue Remedy affects the higher centers of the brain. Dr. Bach was a medical genius; he had tremendous insight in knowing which plant would affect particular conditions."

George MacLeod, DVSM, MRCVS, England;
one of the world's foremost authorities on
the use of homoeopathic remedies for animals;
president, British Association of Homoeopathic
Veterinary Surgeons;
author of four major books on the use of
homoeopathy with animals

"We have found the Bach Flower Remedies and especially Rescue Remedy very helpful in alleviating a wide range of problems and conditions affecting all types of birds and animals. In addition, I have found the Rescue Remedy cream invaluable for insect and animal bites. We regard animals as equal to humans and they deserve equal treatment. In our experience, we have found the Rescue Remedy and the other Bach remedies an invaluable healing tool we would not want to be without."

John Bryant, former manager,
Ferne Animal Sanctuary,
Chard, Somerset, England

"Rescue Remedy, especially combined with Arnica (a homoeopathic remedy), is helpful in various types of animal emergencies, such as shock. I would encourage other veterinarians to try it. I would also like to see more work in testing and assessing the [benefits of] Rescue Remedy, for it has a tremendous potential in veterinary medicine."

Christopher Day, MB, MRCVS,
Stanford-in-the-vale, England;
author of *Homoeopathic Treatment of Small
Animals* (London: Wigmore Publications Ltd, 1984)

In his book, *Dr. Pitcairn's Complete Guide to Natural Health for Dogs and Cats*, Dr. Pitcairn recommends Rescue Remedy, for animals, used along with cardiopulmonary resuscitation, acupressure, external heart-massage, and other modalities, for various conditions.

For information on Dr. Pitcairn's recommendations, consult his book's special guide to handling emergencies, pp. 259-266.

"I have used Rescue Remedy to treat injured birds, newborn puppies, and kittens that are very weak, often with excellent results. I also use Rescue Remedy after difficult surgery, and in many cases this will make a significant difference in the animal waking up more quickly and easily."

> **Richard H. Pitcairn,** DVM, PhD,
> Eugene, Oregon;
> author of *Dr. Pitcairn's Complete
> Guide to Natural Health for Dogs
> and Cats* (Emmaus, Pennsylvania;
> Rodale Press, 1982)

"I use Rescue Remedy especially with newborn animals after a Caesarean section. The remedy seems particularly effective in compensating for the depressing quality of anaesthesia produced in the progeny [offspring]. Further, I consider it an outstanding aid to the harmonious survival of the young animal's family, including an anxious sire."

> **J.L. Newns,** BVetMed, MRCVS,
> Cornwall, England

"I have found the Bach Flower Rescue Remedy extremely effective in postsurgical instances. It is extraordinary in reviving pups after Caesareans. I administer Rescue Remedy during the cleanup stage once the throat is cleared; I find this to be most effective in improving the puppies' respiration and in bringing [the animals] back to normal.

"I use and recommend Rescue Remedy in situations involving the collapse of any young animal. It's a means of buying time. It's an excellent adjunct to any other treatment used for and during an immediate crisis. Try it; don't be concerned with [why or] how it works, since you might deprive yourself of a wonderful healing tool."

J.G.C. Saxton, BVetMed, MRCVS,
Leeds, England

"I use the Bach Flower Remedies on dogs that are under stress and need to relax. I also use the remedies during acupuncture therapy. Ninety percent of the time I get good to excellent results; only ten percent of the cases show little or no effect. I have used Rescue Remedy with animals that have been hit by cars or are in shock after surgery. It really does make a difference. I think that everyone, especially veterinarians, should have Rescue Remedy on hand. It is so effective yet inexpensive that it would be senseless not to try it. If it helps to get the animal out of shock, or even to calm down, it's worth it."

John B. Limehouse, DVM,
North Hollywood, California

"The Bach Flower Remedies are one of the most humane and gentle systems of healing I know. During their development, no animals were required to be sacrificed to prove the remedies' efficacy. They are a tremendous gift of healing for animals. In addition, the Bach remedies can help a person tune in to [himself] and become more sensitive to the animals.

"The more we use the remedies ourselves, the more our understanding of animals' emotions become clear. Careful observation has shown that animals tend to develop the same problems their owners have, especially psychosomatic ones. In addition, animals often have to cope with loneliness, anxiety, and fear. Rescue Remedy is highly recommended for all crises, and especially before and after surgery. We have found, when the remedies are used as indicated, that animals tend to recover very, very quickly."

Rebecca Hall, London, England;
author of *Animals Are Equal:
An Exploration of Animal Consciousness*
(London: Wildwood House, 1983) and
Voiceless Victims (London: Wildwood House, 1984)

"As a veterinary surgeon in general practice, I regularly administer Rescue Remedy for cases involving birth trauma, accident trauma, and post-Caesarean section....

"Often following a difficult birth, puppies or kittens that have been a long time in the birth canal will be slow in taking up the challenge of life. Rescue Remedy dripped on their tongues will give them that impetus to survive.

"Many animals born by Caesarean section often suffer before birth from respiratory depression as a result of the anaesthetic reaching them via their mother's blood stream. Rescue Remedy appears to stimulate their respiration and assist them in eliminating the toxic effects.

"I have had encouraging results using the remedy with lambs that have experienced a difficult birth. This is especially common with small hill ewes. Very often the newborn are suffering from bruising, exhaustion, and shock; their mothers may also be in a similar condition. For both, Rescue Remedy can be a great aid to recovery.

"I also use Rescue Remedy as a standard treatment for wild and domestic birds...[when] the animals are in shock and exhausted: birds that have been attacked by cats or hit by cars; [birds that have] flown into windows, [or fallen] out of their nests; sea birds blown ashore following severe storms; and birds recovering from anaesthetics. In these cases, I will generally administer two to three drops of the Rescue Remedy into the throat, place the bird in a dark box by a heat source, and leave it for about two hours. Often this is the only treatment required. In other cases, it will have helped the bird to be able to cope with further handling and therapy.

"I would encourage all veterinarians to have Rescue Remedy on hand. This is not a miracle medicine, but used regularly where indicated, it has much to recommend it. Inevitably there will be a case, as I have experienced, where Rescue Remedy will have such a profound and startling effect during a crisis that it will leave little doubt as to its efficacy."

Bruce Borland, BVetMed, MRCVS,
Bearsden, Scotland

"I use Rescue Remedy as a routine part of my veterinary practice in pre- and postoperative surgery. In accidents, Rescue Remedy helps animals overcome the shock of strange surroundings and assists with a more rapid recovery. The Rescue Remedy can be administered orally, put in drinking water, or dropped directly on and in the mouth. One of the great benefits of using the Bach remedies, including Rescue Remedy, is that they will not interfere with any other medicine or treatment the animal may be involved in. I would never hesitate using any of the Bach remedies.

"In my experience I have also found that one or two drops of Rescue Remedy will have an almost immediate effect on regulating and deepening an animal's breathing on coming out of an anaesthetic.

"I would further recommend that zookeepers have and use all the Bach remedies, especially Rescue Remedy. Simplicity is the key with the Bach system. I would use them [the remedies] in conjunction with other methods without reservations."

Eileen Wheeler, MRCVS,
Wales, United Kingdom

"I keep both Rescue Remedy cream and liquid available at all times, as I find them an invaluable aid in my veterinary work. They even work on wounds that would usually be slow to heal, as is the case with tortoises. The cream keeps the wounds supple, relieves pain, and speeds up the healing process. As I work with several animal rescue organizations, I am often called upon to treat sick or injured wild creatures, including foxes, badgers, and deer. Rescue Remedy liquid assists greatly by allaying their fear and panic; it also helps them to regain consciousness after being caught in wire snares.

"Birds benefit also from the Rescue Remedy; my standard treatment is to give them Rescue Remedy mixed with honey, then immediately put them into an enclosed box, in a warm, quiet place. After only twenty minutes they are calmer, stronger, and [able to] be handled with less risk of their dying from shock. I have found Rescue Remedy liquid to be extremely effective with creatures suffering emotional traumas and various forms of neuroses....I notice a significant increase in the recovery and survival rates of the wild and domestic species that I have treated since I started using the Bach remedies several years ago."

Sue Smith, veterinary nurse,
Chard, England

Animals: Professional Use

"Not long ago a colleague reported a case of a thoroughbred horse that had gone through long, drawn-out surgery involving the exploration of a tumour in the perineum area. The horse was given Rescue Remedy for three days before, and again after, the operation. During subsequent checkups, the veterinarian was staggered that the animal had recovered so quickly from such a traumatic procedure."

Eileen Wheeler, MRCVS,
Wales, United Kingdom

"Recently while I was carrying out a routine operation on a young toy poodle, it suffered an acute anaesthetic crisis with both the respiration and the heart stopping. The dog was given heart massage, artificial respiration and cardiac stimulants, but to no avail. When all else had failed, I gave the animal a few drops of Rescue Remedy under the tongue. Twenty seconds later the dog took an enormous breath and the heart started pumping. With further doses of remedy, both pulse and respiration were stabilised, the surgery was completed and the dog made an uneventful recovery. My nurse witnessed all this and looked at the poodle with disbelief. This seems a classic case where everything was traditionally done, but Rescue Remedy used as a last resort, saved the day and the dog. I was extremely impressed and continue to use the remedy in my practice."

In another case: "A Labrador bitch was presented for surgery with a ruptured diaphragm, the result of a road traffic accident. This condition always constitutes an extra anaesthetic risk. Once the animal was anaesthetised and surgery was commenced, it suffered respiratory and cardiac arrest. The dog failed to respond to orthodox methods of resuscitation but did respond to a dose of Rescue Remedy . As with the poodle, the heart started beating again and breathing was established voluntarily.

"Even effective procedures do not work in every case and I have had many cases where Rescue Remedy has been of no help. However, I am convinced of its great value and always have it to hand."

Bruce Borland, BVetMed, MRCVS,
Bearsden, Scotland

"I have recently used Rescue Remedy with a bulldog that was having a mild seizure. He was in a state of panic and was having severe respiratory difficulty. I administered Rescue Remedy at half-hour intervals for three to four hours and found it to be more effective than any sedative I could have used."

J.G.C. Saxton, BVetMed, MRCVS,
Leeds, England

"I was visiting a veterinarian friend of mine when another friend brought in a cat that appeared to be quite exhausted. The cat had been out in the rain all day and appeared frightened. We gave it one dose of Rescue Remedy, and within five minutes it was purring, cozy, and friendly."

G.S. Khalsa, MD,
Lathrup Village, Michigan

"I had a case where a dog was quite nervous and the owners wanted to tranquillize him before going on a long trip. I suggested the Bach Rescue Remedy as often as needed. Upon their return, the owners enthusiastically rang back to say that the remedy had helped remarkably to calm the animal down."

P.A. Culpin, MRCVS,
Surrey, England

"Not long ago a dog was brought into my office after being hit by a car. He wasn't very active, his gums were gray, and the time it took for his capillaries to fill was very slow. He had been hit extremely hard, but had no concussion. I gave him two doses of Rescue Remedy fifteen minutes apart. Within a short time his capillary filling time improved, and he began to perk up and recover."

John B. Limehouse, DVM,
North Hollywood, California

"I have often found Rescue Remedy very helpful for my wild bird patients. I particularly remember the case of a jackdaw suffering from severe head injuries. It was blind in one eye, infected with lice and grapeworms, thin and frail, and almost unconscious. I gave it a few drops of the Rescue Remedy on a child's paint brush, then wrapped it in wool and placed it in an electrically heated hospital cage, which I left in the dark. Soon I was handling a 'live' bird, warm and supple, conscious and alert, which I was able to attend to properly and give food. I am convinced that without the Rescue Remedy, this bird would not have regained consciousness or the will to live. In time it made a complete recovery, and its sight was saved. After it was released, it and another jackdaw used the house like a hotel for weeks, dropping in for a meal, for shelter from the rain, or just to look around."

M. Davidson,
The Bird Hospital,
Helston, Cornwall, England

Animals: Consumer Use

In the middle of March we discovered a small copper butterfly just free from her cocoon. We took her indoors, and for a whole week she remained motionless on a vase of flowers. Several times each day I sat her on a drop of Rescue Remedy on my finger. At last she unfurled her proboscis and took a long draught from the drop.

The result was immediate and almost startling. From being almost lifeless, she fluttered strongly about the room, but since the weather was still cold we kept her indoors for two more days, feeding her on fresh hyacinths and Rescue Remedy. One sunny morning at the end of that time, we opened the window and watched her fly on strong wings to freedom.

USA

My friend's dog became very lethargic when its master died. He walked around for days with his head down. Half an hour after I put four drops of Rescue Remedy on his tongue, he perked up and looked quite different. My friend continued putting drops into his drinking water for a couple of days, since then the dog has completely become himself again.

Newton Corner, Massachusetts

I use Rescue Remedy for all minor injuries that my dog and

cat sustain or when I know the animals are emotionally upset for some reason. It is the only medicine my dog doesn't shy away from; he even licks it off me when I use it.

Kansas City, Missouri

A six-month-old cat was brought in with a fishhook lodged in the pad of its right front paw. The cat was frantic and extremely difficult to control. Rescue Remedy, given orally and applied to the affected paw, calmed the cat down somewhat. Repeated applications allowed us to cut its pad with a razor blade and extract the fishhook with tweezers. I wrapped the paw in gauze and kept it wet with Rescue Remedy. During the one-week convalescence, the cat remained calm and chewed very little at the wrapping. The paw healed remarkably well.

Burkittsville, Maryland

I have an eight-month-old Labrador retriever that had cracked paws. I applied Rescue Remedy cream three times a day for one week. Compared to their normal condition, the paws remained in bad shape. But when I took the dog to the vet, I discovered that the paw condition was a result of distemper. The vet said that she had never seen paws in such good shape in a dog with distemper and wanted to know what I had been applying to them.

Madison, Wisconsin

My six-year-old male cat had a chronic abscess problem. No sooner did one abscess heal than another developed. His hair was falling out, and his eyes began to look very wild. A doctor friend told me about Rescue Remedy. I gave Thomas two doses a day, four drops in his mouth plus four drops in his drinking water. In two days the sores had new granulation and were drying; his coat felt smoother, and he was much calmer. Now he has a very smooth new coat; he is back to his normal weight; all the abscess holes are completely healed, and Thomas has his own bottle of Rescue Remedy.

Alameda, California

The Rescue Remedy cream has proved invaluable in a number of instances. A few days ago, I came across a horse that had hurt itself on barbed wire and had not eaten for two days. Its wound was raw and seemed painful to the touch. I gave the owner a jar of Rescue Remedy and told her to apply it to the affected area at regular intervals. She called one hour later, telling me that the horse began to graze. Two days later, the wound healed over.

New Mexico

I have given the Rescue Remedy to injured wild birds that dash themselves against my windows. It seems to bring them to consciousness quickly, and they fly off.

The most amazing recovery, however, was with my cat. Cats in this valley frequently get an intestinal disorder from which they eventually die. We imagine it comes from the field mice they eat. When my kitten developed the trouble, I thought of the Rescue Remedy. I administered the remedy for three consecutive mornings and nights, after which he recovered. A month later, the cat got sick again; I repeated the same treatment, and within a much shorter time he was better. Now eighteen months old, he eats mice and never seems to get sick. I've treated three of my neighbor's cats and got the same permanent results.

Yarrow, British Columbia

Oscar used to be a real fraidy cat, frightened of everything, including his own shadow. He was covered in eczema from head to tail, and we were always taking him to the vet. Six months ago, I decided to put him on the Bach remedies. I gave him the Rescue Remedy plus two other Bach remedies for his great fears. After administering three drops twice a day for nearly a week Oscar has become a changed animal. His eczema has cleared up, and he continues to be braver each week. Also, he has become extremely affectionate.

London, England

One of our Australian shepherds was running in the snow

and stepped on a broken bottle, cutting his foot. After cleaning it thoroughly and washing it in a herbal infusion, we coated the foot with Rescue Remedy cream and wrapped it. We gave the dog Rescue Remedy drops regularly and continued to coat the wound with the salve. We also dropped some of the remedy on his tongue before changing the bandage, and it always calmed him so that he didn't pull his leg away. After less than a week, his foot had completely healed without complications.

Colorado Springs, Colorado

One of my cats came bounding into the house with what looked like a dead baby chipmunk in its mouth. I pried the cat's jaws open, and the chipmunk hit the carpet with a thud. With no real hope of reviving it, I squirted some drops of Rescue Remedy into its mouth, and immediately it began to twitch and move around. It recovered so quickly that I barely had enough time to find a box for it. Fifteen minutes later, it was well enough for me to release it into the woods. Identical incidents occurred twice more during the next two months, one with a field mouse and another with a second chipmunk. Both animals revived after a dose of Rescue Remedy and were released in good health.

Ballston Lake, New York

We found a pregnant wallaby that was hit by a car on a country road. Her tiny, fully furred baby emerged. It was wriggling, struggling, and frantic. We decided to feed it, through an eyedropper, watered-down dried milk and raw sugar. The baby took the first few drops, but as the day drew on he seemed reluctant to take more. The tiny frame became skeletal and his attitude listless and dependent. We feared we were losing him.

It was then we thought of putting four drops of Rescue Remedy in his milk. Whether it was the taste of brandy, Rescue Remedy is in a brandy base, or whether he was just plain hungry, he took it until we were feeding him regularly.

Fortunately, the veterinary office was open the next day, and we took the wallaby by to show him to the vet. The doctor seemed quite surprised at the apparent health and comfort of our little friend and recommended that we continue our treatment.

For the next few days, we included the Rescue Remedy in his mixture. Today we can happily say that we have one healthy, bouncy, and bigger wallaby with us now.

Australia

We have had some marvelous experiences with the Rescue Remedy on animals. Our little Chihuahua once had a bad fall and became ill although the vet could find nothing wrong. The first dose of Rescue Remedy made a tremendous difference—the dog perked up amazingly. It was also a great help when she gave birth to her puppies. I don't know how I could manage without it.

California

Balludur was a twelve-month-old pedigree golden Labrador that completely distrusted people. No one had ever been able to touch him. Several times in a confined space he had lunged at people and bitten them.

This last time I'd gotten the idea of wetting a piece of bread with Rescue Remedy from the bottle I always carry. I did, and threw the dog a bit of the bread, which he ate. Ten minutes later, finding him still there, I wetted some more bread with the Rescue Remedy and squatted on my heels. To my amazement, he came and snatched it from my fingers and ran away. The following day, I fed him several bits by hand, and he let me rub his ears for a second before jumping away. From then on, he fed out of my hand like a normal dog and let me pat him, pull his tail, or put my hand in his mouth.

In three weeks he was behaving quite normally, contentedly stopping to sniff a trouser leg or to accept a pat or a bit of bread.

Farnborough, England

Our cat, Yarrow, caught a bird and was prevented from eating it just in time. The bird was unconscious, evidently suffering from shock. Frequent applications of the Rescue

Remedy to its head, eyes, beak, and feet helped so much that within fifteen minutes the bird was trying to fly. After another quarter of an hour, off it went.

Bermuda

I have used Rescue Remedy on one of my Lhasa Apsos that was terrified of thunder and lightning. She would panic and hyperventilate, run around looking for a place to hide, tremble, pant, and shake all over. About six months ago we began giving her a dose of Rescue Remedy as soon as she heard the first thunder. She's gotten to the point where she survives storms very well now. We don't have to keep treating her all the time. Last night we had a very bad storm, and the dog didn't bat an eyelash.

Down here we also have real flea epidemics, and my dogs get so irritated that they sometimes chew themselves incessantly. I've found that Rescue Remedy, given orally and put on the itchy spots, gives them relief. I use both the liquid and the cream. The remedy also calms them and cuts down on their frantic scratching.

St. Petersburg, Florida

We have a nine-year-old Chinese bantam chicken called Mrs., which had been trodden on by a horse. I carried Mrs. to her usual bed of hay and put Rescue Remedy around her beak and bathed her leg. I repeated this treatment frequently, until the little hen could drink water to which the Rescue Remedy and Bach remedy Crab Apple had been added.

After three days, one eye, which had closed, opened, and the chicken began to take a slight interest in tomato seeds and blackberries. I administered different Bach remedies according to her momentary moods, and her recovery is regarded as a real flower remedy miracle. She has no fear whatsoever of the ponies grazing around her now.

Godshill Ridge, England

A cat in my neighborhood was very lethargic and uncomfortable after delivering her kittens. She was barely eating and drinking, not good for a nursing mother. One night I gave her a dose of Rescue Remedy in her mouth and one during the next day. The following day, she was eating and drinking normally, happily nursing her kittens.

Albuquerque, New Mexico

Our eight-year-old Belgian shepherd, Fritz, had developed dysplasia, which hampered his ability to run and jump. After some time, his movements became more and more difficult. Our vet explained that Fritz's spinal nervous system was deteriorating and that a Vitamin C supplement might possibly improve the dog's condition. This formula worked for a period of time, but after awhile Fritz began to drag his paws, causing his toenails to be rubbed to the quick. He felt so much pain that eventually we had to carry him with a sling wrapped under his stomach. As a last resort, our vet prescribed steroids, but they had no effect.

Then one day a friend told us about Dr. Bach's Rescue Remedy. After obtaining the remedy, we put a few drops on Fritz's tongue, as our friend suggested. Fritz's first reaction was immediate; his eyes lit up, and his ears became erect.

Amazingly after some weeks of daily doses with the Rescue Remedy, Fritz's rear legs became more responsive, and he no longer needed the sling to help him. He stopped dragging his rear paws; his toenails grew back; and his spirit enlivened. Now, a year later, he walks with no difficulty.

The Dr. Bach Rescue Remedy has been a Godsend.

Chicago, Illinois

Recently, we had a bloated lamb that had reached the stage of lying on her side, gasping. She didn't have long to go when I thought of using the Rescue Remedy. I began administering it every few minutes for about an hour, when I was called away. When I returned about twenty minutes later, to my great surprise I found the lamb up and grazing as if nothing had ever happened. Since then we have saved many lambs suffering from bloat.

New South Wales, Australia

My kids were fishing off a pier when a bird fell into the water. They retrieved it and laid it down when our large dog grabbed it suddenly in his mouth. The children rescued the bird again and brought it to me. I could sense its shock and terror. I got two drops of Rescue Remedy into its beak twice before the day was over. The next day it seemed well, so we freed it, and it flew away.

DeSoto, Texas

I used to do foster work for the Great Dane Rescue League, taking in Great Danes that people could not keep. One day I took in a nine-month-old female Dane that had been living with a psychotic woman. The dog was the jumpiest, most neurotic creature I'd ever seen. For the first eight hours I couldn't get near her at all. It occurred to me to put Rescue Remedy into her drinking water, and after a day she calmed down quite a bit. I continued to treat her food and water for some weeks. Having become much more calm and stable, she was shortly thereafter adopted into a good home. I believe Rescue Remedy was the only thing that prevented her from being put to sleep.

Miami, Florida

My tortoise-shell cat, Tina, who is semi-wild, appeared one day with an enormous sheep tick behind her ear. I dropped some Rescue Remedy onto the tick's body two or three times, in addition to adding some to Tina's milk. In three days, the unpleasant parasite completely disappeared! It seemed to shrink in size and then one day just wasn't there. Evidently, ticks cannot withstand the high vibrations of the remedies.

Hampshire, England

My wife was in a hurry when she changed the water in our small goldfish bowl, adding the wrong water temperature. The fish went into shock. They were lying on their sides near the top of the bowl, apparently near death, with only sporadic movement of their gills. We put several drops of Rescue Remedy in the water, and within an hour the fish had completely recovered. The woman who handles goldfish at the pet shop assures me that it is almost unheard of for goldfish to survive the state of shock I described.

Texas

My four-year-old dog had a swollen eye and showed symptoms of allergies such as restlessness, panting, and difficult breathing. I applied several drops of diluted Rescue Remedy over her eyelid, on the tip of her nose, and in her mouth. Within a half-hour the respiratory symptoms and restlessness had abated, although the dog's eye was still swollen. Soon she became relaxed and sleepy, and after two or three more applications around the eye the swelling disappeared entirely.

Albuquerque, New Mexico

My horse's knee became swollen, and he couldn't put any of his weight on it. I rubbed some Rescue cream on it, and within fifteen minutes the horse was able to walk with a light limp. I rubbed more cream on his knee two or three times during the day. By the next day, there was no noticeable limp or swelling.

Albuquerque, New Mexico

Plants

In addition to humans and animals, the Bach Flower Remedies, as well as Rescue Remedy, are reported to be beneficial used on plants.

Plants are often affected by environmental and systemic weakness much in the same way that humans and animals are. For example, uprooting a plant without taking special precautions may result in shock, in which case the Rescue Remedy or the Bach remedy Star of Bethlehem could be helpful. Exhausted or drooping plants may be helped with either the Bach remedy Olive or Hornbeam. Infested or diseased plants may be helped, along with other appropriate treatments, by the Bach remedy Crab Apple. Other remedies may also be chosen, when a plant is 'out of sorts', by careful observation of plant behaviour and 'personality.' For example, a large overbearing plant which might give the impression of taking over the environment, may require the Bach remedy Vine; while a small delicate plant which seems to 'tremble' around people or things, may require the Bach remedy Aspen or Mimulus.

While dusting, I carelessly dropped one of our African violets face down. Sometime later it stopped drinking, its flowers fell off, and its leaves became limp. I thought it had died of shock, and I felt terrible! Shortly after this I decided to give it the Bach Rescue Remedy. In the beginning just a couple of drops at a time seemed to have a beneficial effect, though it did take a month for the plant to revive completely.

Bexhill-on-Sea, England

We had a cypress bush that was badly attacked by frost early this year. We gave it the Rescue Remedy every morning for about two weeks, and it really took a new lease on life. It is quite a happy and healthy bush now.

Manchester, England

So far, I have found several uses for Rescue Remedy in my garden. I am usually bothered with black slugs, especially on my radishes, but this year I sprinkled Rescue Remedy directly on my seeds before I covered them with earth, and I have had almost no slug activity since.

For all transplants, I put a few drops of Rescue Remedy on the roots before putting them into the ground, and then I give them a solution of five liters of water plus eight drops of Rescue Remedy. The transplants always do well after that.

This spring I've had to be away from the garden, sometimes for a week at a time. Often on my return I would find my flowers drooping quite a bit; however, I've found that if I water them that night with a solution of Rescue Remedy, they'd be bright and lovely in the morning.

Amsterdam, Holland

Our anemones were drooping and limp, looking as though they were about to die. We gave them Rescue Remedy, and within three hours they were perky; their stems had stiffened, and they looked jolly and bright.

Acton, England

One of my favourite miniature rhododendrons succumbed to the drought while we were on holiday. Completely leafless and brittle, it seemed a hopeless case. I applied the Rescue Remedy liquid to one-half of the bush. The treated section is now covered with glossy green leaves and flower buds, while the untreated section is completely dead.

Scotland

When we returned from vacation, I discovered that our favorite sansevieria had been traumatized during our absence. Left on a windowsill overnight, it had become chilled when the temperature dropped to twenty degrees. Its leaves were wrinkled and curled tight. We tried everything to revive it, but nothing worked until we watered and washed its leaves with a solution of spring water and Rescue Remedy. The next morning it started to open, and ten days later it was alive and healthy. It is doing fine now, thanks to Rescue Remedy.

Colorado Springs, Colorado

We had a young persimmon tree that was blown down by the wind and was almost completely severed to about one foot above the ground; only one thin thread of bark joined the two sections.

Without much optimism we placed the tree in an upright position, dressed the wound with bandages soaked in a solution of Rescue Remedy, and strapped the two sections tightly between wooden splints.

I kept the dressings moist with the medicine for several days, also watering the roots freely with a weak solution. Now, after this long, severe winter, our little tree is budding normally and shows no signs of the injury at all.

England

Conclusion

The reader may by now have gathered from the preceding pages that the healing effects of the Bach Flower Rescue Remedy on people, plants and animals seem remarkable, if not miraculous. The Rescue Remedy appears to work uniquely on each individual in moments of crisis, giving, for example, soothing relief from the sting of a bee, or quietness to the mind in a time of grief.

It is not the purpose of this work to claim phenomenal cures for serious conditions requiring professional treatments; nor is it to state that the Rescue Remedy should replace standard orthodox medical practice. The intent of this book is to demonstrate that the Rescue Remedy has been consistently used in the past fifty years as an invaluable healing adjunct, which is safe and has no reported side effects.

It has been shown that if standard treatment or first aid measures are not available, Rescue Remedy can make a critical difference in the recovery of the patient, especially by alleviating stressful states of mind. Case histories show that the Rescue Remedy may calm the individual and ease terror, anxiety, and fear involved with illness or injury, thereby helping the person to withstand the trauma while professional help is summoned. Even when treatment is immediately available, Rescue Remedy will augment that therapy by providing a feeling of comfort and safety. Reports indicate that psychotherapists and other health care professionals have found Bach Flower Remedies invaluable for calming anxiety or tension. As well as providing emotional comfort, the Rescue Remedy speeds the healing of physical injuries such as cuts, sprains, bruises, and other physical traumas in people, animals, and even plants.

The Rescue Remedy and Bach Flower Remedies should not be considered as drugs or addictive crutches, but as catalysts that bring about a balance in the individual's emotional and mental levels. The remedies enable some people to become more aware of their inner nature, often bringing insight which helps prevent future recurrence of problems or illness.

In today's society, lack of professional accessibility, high costs, ineffective cures, and undesirable side effects from drugs are some of the many factors contributing to a phenomenal rise of interest in medical self-care. As an indicator of this growing awareness, a report prepared by the Commission on Alternative Medicine in the Netherlands stated that the right of the individual to use an alternative/complementary medicine should be respected. Along similar lines in the United States, Joe Graedon, the Drugs Editor of "Medical Self-Care", and the author of *The People's Pharmacy* and *The People's Pharmacy II*, stated that ". . . if the remedy is harmless and inexpensive and the possible rewards are great, you may decide to conduct your own experiment without waiting for the double-blind studies. Part of self-care is being aware of the no-man's land where some pretty respectable experts say therapy 'x' works, but the final verdict isn't in . . . the final decision is yours."

To date, Rescue Remedy has not had any clinical trials. However, it is anticipated that research work will be carried out using clinical studies to prove the healing effects of the Rescue Remedy and other Bach Flower Remedies. In the interim, the testimonials included in this book from the many scientifically trained medical practitioners may serve to answer any queries concerning the Rescue Remedy's safety and effectiveness. Although some critics may consider these testimonials to be subjective reporting, it should be pointed out that the history of pharmacy is full of examples where folk medicines were subsequently validated.

The case histories reported earlier were based on the use of the Rescue Remedy that is produced by the Bach Centre in Great Britain. As with many successful quality products, there are often imitations which follow and the Bach Flower Remedies are no exception.

A month before he died, Dr. Edward Bach wrote a letter to Victor Bullen, his assistant, on 26 October 1936, foretelling that there would be others who would want to change, add to, and delete from his system of healing. He wrote:

Dear Vic,

I think now you have seen every phase of this Work.

This last episode of Doctor Max Wolf may be welcomed. It is a proof of the value of our Work when material agencies arise to distort it, because the distortion is a far greater weapon than attempted destruction.

Mankind asked for free-will, which God granted him, hence mankind must always have a choice.

As soon as a teacher has given his work to the world, a contorted version of the same must arise.

Such has happened even from the humblest like ourselves, who have dedicated our services to the good of our fellow-men, even to the Highest of all, the Divinity of Christ.

The contortion must be raised for people to be able to choose between the gold and the dross.

Our work is steadfastly to adhere to the simplicity and purity of this method of healing; and when the next edition of the *Twelve Healers* becomes necessary, we must have a longer introduction, firmly upholding the harmlessness, the simplicity and the miraculous healing powers of the Remedies, which have been shown to us through a greater Source than our own intellects.

I feel now, dear Brother, that as I find it more and more necessary to go into temporary solitude, you have the whole situation in hand and can cope with all matters either connected with patients or connected with the administration of this work of healing, knowing that people like ourselves who have tested the glory of self-sacrifice, the glory of helping our brothers, once we have been given a jewel of such magnitude, nothing can deviate us from our path of love and duty to displaying its lustre, pure and unadorned, to the people of the world.

Since then, many "people of the world" continue to benefit from his gentle system of healing.

Without Dr. Bach's deep insight into and understanding of the nature of disease, his gentle system of healing would not have evolved.

As nothing can replace Edward Bach's original writings, *Ye Suffer From Yourselves* and *Free Thyself* are provided for the reader's reflection and upliftment.

APPENDIX A

Ye Suffer
From Yourselves

by
EDWARD BACH
M.B., B.S., M.R.C.S., L.R.C.P., D.P.H.

An Address given at Southport, February, 1931.

I N coming to address you this evening, I find the task not an easy one.

You are a medical society, and I come to you as a medical man: yet the medicine of which one would speak is so far removed from the orthodox views of today, that there will be little in this paper which savours of the consulting room, nursing home, or hospital ward as we know them at present.

Were it not that you, as followers of Hahnemann, are already vastly in advance of those who preach the teachings of Galen, and the orthodox medicine of the last two thousand years, one would fear to speak at all.

But the teaching of your great Master and his followers has shed so much light upon the nature of disease, and opened up so much of the road which leads to correct healing, that I know you will be prepared to come with me further along that path, and see more of the glories of perfect health, and the true nature of disease and cure.

The inspiration given to Hahnemann brought a light to humanity in the darkness of materialism, when man had come to consider disease as a purely materialistic problem to be relieved and cured by materialistic means alone.

He, like Paracelsus, knew that if your spiritual and mental aspects were in harmony, illness could not exist: and he set out to find remedies which would treat our minds, and thus bring us peace and health.

Hahnemann made a great advance and carried us a long way along the road, but he had only the length of one life in which to work, and it is for us to continue his researches where he left off: to add more to the structure of perfect healing of which he laid the foundation, and so worthily began the building.

The homoeopath has already dispensed with much of the unnecessary and unimportant aspects of orthodox medicine, but he has yet further to go. I know that you wish to look forward, for neither the knowledge of the past nor the present is sufficient for the seeker after truth.

Paracelsus and Hahnemann taught us not to pay too much attention to the details of disease, but to treat the personality, the inner man, realising that if our spiritual and mental natures were in harmony disease disappeared. That great foundation to their edifice is the fundamental teaching which must continue.

Hahnemann next saw how to bring about this harmony, and he found that among the drugs and the remedies of the old school, and among elements and plants which he himself selected, he could reverse their action by potentisation, so that the same substance which gave rise to poisonings and symptoms of disease, could — in the minutest quantity — cure those particular symptoms when prepared by his special method.

Thus formulated he the law of "like cures like": another great fundamental principle of life. And he left us to continue the building of the temple, the earlier plans of which had been disclosed to him.

And if we follow on this line of thought, the first great

realisation which comes upon us is the truth that it is disease itself which is "like curing like": because disease is the result of wrong activity. It is the natural consequence of disharmony between our bodies and our Souls: it is "like curing like" because it is the very disease itself which hinders and prevents our carrying our wrong actions too far, and at the same time, is a lesson to teach us to correct our ways, and harmonise our lives with the dictates of our Soul.

Disease is the result of wrong thinking and wrong doing, and ceases when the act and thought are put in order. When the lesson of pain and suffering and distress is learnt, there is no further purpose in its presence, and it automatically disappears.

This is what Hahnemann incompletely saw as "like curing like."

COME A LITTLE FURTHER ALONG THE ROAD.

Another glorious view then opens out before us, and here we see that true healing can be obtained, not by wrong repelling wrong, but by right replacing wrong: good replacing evil: light replacing darkness.

Here we come to the understanding that we no longer fight disease with disease: no longer oppose illness with the products of illness: no longer attempt to drive out maladies with such substances that can cause them: but, on the contrary, to bring down the opposing virtue which will eliminate the fault.

And the pharmacopoeia of the near future should contain only those remedies which have the power to bring down good, eliminating all those whose only quality is to resist evil.

True, hate may be conquered by a greater hate, but it can only be cured by love: cruelty may be prevented by a greater cruelty, but only eliminated when the qualities of sympathy and pity have developed: one fear may be lost and forgotten in the presence of a greater fear, but the real cure of all fear is perfect courage.

And so now, we of this school of medicine have to turn our attention to those beautiful remedies which have been Divinely placed in nature for our healing, amongst those beneficent, exquisite plants and herbs of the countryside.

It is obviously fundamentally wrong to say that "like cures like." Hahnemann had a conception of the truth right enough, but expressed it incompletely. Like may strengthen like, like may repel like, but in the true healing sense like cannot cure like.

If you listen to the teachings of Krishna, Buddha, or Christ, you will find always the teachings of good overcoming evil. Christ taught us not to resist evil, to love our enemies, to bless those who persecute us — there is no like curing like in this. And so in true healing, and so in spiritual advancement, we must always seek good to drive out evil, love to conquer hate, and light to dispel darkness. Thus must we avoid all poisons, all harmful things, and use only the beneficent and beautiful.

No doubt Hahnemann, by his method of potentisation, endeavoured to turn wrong into right, poisons into virtues, but it is simpler to use the beauteous and virtuous remedies direct.

Healing, being above all materialistic things, and materialistic laws, Divine in its origin, is not bound by any of our conventions or ordinary standards. In this we have to raise our ideals, our thoughts, our aspirations, to those glorious and lofty realms taught and shown to us by the Great Masters.

Do not think for one moment that one is detracting from Hahnemann's work, on the contrary, he pointed out the great fundamental laws, the basis; but he had only one life: and had he continued his work longer, no doubt he would have progressed along these lines. We are merely advancing his work, and carrying it to the next natural stage.

Let us now consider why medicine must so inevitably change. The science of the last two thousand years has regarded disease as a material factor which can be eliminated by material means: such, of course, is entirely wrong.

Disease of the body, as we know it, is a result, an end product, a final stage of something much deeper. Disease originates above the physical plane, nearer to the mental. It is entirely the result of a conflict between our spiritual and mortal selves. So long as these two are in harmony, we are in perfect health: but when there is discord, there follows what we know as disease.

Disease is solely and purely corrective: it is neither vindictive nor cruel: but it is the means adopted by our own Souls to point out to us our faults: to prevent our making greater errors: to hinder us from doing more harm: and to bring us back to that path of Truth and Light from which we should never have strayed.

Disease is, in reality, for our good, and is beneficent, though we should avoid it if we had but the correct understanding, combined with the desire to do right.

Whatever error we make, it reacts upon ourselves, causing us unhappiness, discomfort, or suffering, according to its nature. The object being to teach us the harmful effect of wrong action or thought: and, by its producing similar results upon ourselves, shows us how it causes distress to others, and is hence contrary to the Great and Divine Law of Love and Unity.

To the understanding physician, the disease itself points out the nature of the conflict. Perhaps this is best illustrated by giving you examples to bring home to you that no matter from what disease you may suffer, it is because there is disharmony between yourself and the Divinity within you, and that you are committing some fault, some error, which your Higher Self is attempting to correct.

Pain is the result of cruelty which causes pain to others, and may be mental or physical: but be sure that if you suffer pain, if you will but search yourselves you will find that some hard action or hard thought is present in your nature: remove this, and your pain will cease. If you suffer from stiffness of joint or limb, you can be equally certain that there is stiffness in your mind; that you are rigidly holding on to some idea, some principle, some convention may be, which you should not have. If you suffer from asthma, or difficulty in breathing, you are in some way stifling another personality; or from lack of courage to do right, smothering yourself. If you waste, it is because you are allowing someone to obstruct your own life-force from entering your body. Even the part of the body affected indicates the nature of the fault. The hand, failure or wrong in action: the foot, failure to assist others: the brain, lack of control: the heart, deficiency or excess, or wrong doing in the aspect of love: the eye, failure to see aright and comprehend the truth when placed before you. And so, exactly, may be worked out the reason and nature of an infirmity: the lesson required of the patient: and the necessary correction to be made.

Let us now glance, for a moment, at the hospital of the future.

It will be a sanctuary of peace, hope, and joy. No hurry: no noise: entirely devoid of all the terrifying apparatus and appliances of today: free from the smell of antiseptics and anaesthetics: devoid of everything that suggests illness and suffering. There will be no frequent taking of temperatures to disturb the patient's rest: no daily examinations with stethoscopes and tappings to impress upon the patient's mind the nature of his illness. No constant feeling of the pulse to suggest that the heart is beating too rapidly. For all these things remove the very atmosphere of peace and calm that is so necessary for the patient to bring about his speedy recovery. Neither will there be any need for laboratories; for the minute and microscopic examination of detail will no longer matter when it is fully realised that it is the patient to be treated and not the disease.

The object of all institutions will be to have an atmosphere of peace, and of hope, of joy, and of faith. Everything will be done to encourage the patient to forget his illness; to strive for health; and at the same time to correct any fault in his nature; and come to an understanding of the lesson which he has to learn.

Everything about the hospital of the future will be uplifting and beautiful, so that the patient will seek that refuge, not only to be relieved of his malady, but also to develop the desire to live a life more in harmony with the dictates of his Soul than had been previously done.

The hospital will be the mother of the sick; will take them up in her arms; soothe and comfort them; and bring them hope, faith and courage to overcome their difficulties.

The physician of tomorrow will realise that he of himself has no power to heal, but that if he dedicates his life to the service of his brother-men; to study human nature so that he may, in part, comprehend its meaning; to desire whole-heartedly to relieve suffering, and to surrender all for the help of the sick; then, through him may be sent knowledge to guide them, and the power of healing to relieve their pain. And even then, his power and ability to help will be in proportion to his intensity of desire and his willingness to serve. He will understand that health, like life, is of God, and God alone. That he and the remedies that he uses are merely instruments and agents in the Divine Plan to assist to bring the sufferer back to the path of the Divine Law.

He will have no interest in pathology or morbid anatomy; for his study will be that of health. It will not matter to him whether, for example, shortness of breath is caused by the tubercle baccillus, the streptococcus, or any other organism: but it will matter intensely to know why the patient should have to suffer difficulty of breathing. It will be of no moment to know which of the valves of the heart is damaged, but it will be vital to realise in what way the patient is wrongly developing his love aspect. X-rays will no longer be called into use to examine an arthritic joint, but rather research into the patient's mentality to discover the stiffness in his mind.

The prognosis of disease will no longer depend on physical signs and symptoms, but on the ability of the patient to correct his fault and harmonise himself with his Spiritual Life.

The education of the physician will be a deep study of human nature; a great realisation of the pure and perfect: and an understanding of the Divine state of man: and the knowledge of how to assist those who suffer that they may harmonise their conduct with their Spiritual Self, so that they may bring concord and health to the personality.

He will have to be able, from the life and history of the patient, to understand the conflict which is causing disease or disharmony between the body and Soul, and thus enable him to give the necessary advice and treatment for the relief of the sufferer.

He will also have to study Nature and Nature's Laws: be conversant with Her Healing Powers, that he may utilise these for the benefit and advantage of the patient.

The treatment of tomorrow will be essentially to bring four qualities to the patient.

First, peace: secondly, hope: thirdly, joy: and fourthly, faith.

And all the surroundings and attention will be to that end.

To surround the patient with such an atmosphere of health and light as will encourage recovery. At the same time, the errors of the patient, having been diagnosed, will be pointed out, and assistance and encouragement given that they may be conquered.

In addition to this, those beautiful remedies, which have been Divinely enriched with healing powers, will be administered, to open up those channels to admit more of the light of the Soul, that the patient may be flooded with healing virtue.

The action of these remedies is to raise our vibrations and open up our channels for the reception of our Spiritual Self, to flood our natures with the particular virtue we need, and wash out from us the fault which is causing harm. They are able, like beautiful music, or any gloriously uplifting thing which gives us inspiration, to raise our very natures, and bring us nearer to our Souls: and by that very act, to bring us peace, and relieve our sufferings.

They cure, not by attacking disease, but by flooding our bodies with the beautiful vibrations of our Higher Nature, in the presence of which disease melts as snow in the sunshine.

And, finally, how they must change the attitude of the patient towards disease and health.

Gone forever must be the thought that relief may be obtained by the payment of gold or silver. Health, like life, is of Divine origin, and can only be obtained by Divine Means. Money, luxury, travel, may outwardly appear to be able to purchase for us an improvement in our physical being: but these things can never give us true health.

The patient of tomorrow must understand that he, and he alone, can bring himself relief from suffering, though he may obtain advice and help from an elder brother who will assist him in his effort.

Health exists when there is perfect harmony between Soul and mind and body: and this harmony, and this harmony alone, must be attained before cure can be accomplished.

In the future there will be no pride in being ill: on the contrary, people will be as ashamed of sickness as they should be of crime.

And now I want to explain to you two conditions which are probably giving rise to more disease in this country than any other single cause: the great failings of our civilisation — greed and idolatory.

Disease, is, of course, sent to us as a correction. We bring it entirely upon ourselves: it is the result of our own wrong doing and wrong thinking. Can we but correct our faults and live in harmony with the Divine Plan, illness can never assail us.

In this, our civilisation, greed overshadows all. There is greed for wealth, for rank, for position, for worldly honours, for comfort, for popularity: yet it is not of these one would speak, because even they are, in comparison, harmless.

The worst of all is the greed to possess another individual. True, this is so common amongst us that it has come to be looked upon as almost right and proper: yet that does not mitigate the evil: for, to desire possession or influence over another individual or personality, is to usurp the power of our Creator.

How many folk can you number amongst your friends or relations who are free? How many are there who are not bound or influenced or controlled by some other human being? How many are there who could say, that day by day, month by month, and year by year, "I obey only the dictates of my Soul, unmoved by the influence of other people?"

And yet, everyone of us is a free Soul, answerable only to God for our actions, aye, even our very thoughts.

Possibly the greatest lesson of life is to learn freedom. Freedom from circumstances, environment, other personalities, and most of all from ourselves: because until we are free we are unable fully to give and to serve our brother-men.

Remember that whether we suffer disease or hardship: whether we are surrounded by relations or friends who may annoy us: whether we have to live amongst those who rule and dictate to us, who interfere with our plans and hamper our progress, it is of our own making: it is because there is still within us a trace left to bar the freedom of someone: or the absence of courage to claim our own individuality, our birthright.

The moment that we ourselves have given complete liberty to all around us: when we no longer desire to bind and limit: when we no longer expect anything from anyone: when our only thought is to give and give and never to take, that moment shall we find that we are free of all the world: our bonds will fall from us: our chains be broken: and for the first time in our lives shall we know the exquisite joy of perfect liberty. Freed from all human restraint, the willing and joyous servant of our Higher Self alone.

So greatly has the possessive power developed in the West that it is necessitating great disease before people will recognise the error and correct their ways: and according to the severity and type of or domination over another, so must we suffer as long as we continue to usurp a power which does not belong to man.

Absolute freedom is our birthright, and this we can only obtain when we grant that liberty to every living Soul who may come into our lives. For truly we reap as we sow, and truly "as we mete so it shall be measured out to us."

Exactly as we thwart another life, be it young or old, so must that react upon ourselves. If we limit their activities, we may find our bodies limited with stiffness: if, in addition, we cause them pain and suffering, we must be prepared to bear the same, until we have made amends: and there is no disease, even however severe, that may not be needed to check our actions and alter our ways.

To those of you who suffer at the hands of another, take courage; for it means that you have reached that stage of advancement when you are being taught to gain your freedom: and the very pain and suffering which you are bearing is teaching you how to correct your own fault, and as soon as you have realised the fault and put that right, your troubles are over.

The way to set about to do this work is to practise exquisite gentleness: never by thought or word or deed to hurt another. Remember that all people are working out their own salvation; are going through life to learn those lessons for the perfection of their own Soul; and that they must do it for themselves: that they must gain their own experiences: learn the pitfalls of the world, and, of their own effort, find the pathway which leads to the mountain top. The most that we can do is, when we have a little more knowledge and experience than a younger brother, very gently to guide them. If they will listen, well and good: if not, we must patiently wait until they have had further experience to teach them their fault, and then they may come to us again.

We should strive to be so gentle, so quiet, so patiently helpful that we move among our fellow men more as a breath of air or a ray of sunshine: ever ready to help them when they ask: but never forcing them to our own views.

And I want now to tell you of another great hindrance to health, which is very, very common today, and one of the greatest obstacles that physicians encounter in their endeavour to heal. An obstacle which is a form of idolatory. Christ said "Ye cannot serve God and mammon," and yet the service of mammon is one of our greatest stumbling blocks.

There was an angel once, a glorious, magnificent angel, that appeared to St. John, and St. John fell in adoration and worshipped. But the Angel said to him, "See thou do it not, I am thy fellow servant and of thy brethren. Worship God." And yet today, tens of thousands of us worship not God, not even a mighty angel, but a fellow human being. I can assure you that one of the greatest difficulties which has to be overcome is a sufferer's worship of another mortal.

How common is the expression: "I must ask my father, my sister, my husband." What a tragedy. To think that a human Soul, developing his Divine evolution, should stop to ask permission of a fellow traveller. To whom does he imagine that he owes his origin, his being, his life — to a fellow-traveller or to his Creator?

We must understand that we are answerable for our actions, and for our thoughts to God, and to God alone. And that to be influenced, to obey the wishes, or consider the desires of another mortal is idolatory indeed. Its penalty is severe, it binds us with chains, it places us in prisons, it confines our very life; and so it should, and so we justly deserve, if we listen to the dictates of a human being, when our whole self should know but one command — that of our Creator, Who gave us our life and our understanding.

Be certain that the individual who considers above his duty his wife, his child, his father, or his friend, is an idolator, serving mammon and not God.

Remember the words of Christ, "Who is My mother, and who are My brethren," which imply that even all of us, small and insignificant as we may be, are here to serve our brother-men, humanity, the world at large, and never, for the briefest moment, to be under the dictates and commands of another human individual against those motives which we know to be our Soul's commands.

Be captains of your Souls, be masters of your fate (which means let yourselves be ruled and guided entirely, without let or hindrance from person or circumstance, by the Divinity within you), ever living in accordance with the laws of, and answerable only to the God Who gave you your life.

And yet, one more point to bring before your notice. Ever remember the injunction which Christ gave to His disciples, "Resist not evil." Sickness and wrong are not to be conquered by direct fighting, but by replacing them by good. Darkness is removed by light, not by greater darkness: hate by love: cruelty by sympathy and pity: and disease by health.

Our whole object is to realise our faults, and endeavour so to develop the opposing virtue that the fault will disappear from us like snow melts in the sunshine. Don't fight your worries: don't struggle with your disease: don't grapple with your infirmities: rather forget them in concentrating on the development of the virtue you require.

And so now, in summing up, we can see the mighty part that homoeopathy is going to play in the conquest of disease in the future.

Now that we have come to the understanding that disease itself is "like curing like": that it is of our own making: for our correction and for our ultimate good: and that we can avoid it, if we will but learn the lessons needed, and correct our faults before the severer lesson of suffering is necessary. This is the natural continuation of Hahnemann's great work; the sequence of that line of thought which was disclosed to him, leading us a step further towards perfect understanding of disease and health, and is the stage to bridge the gap between where he left us and the dawn of that day when humanity will have reached that state of advancement when it can receive direct the glory of Divine Healing.

The understanding physician, selecting well his remedies from the beneficent plants in nature, those Divinely enriched and blessed, will be enabled to assist his patients to open up those channels which allow greater communion between Soul and body, and thus the development of the virtues needed to wipe away the faults. This brings to mankind the hope of real health combined with mental and spiritual advance.

For the patients, it will be necessary that they are prepared to face the truth, that disease is entirely and only due to faults within themselves, just as the wages of sin is death. They will have to have the desire to correct those faults, to live a better and more useful life, and to realise that healing depends on their own effort, though they may go to the physician for guidance and assistance in their trouble.

Health can be no more obtained by payment of gold than a child can purchase his education: no sum of money can teach the pupil to write, he must learn of himself, guided by an experienced teacher. And so it is with health.

There are the two great commandments: "Love God and thy neighbour." Let us develop our individuality that we may obtain complete freedom to serve the Divinity within ourselves, and that Divinity alone: and give unto all others their absolute freedom, and serve them as much as lies within our power, according to the dictates of our Souls, ever remembering that as our own liberty increases, so grows our freedom and ability to serve our fellow-men.

Thus we have to face the fact that disease is entirely of our own making, and that the only cure is to correct our faults. All true healing aims at assisting the patient to put his Soul and mind and body in harmony. This can only be done by himself, though advice and help by an expert brother may greatly assist him.

As Hahnemann laid down, all healing which is not from within, is harmful, and apparent cure of the body obtained through materialistic methods, obtained only through the action of others, without self-help, may certainly bring physical relief, but harm to our Higher Natures, for the lesson has remained unlearnt, and the fault has not been eradicated.

It is terrible today to think of the amount of artificial and superficial cures obtained through money and wrong methods in medicine; wrong methods because they merely suppress symptoms, give apparent relief, without removing the cause.

Healing must come from within ourselves, by acknowledging and correcting our faults, and harmonising our being with the Divine Plan. And as the Creator, in His mercy, has placed certain Divinely enriched herbs to assist us to our victory, let us seek out these and use them to be best of our ability, to help us climb the mountain of our evolution, until the day when we shall reach the summit of perfection.

Hahnemann had realised the truth of "like curing like," which is in reality disease curing wrong action: that true healing is one stage higher than this: love and all its attributes driving out wrong.

That in correct healing nothing must be used which relieves the patient of his own responsibility: but such means only must be adopted which help him to overcome his faults.

That we now know that certain remedies in the homoeopathic pharmacopoeia have the power to elevate our vibrations, thus bringing more union between our mortal and Spiritual self, and effecting the cure by greater harmony thus produced.

And finally, that it is our work to purify the pharmacopoeia, and to add to it new remedies until it contains only those which are beneficent and uplifting.

Free Thyself

by
EDWARD BACH
M.B., B.S., M.R.C.S., L.R.C.P., D.P.H.

INTRODUCTION

It is impossible to put truth into words. The author of this book has no desire to preach, indeed he very greatly dislikes that method of conveying knowledge. He has tried, in the following pages, to show as clearly and simply as possible the purpose of our lives, the uses of the difficulties that beset us, and the means by which we can regain our health; and, in fact, how each of us may become our own doctor.

Free Thyself

CHAPTER I.

It is as simple as this, the Story of Life.

A SMALL child has decided to paint the picture of a house in time for her mother's birthday. In her little mind the house is already painted; she knows what it is to be like down to the very smallest detail, there remains only to put it on paper.

Out comes the paint-box, the brush and the paint-rag, and full of enthusiasm and happiness she sets to work. Her whole attention and interest is centred on what she is doing — nothing can distract her from the work in hand.

The picture is finished in time for the birthday. To the very best of her ability she has put her idea of a house into form. It is a work of art because it is all her very own, every stroke done out of love for her mother, every window, every door painted in with the conviction that it is meant to be there. Even if it looks like a haystack, it is the most perfect house that has ever been painted: it is a success because the little artist has put her whole heart and soul, her whole being into the doing of it.

This is health, this is success and happiness and true service. Serving through love in perfect freedom in our own way.

So we come down into this world, knowing what picture we have to paint, having already mapped out our path through life, and all that remains for us to do is to put it into material form. We pass along full of joy and interest, concentrating all our attention upon the perfecting of that picture, and to the very best of our ability translating our own thoughts and aims into the physical life of whatever environment we have chosen.

Then, if we follow from start to finish our very own ideals, our very own desires with all the strength we possess, there is no failure, our life has been a tremendous success, a healthy and a happy one.

The same little story of the child-painter will illustrate how, if we allow them, the difficulties of life may interfere with this success and happiness and health, and deter us from our purpose.

The child is busily and happily painting when someone comes along and says, "Why not put a window here, and a door there; and of course the garden path should go this way." The result in the child will be complete loss of interest in the work; she may go on, but is now only putting someone else's ideas on paper: she may become cross, irritated, unhappy, afraid to refuse these suggestions; begin to hate the picture and perhaps tear it up: in fact, according to the type of child so will be the reaction.

The final picture may be a recognisable house, but it is an imperfect one and a failure because it is the interpretation of another's thoughts, not the child's. It is of no use as a birthday present because it may not be done in time, and the mother may have to wait another whole year for her gift.

This is disease, the reaction to interference. This is temporary failure and unhappiness: and this occurs when we allow others to interfere with our purpose in life, and implant in our minds doubt, or fear, or indifference.

CHAPTER II.

Health depends on being in harmony with our souls.

IT is of primary importance that the true meaning of health and of disease should be clearly understood.

Health is our heritage, our right. It is the complete and full union between soul, mind and body; and this is no difficult far-away ideal to attain, but one so easy and natural that many of us have overlooked it.

All earthly things are but the interpretation of things spiritual. The smallest most insignificant occurrence has a Divine purpose behind it.

We each have a Divine mission in this world, and our souls use our minds and bodies as instruments to do this work, so that when all three are working in unison the result is perfect health and perfect happiness.

A Divine mission means no sacrifice, no retiring from the world, no rejecting of the joys of beauty and nature; on the contrary, it means a fuller and greater enjoyment of all things: it means doing the work that we love to do with all our heart and soul, whether it be house-keeping, farming, painting, acting, or serving our fellow-men in shops or houses. And this work, whatever it may be, if we love it above all else, is the definite command of our soul, the work we have to do in this world, and in which alone we can be our true selves, interpreting in an ordinary materialistic way the message of that true self.

We can judge, therefore, by our health and by our happiness, how well we are interpreting this message.

There are all the spiritual attributes in the perfect man; and we come into this world to manifest these one at a time, to perfect and strengthen them so that no experience, no difficulty can weaken or deflect us from the fulfilment of this purpose. We chose the earthly occupation, and the external circumstances that will give us the best opportunities of testing us to the full: we come with the full realisation of our particular work: we come with the unthinkable privilege of knowing that all our battles are won before they are fought, that victory is certain before ever the test arrives, because we know that we are the children of the Creator, and as such are Divine, unconquerable and invincible. With this knowledge life is a joy; hardships and experiences can be looked upon as adventures, for we have but to realise our power, to be true to our Divinity, when these melt away like mist in the sunshine. God did indeed give His children dominion over all things.

Our souls will guide us, if we will only listen, in every circumstance, every difficulty; and the mind and body so directed will pass through life radiating happiness and perfect health, as free from all cares and responsibilities as the small trusting child.

CHAPTER III.

Our souls are perfect, being children of the Creator, and everything they tell us to do is for our good.

HEALTH is, therefore, the true realisation of what we are: we are perfect: we are children of God. There is no striving to gain what we have already attained. We are merely here to manifest in material form the perfection with which we have been endowed from the beginning of all time. Health is listening solely to the commands of our souls; in being trustful as little children; in rejecting intellect (that tree of the knowledge of good and evil) with its reasonings, its 'fors' and 'againsts,' its anticipatory fears: ignoring convention, the trivial ideas and commands of other people, so that we can pass through life untouched, unharmed, free to serve our fellow-men.

We can judge our health by our happiness, and by our happiness we can know that we are obeying the dictates of our souls. It is not necessary to be a monk, a nun, or hide away from the world; the world is for us to enjoy and to serve, and it is only by serving out of love and happiness that we can truly be of use, and do our best work. A thing done from a sense of duty with, perhaps, a feeling of irritation and impatience is of no account at all, it is merely precious time wasted when there might be a brother in real need of our help.

Truth has no need to be analysed, argued about, or wrapped up in many words. It is realised in a flash, it is part of you. It is only about the unessential complicated things of life that we need so much convincing, and that have led to the development of the intellect. The things that count are simple, they are the ones that make you say, "why, that is true, I seem to have known that always," and so is the realisation of the happiness that comes to us when we are in harmony with our spiritual self, and the closer the union the more intense the joy. Think of the radiance one sometimes sees in a bride on her wedding morn; the rapture of a mother with a new-born babe; the ecstasy of an artist completing a masterpiece: such are the moments where there is spiritual union.

Think how wonderful life would be if we lived it all in such joy: and so it is possible when we lose ourselves in our life's work.

CHAPTER IV.

If we follow our own instincts, our own wishes, our own thoughts, our own desires, we should never know anything but joy and health.

NEITHER is it a difficult far-away attainment to hear the voice of our own soul; it has all been made so simple for us if we will but acknowledge it. Simplicity is the keynote of all Creation.

Our soul (the still small voice, God's own voice) speaks to us through our intuition, our instincts, through our desires, ideals, our ordinary likes and dislikes; in whichever way it is easiest for us individually to hear. How else can He speak to us? Our true instincts, desires, likes or dislikes are given us so that we can interpret the spiritual commands of our soul by means of our limited physical perceptions, for it is not possible for many of us yet to be in direct communion with our Higher Self. These commands are meant to be followed implicitly, because the soul alone knows what experiences are necessary for that particular personality. Whatever the command may be, trivial or important, the desire for another cup of tea, or a complete change of the whole of one's life's habits, it should be willingly obeyed. The soul knows that satiation is the one real cure for all that we, in this world, consider as sin and wrong, for until the whole being revolts against a certain act, that fault is not eradicated but simply dormant, just as it is much better and quicker to go on sticking one's fingers into the jam-pot until one is so sick that jam has no further attraction.

Our true desires, the wishes of our true selves, are not to be confused with the wishes and desires of other people so often implanted in our minds, or of conscience, which is another word for the same thing. We must pay no heed to the world's interpretation of our actions. Our own soul alone is responsible for our good, our reputation is in His keeping; we can rest assured that there is only one sin, that of not obeying the dictates of our own Divinity. That is the sin against God and our neighbour. These wishes, intuitions, desires are never selfish; they concern ourselves alone and are always right for us, and bring us health in body and mind.

Disease is the result in the physical body of the resistance of the personality to the guidance of the soul. It is when we turn a deaf ear to the 'still small voice,' and forget the Divinity within us; when we try to force our wishes upon others, or allow their suggestions, thoughts, and commands to influence us.

The more we become free from outside influences, from other personalities, the more our soul can use us to do His work.

It is only when we attempt to control and rule someone else that we are selfish. But the world tries to tell us that it is selfishness to follow our own desires. That is because the world wishes to enslave us, for truly it is only when we can realise and be unhampered in our real selves that we can be used for the good of mankind. It is the great truth of Shakespeare, "To thine own self be true, and it must follow, as the night the day, thou canst not then be false to any man."

The bee, by its very choice of a particular flower for its honey, is the means used to bring it the pollen necessary for the future life of its young plants.

CHAPTER V.

It is allowing the interference of other people that stops our listening to the dictates of our soul, and that brings disharmony and disease. The moment the thought of another person enters our minds, it deflects us from our true course.

GOD gave us each our birthright, an individuality of our very own: He gave us each our own particular work to do, which only we can do: He gave us each our own particular path to follow with which nothing must interfere. Let us see to it that not only do we allow no interference, but, and even more important, that we in no way whatsoever interfere with any other single human being. In this lies true health, true service, and the fulfilment of our purpose on earth.

Interferences occur in every life, they are part of the Divine Plan, they are necessary so that we can learn to stand up to them: in fact, we can look upon them as really useful opponents, merely there to help us gain in strength, and realise our Divinity and our invincibility. And we can also know that it is only when we allow them to affect us that they gain in importance and tend to check our progress. It rests entirely with us how quickly we progress: whether we allow interference in our Divine mission; whether we accept the manifestation of interference (called disease) and let it limit and injure our bodies; or whether, we, as children of God, use these to establish us the more firmly in our purpose.

The more the apparent difficulties in our path the more we may be certain that our mission is worth while. Florence Nightingale reached her ideal in the face of a nation's opposition: Galileo believed the world was round in spite of the entire world's disbelief, and the ugly ducking became the swan although his whole family scorned him.

We have no right whatever to interfere with the life of any one of God's children. Each of us has our own job, in the doing of which only we have the power and knowledge to bring it to perfection. It is only when we forget this fact, and try and force our work on others, or let them interfere with ours that friction and disharmony occur in our being.

This disharmony, disease, makes itself manifest in the body, for the body merely serves to reflect the workings of the soul; just as the face reflects happiness by smiles, or temper by frowns. And so in bigger things; the body will reflect the true causes of disease (which are such as fear, indecision, doubt, etc.) in the disarrangement of its systems and tissues.

Disease, therefore, is the result of interference: interfering with someone else or allowing ourselves to be interfered with.

CHAPTER VI.

All we have to do is to preserve our personality, to live our own life, to be captain of our own ship, and all will be well.

THERE are great qualities in which all men are gradually perfecting themselves, possibly concentrating upon one or two at a time. They are those which have been manifested in the earthly lives of all the Great Masters who have, from time to time, come into the world to teach us, and help us to see the easy and simple way of overcoming all our difficulties.

These are such as —

LOVE.
SYMPATHY.
PEACE.
STEADFASTNESS.
GENTLENESS.
STRENGTH.
UNDERSTANDING.
TOLERANCE.
WISDOM.
FORGIVENESS.
COURAGE.
JOY.

And it is by perfecting these qualities in ourselves that each one of us is raising the whole world a step nearer to its final unthinkably glorious goal. We realise then that we are seeking no selfish gain of personal merit, but that every single human being, rich or poor, high or low, is of the same importance in the Divine Plan, and is given the same mighty privilege of being a saviour of the world simply by knowing that he is a perfect child of the Creator.

As there are these qualities, these steps to perfection, so there are hindrances, or interferences which serve to strengthen us in our determination to stand firm.

These are the real causes of disease, and are of such as —

RESTRAINT.
FEAR.
RESTLESSNESS.
INDECISION.
INDIFFERENCE.
WEAKNESS.
DOUBT.
OVER-ENTHUSIASM.
IGNORANCE.
IMPATIENCE.
TERROR.
GRIEF.

These, if we allow them, will reflect themselves in the body causing what we call disease. Not understanding the real causes we have attributed disharmony to external influences, germs, cold, heat, and have given names to the results, arthritis, cancer, asthma, etc.: thinking that disease begins in the physical body.

There are then definite groups of mankind, each group performing its own function, that is, manifesting in the material world the particular lesson he has learnt. Each individual in these groups has a definite personality of his own, a definite work to do, and a definite individual way of doing that work. There are also causes of disharmony, which unless we hold to our definite personality and our work, may react upon the body in the form of disease.

Real health is happiness, and a happiness so easy of attainment because it is a happiness in small things; doing the things that we really love to do, being with the people that we truly like. There is no strain, no effort, no striving for the unattainable, health is there for us to accept any time we like. It is to find out and do the work that we are really suited for. So many suppress their real desires and become square pegs in round holes: through the wishes of a parent a son may become a solicitor, a soldier, a business man, when his true desire is to become a carpenter: or through the ambitions of a mother to see her daughter well married, the world may lose another Florence Nightingale. This sense of duty is then a false sense of duty, and a dis-service to the world; it results in unhappiness and, probably, the greater part of a lifetime wasted before the mistake can be rectified.

There was a Master once Who said, "Know ye not that I must be about My Father's business?" meaning that He must obey His Divinity and not His earthly parents.

Let us find the one thing in life that attracts us most and do it. Let that one thing be so part of us that it is as natural as breathing; as natural as it is for the bee to collect honey, and the tree to shed its old leaves in the autumn and bring forth new ones in the spring. If we study nature we find that every creature, bird, tree and flower has its definite part to play, its own definite and peculiar work through which it aids and enriches the entire Universe. The very worm, going about its daily job, helps to drain and purify the earth: the earth provides for the nutriment of all green things; and, in turn, vegetation sustains mankind and every living creature, returning in due course to enrich the soil. Their life is one of beauty and usefulness, their work is so natural to them that it is their life.

And our own work, when we find it, so belongs to us, so fits us, that it is effortless, it is easy, it is a joy: we never tire of it, it is our hobby. It brings out in us our true personality, all the talents and capabilities waiting within each one of us to be manifested: in it we are happy and at home; and it is only when we are happy (which is obeying the commands of our soul) that we can do our best work.

We may have already found our right work, then what fun life is! Some from childhood have the knowledge of what they are meant to do, and keep to it throughout their lives: and some know in childhood, but are deterred by contra-suggestions and circumstances, and the discouragement of others. Yet we can all get back to our ideals, and even though we cannot realise them immediately we can go on seeking to do so, then the very seeking will bring us comfort, for our souls are very patient with us. The right desire, the right motive, no matter what the result, is the thing that counts, the real success.

So if you would rather be a farmer than a lawyer; if you would rather be a barber than a bus-driver, or a cook than a greengrocer, change your occupation, be what you want to be: and then you will be happy and well, then you will work with zest, and then you will be doing finer work as a farmer, a barber, a cook, than you could ever achieve in the occupation that never belonged to you.

And then you will be obeying the dictates of your Spiritual Self.

CHAPTER VII.

Once we realise our own Divinity the rest is easy.

IN the beginning God gave man dominion over all things. Man, the child of the Creator, has a deeper reason for his disharmony than the draught from an open window. Our 'fault lies not in our stars, but in ourselves,' and how full of gratitude and hope can we be when we realise that the cure also lies within ourselves! Remove the disharmony, the fear, the terror, or the indecision, and we regain harmony between soul and mind, and the body is once more perfect in all its parts.

Whatever the disease, the result of this disharmony, we may be quite sure that the cure is well within our powers of accomplishment, for our souls never ask of us more than we can very easily do.

Everyone of us is a healer, because every one of us at heart has a love for something, for our fellow-men, for animals, for nature, for beauty in some form, and we every one of us wish to protect and help it to increase. Everyone of us also has sympathy with those in distress, and naturally so, because we have all been in distress ourselves at some time in our lives. So that not only can we heal ourselves, but we have the great privilege of being able to help others to heal themselves, and the only qualifications necessary are love and sympathy.

We, as children of the Creator, have within us all perfection, and we come into this world merely that we may realise our Divinity; so that all tests and all experiences will leave us untouched, for through that Divine Power all things are possible to us.

CHAPTER VIII.

The healing herbs are those which have been given the power to help us preserve our personality.

JUST as God in His mercy has given us food to eat, so has He placed amongst the herbs of the fields beautiful plants to heal us when we are sick. These are there to extend a helping hand to man in those dark hours of forgetfulness when he loses sight of his Divinity, and allows the cloud of fear or pain to obscure his vision.

Such herbs are —

Chicory	*(Cichorium intybus)*
Mimulus	*(Mimulus luteus)*
Agrimony	*(Agrimonia eupatoria)*
Scleranthus	*(Scleranthus annuus)*
Clematis	*(Clematis vitalba)*
Centaury	*(Erythraea centaurium)*
Gentian	*(Gentiana amarella)*
Vervain	*(Verbena officinalis)*
Cerato	*(Ceratostigma willmottiana)*
Impatiens	*(Impatiens royalei)*
Rock Rose	*(Helianthemum vulgare)*
Water Violet	*(Hottonia palustris)*

Each herb corresponds with one of the qualities, and its purpose is to strengthen that quality so that the personality may rise above the fault that is the particular stumbling block.

The following table will indicate the quality, the fault, and the remedy which aids the personality to dispel that fault.

Failing.		*Herb.*		*Virtue.*
Restraint	......	Chicory	......	Love
Fear	....	Mimulus	......	Sympathy
Restlessness	......	Agrimony	......	Peace

Indecision	......	Scleranthus	......	Steadfastness
Indifference	......	Clematis	......	Gentleness
Weakness	......	Centaury	......	Strength
Doubt	....	Gentian	......	Understanding
Over-enthusiasm	......	Vervain	......	Tolerance
Ignorance	......	Cerato	......	Wisdom
Impatience	......	Impatiens	......	Forgiveness
Terror	....	Rock Rose	......	Courage
Grief	....	Water Violet	......	Joy

The remedies are endowed with a definite healing power quite apart from faith, neither does their action depend upon the one who administers them, just as a sedative sends a patient to sleep whether given by the nurse or the doctor.

CHAPTER IX.

The real nature of disease.

I N true healing the nature and the name of the physical disease is of no consequence whatever. Disease of the body itself is nothing but the result of the disharmony between soul and mind. It is only a symptom of the cause, and as the same cause will manifest itself differently in nearly every individual, seek to remove this cause, and the after results, whatever they may be, will disappear automatically.

We can understand this more clearly by taking as an example the suicide. All suicides do not drown themselves. Some throw themselves from a height, some take poison, but behind it all is despair: help them to overcome their despair and find someone or something to live for, and they are cured permanently: simply taking away the poison will only save them for the time being, they may later make another attempt. Fear also reacts upon people in quite different ways: some will turn pale, some will flush, some become hysterical and some speechless. Explain the fear to them, show them that they are big enough to overcome and face anything, then nothing can frighten them again. The child will not mind the shadows on the wall if he is given the candle and shown how to make them dance up and down.

We have so long blamed the germ, the weather, the food we eat as the causes of disease; but many of us are immune in an influenza epidemic; many love the exhilaration of a cold wind, and many can eat cheese and drink black coffee late at night with no ill effects. Nothing in nature can hurt us when we are happy and in harmony, on the contrary all nature is there for our use and our enjoyment. It is only when we allow doubt and depression, indecision or fear to creep in that we are sensitive to outside influences.

It is, therefore, the real cause behind the disease, which is of the utmost importance; the mental state of the patient himself, not the condition of his body.

Any disease, however serious, however long-standing, will be cured by restoring to the patient happiness, and desire to carry on with his work in life. Very often it is only some slight alteration in his mode of life, some little fixed idea that is making him intolerant of others, some mistaken sense of responsibility that keeps him in slavery when he might be doing such good work.

There are seven beautiful stages in the healing of disease, these are —

PEACE.
HOPE.
JOY.
FAITH.
CERTAINTY.
WISDOM.
LOVE.

CHAPTER X.

To gain freedom, give freedom.

THE ultimate goal of all mankind is perfection, and to gain this state man must learn to pass through all experiences unaffected; he must encounter all interferences and temptations without being deflected from his course: then he is free of all life's difficulties, hardships and sufferings: he has stored up in his soul the perfect love, wisdom, courage, tolerance and understanding that is the result of knowing and seeing everything, for the perfect master is he who has been through every branch of his trade.

We can make this journey a short joyful adventure if we realise that freedom from bondage is only gained by giving freedom; we are set free if we set others free, for it is only by example we can teach. When we have given freedom to every human being with whom we are in contact; when we have given freedom to every creature, everything around us, then we are free ourselves: when we see that we do not, even in the minutest detail, attempt to dominate, control, or influence the life of another, we shall find that interference has passed out of our own lives, because it is those that we bind who bind us. There was a certain young man who was so bound to his possessions that he could not accept a Divine gift.

And we can free ourselves from the domination of others so easily, firstly by giving them absolute freedom, and secondly, by very gently, very lovingly, refusing to be dominated by them. Lord Nelson was very wise in placing his blind eye to the telescope on one occasion. No force, no resentment, no hatred, and no unkindness is necessary. Our opponents are our friends, they make the game worth while, and we shall all shake hands at the end of the match.

We must not expect others to do what we want, their ideas are the right ideas for them, and though their pathway may lead in a different direction from ours, the goal at the end of the journey is the same for us all. We do find that it is when we want others to 'fall in with our wishes' that we fall out with them.

We are like cargo-ships bound for the different countries of the world, some for Africa, some for Canada, some for Australia, then returning to the same home port. Why follow another ship to Canada when our destination is Australia? It means such a delay.

Again, we perhaps do not realise what small things may bind us, the very things that we wish to hold are the things that are holding us: it may be a house, a garden, a piece of furniture; even they have their right to freedom. Worldly possessions, after all are transient, they give rise to anxiety and worry because inwardly we know of their inevitable and ultimate loss. They are there to be enjoyed and admired and used to their full capacity, but not to gain so much importance that they become chains to bind us.

If we set everybody and everything around us at liberty, we find that in return we are richer in love and possessions than ever we were before, for the love that gives freedom is the great love that binds the closer.

CHAPTER XI.

Healing.

FROM time immemorial humanity has recognised that our Creator in His love for us has placed herbs in the fields for our healing, just as He has provided the corn and the fruit for our sustenance.

Astrologers, those who have studied the stars, and herbalists, those who have studied the plants, have ever been seeking those remedies which will help us to keep our health and joy.

To find the herb that will help us we must find the object of our life, what we are striving to do, and also understand the difficulties in our path. The difficulties we call faults or failings, but let us not mind these faults and failings, because they are the very proof to us that we are attaining bigger things: our faults should be our encouragements, because they mean that we are aiming high. Let us find for ourselves which of the battles we are particularly fighting, which adversary we are especially trying to overcome, and then take with gratitude and thankfulness that plant which has been sent to help us to victory. We should accept these beautiful herbs of the fields as a sacrament, as our Creator's Divine gift to aid us in our troubles.

In true healing there is no thought whatever of the disease: it is the mental state, the mental difficulty alone, to be considered: it is where we are going wrong in the Divine Plan that matters. This disharmony with our Spiritual Self may produce a hundred different failings in our bodies (for our bodies after all merely reproduce the condition of our minds), but what matters that? If we put our mind right the body will soon be healed. It is as Christ said to us, "Is it easier to say, thy sins be forgiven thee or take up thy bed and walk?"

So again let us clearly understand that our physical illness is of no consequence whatsoever: it is the state of our minds, and that, and that alone, which is of importance. Therefore, ignoring entirely the illness from which we are suffering, we need consider only to which of the following types we belong.

Should any difficulty be found in selecting your own remedy, it will help to ask yourself which of the virtues you most admire in other people; or which of the failings is, in others, your pet aversion, for any fault of which we may still have left a trace and are especially attempting to eradicate, that is the one we most hate to see in other people. It is the way we are encouraged to wipe it out in ourselves.

We are all healers, and with love and sympathy in our natures we are also able to help anyone who really desires health. Seek for the outstanding mental conflict in the patient, give him the remedy that will assist him to overcome that particular fault, and all the encouragement and hope you can, then the healing virtue within him will of itself do all the rest.

Photographs

Dr. Bach rowing, one of his favourite forms of relaxation.
(Courtesy Bach Centre) date unknown

Edward Bach as a young man, circa 1905.
(Courtesy Bach Centre)

Edward Bach, circa 1922.
(Courtesy E. Varney)

Victor Bullen
(1887-1975)

"Victor Bullen, friend and partner of Dr. Bach, for over 40 years had dedicated his life to bringing back happiness and health to a great number of people, not only with the Bach Flower Remedies but by his own happiness, kindness, and understanding. Dr. Bach called him 'the soul of honour and integrity' and trusted him to carry on his work in all its simplicity after his own death. This Victor did most faithfully."

Nora Weeks, 1975

(Courtesy Bach Centre)
c.1950

Nora Gray Weeks
(1896-1978)

Nora Gray Weeks witnessed the whole spectrum of Dr. Bach's discoveries first hand — proving herself to be not only his right hand helper, but someone he could rely on to nurture him during the great development of his increasing sensitivity through the latter 4 years of his life. Her dedication and loving respect for the doctor must be recorded as perhaps the back-bone of his endeavour, for without her supportive resilience it can safely be assumed that the doctor's work might have faltered before completion — for he did indeed suffer greatly, both mentally and physically as an integral part of his great discovery. The doctor bequeathed to her the whole responsibility of his work. For over 40 years Nora, with the help of Victor, continued steadfastly to offer the Bach remedies to the world honouring the simplicity and purity of Dr. Bach's vision.

(Courtesy Bach Centre)
c.1923

c.1920

Dr. Edward Bach with his daughter Bobbie
(Courtesy E. Varney)

c.1917

c.1919

The Authentic
Bach Flower Remedies

Because of the extensive use and popularity of the Bach Flower Remedies and Rescue Remedy, similar products have begun to appear on the market. The following will help you to distinguish the authentic Bach remedies and Rescue Remedy from other products and clear up some of the misconceptions surrounding the differences.

The name **Rescue Remedy** is a federally registered trademark, as is **Bach Flower Remedies**, with the latter applying to 38 specific preparations and the unique philosophy and system of their use. All 38 of the Bach Flower Remedies are officially recognized as over-the-counter homoeopathic medicines and are listed as such in the *Supplement to the Eighth Edition of the Homoeopathic Pharmacopeia of the United States.*

The Bach Flower Remedies and Rescue Remedy are prepared at only one location in the world, the Bach Centre in England, where to this day the same wildflower locations originally discovered by Dr. Bach are still used. Similar products prepared anywhere else in the world that claim to be Bach Flower Remedies or Rescue Remedy are not, nor are they proven to be, Bach remedy 'equivalents.'

Some of these newly released products are not made from real flowers at all, but are prepared by radionic methods or other devices said to duplicate or enhance the 'vibration' of real flowers. Some of these other products are made from real flowers, but not from the species used for the actual Bach Flower Remedies.

In addition, there are products on the market that are actually unauthorized dilutions of the authentic Bach remedies and Rescue Remedy. Unfortunately, some of the literature and occasionally the labeling of these products makes reference to Dr. Bach's name. This tends to create the false impression that they are genuine Bach remedies or Rescue Remedy. They are not.

All authentic Bach Flower Remedies, including Rescue Remedy liquid, come bottled in concentrated liquid form. Rescue Remedy also comes in cream form. These officially recognized preparations all meet stringent FDA and homoeopathic labeling and quality-control laws. Unauthorized dilutions (even by retail stores) of the Bach Remedies or Rescue remedy, resold over the counter, often do not meet these stringent requirements. Furthermore, though appearing smaller in size, one ten-milliliter (one-third ounce) bottle of Bach remedy concentrate may produce as many as seventy bottles of these watered-down products. Additionally, these products have a limited shelf life, and cost the end consumer substantially more money than if they purchased the authentic Bach remedy concentrate directly.

Ultimately, what distinguishes the real Bach Flower Remedies, including Rescue Remedy, from similar products is more than just the name *Bach*. The Bach Flower Remedies and Rescue Remedy have been used worldwide for over fifty years and have consistently proven themselves safe, gentle, and effective by countless numbers of physicians, health care professionals, and the general public. To make sure you are getting the genuine Bach Flower Remedies or Rescue Remedy, look for the manufacturer's name, the **Bach Centre**, England, appearing on the front or side of every label.

The freedom and right to choose are important to us all; equally important is the information and knowledge needed to choose wisely.

Where to Obtain Rescue Remedy and the Other Bach Flower Remedies

In England, and to inquire about distributors in other parts of the world write:

DR. EDWARD BACH CENTRE
Mount Vernon
Sotwell, Wallingford
Oxon., OX10 0PZ, England

This was the home and workplace of Dr. Edward Bach during the latter years. Today, the Dr. Edward Bach Centre still carries on Dr. Bach's work of helping those in need, manufacturing and distributing the Bach Flower Remedies used around the world. Additionally, individual booklets such as Dr. Bach's *The Twelve Healers* and *Heal Thyself*, as well as other materials related to the work may be obtained here.

In North and South America and Japan write:

ELLON (BACH USA)
P.O. Box 320
Woodmere, New York 11598, U.S.A.
516-593-2206

In Germany, Austria, and Switzerland write:

THE GERMAN OFFICE
OF THE BACH CENTRE ENGLAND
c/o M. Scheffer
Eppendorfer Landstr. 32
2000 Hamburg 20
West Germany

Further and Recommended Reading

NOTE: Copies of the books listed below may be ordered in their individual (pamphlet) form, published by C.W. Daniel. These as well as additional information on where to locate Dr. Bach's books in other languages may be obtained from: **The Bach Centre**, Mount Vernon, Sotwell, Wallingford, Oxon., OX10 OPZ, England.

In North and South America including Japan, copies of the above books in English may be obtained from: **Ellon (Bach USA)**, P.O. Box 320, Woodmere, New York 11598, U.S.A.

1. *The Bach Flower Remedies* (three volumes in one) includes *Heal Thyself* by Dr. Edward Bach, *The Twelve Healers and Other Remedies* by Dr. Edward Bach, and *The Bach Remedies Repertory* by Dr. F.J. Wheeler (New Canaan, Connecticut: Keats, 1977). All three volumes originally published by C.W. Daniel, Saffron Walden, Essex, 1931, 1933, and 1952, respectively.[1]

2. *The Medical Discoveries of Edward Bach, Physician* by Nora Weeks (New Canaan, Connecticut: Keats, 1979). Originally published by C.W. Daniel, Saffron Walden, Essex, 1940.

3. *The Handbook of the Bach Flower Remedies* by Philip M. Chancellor (New Canaan, Connecticut: Keats, 1980). Originally published by C.W. Daniel, Saffron Walden, Essex, 1971.

4. *The Guide to the Bach Flower Remedies* by Julian Barnard (C.W. Daniel, Saffron Walden, Essex, 1979).

5. *Introduction to the Benefits of the Bach Flower Remedies* by Jane Evans (C.W. Daniel, Saffron Walden, Essex, 1974).

6. *Dictionary of the Bach Flower Remedies* by T. H. Jones (Surrey, England: Published by author, 1976).

---

1. These separate books as well as all the above are available through the Bach Centre, England.

Contributors Index

Index

Index

ABOUT THE AUTHOR

Over the years, Gregory Vlamis has written numerous articles and organized educational seminars in the field of awareness and natural healing. A tireless worker, he has devoted much of his personal time to assisting non-profit organizations to accomplish their various projects and goals.

In addition to writing *Bach Flower Remedies to the Rescue,* Mr. Vlamis spent two years researching throughout the United Kingdom. He interviewed those who knew Dr. Bach and uncovered rare letters, photographs, and other biographical material previously unavailable.